DEFLECTED

Published by SwaNi

About the Authors

First-time novel writers Swapnonil Banerjee and Nivedita Majumdar grew up in West Bengal, India. After completing undergraduate degrees in engineering, they arrived in the United States in the early 2000s. For the last two decades, they have lived and worked in various cities across North America, and currently reside in the Bay Area.

Swapnonil Banerjee, PhD

https://www.linkedin.com/in/swapnonil-banerjee-phd-5597553b/

Nivedita Majumdar, PhD

https://www.linkedin.com/in/nive-majumdar-phd-5523b07/

Authors' Note

Historical records suggest that around the mid-nineteenth century, Radhanath Sikdar, who worked for the Great Trigonometric Survey of India, had likely calculated the height of Mount Everest for the first time, thereby discovering the tallest point on Earth. Sir George Everest, after whom the peak is named, had retired, and returned to England almost ten years before Sikdar arrived at his groundbreaking result.

Educated at a prestigious Calcutta school, Sikdar was mentored by British teachers from a young age. At eighteen, he joined the Survey and started working directly with British supervisors and colleagues. He was highly regarded for his mathematical prowess and his admirers included Surveyor Generals Sir George Everest and Sir Andrew Waugh, whose tenures he served. Sir George Everest, known to be sparing with his compliments, had written the following about Radhanath Sikdar: "There are a few of my instruments that he cannot manage; and none of my computations of which he is not thoroughly master."

Born at a time when there were no computers, Sikdar was a forefather to modern-day Data Scientists, who derive insights from large amounts of physical measurements by mathematical modeling using computers. Sikdar's modeling was of course, all done manually. In fact, Sikdar's official title named him as the Chief Computer!

About the time when Sikdar's discovery became public, India was nearing the completion of one hundred years of British rule. A volatile socio-political environment had built up with both the nobility and the masses grappling to come to terms with their rapidly changing worlds. It soon culminated in a violent rebellion that took the British completely by surprise. With a compelling cast of Indian and European characters, the historical fiction DEFLECTED unfolds in this tumultuous backdrop, over the years 1856, when the news on Mount Everest becomes public, and 1857, when the mutiny breaks. In addition to available historical information, we have used our decades of cross-cultural experience, our appreciation of a scientist's temperament, and our intimate understanding of Bengal where Sikdar is from, to write this novel. We have resurrected a forgotten, exotic era where early experiments in diversity, equity and inclusion had happened, and whose successes and failures are of urgent relevance today, when questions of understanding and acceptance between cultures have amplified in importance.

Swapnonil Banerjee
Nivedita Majumdar

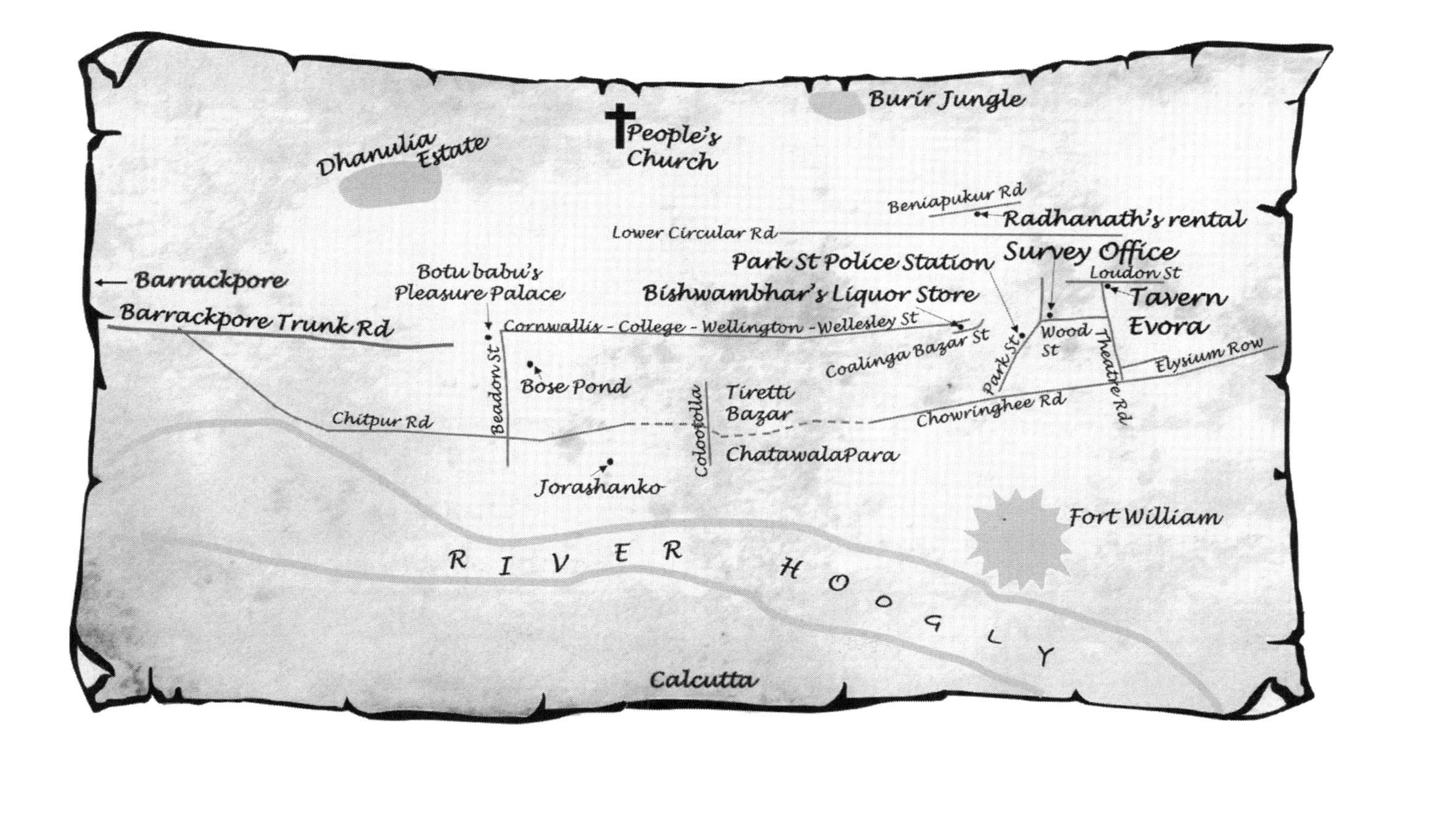

Burir Jungle
People's Church
Dhanulia Estate
Beniapukur Rd
Radhanath's rental
Lower Circular Rd
Survey Office
Park St Police Station
Loudon St
← Barrackpore
Botu babu's Pleasure Palace
Bishwambhar's Liquor Store
Tavern Evora
Barrackpore Trunk Rd
Cornwallis - College - Wellington - Wellesley St
Wood St
Coalinga Bazar St
Park St
Theatre Rd
Elysium Row
Beadon St
Bose Pond
Tiretti Bazar
Colootolla
Chitpur Rd
Chowringhee Rd
ChatawalaPara
Jorashanko
Fort William
RIVER HOOGLY
Calcutta

Part 1

Chapter One

17th May 1856

"They added the two feet!" mouthed a tall, broadly built, intense-looking man, his eyes racing through a prominent article on *India Chronicles*. "Surveyor General Andrew Waugh Declares Himalaya's Mount Everest as the Tallest Point on Earth!" read the headline.

Soaring walls of ice-capped mountains formed a fitting backdrop for Radhanath Sikdar reading the paper, while seated on the terraces of Russell Teahouse in a remote Himalayan hill station called Mussoorie. As Chief Mathematician at the Great Trigonometric Survey of India (GTSI), Radhanath worked for Andrew Waugh. Radhanath was the mathematical prodigy responsible for establishing the new world record on tallest point on Earth, beating the old record by more than eight hundred feet! In a recently penned letter to his deputy, General Waugh had proposed to name their precious find after George Everest, GTSI's most famous alumnus. *How did the Chronicles get this*? Radhanath wondered, as he read excerpts from that letter. Generals Waugh and Nicholson were praised for spearheading the effort. No one else got a mention. As Radhanath finished reading, still trying to wrap his head around the article, a tiny, resigned smile lit his sharp-featured, dark-skinned face. The height of Mount Everest reported was different from the value he had originally computed – by two feet.

As a *pagri*-cummerbund clad waiter came to serve more of the aromatic black tea that Russell Teahouse was famous for, Radhanath, snug in his usual high-necked *galabandh* and *ushnish,* set the newspaper down. He turned to look at his breakfast partner and childhood friend Chandrakanta, a curly-haired, lithely built Bengali aristocrat – a landed *zamindar* – seated across the table from him. Both bachelors in their early forties were on vacation – glad to escape their home city Calcutta's terrible summer weather for a few weeks.

With a sardonic smile twisting his lips, Chandrakanta drew his embroidered Kashmiri shawl close and pointing to the newspaper, remarked, "So how does it feel to have your work featured in the news, Radhanath?"

Leaning back into his chair with an inscrutable look, Radhanath responded, "At least it is out! Waugh has been sitting on that result for years."

Chandrakanta mused aloud, "When was it? Wasn't it 1850 when you first calculated it? You used to call it Peak XV then. Gosh! Has it been more than *five years* already?" Chandrakanta's brows had risen with surprise.

Nodding to confirm, Radhanath reached for his cup. After taking a sip, he said, "It was a difficult result to sell!"

"Oh yes, you've told me that," Chandrakanta interrupted. "Peak XV, or I should say Mount Everest now, *looks shorter* than the peaks around it!" Leaning forward to add extra sugar to his cup, Chandrakanta continued, "Well, had it not been for your mathematics, no one would know that Peak XV is the tallest!"

"You see why Waugh was dragging his feet?" rejoined Radhanath. "For such an important landmark, mistakes in the mathematics could put Waugh's reputation at risk." With a low chuckle, he reminisced, "How Waugh hated the number twenty-nine thousand!"

Promptly, Chandrakanta quipped, "And how you hated those two extra feet!"

"Of course, I did!" Radhanath shot back. "I have repeated those calculations many times. The height always comes very close to twenty-nine thousand." Then, the mathematician lamented, "Waugh had got it in his head that a perfect round number like twenty-nine thousand looks unconvincing as the height of a mountain! He pushed to add two ad hoc feet, insisting that measurement noise in the data justified the step."

Though Radhanath never agreed, the figure of twenty-nine thousand and two in the news showed that Waugh had ultimately gone ahead and added the two feet.

"Do you think you'll get a promotion now? Deputy Surveyor General perhaps?" Chandrakanta sounded curt.

"We will see!" Radhanath retorted, before quietly adding, "I may have done the calculations Chandrakanta, but many people contributed to this result!"

Chandrakanta's face hardened. He found it difficult to understand Radhanath's loyalty to his employers after being repeatedly denied raises and promotions he had earned many times over. To Chandrakanta's chagrin, he had recently discovered that while Radhanath was paid a meagre four hundred rupees as Chief Mathematician, his immediate boss, the Surveyor General, drew almost four thousand in monthly salary! However, knowing how much Radhanath cared about the science he got to do at GTSI, Chandrakanta decided to say nothing. To calm himself, he turned his face toward the Himalayas. Tucked under ancient blankets of ice, the endless, barren mountain ranges reclined in divine splendor on their horizon. Nestled among the Himalayan foothills, Mussoorie was looking particularly delightful this day with its wildflower-strewn meadows and hillside-hugging trails. Sweet strains of piano coming from the club's morning room brought Chandrakanta's attention back to the terrace. Several new guests, mostly European, had arrived by this time. They were enjoying their tea, warmed by the fire crackling in a great iron brazier at the center of the terrace. Turning to Radhanath, Chandrakanta asked, "What time are you expecting Dubois?"

He was referring to Radhanath's colleague, the Frenchman contractor for GTSI who dealt in optical parts. Dubois was supposed to join them for breakfast this morning. *Raja* Uday Singh of Jainagar, a nearby princely state, had commissioned Monsieur Dubois to build an observatory. Upon discovering defects in the telescopic gauge that he was using, Dubois had written to Radhanath asking to borrow one of the more advanced models from GTSI. Since Radhanath was coming to Mussoorie, a city only about a hundred and fifty kilometers to the north of Jainagar, they had arranged for Radhanath to bring the part with him. Dubois was going to return it the next time he was in Calcutta.

Radhanath did not answer Chandrakanta's question because his eyes at that moment had fallen on a new arrival at the entrance to the terrace.

"There's Dubois!" Radhanath said.

Chandrakanta saw a dark-haired, sprightly gentleman, somewhere in his late twenties, in a long frock coat of dark striped wool, looking inquiringly around the patio. Spotting Radhanath who had raised his hand, Monsieur Dubois smiled and headed toward their table. As they exchanged introductions, Dubois shook their hands. Then his eyes fell on the *India Chronicles*.

"A truly astonishing feat, that!" Dubois exclaimed, having already read that piece of news.

"Congratulations to Rady!" he added, before turning to Chandrakanta with a wide smile. "Anyone at GTSI will tell you how much of this is owed to Rady Sikdar here!" Dubois said, as he took one of the vacant chairs at their table.

Chandrakanta's lips lengthened to one side as he responded to Dubois' comment, "Really? Well, whoever leaked General Waugh's letter to the press, didn't seem to think so. There's no mention of Radhanath anywhere in that article."

Although Dubois looked surprised by the insinuation that the GTSI had deliberately leaked Waugh's letter to the press, he chose only to protest a part of Chandrakanta's comment. With a dismissive wave, he said, "*Ah, non*! Everybody at GTSI knows Rady Sikdar by reputation. He is the man behind their numbers!"

A waiter had approached their table to serve tea for Dubois. As he poured, Chandrakanta sat with an eloquent expression (leaving little doubt about where he stood on the matter). Radhanath, not too happy to be discussed in this light, reached for the package he was carrying. As the waiter departed with their breakfast orders, Radhanath extended it toward Dubois.

Eagerly taking the package, Dubois started to unwrap it, and simultaneously broke into an energetic monologue on the long-range, refractor telescope he was building for Uday Singh. It had a custom-design, American-made lens that he had personally brought over from Europe on his ship earlier this year. Upon Dubois' request, Radhanath started explaining how to operate the gauge. Chandrakanta noted, the usually reserved Radhanath transformed as he described the technical nitty-gritties with effortless confidence. It occurred to Chandrakanta that his charismatic friend's very personality could be making things difficult for him. Radhanath's self-confidence was easy to misconstrue as condescending. Whilst this might be tolerated in a white man, Radhanath's European colleagues could be hard-pressed to stomach such airs from an Indian.

After they finished, and Dubois was putting the piece away, Radhanath inquired, "So when are you expecting to be done? I hear you'll be in Calcutta in July?"

"*Oui*!" Dubois confirmed. "I am almost done. And now with the gauge here, it shouldn't be long. In fact, I could have been back in Calcutta earlier, but his royal highness has invited me to a hunting party. That's where I'm headed after here."

"Did I hear you right? You've been invited to Uday Singh's *shikar* party?" burst Chandrakanta, his voice gone a tad shrill with excitement. "From what I have heard, those are really grand occasions! Important members of India's aristocracy attend. European diplomats attend. It is not easy to get invited." Radhanath eyed Chandrakanta askance, amused by the wistful note he detected from his trophy-hunting enthusiast of a friend.

Dubois was more than delighted to elaborate. The famous expedition was set to take place in the forests of Barnala, on a spectacular bit of the Garhwal Himalayas this year. The spot was not more than four to five days from Mussoorie on horseback. A royal campground had been constructed on the alpine meadows of Ananta Bugyal, adjoining the forests.

Beaming at Chandrakanta, including Radhanath in his glance, Dubois said, "If you are interested, you are both very welcome to join as my guests. You see, the king is very pleased with me. I have carte blanche to invite friends along!"

Chandrakanta noticed Radhanath smiling evasively, clearly not as moved by Dubois' invitation as he was. Chandrakanta then started to pepper Dubois with questions, hoping that the added color on Uday Singh's hunting party might pique Radhanath's interest. Over the next hour or so, as the three enjoyed toast, eggs, and sausages the waiters had brought out for them, Dubois happily unveiled what he knew of the plans for the *shikar* party this year. It was going to be a lavish, multi-day affair. Apparently, activities had spread over the whole of last year to prepare for the event. Veritable palaces of bamboo and cloth furnished with the finest luxuries have been constructed to host the guests. Sumptuous food, an abundance of wine and first-rate entertainment were on the cards. Many *nach* girls from all over India have been invited. Out of all he heard, Radhanath was particularly surprised to learn that to make the hunts more exciting, the *Raja*'s men supplemented the natural wildlife of the area with additional exotic creatures transported to the hunting location in cages. The rumor was that for this year they were bringing Asiatic cheetahs all the way from Persia.

Nevertheless, when Dubois left that morning, Radhanath, not nearly as keen on hunting as a sport as his bourgeois friend, had yet to decide on whether going to *Raja* Uday Singh's hunting party made sense for him. Dubois said they could take the day to think it over; once they reached a decision, all they needed to do was send word at the Crown (a white-only guest house where he was staying). Dubois indicated that if they wished, they could ride with him; he already had servants riding ahead with instructions to setup camp at various spots along the way; Radhanath and Chandrakanta were, of course, also free to make their own arrangements.

Dubois' eagerness to join the *shikar* was owed not just to the thrill of a grand party; it had also to do with a young British woman he met six months back on the P&O vessel *Hindustan*. Sara Langley was on her maiden voyage to India on the same ship. One evening, while Dubois was trying out the lenses that he was carrying for *Raja* Uday Singh's telescope, he ran into the lovely Sara strolling by herself. A spontaneous friendship developed between the two. Over the remainder of their journey, they were often found together stargazing, stretched on their backs on the deck. Dubois was thrilled to discover Sara staying in Jainagar, with her Uncle Dick, a British Officer posted there. The two remained in touch over the next six months, meeting up whenever Dubois was in town. As an army man, Sara's uncle was automatically invited to the *Raja*'s hunting party, and she was going be there with her uncle. Dubois had therefore jumped at Uday Singh's invitation when it landed on his lap.

Radhanath's resistance to the royal hunt melted in the heat of Chandrakanta's barely contained enthusiasm; whereupon, cutting their vacation at Mussoorie short, they informed Dubois that they will meet him directly on site. Aided by those who helped Dubois plan his trip, Radhanath and Chandrakanta gathered a map, a compass, rifles, and other supplies. Exactly two days after their meeting at the teahouse, the two friends started for the royal campground from Mussoorie. Both were expert horsemen: Chandrakanta having learned it as a sport fashionable in his aristocrats' circle and Radhanath having picked it up during his years on GTSI field trips.

The route to Ananta Bugyal lay to the northeast of Mussoorie. The serpentine trails they crossed curved back and forth, up and down, straddling over several steep ranges. The experienced groomsmen had put blinders on the horses to prevent them from seeing sideways. This allowed the horses to proceed safely when precipitous drops flanked their trails. For most of the journey, the Himalayan Massif Bandarpunch dominated the horizon. The two travelers saw spectacular waterfalls, crossed tumultuous riverbends, heard unique birdcalls and insects. Occasionally, they saw great herds of yak and wild deer, especially when the mist thinned, and the floating masses of cloud shifted clearing the view to the valley floor below them. This would occasionally also reveal huge spreads of spring wildflowers. The temperature fluctuated quite a bit between night and day. With the warm sun on their back, they tried to cover as much distance as possible. They spent the significantly colder nights at various Garhwali hamlets, enjoying the villagers' hospitality, and feasting on lentil stuffed *parathas*, a specialty of this region.

On the way, Radhanath frequently reminisced about his time working for the GTSI among these lower Himalayan terrains, particularly of the time he was working in the Sal forests near Mussoorie. Those days, George Everest had turned his personal residence at Hathipaon, not too far from Mussoorie, into a temporary office for the Survey. Radhanath, like the other GTSI personnel, was living in tents outside his house. If there was anyone at GTSI, whose brilliance, dedication, and integrity Everest held in high esteem – it was undoubtedly Rady Sikdar. Conversely, despite having butted heads many times with his ill-tempered boss, Radhanath remembered the legendary Everest with respect and fondness.

While Radhanath talked, a thought that had niggled Chandrakanta since he first read about Mount Everest in print, swirled in Chandrakanta's head. *Did his friend not realize how ridiculous it was to name the highest peak found in Asia after an Englishman? Especially since having retired almost ten years before it was ever measured, George Everest had had nothing to do with it?*

Around mid-morning five days since they started, Radhanath and Chandrakanta finally caught sight of Jainagar's flame-colored flags fluttering high above them. They still had some climbing to do, but the knowledge that they were close immediately lifted their spirits. Over the last day or two, the rigors of continuously riding at these altitudes had started to take its toll. They were beginning to get frequent headaches. After climbing for a further few hours through lush forests of rhododendrons, it was late in the afternoon when they finally emerged from the tree line. And the vast, verdant meadows of Anant Bugyal, cradled by the imposing Himalayas, took their breath away.

An enormous, fenced campground stood to one side of the meadow, with tall poles bearing the flags they had seen from down below. Nearing the campground, they spotted armed guards standing at regular intervals along the perimeter fence. The king's welcome party came forward to direct them to the reception. Their horses were taken away to be watered and fed. The *Raja*'s men informed Radhanath and Chandrakanta that Dubois was out exploring the region. The guests were then asked to choose between the large-scale marquees or single occupancy tents. The marquees were ready to go, and wedge tents were available for guests who preferred private accommodation. Opting for the latter, as the two waited to be led to the spots they were allocated, they noticed an elaborate looking pavilion visible only from the side. They learned that it was the venue for the inauguration dinner slated for later tonight. Soon, leaving the pavilion to their left, they followed the *Raja*'s men across the busy campground, crossing the big marquees, to an area with smaller tents. The servants put their luggage and tenting equipment on the ground to start work. The two friends drifted a short distance away, finally free to focus on the partying in full swing around them.

Chandrakanta doubted that anyone was inside their tents. The carefree crowd consisted of brocaded *sherwani* and embroidered shawl clad Indians and shiny suit, boot and hat clad Europeans – all taking leisurely strolls or holding court excitedly among themselves. Their animated chatter and infectious enthusiasm refreshed the exhausted travelers whose fatigue and headache were soon forgotten. Feeling ravenous, the two helped themselves to the beautifully crafted hors d'oeuvres, mince pies, and deviled eggs that pink-turbaned, *kurta-pajama* clad royal waiters carried around in trays. Others carried trays bearing tall flutes of *sherbet* or sparkling champagne. Several European women turned heads in elaborate, high-fashion gowns, holding their skirts up ever so daintily. Suddenly, Chandrakanta became amused by a childish thought. *The gorgeous headgear worn by the Eastern gentlemen could give the extravagant hats adorning the European ladies a run for their money.* Around the campground, Chandrakanta noticed many artists, the majority of them women, who were eager to capture the curiosities of this exotic assembly on their easels.

Admiring the grandeur around him in this thoroughly remote place, Chandrakanta marveled at what a great contrast it was to the hardship of their journey. He lost track of how much time he stood enthralled by his surroundings when abruptly coming back to himself, he noticed that Radhanath was no longer next to him. Looking around, he soon located his friend where the *Raja*'s men were setting up their tents. Radhanath seemed busy providing instructions to the laborers.

Walking over to Radhanath, Chandrakanta said, "Why don't you let them do their work? Why do you need to get involved?"

Radhanath responded, "I was watching them from the moment they started. They don't know what they're doing. I am convinced those who really know how to do this aren't available." He further added, "I know how to construct tents that can withstand the elements. Would you prefer our tents collapse on us in the middle of the night?"

Aware of his friend's penchant for perfection, Chandrakanta hid his smile and decided to leave Radhanath alone. "I'll go have a look at the menagerie," he said. He was curious about the additional animals the *Raja*'s men were going to release for the hunt.

Chandrakanta asked a passing waiter which direction to head. To Chandrakanta's disappointment, the man indicated that the animals were being held at a spot several miles away, near the village of Barnala. Chandrakanta would have to cross the meadow and then a section of the forests to get to them. Instead, Chandrakanta decided to satisfy himself with an exploration of the campground. As he started to walk away, he heard Radhanath assuring that come high wind, hail, or highwater, or even an escaped rhino from the *Raja*'s collection, their tents will remain standing. Chandrakantha shook his head without turning to look at his incorrigible friend, an indulgent half-smile materializing on his face.

Indeed, trained by none other than his idiosyncratic mentor George Everest, Radhanath knew all about constructing sturdy tents. Everest never tired of reminding them how the tents protected their all-important notes and equipment, along with providing shelter in inclement weather and sickness. Watching the *Raja*'s men fumble this evening, Radhanath had felt compelled to show them what they were doing wrong. As his exertions made Radhanath hot, he removed his coat and *ushnish,* laying them on the ground by his side. He rolled up his sleeves and trousers, getting down on his knees to work alongside the men. When the laborers moved to start on the second tent, Radhanath stood up, giving a final once-over to the one they had just completed. Noticing some wrinkles on the tarp that might cause someone to trip, Radhanath, hammer in hand, bent down again, intending to stretch the sheet with additional nails. Suddenly, a female voice from behind him broke his concentration, causing him to hit his own thumb. With a soft yelp of pain, Radhanath dropped the hammer and turned around. A British girl, in her early twenties, stood looking at him. Caught off guard, Radhanath forgot his pain, vaguely registering it was her voice that had distracted him.

Over the years, Radhanath had interacted with many European women, in parties with GTSI employees and their families. He was at ease around them. However, today, something unusual happened. The way this girl's eyes seemed to take him in got under his skin. The lady was pretty – about five feet four, with golden hair and radiant skin, wearing a modest brown dress with a dainty bonnet – but Radhanath didn't notice all that until later. At that moment, foremost in his mind was the thought that he had never seen eyes that clear, or beautiful, in his entire life. Oddly enough, perhaps for the first time in his life, he felt *seen*.

As the silence between them lengthened awkwardly, Radhanath stood in the throes of unfamiliar emotion. Mercifully, the girl broke into a melodious chuckle – a moment that got deeply imprinted on Radhanath's unaccustomed heart. His effortless recollection of this moment would astonish Radhanath in the future when a whole year later, the two were fated to meet again.

Presently, the girl's laughter shook Radhanath out of his paralysis. Becoming conscious, he straightened his trousers. The girl had started to repeat her question in broken Hindi. "Since you seem to know how to fix tents, I wondered if you could help me with mine?" Responding in perfect English, Radhanath indicated he would be happy to, if the lady kindly shared what the matter was with it.

The girl was astonished to hear British accented English spoken by this sweaty, muddy, dark-skinned man. She had assumed he was one of the working-class natives, who in her experience, did not speak English. She stood feeling a tad embarrassed for having jumped to that conclusion.

Brushing his hand vigorously clean by the side of his coat, Radhanath bowed politely before offering the girl his hand in greeting, "Rady Sikdar at your service, miss."

As the girl extended white gloved hands to shake Radhanath's, her face warmed with a smile. She gave her name as Sara Langley. Radhanath learned that when Miss Langley had returned to her tent moments ago, she had found it starting to lean to one side. Fearing that a good strong wind could be its undoing, she had ventured to find a laborer she could ask for help. No one seemed around. There seemed a shortage of staff, with everyone pulled away to perhaps prepare for the inauguration.

With daylight going soon, and the second tent not quite done yet, Radhanath decided to check Miss Langley's tent himself. He gave final instructions to the men he was supervising. Then, picking up one of their tool sets, he asked the lady to lead the way. On the short walk through the maze of tents, Radhanath learned that Miss Langley, like them, had arrived earlier today with an Uncle Dick. The two were soon standing in front of Miss Langley's tent, leaning uncomfortably to its left.

A quick inspection told Radhanath that a few of the stakes that anchored the tent had become loose causing the tension to slacken.

He turned to the girl, then smiled and shook his head, "They are evidently sending all kinds over to pitch tents. These stakes need to go deeper. It won't take me long to secure them."

Hammer in hand, Radhanath went around the tent, working with precision and confidence. Having a few moments to herself, Sara wondered, *who is this man? From his appearance, he did not look like royalty*. From her last six months in India, Sara had noticed that the common Indians were either the type to outright avoid her, or they spoke with exaggerated deference. This man hadn't done either, which Sara thought unusual. *How old was he?* Sara became amused catching herself feeling a bit extra keen. She thought he might be in his late thirties or early forties. She was surprised she hadn't hesitated to make that guess. Usually, she struggled to guess the age of Indians. *It was a cultural thing*, she felt. Sara reasoned that perhaps Radhanath's decidedly Western body language had allowed her instincts to come to her aid. She was feeling intrigued by this man, with his direct stare, under which she had burned moments ago, but who, nevertheless, exuded an attractive mix of vulnerability and optimism.

Sara's tent looked miraculously upright by the time Radhanath was done with it. As she thanked him, both realized there was no further reason for Radhanath to stay.

Not quite ready to part ways, Sara tried to start a conversation, "I am curious how you know so much about tents, Mr. Sikdar!"

"From my years spent outdoors, Miss Langley. We survey public lands as part of the Trigonometric Survey," responded Radhanath.

"You don't say!" Sara exclaimed. "You really work for the GTSI, do you! I have a good friend, Monsieur Francois Dubois, who works there. Do you know him?" she questioned eagerly.

"Certainly!" said Radhanath, his eyebrows raised. And then, as he waited for Sara to say some more on the matter, he noticed her hesitate.

"I am currently living in Jainagar, as is Mr. Dubois. We often run into each other at social functions. Mr. Dubois has told me a great deal about the work the GTSI does in India," she explained.

Radhanath maintained a poker face, appropriately tempered with a show of polite interest. Internally, he felt both surprised and disconcerted to discover the girl's connection with Dubois. He watched her, trying to assess if the two were romantically entangled.

Sara next said that Radhanath must be very proud of the news on Mount Everest. "What a great feather in the cap for nineteenth century science!" she said.

"Of course!" said Radhanath, rather curtly.

Sensing that Radhanath was not keen to discuss the topic, Sara stood wondering what to say next, her curiosity about Radhanath not quite satisfied yet. Meanwhile, her restraint wasn't lost on Radhanath, who understood that the girl was interested to hear more. He appreciated that it must look odd, in fact downright rude, to say so little on such historic news, especially after disclosing that he worked for the GTSI!

Though the sun had gone down, there was still light. One or two stars were beginning to bloom. The throngs around them had thinned, with most either headed to the pavilion or inside their tents, preparing for the dinner. A light breeze had started to whisper in their ear. For a moment, Radhanath's eyes rested on the fireflies glowing like powdered gold around them. Then, he turned to look at Sara again.

Words that tore out of him next, seemed to do so with a mind of their own. "I computed the precise height of Peak XV, now called Mount Everest," Radhanath said. "As Chief Mathematician of GTSI's Calcutta office, it is my job to calculate the heights of, and distances between, various landmarks, mathematically correcting the noise that cannot be avoided when making measurements. Several years ago, when I uncovered that Peak XV is taller than any known landmark in the world, I had the privilege of sitting alone with that knowledge for some time."

Radhanath stopped. He could hear his own heart thump with emotion. He had denied himself these exact words, particularly since the news emerged in print without his name associated with it. Sara stared at Radhanath in utter astonishment. In the next few moments, Radhanath held Sara spellbound with the ferocity of his gaze. The moment was shattered by a jovial call that came from their left.

"There you are!"

Radhanath and Sara jumped, before turning to find Dubois and Chandrakanta walking toward them. "I met your friend totally lost and wandering by the grand pavilion!" exclaimed Dubois. He continued, "Then we found your tents but no Monsieur Sikdar in sight. It was your coolies, thankfully, who were able to tell us that you had gone in this direction." With his brows raised playfully, Dubois added, "With a *memsahib*."

Turning to Sara next, he asked how *memsahib* was doing. After the introductions, Dubois said he wished they could chat further now, but that everyone should get going. He did not want to be late for the inauguration dinner set to start at seven.

Chapter Two

In 1757, East India Company's Robert Clive and his three thousand men faced Bengal's *Nawab* Siraj-ud-Daulla's army of fifty thousand on the battleground at Plassey, on the eastern Gangetic Plains. Clive's nerve rested precariously on one man's traitorous ambitions for the throne of Bengal for himself – Mir Jafar – the commander of Siraj-ud-Daulla's forces. Mir Jafar had secretly sworn not to join the fight against Clive – withdrawing his support for the *Nawab* at the eleventh hour – a treachery that ultimately did not serve him well. Before the turn of the century, the East India Company had transitioned from humble traders to Queen Victoria's empire builders, seizing complete control over vast swathes of the country. Simultaneously with the fortunes of the British, rose the fortunes of Calcutta, which started life as a fishing village bordering the British outpost at Fort William, on the eastern banks of the Hooghly River. In the latter half of the 1700s, Governor General Wellesley spearheaded the development of the city by draining its marshes, laying out streets, and building public infrastructure, which was all funded by lucrative opium trade. By the mid-1800s, Calcutta had burgeoned with thriving British and native communities in a vibrant patchwork of white and brown neighborhoods.

24th May 1856

Bishwambhar's native liquor joint stood at the edge of Coalinga Bazaar Street, about four miles to the east of Fort William. While the grand Wellesley Street stood to one of its sides, a colorful chunk of native slums bordered the other. The lines between the whites and non-whites were at their fuzziest in this part of the town, which was not entirely unexpected, as these shops catered to the working class, indistinguishably drunk, poor, and dirty.

That hot, humid evening, Park Street *thana* Police Chief Lawrence Cockerel sat at Bishwambhar's liquor store at the edge of the bazaar, savoring small sips from a bowl full of delicious *bhang-sherbet.* From the corner of his eyes, he watched a thin, native man called Pannalal, who had just drunk his bowl dry in one biggish gulp. After, Pannalal sat with his arms linked around his knees, hugging them to his chest. A hookah pipe sat loosely in one of his hands. Drowsy with drink, he kept nodding off, but just before falling over, he would arduously force his eyes open and drag on the pipe he held.

Lawrence observed Pannalal with private amusement. As far back as Lawrence can remember, downing his *bhang* in one go and then smoking as he catnapped thereafter was classic Pannalal. However, Lawrence knew, despite looking thoroughly inebriated, Pannalal was far from gone. The man could hold his *bhang* exceptionally well. Pannalal had once declared that *bhang* had the effect of heightening his senses to razor sharpness. Soon after, Lawrence had tested the claim by attempting to extract the hookah pipe sitting in a sozzled Pannalal's grip. Perking up immediately, Pannalal had looked at Lawrence from under his lids with a self-satisfied smile.

"Nuh-uh!" he had said, genially shaking his head.

Lawrence Cockerel was a tall, thickset man in his early thirties, with a prominent moustache. He worked for the East India Company and shared an unlikely camaraderie with sepoy Pannalal Chettri, also with the East India Company and posted at their cantonment in Barrackpore, twelve miles from Calcutta. When Pannalal's father, a sepoy of the Bengal army, learned of his squadron leader's wife's demise at childbirth, he had sent his own wife to General Cockerel's household in Calcutta to work as an *ayah* for the newborn. The then nine-year-old Pannalal had accompanied his mother. Little Lawrence had become inseparable from the older Pannalal in those early days of boyhood. The British worried that if their children grew too close to the natives their English may become accented like an Indian's, which is why an education in England was considered almost obligatory. When Lawrence turned nine, he was indeed sent away to England to study, later than usual perhaps because his father had hated to part with his beloved, motherless son. That same year, following his own father's footsteps, the then nineteen-year-old Pannalal joined the Bengal native infantry.

In all his years abroad, Lawrence never integrated too closely with British society. His blissful childhood spent with Pannalal as a constant companion and his early adolescence spent camping in the jungles of India with his father kept him mentally tethered to the India he had left behind. He wrapped these memories around himself like a blanket each night, and they grew thin and weary, but he never let them go. Ten years later when he returned to India, Lawrence looked Pannalal up in Barrackpore. Though he found their old familiarity gone, something of their unusual understanding had persisted.

Lawrence and Pannalal had fallen into a habit of coming to Bishwambhar's for *bhang* and hookah on Saturday evenings that summer. Pannalal's family was originally from the predominantly native neighborhood of Jorashanko, not far from Bishwambhar's shop. Pannalal often spent his Saturday nights in the room of his ancestral house, reporting to Barrackpore for duty late on Sundays.

If Lawrence got drunk silly during one of their Saturday bashes – to the point that returning to his quarters at Elysium Row by himself seemed impossible – he would come over to stay the night at Jorashanko, bunking with Pannalal in his room. Nobody bothered them. In fact, the two planned on it for tonight. But that wasn't because Lawrence expected to be too drunk to get back. After Bishwambhar's, the two planned on going to a *khemta* function. Both were fans of the sensuous *khemta* tradition, with its abundance of jerky pelvic movements and raucous singing, set to lascivious themes. Lawrence's excellent grasp of the vernacular language allowed him complete appreciation of its nuances. Fully expecting tonight's event to continue into the wee hours of the morning, Lawrence had come mentally prepared to crash at Pannalal's, a short distance from the venue of the function.

A crowd was starting to form at Bishwambhar's. Through eyes half-open, Lawrence watched them in the haze of frankincense smoke, burned as much to drive out mosquitoes as to make the air smell good. He knew many of the regulars by face these days. People were enjoying *bhang*, or hookah, or both. Lawrence breathed the fragrant air with languid pleasure, picking up the distinctive aromas of strong frankincense and tobacco. He kept looking at the woozy, brown faces; some were smoking alone while others had formed groups of twos or threes, sharing one hookah between them. Lawrence knew those sharing their hookah must be of the same caste. Bishwambhar's shop segregated the hookahs that way. People were very conscious of their castes in India. A *Kaistho*, like Pannalal, would never smoke from a hookah meant for *Boishyos*. Pannalal would not use hookah kept aside for *Brahmins,* who were above his caste, nor those kept aside for *Boishyos* or *Shudros,* who were below. In fact, Lawrence noticed Pannalal had his own hookah at Bishwambhar's and wouldn't touch any other, even from his own caste. *Silly old fool!* Lawrence smirked to himself. *Perhaps hobnobbing with the East India Company had given him his airs.*

After drinking the remaining *bhang* to the lees, Lawrence set his cup down on the mattress where he was seated. It was growing stuffy inside. He eyed the *punkahwallah* tiredly pulling the rope attached to the manual fan, which did nothing to clear the air. Rearranging the pillows that he was resting against, Lawrence shifted his weight such that he had a clearer view to the outside, hoping the more direct airflow will ease his breathing. In the declining daylight, he spotted a *dhuti* clad lamplighter up his ladder on the street. The man had opened the lantern sitting at the top of the pole to light the flame.

A landaulet passed by the front of Bishwambhar's shop. *There goes a debauched babu, one of those neo-urban, affluent class of fun-loving Bengalis for a night out in town. Perhaps this one was off to one of the brothels to the west.* Inspector Cockerel was no stranger to Calcutta's intemperate nightlife.

Hearing raised voices, Lawrence turned his attention to two female fishmongers who had set up shop by the roadside. They had fresh fish in shallow iron cauldrons on display in front of them. The dark skin on their bare shoulders shone in the candlelight they had burning by their side; they were a happy-go-lucky pair, calling heartily on those walking by to purchase fish from them.

Lawrence's wandering eyes came to rest on a little girl he found kneeling to the extreme left of Bishwambhar's, on the opposite side of the street. She was a flower girl, likely having arrived in the past couple of minutes from the alley that intersected the main street on which the shop was located. Lawrence had seen her at that same spot before. Last time, he had found her soaking scented tuberose sticks in a bucket of blue colored water (probably indigo). Lawrence knew that trick; it made the tuberose appear fresher than they were. Tonight, it wasn't tuberose. The girl had conspicuous orange and yellow marigold garlands on display.

Shifting his weight on the mattress again, Lawrence now leaned his tall frame over toward Pannalal and gave him a poke. The intoxicated Pannalal promptly opened his eyes and blinked inquiringly at Lawrence.

"Let's go. It will take some time to get to the *khemta*," said Lawrence.

The inspector watched Pannalal swiftly packing his hookah to be stowed away by the shop's bellboy. Then, tightening his habitual cotton shawl around his waist, Pannalal stood up ready to go. His eyes were red like hibiscus from the copious amounts of *bhang* he'd drunk. As Lawrence also got up to exit, he realized his feet were not exactly steady. In contrast, noted Lawrence with a touch of envy, other than the red eyes, Pannalal appeared to be his usual rock-steady self.

As the two paid Bishwambhar, the pot-bellied proprietor seated on a low stool by the entrance inquired, "Is sahib going to the *khemta* dance at Botu *babu*'s?"

The colorful Bishwambhar knew his clients. He knew Lawrence and Pannalal usually had plans after they left his shop – *khemta*, *jatra*, or some other entertainment. Knowing how widely Botu *babu*'s bashes were attended, Bishwambhar was sure they had heard of it.

Turning to Pannalal without waiting for Lawrence sahib to respond, Bishwambhar added, "Botu *babu* has commissioned a top-notch dancer. The luscious Shashibala!"

Bishwambhar had raised his brows, his eyes almost closed with pleasure, a wide, suggestive smile flourishing on his face.

After stepping out from Bishwambhar's with Pannalal, Lawrence walked over to the flower girl, intending to purchase some of her marigold. He had observed, when *babus* met their paramour, they always carried garlands with them. In an opportune moment, they either flung the garland toward the woman or put the garland lovingly around the woman. Lawrence was going to be ready for Shashibala tonight.

Botu *babu*'s pleasure palace, where the *khemta* was arranged, was on Beadon Street, further north. Lawrence and Pannalal decided to head up along Wellesley Street in that direction. As they went by the bazaar toward Wellesley Square, they passed the two fishmongers Lawrence had seen before.

One of the women looked at Lawrence with a beguiling smile and asked, "*Aye gora*! Do you want some fish? It is very fresh. Big *bhetki*."

With a kind smile so as not to offend her, Lawrence shook his head indicating that he didn't want fish. With a meaningful smirk, the woman looked at her companion, "See those unsteady feet? Sahib has come loaded from Bishwambhar's, probably daydreaming about the woman he will visit in a brothel tonight."

And then with an exclamation she interjected, "*Oh-ma*! Look! Sahib has bought garlands!"

She had spotted the dried Sal leaf wrapped package Lawrence held, with marigold peeking from its corners. The women were now grinning broadly, having drawn a juicy conclusion on why a sahib should be carrying Sal-wrapped marigold at this time of the night.

Pannalal, who had been quiet so far, barked a warning at thc frolicsome girls, "Shut up and do your work. Talking rubbish!"

Lawrence knew Calcutta's female fishmongers had a reputation for being sharp-tongued. These women could get downright nasty. He smiled placatingly at the pair, as he and Pannalal walked past them.

By then, a half-moon had risen on the clear summer skies. After the smoke-filled atmosphere at Bishwambhar's, the evening air felt pleasant to Pannalal and Lawrence. They walked side by side quietly, unwilling to interrupt the sweet buzz from the *bhang* working its magic in their system. Looking at Pannalal from the corner of his eyes, Lawrence marveled once again. *The man showed no outward signs of intoxication.* For the next twenty minutes, they stayed on the main road, flanked by palatial British constructions. Lawrence admired the open waters of Wellington Square with its stocky ducks and long-necked swans visible in the fading light of day. Next, they passed the grand pillars of Calcutta's first hospital – the Medical College building. After a while, they slipped into one of the alleys forming a shortcut to Botu *babu*'s palace on Beadon Street.

The exposed drain-lined alleys, with visible mounds of rubbish to the sides, did not make for pleasant walks. While Lawrence brought out his handkerchief, Pannalal held the loose cuff of his *kurta* to his nose. Lawrence knew it got much worse in the rainy season with the water from the sewers overflowing. The government's expenditure to build Calcutta had historically focused on its European neighborhoods, with the native areas struggling under dual onslaughts of poverty and a burgeoning population. As the stench got worse, Lawrence tried to distract himself by wondering about the dancer Shashibala. He was looking forward to her *khemta*, a tradition known to walk a fine line between art and vulgarity. Lawrence remembered Bishwambhar's excitement. "Top-notch dancer! " he said.

"Hmph! See that native Christian?" pointed Pannalal, breaking their long silence and bringing Lawrence, lost in thoughts of *khemta* dancers he had known in the past, back to the present.

Lawrence noticed they had exited the foul-smelling alley. Pannalal was pointing to a dark, curly haired, native man in his sixties, sitting under a banyan tree, surrounded by a handful of other working-class men.

"He talks to the natives here," elaborated Pannalal with his eyes glinting cynical amusement. "They come to him under that tree, and he tells them whatever he fancies about your Lord Jesus Christ."

Had Pannalal not drawn his attention to the man, Lawrence wouldn't have noticed this character who went by the name Gokul. But now, Lawrence recognized Gokul, having seen him often at the People's Church Lawrence himself frequented. Gokul had a certain nondescript quality that made it easy to lose him in the crowd. Then again, if you looked closely, he had a peculiar seductiveness. Something about him always made Lawrence uncomfortable. Lawrence knew that many years ago, his friend, Reverend Stuart of the People's Church had recruited Gokul to spread the word of Lord Jesus among the masses. His Christian name was Gary, but it didn't stick.

Abruptly, Lawrence was distracted by a friendly nudge from Pannalal who danced his brows and jeered, "Sahib, you are Christian and so is Gokul!"

After walking another couple of minutes, the two arrived in front of the ornate, whitewashed walls of Botu *babu*'s pleasure palace. Oil lamps flickered along the terrace, the balcony, and the perimeter of the building. *Babus* in fine *dhuti panjabi* looked busy, running in and out of the house and supervising various activities. They did not take much notice of the new arrivals. Entering through the relatively modest gate, Lawrence and Pannalal found themselves in a square hall, lit by a grand overhead chandelier. Large columns stood on all four sides of the hall. The central portion had been raised to form a stage. Thick, sheet-lined mattresses and pillows lay around the stage for the guests. As some eyes turned to look at the sole British man entering the hall, Lawrence spotted a fish-eyed, tumid-lipped man, presumably sponsor Botu *babu*, reclining in luxury among his entourage at one end. Lawrence nodded to acknowledge the *namaskar* that man held toward the officer in greeting. Currently, two groups sat on the stage, engaged in *kobir-larai*, a type of a verbal duel where each party has to say their bit in extemporal rhymes. Lawrence checked that the next item was Shashibala's *khemta,* tonight's main attraction. Afterward, there was more. *Tappa* songs, of high wit and luscious tunes, and a *jatra*, where they were going to enact some undoubtedly spicy, indigenous drama. The air was thick with the evening's excitement. No one was expecting it to finish anytime soon. Feeling hungry, Lawrence proposed they get some food before settling down inside the palace.

They were shown to the side of the palace building with the ad hoc tents serving food. *Babus* stood outside, energetically supervising the stall owners. Pannalal pointed to one frying hot potato chops. Another right next to it, was frying sweet, crisp *jeelipi*. The mounds of food on display attracted humans and flies alike, but the guests did not seem to mind. A few perky urchins could be seen around the stalls. They were reminded that the programs tonight were for adults only.

"Take the food and go. If you're found here after, you'll get a beating you won't soon forget!" threatened the adults amiably.

The *kobir-larai* team finished up. There was a short break with people milling in and out. The kids were chased away. Then, from a row of landaulets waiting by the side of Botu *babu*'s house, several deep aluminum basins holding a large number of whiskey bottles were brought out and carried inside the house. Around the same time, three phaetons came and stopped in front of the palace; the celebrated Shashibala and her team of musicians stepped out from them. Those eager to catch a glimpse found the dancer concealed head-to-toe by a shiny silk covering. Shashibala slowly made way to the center of the stage to begin setup for the evening. Shortly thereafter, Shashibala began her *khemta*.

The teenage dancer was stunning. More than perfect features, her attraction lay in her sex appeal. Her juicy expressions and energetic pelvic thrusts, metered by the rhythm of her skillful footwork, drove her admirers wild. Sponsor Botu *babu* shouted ecstatic compliments. The other *babus* followed his lead, with bottles of whiskey in one hand and money in the other, while making raucous calls to her. If she desired to collect the money that they were waving at her, the dancer was to approach them and kiss them on their lips. Initially, the lady did not show enthusiasm for this proposal, keeping her devotees on the hook. But soon, she relented, accepting the scandalous deal.

Lawrence was watching Shashibala perform with admiring eyes, taking swigs out of the bottle of whiskey Pannalal extended toward him from time to time. They were sharing that bottle because when the initial supply of whiskey arrived, there was almost a stampede to purchase the bottles, and Pannalal only managed to get one.

As the young belle swayed her hips, a delighted Pannalal turned to look at Lawrence with his eyebrows raised, seeking his companion's response. Lawrence nodded enthusiastically, reacting with spontaneous appreciation;

Shashibala was undoubtedly irresistible, and his blood was on fire, like every other male in the audience.

Lawrence extracted some money from his pocket and waved them to attract Shashibala's attention. Noticing him, the dancer rewarded him with a smile. As the lady neared, Lawrence extended the money toward her. This surprised Shashibala, who wasn't expecting to get the money without working for it. The other *babus* weren't parting with their cash without getting the maiden to kiss. Recovering from her initial surprise, Shashibala took the money from Lawrence's hand. Then, after a brief hesitation, she moved closer intending to give him a kiss. However, Lawrence turned his head away. As he looked back at her, he saw the young woman's eyes flash with annoyance. *Where everyone was hoping to win her favor, how dare this ungrateful Englishman reject her kiss!* Lawrence locked his eyes with those of the delicious wench. Holding Shashibala captive with his gaze, Lawrence began to bring out all the money he had on him, taking his sweet time doing it. By then, every eye in the room was on the two, including Botu *babu*. Pannalal also sat gawking.

In immaculate Bengali, Lawrence said, "I am not happy with just a kiss. You are too beautiful! If you remove your clothes and then do your *khemta*, then all this money is yours, along with my heart."

The musicians had faltered to a stop. No one moved or spoke. Shashibala's eyes flashed as she stared at Lawrence for what seemed like an eternity. The amount he offered stoked her ego, but his initial rejection had hurt. Finally, the headstrong young woman leaned forward and took all the money from Lawrence's hand. Summoning a servant with a flick of her eyes, she handed off the money she had collected. Facing her audience, she started to retreat toward the stage, walking back, one step at a time. Off came her stroll, blouse, and skirt, one by one in an unhurried strip tease. Soon, not a thread lay on young Shashibala. Her flowing, dark hair and ample gold jewelry shone against her smooth, brown skin.

Looking directly at Lawrence, Shashibala said, “Do not think this is for your money, sahib. Remember, you also promised your heart.”

As the crowd who had never seen *khemta* by a naked woman, erupted in roaring approval, Lawrence winked good-naturedly at Pannalal.

Shashibala put one hand on her waist, the other behind her head, and resumed thrusting her pelvis to the beats she kept with her feet; the nipples on her full, jiggling breasts had hardened with excitement. The audience showered the performer with generous amounts of cash, and an avalanche of compliments. As she spun around in circular motions, her sweat-slicked body glistened in the light of the overhead chandelier. Lawrence savored the sight of the youthful, eastern beauty. The Sal leaf wrapped marigold that he had brought with him lay forgotten on the mattress. Before Shashibala’s dance was complete though, Lawrence leaned over to Pannalal to tell him he was stepping out for a bit; it was too hot inside. Pannalal inclined his head to indicate he had heard without turning to look, giving Lawrence the impression that he didn’t want to be distracted from the performance.

As the inspector emerged from the stuffy atmosphere of the hall, the pleasant night air washed over him. Though it took a moment for his eyes to adjust, the half-moon was bright enough for Lawrence to see. Most of the oil lamps were dead or dying. He eyed the deserted food stalls with empty aluminum basins stacked away. A mound of used Sal leaf food plates stood in one corner. Lawrence started to walk toward the Bose Pond, located about ten minutes from the pleasure palace. While he was perspiring among all those people inside, the cool waters of the pond had called to him.

Chapter Three

24th May 1856

With Radhanath's job on Sara Langley's tent completed, the four parted ways to change for the *shikar* party's inauguration dinner which was set to start in another half hour. Having witnessed Sara thank Radhanath for coming to her rescue, Chandrakanta showed no further curiosity about the Englishwoman. Foremost on his mind was the upcoming dinner, and he was eager to be there on time. Noticing the long strides Chandrakanta was making, Radhanath asked his friend to go ahead, proposing to join him directly at the pavilion. Chandrakanta agreed, supposing Radhanath was tired from working on the tents, not to mention their long journey on horseback up until late afternoon today.

As Chandrakanta vanished ahead, Radhanath relaxed his pace, walking almost lazily among the frequently empty tents. Fresh, woodsy scent of the outdoors enveloped his senses. A nocturnal chorus of chirping crickets filled his ears. Reaching his own tent, Radhanath stood inspecting it in the light of the lantern the *Raja*'s men had placed outside the entrance. Momentarily, his eyes strayed to the light coming from Chandrakanta's tent, next to his. Picking up the lantern, Radhanath entered his own tent. He saw a clean camp bed with a folded plaid blanket resting at one end. His knapsack lay on the ground next to the bed. A pot of water on a little stool and a folding chair completed the furnishings. Eyeing his bag, Radhanath decided unpacking and organizing would have to wait till tomorrow.

Absentmindedly, Radhanath sat on the chair by his bed. The events of the last hour or so filled his thoughts. He found the color of his mind completely changed from how it was when he first arrived at the camp today. In the brief moments with the girl Sara Langley this evening, an alien feeling of masculine possessiveness had come over him. He had wanted to know Sara in a way he had never wanted to know anyone else before. Perhaps it was the exquisite life in her eyes, the promise he imagined in them, that set him off. He glanced at his thumb where the hammer had fallen, nursing it idly. He sighed, wishing he understood why he was feeling so overwhelmed. After a while, pulling his pocket watch out, he saw it was ten to seven. He felt regret that he could not sit and continue like this. Slowly, he got up to get dressed.

By the time Radhanath stepped out in an embroidered *galabandh* suit, night had fallen thickly around them. The path to the pavilion, however, was well illuminated. Torches on tall poles stood burning throughout the campground. Members of the royal staff were available at various points to direct the guests. The night air had become an exotic mix of aroma – spicy biriyani, attar, and incense, alongside scents from wildflowers and fresh cut grass. Radhanath couldn't help feeling astonished by the rich aura of the place. Soon, he found himself in front of the walled pavilion that he and Chandrakanta had only briefly seen from the side when they got here earlier today. Floodlit by golden light from the torches standing around it, the pavilion looked stunning, delineated grandly against a clear night sky. Radhanath recognized the *bandhani* artwork depicting folklore from Jainagar, displayed on the long canvas formed by the walls of the pavilion. He estimated the structure could easily seat a couple hundred guests.

As he stepped inside, Radhanath's eyes were dazzled. He saw several chandeliers spanning the roof, but that couldn't have explained this much light. Then he noticed the highly reflective brass plates cleverly placed at various points on the roof. *That's what amplified the light!* The enormous pavilion was rectangular in shape, with two entrances located on opposite sides of its shorter walls. A continuous curtain of red velvet hung down its length, splitting the space into two halves. Radhanath assumed that the other side must be where the typical long-running dinner table was being set. On the side where he stood, couches and chairs were arranged to accommodate the guests. Radhanath had been hearing faint music as he was walking toward the pavilion. He now located the source of it. A raised platform stood near the entrance away from him. Several women seated on that stage were playing the *sitar* to energetic beats of *dholaks*. Behind them, the king's imposing throne stood empty; the king hadn't arrived yet. Radhanath could see musicians sporting both European and Indian instruments, seated in an enclosed area to the side of the stage.

At this time, one of the *pagri*, cummerbund clad waiters approached Radhanath with a tray of beverages. Picking up a brandy, Radhanath continued to walk among the guests. The European men were mostly in military apparel, red coats, or gold embroidered black velvet; next to them, their women were elegantly gowned and coiffured. Engrossed in conversation, their faces gleamed with the evening's excitement. The royally-attired Indians were engaged in their own discussions, standing around or sitting on couches. As before, both the European and Indian guests seemed to prefer congregating mainly among themselves. Radhanath spotted a bowtie, tailcoat and pantaloon clad Chandrakanta in animated conversation with a distinguished looking Indian gentleman.

As Radhanath approached, Chandrakanta introduced him to his companion, "Radhanath, meet his excellency, my friend Nana sahib – son of his highness, the Peshwa Bajirao of Bithoor."

The man immediately raised his hand to correct Chandrakanta, "Nuh-huh, *adopted son*, sir!"

His silk suit and bejeweled *pagri* paled in comparison to the fiery eyes he turned to greet Radhanath. Nana sahib was a polished man, several years younger than the two friends – *with a rather disconcerting aura,* thought Radhanath, his brandy forgotten. The words *adopted son* were still ringing in his ears.

When Chandrakanta introduced Radhanath as the man who discovered Mount Everest, Nana sahib's face lit up with pleasure, "*Arreh*! Everyone's talking about Mount Everest!"

With a bow, Nana sahib added, "I am deeply honored to meet the protagonist of that story."

Radhanath inclined his head to politely acknowledge the compliment, but he wasn't prepared for what came next. With his eyes unmistakably mocking, Nana sahib said, "They didn't bother to include you in their announcement, did they? If memory serves, there was no Indian name in that article?"

Taken aback, Radhanath exclaimed, "Nana sahib, there's been no official announcement yet. A private letter simply…"

A sudden burst of bagpipes from the musicians' enclave near the stage interrupted their conversation. The British redcoats were taking part in some ceremonial activity. Ignoring them, Nana sahib turned back to Radhanath.

"Ah Mr. Sikdar, this is no news to me!" Nana sahib said, taking the disapproval in Radhanath's expression smoothly in his stride. "I have known the British long enough to appreciate how these things work. I bet you're a hero in some of their internal circles."

Radhanath glanced at his friend before moving to finish the brandy he held, quietly wondering how much the two have discussed him before he showed up tonight.

Touching Radhanath's arm with a wry smile, Nana sahib pointed to Chandrakanta and said, "Remember, how I corrected him that I am the adopted son of my late father? Throughout our history, India's royal families have adopted heirs in the absence of a direct male child. But now, the British have decided to strip me of all honors, refusing to recognize me as rightful heir to the Peshwa. Why? Because I was not *born* from him!"

With eyes narrowed, lips thinned frustratedly, Nana sahib drawled on his words for effect, "The doctrine of lapse, they tell me! A completely ad hoc law that they passed without consulting a single Indian. They've decided I can live in the royal premises and maintain a fort and army, *but* I am to be denied all recognition and all honors that would have come to the Peshwa, including the pension they paid my father."

Earnestly looking at Radhanath, Nana sahib insisted, "It's not just about the money, mind you. In a sense, your situation and mine are the same. You are recognized, then again, *not*. In important ways, we have been made invisible!"

Chandrakanta savored what Nana sahib was telling his difficult friend. He had never been able to quite so succinctly express why he felt upset with Radhanath's loyalty to the GTSI. Unable to resist pulling Radhanath's legs, Chandrakanta rejoined, raising his brows in a lighthearted vein, "Nana sahib, Radhanath really enjoys working with the British. He has nothing but high praise for their George Everest."

"Look," said Radhanath, gazing directly at Chandrakanta, "how can you not respect the man who has devoted his life to measuring the length and breadth of our country? On innumerable field trips, he never hesitated to expose himself to the elements. Sometimes he paid for that by contracting life-threatening disease that left him sick for months. But he persisted! How can you not respect that?" Shaking his head, Radhanath said, "Without George Everest, GTSI would not be where it is today!"

Nana sahib countered, "Is that enough reason for the GTSI to name the highest mountain peak in the world, found in Asia, discovered by an *Indian* man, after George Everest?"

No one missed his smooth emphasis on Indian.

Radhanath looked at Nana sahib in silence, surprised that a casual dinner conversation had become so provocative. Cued by Radhanath's evident uneasiness, Nana sahib began again, "Mr. Sikdar, I am not suggesting the British are entirely without honor. I have hobnobbed with them long enough to know a few I would trust my life with. However, no matter how interesting they are as people or how admirable their qualities are, at the end of the day, they are very clear about what it is that they want from us. They want to have the last word on everything, and you have to dance to their tune to get anywhere with them."

Nana sahib was making a conscious effort to speak up, to be heard above the loud cacophony of bagpipes and drums he had been trying to ignore since it started. He now looked to the source with a pained expression again. It had become too loud to continue. Radhanath didn't mind the interruption, feeling awkward about openly criticizing the English within earshot of so many of them.

At this point, a man ascended to the stage. Beating on a gong he held, he announced that his royal highness, *Raja* Uday Singh, the sovereign of Jainagar has arrived. The Indian musicians seated to one side of the stage started to play a welcome song. Radhanath spotted a man in a peacock-feathered crown, heading toward the stage, leading a retinue of important others. It was not hard to guess this was *Raja* Uday Singh. Next to the king was a British officer, possibly the guest of honor who looked vaguely familiar to Radhanath. As the *Raja* climbed on the stage, the applauding crowd rose to its feet. Members of the *Raja*'s entourage moved to take their positions on and around the stage. Radhanath surveyed the audience cheering for the *Raja*. His eyes stopped on a face he had seen not too long ago. Sara Langley looked magnificent in an embroidered gown of midnight blue, her golden hair pulled back in a chic chignon. Radhanath felt her severe hairdo accentuated her womanliness. Dubois, who was standing next to her, was saying something to Sara. As

Radhanath's eyes lingered on Sara, he found it incredible that feelings similar to that first time he saw her, seemed to wash over him again.

When he looked back at the stage, Radhanath was thoroughly surprised. He now clearly saw the face of the British man next to the *Raja*. It was his own boss – Surveyor General Andrew Waugh! No wonder he had looked familiar from the side. Radhanath shouldn't have been surprised to find Waugh here. Since this *shikar* was a key diplomatic event on India's sociopolitical stage, as the head of GTSI, Waugh would've been automatically invited. A sudden suspicion crossed Radhanath's mind. *Was Waugh's letter on Mount Everest purposely leaked targeting coverage at this event?* The attention Jainagar's *shikar* party got from the European press made this a great occasion to talk about GTSI's achievements.

Uday Singh, who had come to the front of the stage, held his hands in a traditional *namaskar*, savoring the cheering crowd. Then as he raised his hands, a pregnant silence fell. When Uday Singh began, Radhanath found the *Raja* was well-spoken, skillfully engaging his audience.

Uday Singh started with the history of this hunt. When his great grandfather killed a seven-foot tiger with a mere dagger in the early 1700s, Jainagar's royal family had started these elite safaris to commemorate the occasion. It was only after the *Raja*'s grandfather signed a treaty of friendship with the English in 1818 that the *shikar*'s guest list started to include European guests. The *Raja* joked that the *shikar* used to be a simple affair in the early days – with his guests content with the natural reserves of wildlife from the area. His pointed reference to the growing demand for supplies of exotic animals evoked polite laughter from his audience.

It was the perfect segue to the specialty game the *Raja*'s men had brought to the area this year. To everyone's delight, Uday Singh declared that in addition to Asiatic cheetahs all the way from Persia, they planned to release markhors, prized for their spectacular horns. Of course, he neglected to mention the open secret that the more dangerous animals were usually drugged to make it easier to hunt them. The *Raja* added that although transportation between the campground and the hunting ground has been arranged, should the guests choose to ride by themselves, they were more than welcome to check out his stables. He also told them of the various *tamashas* and *mujaras* being hosted inside the campground to entertain his guests. The sovereign wound up his speech with an important reminder. All major meals were going to be served at this pavilion.

Then, Uday Singh said, "Ladies and gentlemen, it is now my privilege to welcome the honorable Surveyor General Andrew Waugh, head of the Great Trigonometric Survey of India, to speak from this podium. As you may know, having measured Earth's tallest peak on our Himalayas, he appears on the front page of newspapers around the world today!"

As Waugh stepped forward amidst claps and cheers, Radhanath felt both Chandrakanta and Nana sahib's eyes on himself. He nodded to admit he knew the man; Chandrakanta, of course, knew their exact relationship. Of their own accord, Radhanath's eyes went to where he had spotted Sara moments ago. He saw Dubois beaming at Sara, possibly titillated by Waugh's unexpected appearance. She acknowledged Dubois, then turned her face to the crowds, searching for something.

Meanwhile, General Waugh stood smiling, occasionally bowing, and waited for the crowd to settle. Then he began his address, starting with a warm thanks to *Raja* Uday Singh for the gracious invitation to this event. Waugh said he had planned to attend the *shikar* as a regular soldier, with no intention of making speeches. But then, with a mock, pained expression, Waugh added, "You see, the cat got out of the bag earlier than we wanted!" His oblique reference to the unauthorized news of Mount Everest in the papers drew chuckles from his audience. "Ah, just as well!" he shrugged.

Waugh began with words introducing GTSI's mission. Back in the eighteenth century, the Indian sub-continent was mostly a blank page, with its layout, major cities, rivers, and mountains, existing only on very rough maps, built partly based on hearsay and partly from written accounts by the occasional traveler to the region. Large chunks of the land were literally blank, with no information available about them. Waugh said, with unmistakable pride, that the GTSI has changed all that forever. GTSI's men, British and Indians alike, have walked a hard, tortuous path to measure the length and breadth of the country and develop its first accurate maps. It had all been very worth it, Waugh asserted, serving the people of India, assisting the English administration, and, at the same time, furthering the cause of science.

Waugh went on to say that originally, the GTSI never intended to measure mountain peaks so far up north on the Himalayas. Lady luck, he acknowledged, had played a hand. Mount Everest was a very difficult peak to measure, perpetually covered in mist and totally inaccessible. There was no particular reason to think it was the tallest as it appeared shorter than other peaks near it. Nevertheless, driven by some kind of instinct, enthusiastic field personnel led by General Nicholson went ahead and took measurements.

"However, my esteemed friends, I should tell you, the direct measurement wasn't enough. You simply cannot trust a direct measurement in these circumstances. One day it is one number. The next day, when the atmospheric conditions have changed, the direct measurement will give you a different number for the same peak. In fact, you don't even have to wait till the next day. Within a span of hours, you could get a different value. There are a lot of variables beyond human control," explained Waugh with mock disappointment. "So? What could we do? We called on our mathematicians!"

The lighthearted tone of his last words inspired vague chuckles from his audience, not necessarily able to appreciate the connection. Continuing to use a carefree tone, Waugh clarified, "Seriously, their contribution to this discovery was no less than those of the field surveyors who made the actual measurements."

To Radhanath's irritation, the audience found this comment funny as well. With a smile reflecting private amusement, the Surveyor General started to wrap up his speech, "I'll assume our esteemed guests will thank me for sparing them the intricacies of why we needed mathematics, yes? Especially since that would be what stands between you and this grand dinner!" The audience roared its approval. With a dignified bow, Waugh stepped back as Uday Singh stepped forward to take over from him.

Without consciously meaning to, Radhanath found himself looking toward Sara a third time this evening. *The lady was looking directly at him!* His heart skipped a beat. It thrilled him to realize that she had taken the trouble to locate him amid the sea of faces. He inclined his head briefly acknowledging Sara Langley, as did the lady, before both looked away. In the very next moment, Radhanath felt an uncharacteristic angst. Waugh had only briefly mentioned mathematics, with no details on his chief mathematician. *Did Sara believe his grand claims of having discovered Mount Everest pretty much by himself?*

Soon after, the curtain running down the middle of the pavilion was drawn back revealing a sumptuously laid table. The soaring candle flames, the grand fresh-flower arrangements, and the elegant silverware sparkled with the evening's promise. Radhanath's eyes were drawn to some structures along the opposite wall of the pavilion. It looked like a set of anterooms, presumably being used as temporary kitchens to organize the food. The staff began ushering the guests to their assigned seats. Upon discovering that Nana sahib was seated away from them, Chandrakanta requested one of the staff to reconfigure their placements such that the group did not have to disperse – a request they were able to accommodate. As the three settled into their high-backed chairs, Radhanath was astonished by the vegetable sculptures he saw, placed at frequent intervals along the length of the table. There were lions, wolves, swans, and owls carved from melons, potatoes, brinjals, and gourds. Uday Singh had artisans from Siam to thank for this display, that cleverly accentuated the main theme of the event.

The dinner constituted a delightful blend of Indian and continental cuisine with many varieties of spicy meat and vegetables, paired with delectable wines. As they went through the courses, Chandrakanta and Nana sahib discussed East India Company's administrative policies, causing Radhanath to fall silent. Since both were landed gentry, they had tenants living on their estates. Their conversation revolved around various issues they were facing, particularly the East India Company's meddling with indigenous property laws, often without a full appreciation of the consequences. Radhanath was surprised to register Chandrakanta's vigorous interest in politics, a side of him that had remained rather hidden from Radhanath, in all the time he knew his friend.

Nana sahib had been looking at Radhanath from time to time throughout the evening. Radhanath noticed that Nana sahib refrained from bringing up the GTSI a second time in their conversation. He didn't ask a single question on how well Radhanath knew Surveyor General Waugh. His silence seemed to say, he had felt duty-bound to mention what he did, one Indian to another, but he didn't want to make Radhanath uncomfortable. As Radhanath watched Nana sahib talk with Chandrakanta, he wondered how well they knew each other.

After the dinner, the guests were ushered back to the couches on the side of the pavilion where they had been earlier in the evening. The separation curtain was dropped while the dinner table was being cleared. The guests were served madeira, port, whiskey, coffee, or tea and left free to broadly mingle. When a waiter approached the three with a tray of drinks, Nana sahib chose an aromatic *sherbet* prepared with milk, cardamom, and dried rose petals. Chandrakanta took a few moments debating the choices, and then settled for the same thing as Nana sahib. Meanwhile, Radhanath had picked up and emptied a shot of cognac. He picked up a second shot glass just as the waiter was leaving, causing the man to stop and wait hesitantly, wondering if he'd like a third. Radhanath nodded to the man and grabbed one more for later. Seeing Radhanath drink like this, Chandrakanta was reminded of their school days.

He broke into a soft chuckle, causing both Radhanath and Nana sahib to look at him curiously.

"We used to play a game, when we were boys studying at the Hindu School together more than twenty-five years ago now," said Chandrakanta. "It involved alcohol and mathematics."

Nana sahib looked at Chandrakanta expectantly, waiting for him to continue. Radhanath sat with a quiet smile on his face.

"There were many from affluent families at our school, so purchasing liquor was no big deal. In our game, each participant got a shot of whiskey and a geometrical problem to solve. You drank, and then you had to solve your problem. If you did both properly, you qualified for the next round. Otherwise, you were eliminated. Being good at both, my friend here was often the last man standing, to the utter vexation of those who challenged him," Chandrakanta finished fondly. Nana sahib sat looking highly amused.

Radhanath broke into a chuckle himself. Then a tad defensively said, "It happened only a few times and was arranged in secrecy of course!"

Chandrakanta turned to Nana sahib and said, "Radhanath had produced proof of his extraordinary mathematical aptitude while still in school! He was one of those rare Indians whose work had come out in an international journal at that time!" Chandrakanta looked toward Radhanath, having forgotten the name of it, "Do you remember the name of the journal?"

"*Gleanings in Science*," responded Radhanath softly.

Abruptly, Nana sahib asked, "Won't you say hello to General Waugh tonight?" Radhanath was startled with the suddenness of the suggestion.

Nana sahib pointed in a direction behind Radhanath and said, "There he is!"

Radhanath craned his neck to where Nana sahib pointed, with slight discomfort. Indeed, there was a crowd starting to accumulate around the red-coated Andrew Waugh. While there was nothing wrong with Nana sahib's question, Radhanath sensed a silent rebuke in it – rebuke for Radhanath's implicit willingness to settle for less than he deserved. Radhanath mulled over what his next steps should be with his face still turned away. Then looking back at Nana sahib, he said, "Of course I will. Since we are both here!"

"I am in no hurry though," he added. Pointing his head in the direction where Waugh stood, Radhanath explained, "As you can see, he's quite popular at the moment." That's when Radhanath finished his third shot of cognac and stood up, abruptly. He begged their leave, telling them he would go around a bit by himself.

When looking toward Waugh, Radhanath's eyes had caught another person. Sara Langley was standing on her own. He had decided he was going to go say hello to her then. As he headed in her direction, the three shots of cognac he had downed began to make its presence felt in his blood. He hadn't drunk so much in a while and felt transported back to his teen years. Tongue-in-cheek, he thought, *if he could hold his liquor and tackle mathematics, he was ready for the young lady tonight.*

Sara turned to watch Radhanath approach. When he got close, she spoke with intriguing playfulness, "I have never had so much of the GTSI in such a short span. The newspapers are talking about it. Then I meet you at the camp. Then we have General Waugh give a speech. I am beginning to feel like I work for the GTSI myself." Radhanath noticed she did not mention Dubois.

"What are you doing on your own? Wasn't Monsieur Dubois here with you?" Radhanath inquired.

With her eyes glinting, Sara agreed, "Yes, he's gone now to get more crème caramel. I believe you can get drinks and dessert as you like, from those anterooms on the other side of the dining table." Then, leaning her head toward Radhanath in the manner of one sharing a secret, she pointed out, "And there on the stage is Uncle Dick." Radhanath looked to where Uday Singh was seated on his throne surrounded by what looked like members of his ministry and important guests.

"Ah, there is Mr. Dubois!" said Sara. Dubois was walking toward them holding a dessert bowl in hand.

"*Bon soir, mon ami*! I was thinking of you," Dubois greeted Radhanath. "The *Raja* never said General Waugh was going to be here! Did you know?"

Without waiting for a response, Dubois next invited, "If you haven't already, would you like to come with me to meet the General?"

"What do you say Miss Langley?" Radhanath asked Sara, "I presume you want to meet our illustrious head and tell him how much you have enjoyed hearing about us all evening?"

Acknowledging Radhanath's reference to her earlier remark with a twinkle in her eye, Sara nodded in agreement, "Yes, I would love to come."

Dubois was eyeing his crème caramel with fond hesitation and then a tad friskily, decided to bring the bowl with him. Noticing Radhanath watching him with amusement, he added, "This is incredible! They have even laced it with rose water. *Parfait!*"

There were quite a few people around Waugh by the time the three neared the Surveyor General. As they waited their turn, Radhanath watched the formally attired Waugh, many military medals hanging from his lapels. He thought of their time together, poring over sheets of data and complicated mathematics, in his airy Wood Street office in Calcutta where all formalities were kept aside on Waugh's explicit orders. Waugh used to say, "Here, we are as servants of science. If there are intellectual battles that drive us to very edge of civility, so be it. There is no need to fret over that. Within these walls, the truth is the only master."

The group that stood separating the three from Waugh moved unexpectedly. The three now got a direct view of the General, intent at that moment on listening to a stranger. As they moved in, Radhanath heard the man telling Waugh, "It makes plain sense! Not a round approximate figure like twenty-nine thousand feet, but exactly twenty-nine thousand and two. I mean if someone said twenty-nine thousand, I would have thought that's not right, that's too perfect! Nature doesn't work like that!" Waugh shrugged his shoulders as if he couldn't agree more. Then his eyes fell on the newcomers.

The illustrious head of GTSI looked bewildered, finding of all people Radhanath standing in front of him at this precise moment. Then he recovered, and his face lit up with a smile. Exchanging pleasantries with the three, including the lovely Miss Langley who had introduced herself to him, Waugh raised his voice to draw the attention of those standing around them, "Ladies and gentlemen, you have heard much from me about the GTSI. I didn't know we had more members of our team here tonight. Meet Monsieur Dubois, all the way from France, an optician par excellence. And Mr. Sikdar, our chief mathematician. I was telling you how mathematics has been an essential tool to accurately estimate the height of Mount Everest. Rady Sikdar was the main man on that job."

As Waugh spoke about him, Radhanath's demeanor became stiff. Some of the Europeans standing near them had started to raise hesitant toasts and then fell silent. Radhanath's mathematics background, imposing physique and reserved expression were a bewildering combination in a native man. The hunting party audience, largely here for a good time, felt a visceral resistance. They didn't want to bother with what this strange character may or may not have achieved. Soon they started to fidget, some smiled. This was not the first time Radhanath faced this sort of reception. He had seen this play out on other occasions where his work may have come up in discussions with a general audience. In fact, levity was surprisingly common. Radhanath's hypothesis was, *it came from a need to hide behind something*. As a case in point, right now, these people were possibly feeling both out of depth, and uninterested in the mathematics Waugh advertised. And these feelings were perhaps magnified because Radhanath challenged their expectations on many levels. Somewhere though, realizing the unfairness of it, they tried to hide behind lightheartedness.

Waugh was about to resume conversation, when a stocky man among the audience, good-naturedly pointed to the bowl of dessert Dubois held and asked, “You like it, Frenchman?”

“*Delicieuse*!” Dubois enthusiastically responded. “The kitchen staff here are miracle workers. I don’t know how they are serving these things in the middle of nowhere.” The Frenchman sank his teeth into yet another delicious bite before continuing, “My only regret is that I might have to remake all my clothes!” His comment drew polite laughter from his audience. Dubois continued, “That, ladies and gentlemen, is no small horror, I swear to you. I sent my favorite tailcoat to Calcutta’s Roshan Ali and received a perfect copy, down to the patched-up tear on my coat front!”

Everyone looked at Dubois blankly for a moment, and then people started to laugh. Genuinely incredulous, one blurted, “You cannot be serious!” Others shook their head – just the thing you’d expect from those native tailors, they seemed to say.

“I am serious, sir!” insisted Dubois, “I am scared to visit Roshan Ali again! The last I checked, I was a hundred and sixty pounds. I don’t know how much I will be after all this crème caramel.”

While Dubois stood wearing an insincere expression of anxiety on his face, Waugh couldn’t resist joking, “We may not meet the fashion standards of Paris, Monsieur Dubois, but you are too harsh on Roshan Ali. He is a fine tailor. He is my tailor in Calcutta.”

The stocky man spoke up again, “Did I hear you say a hundred and sixty *pounds*? Now, now, I thought the French were all about the metric system! Why am I not hearing kilograms?”

Waugh laughed out loud and rejoined, “It shows Dubois has rubbed shoulders with us for a little too long! But pray Frenchman, you’ve got to tell us exactly how many kilograms a hundred and sixty pounds is.” Waugh’s comment was met with loud chuckles, as the largely English audience delighted in needling the Frenchman.

Before Dubois could respond, a female voice cut through this laughter, and people turned to look at young Sara Langley responding to Waugh's challenge. "If I remember my math lessons, it is roughly 2.2 pounds to a kilogram. That means you must divide 160 by 2.2. And let me see," continued Sara, trying to do the calculations out loud, "since 160 divided by 2 equals 80, this result should be something shy of 80 kilograms..."

Waugh interrupted, "That is correct, Miss, well done!" Seeing a lovely young lady attempt mathematics, the men had produced patronizing smiles. Waugh continued, "However, as you can probably appreciate, the challenging part of this calculation is to figure out exactly how much less than 80 kgs is this going to be. You and I are in the same boat on that one, without pen and paper to work it out."

The amused laughter Waugh's response had evoked had not all abated when a male voice spoke up, "72 kgs approximately." Radhanath had spoken.

Chuckling uncomfortably, Dubois looked at Radhanath and said, "*Oui*, sounds about right. That was my weight when I last left France. And I haven't changed much since then."

From among those now looking at Radhanath once again, the earlier thickset gentleman spoke, "Did you do the division in your head?"

Radhanath responded, "Not quite!"

Both Sara and the man simultaneously countered, "How do you mean?"

Radhanath certainly felt happy with Sara's interest. He expanded, "As Miss Langley was saying, you divide 160 by 2 and get 80. Now, divide that 80 by 10, which leaves you with 8. Finally, subtract the 8 from 80 to get 72 kilograms. Of course, this is an approximation, not exact, but if you work out the actual division, you will see it gets pretty close." The thickset gentleman had produced a small leather-bound diary and pencil. He started to work out the sum to ascertain the match between the result from Radhanath's trick formula and the exact result. Upon confirming their close agreement, he looked up at Radhanath with pleasant surprise.

Sara had been looking at the man's notebook and now spoke excitedly, "What about another number, say 187 lbs.? Will it work?"

Relishing her eagerness, Radhanath said, "It's the same rule. Let's do it together, shall we? If you divide 187 by 2, you will get, …"

Sara completed the sentence, "Let me see… I think, 93.5."

Radhanath nodded, "Correct, now divide the result by 10, and you get..."

Sara resumed, "9.35. So, we should subtract 9.35 from 93.5."

Radhanath said, "Ignore the digits after the decimal to keep things simple."

Sara continued, "Okay. So, it will be 93 minus 9 which is 84. The 187 pounds should be roughly equal to 84 kilograms."

The thickset man worked out the second conversion in his notebook. As he showed it to Sara, they looked at each other – it was indeed close. Sara looked at Radhanath, her eyes shining with excitement.

Dubois asked, "But how did you get the rule?"

Radhanath smiled but did not immediately answer, "That my friend, is a bit too technical. It will require an understanding of Calculus and Taylor expansion. I think I will follow General Waugh's example and spare you those details."

After a brief silence, Waugh pointed toward Radhanath and said to the others, "Gentlemen, as I was telling you earlier, our man Rady knows his numbers. All of us at the Survey are humbled from time to time by Rady's wisdom."

The audience who had not showed much interest in Radhanath earlier, now looked at him again. The thickset man had his mouth held slightly open. And in those brief moments, they went through a strangely visceral experience. Insignificant as this simple mathematical trick was, compared to the mastery of mathematics Radhanath had needed for calculating the height of the tallest point of Earth, the audience was finally waking up to Radhanath as someone who had accomplished a task of incredible scale and magnificence.

As the night deepened, the buzz from the dinner guests began to subside. Many of the Indians had left and the remaining had coalesced into one large group. They seemed determined to drink the night away, including Chandrakanta. The intervening curtain started to move. As it drew back, Radhanath saw that the dining tables had been dismantled. Apparently, despite the grassy floor, they were inviting folks to enjoy some European style dancing in the other half of the pavilion. As the orchestra started a delightful reel, Radhanath spotted Sara with Dubois walking toward the cleared area. Feeling pangs of an unfamiliar, ugly emotion that he recognized as jealousy, Radhanath grew irritated at himself and deliberately moved his eyes away. The reel picked up. The grass floor notwithstanding, the energetic and graceful dancers swung to the music, reel after reel. Just when a new dance was about to start, Radhanath noticed a couple emerge from one of the anterooms at the back of the pavilion and join the dance. Feeling curious, Radhanath headed in that direction. He was stopped by a pair of sentries, apparently guarding access to those rooms.

As Radhanath looked at the sentries in confusion, they enlightened him with a leery smile. "*Kala jaiga, babu.* Only for *gora-gori.* You cannot go in there."

Ah, kala jaiga meaning dark corners – reserved for European couples, should they wish for some privacy after a titillating round of dancing! This was the first time Radhanath learned of such a thing, probably because he hadn't ever been to a party of this scale before. Abruptly, his eyes rushed to look for Dubois and Sara on the floor. *Would they feel as close as that afterward?* He felt a sudden urge to laugh out loud, a reaction he wasn't quite prepared for. He felt supremely confident that Dubois was no match for Sara. Although he didn't know Sara at all, he condescendingly contemplated that if Sara did not see how incompatible they were, then he had no sympathy to offer.

Radhanath left the pavilion and started walking down the path marked by the dying torches quivering in the wind. A lot had happened this evening.

Images from the past few hours flashed in his mind. Bittersweet, unfamiliar emotions coursed through his body. He walked faster. It was a bit of a walk to his tent. Leaving the large marquees behind, he continued toward the maze of smaller tents. After a while, his restlessness abated. The walking had helped. That's when he noticed the winds had grown stronger; their soft whispers had turned to growls. The temperature had also plummeted. Notwithstanding the cold, Radhanath found, one thought from earlier this evening was generating an uncharacteristic warmth inside him – the thought of the exquisite Sara Langley appreciating his mathematics.

Chapter Four

25th May 1856

When Lawrence opened his eyes, a bright morning had come in through the open window warming his cheeks. Moving his head to avoid the sun, Lawrence blinked with confusion. His eyes burned with unfinished sleep. His body felt damp from heat, and it was not mid-day yet. Then, last night started to come back to him. In the small hours today, Lawrence and Pannalal had returned to Pannalal's room in Jorashanko, from Botu *babu*'s, where Shashibala had mesmerized everyone with her *khemta.* Although Lawrence had stepped out in the middle of the function, it wasn't until the very end that he was able to get to bed because Pannalal, engrossed in the *jatra* afterward, had refused to budge from the scene.

Extending his hand without sitting up, Lawrence felt for his pocket watch, which he had kept on the stool by the bed. It read about nine thirty a.m., jarring Lawrence into sudden wakefulness. Wiping the beads of sweat from his forehead, Lawrence sat up with thoughts of the Reverend Stuart's Sunday mass, where he was expected by ten thirty a.m. He had missed several Sundays in a row and wanted to be there today. Lawrence knew Stuart's church was not more than a ten-minute *tanga* ride away. Still, he needed to move quickly to be there on time.

Having been at Pannalal's house before, Lawrence knew that Pannalal's siblings, cousins, aunts, and uncles lived with their families in the various rooms of this large family home. Pannalal's share of the property was this one room where he spent the occasional night. When Lawrence came, Pannalal dragged an additional rickety charpoy into their room, giving up his own which was in marginally better shape, for Lawrence to use.

Indistinct voices of children having an argument floated up to Lawrence. Giving in to pleasurable lethargy, he tried to figure what their argument was about, wishing everyone wouldn't speak at once. His eyes were lightly closed as he tried to concentrate on what they were saying. Picking up the word *lattu* several times, a quiet smile bloomed on Lawrence's face; the wooden spinning tops are certainly part of every boyhood. Tuning out further chatter, Lawrence searched for a half-smoked cheroot in his pockets. After he lit it and inhaled, he looked outside the window. A dense growth of undisciplined taro root leaves gleamed in the sunlight. Looking there for a few moments and finding nothing to amuse him, Lawrence turned his attention back to the insides of the room.

Other than the two charpoys, a stool, and a wooden box where Pannalal kept his clothes, there wasn't much else in the room. After all, Pannalal was rarely here. The walls had quite a few cracks. Lawrence eyed the shape formed by a spot of damp, which he recalled having seen the last time he was here as well. It looked a little bit like the Italian coastline, *the boot*, affirmed Lawrence to himself. Idly, he gazed up at the ceiling lined with wooden beams.

Lawrence's cheroot was almost done when the door to the room opened noiselessly, and Pannalal entered. He had just finished his bath. The two smiled at each other, enjoying the comforts of quiet camaraderie. Lawrence took a final puff and got up to chuck his cheroot out the window. Meanwhile, Pannalal had stepped out again. When he returned this time, his hands held a shiny bronze plate with handmade chapatis and vegetable curry, stuff from their family kitchen where Pannalal ate his meals when he was visiting. The food reminded Lawrence that he hadn't eaten in a while. As Pannalal extended the plate to him, Lawrence took it eagerly. He started to gulp down the food, eating with his hands and realizing how hungry he was. After his initial craving was sated, Lawrence spoke his first sentence of the day, "We had a great time last night, didn't we?"

"No doubt," nodded Pannalal, but then started to complain, "you went swimming in the dark, huh? The area around Bose Pond is overgrown and infested with snakes. Have I not told you this before?"

Lawrence smiled and said, "The *khemta* was too much for me! I was burning, man. She was as sweet as she was wild!" After a pause, he added, "I did not expect her to take me up on my offer and dance naked. Did you?"

"No, I did not," said Pannalal, a tad harshly. Lawrence stopped eating and looked at Pannalal, bewildered. Pannalal looked annoyed with his face turned away toward the half-closed doorway. *Was Pannalal offended that Lawrence had asked Shashibala to dance naked?* wondered Lawrence.

As he resumed eating, a sharp irritation rose inside the inspector, having figured exactly what had ticked Pannalal off. *The precocious native has decided the white man went too far last night, baiting Shashibala to strip.* Easygoing Cockerel, who never for a moment would think of himself as a racist, reacted to Pannalal's behavior with obvious racial chauvinism. *Pannalal's fancy Bengali babus were content with their dull ogling. When Lawrence pushed things to a whole new level with his spontaneity, with his boldness – that got Pannalal's goat. How dare Pannalal judge him unfairly,* fumed Lawrence in silence. As the food settled in his belly however, Lawrence's frustration mellowed. Pannalal was a good bloke, loyal to Lawrence; *the old fool couldn't help himself.*

"How are things at Barrackpore?" Lawrence asked. Pannalal lived right outside the Barrackpore cantonment in the Sepai Para neighborhood during the week. As an ex-officer of East India Company's Bengal army prior to joining the police, Lawrence had first-hand experience of living on army barracks himself. Occasionally, he pumped Pannalal for the latest anecdotes on life at the cantonment. Following Lawrence's lead, Pannalal started to describe the happenings around the recent arrival of a garrison of eighteen and nineteen-year-olds from Britain. Stranded far from family for the first time in their lives, they seemed to have sprouted an unnatural fondness for pets. No stranger to the comforts a companion animal can bring to the lonely soldier, Lawrence nodded with a knowing smile. He was thoroughly amused to learn that their practice had spiraled quite out of control, with each now having several animals in their possession. Pannalal remarked that the barracks have taken on new life as a mini zoo. Apparently, all that was to end soon. The newbies had been served notice, restricting the number of animals they can keep to one. They were going around with long faces, forced to either sell or donate the rest of their collection.

Lawrence had finished eating, and the two were chuckling merrily when Lawrence checked his pocket watch again and exclaimed, "Oh gosh! Is that the time? I am going to be late for church. Reverend Stuart has been threatening to fine late comers!" Lawrence mock complained.

At first, Lawrence did not notice Pannalal growing stiff at the mention of the Reverend. When Pannalal cleared his throat to draw Lawrence's attention, Lawrence paused to look at him confusedly a second time this morning. He realized Pannalal was struggling to get out something difficult. After a pause, Pannalal spoke in a tone that underlined the gravity of what he had felt compelled to share, "There is a growing dissatisfaction among people about the Reverend and his missionaries. There is a belief that they are plotting with the government to coerce native sepoys to become Christians."

Alarmed by what he heard, Lawrence told Pannalal that their suspicion was baseless; that as far as he knows, the British government has no interest in converting the people of India into Christians. From his look, Lawrence knew

Pannalal wasn't convinced. And while he smiled toward the end and nodded through Lawrence's explanation, there was unmistakable warning in his eyes. "The native soldiers, particularly those from the upper castes take religion very seriously, sahib – something the government will do well to remember," Pannalal had murmured in parting.

Having given away the last of what he had on him to Shashibala, Lawrence needed to borrow money from Pannalal before walking to the main road from Pannalal's house on foot. As the landaulet he hired to take him to Stuart's church hurried along the main road, he sat inside, unable to get over a feeling of disquiet. He had told Pannalal that the sepoys' private religion was not at risk. But even as he said those things, he felt uneasy, somehow having known this was coming. It was true that the East India Company had no interest in persecuting people's religious beliefs. But with the heightened activity of the missionaries, how many really understood that the government was not necessarily endorsing it. As someone with intimate awareness of the Indian psyche, Lawrence knew how strongly the Indians felt about their religion. Lawrence feared, if somehow the idea that the British intend to convert them into Christianity gained a strong foothold among the natives, that could become a serious threat and even signal the beginning of the end of the British Empire in India.

The Reverend firmly believed his fight was to show the natives the one true path of light. He made no secret of his agenda to convert the natives into Christianity. Lawrence wondered if the Reverend had considered some of the more extreme consequences of his missionary zeal. At his earliest opportunity, perhaps today, Lawrence resolved to gently bring the matter up with the Reverend. He should be made aware of the emotions he was stirring.

The People's Church, sometimes called the Bengali Church because of its wide native attendance alongside the Europeans, was established about a decade ago, drawing parishioners from all walks, both affluent and poor. It has grown increasingly popular over the years. The modest church grounds and vicarage were lovingly tended and always sublimely peaceful. As much as it was a religious duty he desired to fulfill, Lawrence thought of his Sundays here as a social occasion as well.

This morning, as he sat inside the church with a sermon in progress, Lawrence eyed the deity of Christ, decorated with tuberose garlands, which is how they worshipped Christ here in Bengal. The air was heavy with the scent of candles and incense, despite the labors of the *punkahwallah*. Reverend Stuart, a short, elderly man, who had put on weight in recent years, was at the pulpit. Stuart had quite a presence, his white hair unbridled like a lion's mane, but he could be as gentle as a lamb. Lawrence was amused by the fact that the young Reverend Banerjee, helping Stuart deliver his sermon, was adding his own color to the translations he was making as the Reverend spoke. *Did Stuart get that?* wondered Lawrence. Stuart did not know the language well enough to appreciate the nuances. Lawrence turned his attention to the gathering inside the church. His eyes stopped on Gokul seated in the native block. It was the same native Christian man that Pannalal pointed to him on their way to the *khemta*. Gokul likely did not understand a single word of Stuart's English and waited for the explanations from Reverend Banerjee. However, he listened to Stuart's words with a singular expression of ardor. Lawrence had occasionally seen Gokul in private conference with Stuart after the mass. The man seemed to hang on to every word that came out of Stuart. Perhaps feeling eyes on himself, Gokul turned to look at Lawrence. As their eyes met, Lawrence tried to offer a smile, but the shifty Gokul turned his eyes away.

After the mass, Lawrence went to find Stuart in the anteroom next to the pulpit. He discovered Gokul had had the same idea and was in conversation with the Reverend. Lawrence waited for them to finish, casually noting the long scar on Gokul's right arm. From where he stood, bits and pieces of their discussion floated up to him, mainly Stuart's words, since he was doing most of the speaking. What he heard made Lawrence smile, just like it did many natives that Stuart attempted to speak with in Bengali. Even after all these years, Stuart spoke in formal Bengali, which is only ever used in written prose and never spoken. Stuart had never bothered to master colloquial Bengali. Lawrence gathered the two were making plans to meet later in the afternoon today. Gokul was to round up an audience at the open meadow next to Burir Jungle, six miles to the west of the church. Stuart along with Reverend Banerjee were going to meet them there to deliver a lecture and then distribute free milk among the poor. On his way out, Gokul walked hastily past Lawrence avoiding eye contact. Lawrence eyed the shiny cross the man wore around his neck.

Meanwhile, Stuart had turned to beam at Lawrence. The two had become friends in the early days when Lawrence returned to Calcutta after completing his education in England. Young Cockerel had fallen in love with Stuart's daughter, Emily, and was a frequent visitor to their house in those days. Unfortunately, Emily did not reciprocate his feelings and chose to settle down with an officer of the British army, currently posted in Kanpur, in the north of India. Even if the romance between Lawrence and Emily failed, the warm friendship between the padre and the inspector continued over the years. The father in Stuart used to urge Lawrence, "Young man, I do sincerely hope you have not given up on love altogether. You must try again."

With his Sunday mass completed, the relaxed Reverend asked his friend why he had been missing from the church over the past few weeks. Lawrence avoided a direct answer with a shy smile, but the Reverend in a cheerful mood, wouldn't let it go. "Are you going to tell me it was some fair maiden that monopolized your time – which would be entirely forgivable and in fact wonderful news?"

Thoughts of the temptress Shashibala came rushing to Lawrence darkening his face with complex emotion. Noticing the unusual discomfort on Lawrence's face, Stuart smoothly changed topics. "What do you think of Gokul?" the Reverend asked. He had noted Lawrence eyeing Gokul as the man was leaving. “Have you ever spoken with him? I have made great progress with the natives – far better than I expected – with Gokul’s assistance.”

Lawrence had meant to discuss the church’s initiatives with Stuart today. Seizing the opportunity, Lawrence said, “Reverend, I am really happy for those who have found comfort in your teachings. But not everyone has. Is Gokul telling you about them?” There was a sharpness in the way Lawrence’s remark came out that took both by surprise, creating an awkward pause in their conversation. Stuart asked Lawrence to explain himself.

It was hot in the anteroom. Wiping sweat off his forehead with the kerchief he carried, Lawrence said, “I am afraid not everyone is as contented with the spread of these ideas as you might like to think.” Taking a pause to organize his thoughts, Lawrence repeated what he had heard from Pannalal to Stuart. If the sepoys begin to believe the British government is going to force them to give up their religion, that can get ugly, warned Lawrence. The padre stood quietly for a few moments. Then, with one of his hands outstretched to indicate Lawrence should follow him, he started to walk toward the gardens that are part of the vicarage right next to the church. They walked quietly side by side on a path lined with flowering creepers. A six feet by three feet, patina-coated brass bell stood at the end of their path. As Lawrence’s eyes fell on the bell gleaming in late morning light, he was reminded of the hours he spent at this place when he was love-sick and recovering from Emily’s rejection. Stuart started to speak, “My son, the natives of this land do not know Christian kindness. Our work here is to awaken those noble feelings in them. We must continue this work for their sake as much as for ours and find a way to deal with their fears and suspicion.”

Lawrence remembered Pannalal who gave him his own charpoy to sleep and brought him food the first thing this morning. He looked back at Stuart and said, “Father, there is no lack of kindness in them. As I once told you, my native *ayah* was the only mother I ever knew. And her son has always been a loyal companion to me.”

Looking Lawrence directly in the eye, Stuart said, "Not thirty years ago, they burned their widows on the funeral pyres of the dead husband. They still sacrifice live animals and mark themselves with warm blood from the carcass in the name of veneration. I am sorry, but where exactly do you find compassion in these practices?" Stuart had stopped in his tracks to speak. Calmly, composedly, he looked at Lawrence in the manner of one resigned to battle.

Lawrence had no desire to spar with the Reverend. He spoke matter-of-factly, as a messenger relaying what he considered important. "The Indian sepoys are the legs of British rule in India, Reverend. We do not have the number of British officers we need to govern this country with British force alone. To say we depend on the sepoys, that our lives depend on them, is no exaggeration. We cannot ignore the possibility that if pushed, especially on religious issues, they may refuse to cooperate. And worse, they may turn against us."

Stuart countered, "Excluding whatever your short-term misgivings are, Lawrence, the best way to breed long term loyalty is to bring them under one God. Until and unless that happens, not just the sepoys, but from every one of them, the best we can expect is superficial allegiance, easily shaken, easily broken. I do not know how confident you feel of the loyalty of this native man, your *ayah*'s son. But I can assure you, that native Gokul, will remain faithful to me for the rest of his life. Do you know why? Because he is now Christian. Gokul knows little of the English, but he feels connected to the British empire because regardless of the color of his skin, he knows he is Christian."

As the Reverend continued to speak his mind, Lawrence realized Stuart wasn't open to ideas that contradicted him in matters of faith. Feeling reluctant to push the old man further, Lawrence kept quiet, neither agreeing nor disagreeing. He let the Reverend say his piece and then took his leave. In the landaulet Lawrence hired to return to his quarters at Elysium Row, Gokul came to his mind again, perhaps because of the Reverend's many references to the man in today's conversation. *Where did Stuart meet this strange character?* Lawrence reflected that Stuart never told him how Gokul became a Christian.

Though Lawrence will not learn about it until later, Gokul and the Reverend did go a long way back. They had met nearly two decades ago when the padre was just starting his career in India. Today, Gokul is a devoted ally to the pastor, so much so that Jesus and the Reverend are probably the one and the same for him. But back then, Gokul was part of a group of *thugees* – sinister, nomadic assassins who preyed on unsuspecting passersby and strangled them to their deaths.

The *thugee* network thrived in the early part of the nineteenth century, plaguing travelers all over the country. They were a real menace, with their network of informers keeping tabs on the vulnerable on the road. A benign looking handful made initial contact with the intended victims, befriending them as fellow travelers, advocating safety in numbers. Clearly, these rascals had the skills to win people's trust. Then, in an opportune moment, they would attack using a simple kerchief as weapon. After strangling their victims, the *thugees* looted their possessions. Shockingly, after these horrendous crimes, the *thugees* went back to families and homes in regular society and reintegrated without a hitch; their identities were kept a religiously guarded secret known only to those in the clan. Back then, this centuries-old practice was rampant in Indian society. In his days as a *thugee*, Gokul had been a remorseless murderer like the others of his clan. However, in the early 1800s, the iron jaws of British rule had started to clamp down on members of this violent cult. Those caught were hanged without mercy. Those suspected but not convicted were shipped overseas with life imprisonment. Gokul began to live his days in abject fear of punishment.

In those days, Reverend Stuart was beginning to appreciate the enormity of the challenge he had embraced in attempting to spread Christianity among the natives. It wasn't going to be easy to convert a people he hardly understood. Stuart trudged on, ignoring the sly smiles and insubordination he was commonly shown when giving his sermons. When Stuart was out doing his work, people would come and stand around him. Stuart understood they had minimal interest in his message but were greatly amused by the spectacle of a British padre attempting to speak to them in poor Bengali.

One fateful day of both their lives, Gokul was among the people listening to Reverend Stuart. The troubled Gokul was touched by the Reverend's words of kindness and forgiveness. He started following the Reverend around. And then one day when Stuart was alone, the ruthless *thugee* finally broke down, confessing his sins to the padre. Gokul also told Stuart he wanted to embrace Christianity. Gokul's breakdown and desire to become Christian moved the Reverend. Stuart felt that Gokul could become their poster boy on how a pagan man could be redeemed by Christian faith. Tormented by the barrier that language presented for him, the shrewd Stuart also saw potential in Gokul as a man who could help him deliver Christ's message. The Reverend agreed to save Gokul's neck. He took Gokul to the police and negotiated a deal on his behalf with them. In lieu of immunity for himself, Gokul revealed the names of several members of his gang. Then he became Christian.

After the Sunday mass Gokul attended with Lawrence and others at the People's Church this morning, Stuart's trusted servant had gone off to round up the natives for Stuart's lecture later in the day. However, Gokul did not directly get to it. He took a detour to the spot in the open space at the edge of Burir Jungle where the event was set to happen. These days, with the ever-expanding city, this location had become more easily accessible, but it used to be quite out of people's way, back in the day. Gokul stood under a great banyan tree that dominated the landscape, imagining the Reverend lecturing from there. It was Gokul who had suggested this site to Stuart. Had he not been so fascinated with the place, his good sense might have prevailed. The ugly secret was, in his *thugee* days, Gokul used to bury his victims at this location. The soil here has soaked the blood of many bodies. Gokul knew, if one were to dig under the very spot where he asked Stuart to deliver his sermon, they would find human skeletons. However, he wasn't exactly worried because the last of those who knew his secret, were all by now dead or deported. Gokul felt a strange pleasure in having the Reverend he held in God-like esteem speak from here, oblivious to the dark secrets of the place.

Chapter Five

In the year 1856, Jainagar's hunting party was staged in lush forests of oak, maple, and deodar cloaking the hills of Barnala. At the edge of the forests, lay the alpine meadows of Ananta Bugyal, offering breathtaking views of the Himalayas. The plan was for the beaters' drumbeats to drive the animals up the jungle-covered hills toward the hunters on higher ground. The hunters were going to enter the jungle from the direction of the meadows. The royal campsite was constructed on the other edge of the meadow, with the camping and hunting zones effectively separated by vast stretches of open ground. Comfortable transportation was available to go back and forth between them.

25th May 1856

On the morning after the inauguration dinner, Radhanath rose early, an effect the outdoor air seemed to always have on him. Emerging from his tent in semi-darkness, Radhanath stood shaking in the cold, his breath rising in billowing mists. A lively chorus of birdcalls filled the air. Glimpses of the magnificent Himalayas greeted him from what he could see of the purple-pink horizon. Few guests were up at this hour, and the only signs of movement were servants clearing their flimsy, makeshift *jhupris* where they had sheltered the night before. After returning to his tent from a trip to the communal bathrooms, Radhanath donned his *galabandh* suit before stepping out again. Walking up to Chandrakanta's tent, he stood to listen for a moment. When he last saw his friend yesterday evening, the man was happily drunk with a gang of Indian royals. Detecting no sounds of movement from inside the tent, Radhanath concluded that Chandrakanta was still fast asleep. He decided to head toward the pavilion, looking forward to breakfasting by himself. On his way, despite the early hour, he caught sight of servants ferrying water to the campground on the backs of mules, presumably from some nearby alpine lake.

Breakfast, an informal affair, was indeed waiting at the pavilion. With the dividing curtain pulled back, several smaller tables with open seating had been laid, able to accommodate up to groups of ten. Large steaming food platters on long tables stood against the walls, inviting the guests to help themselves. The chandeliers had not been lit, but large silver candelabras adequately illuminated the interior. Waiters moved around, serving tea, coffee, juice, milk, or water and clearing the used dishes as needed. There were several people breakfasting and sounds of conversation filled the air. Radhanath chose to sit alone, cruising through hot cutlets and eggs. He was nearing the end of his meal, when suddenly, he heard faint sounds of trumpeting. The guests looked at each other in astonishment. Drinking the last of his tea, Radhanath hurried to exit the pavilion. Outside the perimeter of their campsite stood a fleet of elephants. Much to everyone's delight, *Raja* Uday Singh had planned this grand ride to transport his guests to the hunting area.

With no sign of Chandrakanta, Radhanath, who had witnessed his friend get along famously with the royals last night, decided Chandrakanta would be fine among his newfound friends. Choosing not to wait, Radhanath started walking toward the elephants, eager to start what he could already feel was going to be an exceptional day.

The majestic cavalcade, fitted with gaudy, bejeweled howdahs, accompanied by uniformed mahouts, stood fidgeting – waving their long ears, curling up their trunks, and occasionally letting out shrill calls in excitement. Radhanath noticed the crowd had grown, and the enthusiastic souls included women, buttoned up and ready to go in dark riding habits. The elephants were going to take almost two hours to reach the hunting area. One could alternatively ride a horse along the mud trail by the side of the ridge. The trail was at places too narrow for the elephants, but it promised picturesque views of the valley and was in fact, a shortcut. Radhanath, in no hurry this morning, queued up for the first elephant ride of his life.

Radhanath found that guests were being paired with companion hunters. Those with no hunting experience were required to take on companion hunters for their own safety. These were men on the *Raja's* payroll, not permitted to directly participate in the hunt, except in rescue situations. When Radhanath declared he had no hunting experience, he was paired with a native man. Radhanath quickly realized that the native guests were being paired with native companion hunters and European guests with European hunters, possibly to minimize awkwardness. Radhanath's companion introduced himself as Baburam from Bihar, a marksman who made a living as a *shikari* for hire.

As their mahout got their elephant to bend his right hind leg, Baburam expertly climbed onto the howdah using the elephant's bent leg as a stepping stool. Next, Radhanath mounted with Baburam's help. The mahout took position, sitting astride just behind the elephant's head. Soon, the gently swaying creatures started crossing the meadow.

The howdah was large enough for the pair of them. Radhanath eyed the loaded Brown Bess musket Baburam held. Two additional howdah pistols, cartridges, and gun powder supply for all the firearms, sat within easy access. A basket of food and leather waterskins with drinking water stood against the howdah wall. All the articles had been secured with rope to prevent sliding. As a first-time elephant rider, Radhanath did not find the undulant motion atop the beast entirely comfortable. However, the grand views of the ice-capped Himalayas bathed by the rays of the rising sun, more than compensated any inconvenience.

Radhanath began to hear the beaters as they neared the hunting area. Upon entering the forests, the guests looked around excitedly, but the sounds of commotion had riled up the elephants. The beasts started to slow, shaking their huge heads from side to side, trumpeting in protest. The mahouts slapped them on their heads, and the sharp hook on the goads dug painfully into their skin. As they stomped forward, the low branches of overhead trees tugged at the howdahs; leaves and twigs on the forest floor crackled noisily beneath their feet. Perhaps his mind was playing tricks because to Radhanath the low bushes seemed to pulse with movement. Reflexively, he reached for the knife in his trouser pocket and then smiled. *How useless is a knife in this environment!* As he pushed his knife back, his hand touched a matchbox, the other thing he also always had on him. Radhanath picked up a howdah pistol although he did not intend to hunt.

That's when a warthog emerged from under one of the shrubs and following its own pair of curled tusks, beelined for the bush opposite the minor clearing where they were standing. More than one rifle went off. However, the warthog wasn't killed, and they could hear its squeals fading into the distance. Suddenly, Radhanath's elephant threw its front legs in the air, trumpeting loudly. Radhanath lost his balance, and had it not been for Baburam, he would have fallen. While their mahout tried to control their elephant, Baburam growled that the elephant must have sensed big cats near them. As if on cue, Radhanath saw a surge of black and gold among the trees, charging toward them. The tiger ground to an abrupt halt about thirty yards away. Confused by the sight of several elephants at once, it hesitated for a moment, taking a step back. Then it pivoted, going for the elephant to its right. The shots fired by the sole hunter on that elephant kept missing its target until the leaping tiger's paw was within inches of his elephant's tusk; that was when the hunter's bullet finally struck the tiger dead.

For the next two hours Radhanath's heart thumped with an adrenalin rush from the beaters' rousing cacophony, the animals' angry growls, and cracks of gunshots filling the air. The jungle began to smell hot and dry; the air grew hazy with dust. Animals ran helter-skelter, charging or in retreat. A chorus of tree-borne langurs following their progress made the experience especially disorienting. At one point, a shrieking peacock swooped from a top branch down to a bush, covering quite a distance. Radhanath was following its course, when his eyes became transfixed on a bare outcrop of rock on the top of a natural ridge, not twenty yards from them. A big cat was advancing along its length, its taut body held low on the ground. Its powerful muscles rippled under a smooth golden skin dotted with shiny, black teardrops. Abruptly, the feline sprang on an elephant coming into view from behind the ridge. The companion hunter on that elephant was quick! Twisting his body, he took a shot at the animal, in motion, mid-air. With an angry howl, the animal tore flesh from the hind of the elephant as it crash-landed. Baburam had to raise his voice above the elephant's shrill cries of pain, to tell Radhanath that this was the Asiatic cheetah, not native to these jungles. The cheetah lay writhing and roaring on the ground; the bullet had only managed to injure! A second shot put the animal to rest.

Feeling tired, and also pangs of hunger, Radhanath pulled his pocket watch out and saw that the lunch hour had creeped up on them. He was surprised by how he had lost all track of time. Radhanath suggested they take a break, and the mahout steered their elephant to the edge of the forest. They found that several other hunters had had the same idea. Pulling the picnic basket, Radhanath brought out a packet of bread layered with spicy meat. Baburam joined Radhanath for his mid-day meal with a bunch of chapati and jaggery. Radhanath noticed their mahout serving soaked lentils to their elephant before the man started eating himself. With the beaters' sound fainter here, Radhanath began to hear a variety of birds.

Baburam broke the silence and said that although he was attending on the *Raja*'s payroll, as a well experienced hunter he would have loved to participate in the hunt himself. In fact, he good-naturedly declared, he would welcome a competition between the English and Indian *shikaris*, where they could tally the trophies from each team – skins, skulls, horns, everything. Then he pointed to the British man and woman on an elephant at a distance from them and said, "I trained the man on that elephant just a few weeks ago to serve as companion *shikari* like me." He then cheekily added, "And now he gets to ride next to the chic *memsahib*." Baburam smiled at Radhanath guilelessly, implying that he, a much better shot than that English fellow over there, would have been more than happy to ride in the howdah with the *memsahib*. Noticing Radhanath's lack of a response, Baburam hastily added, "Not to suggest that I am disliking your company, Radhanath sahib."

Radhanath had been maintaining a reserved facade so as to not unduly encourage Baburam. However, the mention of a *memsahib* had made him self-conscious, reminding him of Sara Langley. He wondered if she had come to the hunt; he was quite certain he hadn't seen her yet. After finishing their lunch, just as they were getting ready to return to the hunt, Baburam drew Radhanath's attention to a Markhor sheep with beautiful, curled horns grazing out on the meadows. He lamented that this one wasn't mature yet, its horns not large enough to make it worth killing.

Later in the afternoon, Radhanath's elephant arrived at a spot where a cluster of Gulmohar trees, lush with red blooms, arrested his attention. As he stood admiring the flowers, his eyes fell to a point under one of the trees, and he was left speechless. A warthog lay noiselessly with its skull cracked open, part of its brain lying out on the forest floor. One of its eyes had been knocked out of its socket and lay covered in blood and dust next to the animal's head. The warthog was still alive and seemed to be looking at them with its other eye. Radhanath guessed the animal had carefully pulled itself into that spot hoping to hide. As Radhanath prepared to aim with a howdah pistol, he heard Baburam, who had also seen it by this time, swear under his breath at the incompetent hunter who had done the damage and then abandoned the poor animal. Before Radhanath could shoot though, another bullet went past them and completed the act of mercy.

With the beaters going full steam, Radhanath hadn't heard Sara Langley arrive on horseback behind them. Now he saw her, narrow-eyed, thin-lipped and atop an Arabian mare. She wore a grey-green riding habit, a top hat, shirt, and cravat and was holding a smoking rifle. It was her bullet that had laid the warthog to rest. A beam of sunlight through the foliage overhead had fallen on her face, revealing an inscrutable expression. Their eyes met for a brief instant before Sara turned her horse and trotted away.

Radhanath turned to look at the warthog, finally at peace. The sight of it left him feeling drained. What all the previous sightings of animals getting killed hadn't done, hit him now. He had had enough for today. Baburam was glad to hear Radhanath's decision to retire early. He was justifiably disappointed with his day spent on the sidelines and looked forward to enjoying a sound nap before dinner. On their way out, Radhanath thought he caught a glimpse of Chandrakanta with Nana sahib at some distance, but as exhausted as he was, he didn't try to contact them.

When Radhanath's elephant returned to the meadows, he noticed the *Raja*'s men had lined up the day's kills to take back to the camp. The sight of these magnificent animals, cold and dead, depressed him. Next to them, Radhanath saw the *Raja*'s men had set up an impromptu horse stand. Armed guards stood around the horses. From them, Radhanath learned that the horses had been walked over for the guests. If anyone changed their minds about the longer elephant ride, they could avail this alternative. Returning to the campground sooner rather than later sounded quite attractive to Radhanath right then. Therefore, after thanking Baburam and the mahout, Radhanath got off his elephant. Borrowing a stout *Marwari* horse and a rifle from the *Raja*'s men, Radhanath started down the supposedly straightforward mud trail he had heard about this morning. When he returned to the campground within the next hour, he felt rather pleased with his decision. Besides saving time, the trail had lived up to its promise of spectacular views along the way.

26th May 1856

Radhanath woke at his usual five thirty a.m. He had planned to sleep in today, and so he stretched lazily, making no attempt to leave the warmth of his camp bed. He knew Chandrakanta and his companions would be getting up now, or soon, and beeline for the hunting grounds. At least that's what they had discussed last night, when flushed with whiskey, Chandrakanta couldn't stop thanking Radhanath for coming to the *shikar* with him. They had been sitting around the large campfire the *Raja*'s men had lit, where they'd dined alfresco with meat from the *shikar,* cooked to perfection in open fire pits. The campground, meanwhile, was alive with sounds of various performances. Radhanath had watched the fire-jugglers and the tightrope walkers from a distance. Having chosen to stay put by the campfire, he enjoyed the ethereal evening under the starry skies, set against the moon washed white mountains. Thoughts of last evening stayed with Radhanath as he fell asleep again. When his eyes opened next, it was past noon!

After a big, leisurely lunch at the pavilion, Radhanath decided to explore the campground. There was clearly no dearth of entertainment for those that had opted to stay behind. Radhanath eyed the dexterous tightrope walkers he had seen last night only from a distance. On his way past a tent, Radhanath heard sounds of female singing; a *mujara* was in progress. As he stuck his head inside, his eyes and nose were hit with a heavy mix of tobacco and incense. Through the haze, he saw a pretty *Lucknowi* girl, skillfully doing a *thumri*. Her luscious song about the lover who has stolen her peace enthralled her audience.

Radhanath noted most of the audience were members of India's royalty, and a handful were European guests.

Soon, Radhanath stepped back out and resumed wandering the campground. The artists were back on their easels sketching. He noted several stalls around the site serving drinks. Radhanath stopped for a while to watch a man perform a number of curious tricks with a bevy of Mynah birds. Then he meandered to a gathering around a *pagri*-clad man who seemed to be gently guiding a thread like object into one of his nostrils. Radhanath was shocked to discover that it was a thin, green, vine snake he held! After disappearing for a few seconds, the snake would emerge of its own accord from his other nostril. Radhanath stood spellbound by this bizarre spectacle. After a while, extracting his pocket watch, he saw it was close to three p.m.

"Rady!" A familiar call caused him to turn around. His boss, Surveyor General Andrew Waugh was walking toward him, looking sharp in his riding clothes. "My dear man, I am going to the royal stables to pick me a ride. They say the *Raja*'s collection is among the finest. Would you like to join me?"

Radhanath cordially responded, "Thank you for asking, sir. But I must pass. I am feeling lazy with all the wine and dine."

Waugh responded with a show of mock surprise, telling Radhanath the word "lazy" simply didn't fit the hard-working soldier he knew Radhanath to be. "Don't forget young man, I have seen you work all night looking fresh as a cucumber in the morning!" he teased.

With his brows knit playfully, Radhanath shot back, "A young man, sir?"

"But of course, dear Rady!" perked up the near half-centenarian. "I'm still a young man myself!" As their laughter abated, Waugh declared, "If you aren't coming, that's fine. I will get going. Let me ask though," raising his brows, Waugh inquired, "Have you been on the trail behind the campground yet?" Radhanath nodded, indicating that he had returned from the hunting ground by that one yesterday.

Nodding, Waugh said, "Well, then you already know of the amazing views it offers." As Waugh prepared to leave with his hand raised in farewell, he cautioned, "Don't forget a rifle if you change your mind about stepping outside the camp."

When Radhanath told Waugh that he was feeling lazy, what he really meant was that his spirit was somehow low this morning. Flashes of yesterday's near-dead warthog with its brains exposed and an eye knocked out of its socket were making him nauseated. Feeling parched, Radhanath started to look for somewhere he could get a drink and soon located a stall serving alcohol. Requesting the bartender for a double shot of whiskey, he stood waiting by the side. Among the crowd around the stall, his eyes fell upon the thickset gentleman he had met two nights ago at the inauguration dinner – the one who was checking if Radhanath's trick formula to convert pound to kilogram worked. As their eyes met, the man's face also lit up with recognition.

"Hello Rady! Good to see you again!" he said energetically. Michael Carmody, an accountant who worked for the East India Company, was here as secretary to one of the Company's Generals. Turning to his friends, Michael introduced Radhanath to them, "Gentlemen, I assume you remember General Waugh announcing the discovery of Mount Everest. Meet Rady. He is a mathematician from the Survey and was a key contributor in measuring the height of that mountain. Can you even imagine how one measures a mountain? Especially one that is constantly shrouded in mist and impossible to approach. It is beyond my understanding! But not for Rady; he is a genius." Radhanath found Michael oddly inclined to praise him.

Michael's friends gathered around Radhanath offering their congratulations. Radhanath could see that they were all flushed with drink, and if you asked him, he would attribute their effusive appreciation of his mathematical talents mainly to that. Michael continued, "Get this, Rady has this neat trick to convert pounds to kilogram mentally. It's uncanny how that works. Do you want to see?"

The audience was happy to stand admiringly with the pleasant buzz of whiskey humming in their ears. They had no interest in getting into mathematics at that moment. Without skipping a beat, one of them seized the floor with the words, "I know a *fakir* that can read your thoughts. The natives are all geniuses!"

Radhanath did not know whether equating the two was the genius of whiskey. He wouldn't put it past these men to say the same even if they were sober. Sipping the whiskey in his hand, Radhanath stood thinking how glibly they attributed a supernatural dimension to anything extraordinary an Asian did. The Europeans thought the East was about mysticism, and they didn't care to be contradicted.

Deciding it was time to cut this conversation short, Radhanath finished the rest of his drink. Pointing to the direction where he had just visited, Radhanath recommended they check out the Indian *psychic* on this very campground running a live snake through the cavities of his nose. Then, with a friendly pat on Michael's back, Radhanath started to walk away, heading for the royal stables. Perhaps it was whiskey in his system that changed his mind because riding a horse seemed the very thing to do next.

Radhanath knew where the stable was, having returned his ride there when he got back from the hunt yesterday. He was surprised to find a British man minding the stable today, who eyed Radhanath's high-necked, eastern-style coat askance. Taking the paper ticket Radhanath handed him, the man went to fetch his animal, walking it around to where Radhanath was waiting. As the man handed him the reins, Radhanath got the feeling that he had intended to say something but decided against it in the end, copping to a blank smile instead. With a new man arriving, British, the stable keeper rushed away to assist him.

About to mount the animal, Radhanath found the scabbard containing his rifle had become somewhat loose, probably from the wear and tear over the course of their journey here. He took a few moments to secure it properly, during which he overheard bits of the stable keeper's conversation with the newcomer. The stable keeper asked the man to keep an ear out for the beaters. If the beaters grew loud, it would mean the rider was too close to the hunting ground. Radhanath immediately understood, his instinct had been right – this was a reminder the stable keeper was supposed to give anybody who came for a horse. He had decided against speaking up because somehow, Radhanath had made him uncomfortable. Indeed, Radhanath had had similar experiences at his workplace. Europeans, especially those who didn't know him, were sometimes not at ease around him. The unfortunate consequence was that Radhanath missed out on important information simply because the person who was supposed to deliver the message had chosen to stay silent when they saw his face. Seated on his horse at this point, Radhanath kicked the animal lightly on its sides. The horse started on a gentle trot and Radhanath guided it toward the head of the trail.

As Radhanath followed the path running along the edge of the meadow, he realized that though he had been on this same trail the day before, it looked unfamiliar riding from the opposite direction. He couldn't remember seeing the vibrant swathes of yellow Himalayan flax, way down on the valley floor yesterday. *What a difference a change of perspective made*, mused Radhanath. Estimating he had enough time until sunset, he gave himself up to the warmth of the sun and the chill from the breeze on his skin. As he passed the rhododendron forests below, he made a mental note to go down to take a walk among those sometime. He did pass a rider or two on the trail, but traffic was rare. Most of the time he had the trail to himself. Time seemed to fly until suddenly he became aware of the beaters' sounds, implying he was approaching the hunting area. Radhanath eyed the gun hanging to the left of his horse. He was debating whether to turn around when a rider on horseback appeared on the trail coming from the opposite direction. Radhanath slowed to let him pass, as the trail was rather narrow at this point. When the silhouette of the rider became clearer, Radhanath recognized it was a woman, in fact a woman he knew. There she was – Sara Langley – clad in full-sleeved grey-green habit and top hat like yesterday.

In the few interactions Radhanath had had with Sara, he had found himself reacting to her presence in ways that wasn't usual for him. Though normally a reticent man, he had declared he calculated the height of Mount Everest to her the very first time they met. At the inauguration dinner, he had not been able to resist showing off his trick formula to go from pounds to kilograms, probably influenced by her presence. Today, as he greeted her, he found himself dismounting from his horse, for no obvious reason. Sara Langley ground to halt, watching him noncommittally. After a pause, she also got down and stood quietly by her horse, looking at him. Her self-possession did little to reduce Radhanath's embarrassment for having done something that now felt silly to him. Sara's face was composed, but Radhanath thought her eyes looked amused and seemed to ask, what next.

Sara broke the silence and suggested, "Shall we take a turn together?"

Without waiting for an answer, she turned her horse around. Radhanath said, "How…" Sounding hoarse and peculiar, he cleared his throat before starting again, "How did your hunting go?" He also mumbled, "Sorry, I probably should not have gotten off my horse."

Sara ignored the apology remaining silent for a moment. Then, she responded to his original question, "Ah, it was nothing to write home about. But I wouldn't mind a walk now." Radhanath didn't know if that was what he had in mind when he got off his horse. Sara put words into his mouth, suggesting she was accommodating what Radhanath had wanted. Radhanath felt a bit awkward, recognizing the young lady was amused, but he couldn't gauge exactly how much.

The two started walking, the leash of their respective rides in hand while their animals came behind them. Following up on Sara's last statement, Radhanath asked, "Did you not enjoy the hunting? I hope nothing untoward happened?"

Radhanath had noticed Sara's face assumes a somewhat defiant expression when she concentrates. With that same look coming to her face, she admitted that while aiming her rifle at a warthog at the hunt today, she had remembered the warthog from the day before. "And that awful image seared in my brain seems to have killed my appetite for sport for the moment." She looked at Radhanath with an uncertain smile, revealing her uneasiness.

Radhanath could not think of anything appropriate to say. He noticed she refrained from asking why he hadn't gone hunting himself, which was perhaps not hard to surmise because he was riding toward the hunting ground at this hour of the day.

Abruptly, Sara threw him a question, "Mr. Sikdar, do you think you could help me understand what you exactly did to calculate the height of Mount Everest?" Radhanath assumed Sara changed topics because she did not want to talk about hunting anymore. At the same time, he was pleased by the genuine curiosity he sensed behind her question.

Radhanath stopped walking and started looking around. The trail had flattened, and they were passing by a grassy patch about a mile wide, bordered by tall deodars blocking a direct view of the valley.

"Come," he invited, taking the reins of both their horses in his hands and getting on the grassy patch. As he tied their animals to the nearest tree before returning to Sara, she stood on the grass by herself, curiously watching his movements. Pointing to a tree some distance from them, Radhanath said, "See that deodar? Let's say you want to measure how tall that is. How would you do it?"

"First, you need to measure the angle to the top of the tree with respect to the flat land here." As Radhanath said this, he held one palm flat and the other at an angle to the first, such that the two resembled a half-open book. He looked at Sara and asked, "Do you know what an angle is?"

Sara nodded. "I have some introductory understanding of Euclidean geometry." Seeing Radhanath still holding his palms together, Sara added looking amused, "Thank you for asking, but you needn't start all the way from there."

Relaxing his palms with slight embarrassment, Radhanath resumed, "Alright. You have to make two measurements. Both are measurements of angles to the top of that tree whose height you want to know. Note that no matter how far the actual object is from you, it is simple to make an angular measurement. You just point your telescope to the top of your object of interest, and you can read the angle directly from the markings on the instrument."

"Now, the two angular measurements we need must be made from different positions on flat ground. For example, I make a first measurement from where we are standing right here." Taking several long strides toward the deodar tree, Radhanath called out to Sara in a raised voice, "I am going to make a second measurement of the angle to the top of the tree from this new location I am at."

Then walking back to Sara, Radhanath said, "Using these two angles measured from the two different locations I indicated and the distance between the two locations, you can apply mathematics – trigonometry, in particular – to estimate the height of the tree. We apply this same basic principle to estimate the height of a mountain."

Sara seemed genuinely surprised with this information. "Just this?" she asked.

Nodding his head to affirm, Radhanath elaborated, "This picture, Miss Langley, is over-simplified and idealized, but in its defense, it is essentially correct. However, there are many additional considerations that complicate matters when measuring the heights of mountains."

Radhanath saw Sara look at him expectantly, hoping he would continue. Feeling stimulated by her curiosity, Radhanath expanded, "One of the key considerations is the atmosphere. The light that comes from the top of the mountain travels through the atmosphere before it reaches the instrument that we are using to make the measurement. It's actually quite a tricky business,

Miss Langley. There are two main effects. First, the atmosphere here is different from the atmosphere at the top of the mountain; in fact, it is changing continuously between here and there. As a result, light does not travel in a single straight line, giving a false impression about the location of the peak. Second, the atmosphere is also changing constantly with time. Each time we make the measurement, we will get different values for the height of the same thing. Besides, the earth being round can also complicate things."

Sara had been listening to Radhanath intently. Now she rejoined, "So you came to the rescue with your bag of mathematical tricks to estimate the true height from these imperfect measurements. I bet some of these measurements were way different from the final figure you postulated. It's quite remarkable, Mr. Sikdar! You must have incredible confidence in your skills to reconcile all that data, simply based on calculations, especially as it sets a new record as the highest point on Earth."

Radhanath remembered feeling anxiety right after Waugh's speech at the inauguration dinner, wondering whether Sara believed his claim to be the one who first computed the height of Mount Everest. *Those doubts could be put to rest.* He was feeling gratified as he glanced at Sara, her youthful freshness speaking directly to his heart. Abruptly, he became conscious of the beaters that he had completely forgotten about since he ran into Sara. Remembering the implication, an outpouring of concern for Sara's well-being made him nervous; it wasn't safe to hang so close to the hunting grounds this late in the day.

Radhanath was about to relay his concerns, when Sara let out a cry, and Radhanath observed her face contort with pain. Without being conscious of it, he found himself inches from her face in the next instant to ask what the matter was. Radhanath's automatic concern was not lost on the sharp young woman as she pointed to the back of her neck with the words, "Something stung me!"

As Radhanath looked at the reddening wound on the exposed skin above the neckline of her shirt, both first heard a bee and then saw it buzzing away from them. Swiftly recovering her verve, Sara's eyes moved past Radhanath's shoulders, combing the jungle behind them. Soon, squealing triumphantly, she pointed to a yellow blob on a tree about a half a mile away, "Look Rady, there, right there! Can you see it?"

As Radhanath turned to look, he heard Sara asking, "Have you ever eaten honey directly from a beehive?"

Marveling at her eyesight for recognizing the hive from so far away, Radhanath turned back to Sara, shaking his head. He hadn't eaten honey directly from a hive before.

"It's heavenly!" Sara offered, before jumping to, "By any chance, do you have a matchbox on you? Do you smoke?" A mischievous look had dawned on her face.

Radhanath said he did not smoke, but that he did have matches on him, struggling to understand the import of her questions. Without bothering to explain, the girl simply said, "Good. Let's go!"

She broke into a run, headed toward the hive. Radhanath was conscious of not having communicated that they may be perilously close to the hunting ground right this moment. With Sara sprinting ahead, he had little choice but to follow her. Both arrived near the tree, somewhat out of breath. A number of stray insects went zigzagging past them.

"Can I have the matches please?" Sara extended her hand toward Radhanath with a bright smile, still out of breath.

Radhanath dug into his pocket but tried to use the moment to bring up the beaters. "Listen Ms. Langley," was all he got out.

"That too!" said Sara, pointing to the small knife that had slipped out and fallen from his pocket, while Radhanath retrieved the matchbox in his hand.

Genuinely curious, Radhanath handed both over with the words, "Exactly what do you want to do?"

Taking her time to respond, Sara offered, "When I visited my grandparents, we often would go to the woods near their home and collect fresh honey. If you want a taste of wild honey, we need to hold a fire beneath that hive. It will drive the bees away. Then we can bring the hive down!"

Radhanath stood dumbfounded. Coolly, Sara continued, "Rady, I will also need that cloth you have draped on your head. I must cover my face with something to avoid the bees."

Radhanath croaked, "You are planning to bring that beehive down?"

Sara looked at Radhanath for a few moments, neither accepting nor denying the charge, before starting to collect dry leaves and twigs from the ground. Finding his voice, Radhanath said, "Listen lady, that is out of the question; bee attacks can be dangerous! Besides, can you not hear the beaters? We are too close to the hunting ground. We should head back immediately!"

Ignoring Radhanath's outburst, Sara responded with playful outrage, "Sir, did I not tell you, I have done this many times before! Please do not worry yourself. And yes, I can hear the beaters, but I promise it won't take but a moment." As she spoke, Radhanath watched her deftly making twine from creepers she was pulling free, expertly removing the leaves off of them with his knife. Sensing she was not one to be easily dissuaded, Radhanath decided to say nothing more. Besides, the sooner she was done, the quicker they could leave. Presently, tying the sticks and the leaves with the twine she had harvested, Sara held up a fairly reasonable looking torch that was ready to be lit.

Radhanath unwrapped the *ushnish* from his head to handover to the determined young woman. Stowing the matchbox and the knife in the folds of her dress, Sara removed her top hat and started to wrap the light blue cloth of the *ushnish* around her face. Her riding clothes covered the rest of her skin adequately. Radhanath could not escape how pretty the blue looked against her radiant complexion. As Sara exerted herself, the profile of her youthful breasts became prominent, triggering a helpless arousal in him. He turned his head up to look at the hive where the bees continued to buzz. Then, the thought that should have come to him already, but probably didn't because he had become overwhelmed with one thing after another, came. *The hive was at least twelve feet away. How was Sara going to reach it?*

Intending to ask this question, Radhanath turned and found Sara ready to light up the torch she had improvised. He noted the bits of eyes, nose, and lips visible through the cute cocoon of his *ushnish.* "May I ask how you are planning to reach the hive?"

Sara looked around as if she was hoping to discover something useful near them. Then she proposed the idea she had already formed soon after they first arrived at this spot. "I don't see an alternative to standing on your shoulders, do you?"

Radhanath, not quite able to believe his ears, stood quietly. *What an insane idea!* He wanted to laugh out loud. "You are planning to stand on my shoulders to reach the hive?"

Chuckling lightly, Sara said, "Of course, only if you agree. I am light, Rady. You don't have to look so worried!" As Radhanath stared, Sara added, "Your height plus mine will get me to the hive."

Carrying Sara on his shoulders was the least of his concerns. Radhanath squatted on the ground next to the tree. After handing the smoldering torch to Radhanath, Sara removed her boots and climbed on him, oddly without self-consciousness. She soon stood with her feet spread across his shoulders, holding the trunk next to them for support. Radhanath passed back the torch. Then, holding one of her legs with one hand and the trunk of the tree with the other, he stood up slowly. Radhanath understood Sara had reached the hive from the amplified growl of the bees. He stood stiff and tensed, fearful of losing their precarious balance. Gradually, the noise from the bees seemed to peak. From the corners of his eyes, he caught sight of hundreds of bees escaping like a brown plume of smoke. Although he was located further away from the hive, a few bees stung Radhanath. Amidst the discomfort of it, a new respect for the girl's courage dawned inside Radhanath. And with that, he thought that his *ushnish* could hardly be protection enough. With an abrupt, anxious squeal, he asked if she was alright. Her response from above his head, came calmly – she was all done.

Sara passed a chunk of the hive which Radhanath dropped on the ground by his side. Then she passed him the torch, which Radhanath now held in his hand. As soon as he had helped her get off of him, he tried to discern whether Sara was alright. She was busy unwrapping the *ushnish*, and soon held it up for him smiling. Radhanath felt relieved that but for a few red welts where the bees had stung on Sara's nose, there didn't seem any real damage. The sweaty locks of her hair were starting to blow out in the breeze. Sara bent down to put her boots on. Radhanath now dropped the torch he was holding on the ground and started stomping on it to kill the flame.

When Radhanath looked back, he found Sara kneeling on the grass, closely inspecting the reddish-yellow mass of the hive she now held with both hands. Extracting the knife from the folds of her dress, she started cutting out pieces from it. As Radhanath's eyes strayed to the long, gold-flecked lashes on her downcast eyes, she looked up at him and extended a square of the oozing beehive with a triumphant smile. Radhanath accepted the morsel and drew it close, carefully observing the dark red honey coating the hexagonal compartments of the hive. *It had a curious fragrance*, he noted. He heard Sara urge, "Just bite into it, hive and all – every bit of it is edible."

As he watched Sara relishing her mouthful, Radhanath took a small bite himself and experienced an extraordinary sensation. He had never tasted anything so delicious. The honey had an interesting bitter aftertaste. He wondered if that was because it came directly from the hive. Radhanath continued to observe Sara from the corner of his eyes, simply gorging herself on the honey. Every bit of her seemed to be glowing with happiness.

As Radhanath finished his square, he suddenly realized he couldn't hear the beaters anymore, which probably meant that the hunting was done for the day. Scanning the ambient light, he was surprised at how quickly dusk seemed to be falling; nervously, he estimated they had at the most a half an hour of daylight remaining. With everything moving so fast, his uneasiness from their proximity to the hunting ground had become eclipsed yet again. As it returned to him, Radhanath glanced toward where their horses stood, some distance away. Both their firearms were sitting on those horses. With renewed urgency, Radhanath turned toward Sara, "Miss Langley, it will get dark soon. We should head back."

Sara sat staring at the piece of the beehive she held as if she did not hear him. Radhanath raised his voice, "Miss Langley!"

When Sara finally responded, a jolt of fear ran through Radhanath. The girl had slurred her words, "This honey is wonderful!"

"Come on, Miss Langley! We need to get going!" urged Radhanath, hurrying toward her. Bending to check on the girl, he touched her shoulders. Sara tried to stand up and then clutched his arms, seeming unsteady on her feet. And then, to his utter astonishment, he felt dizzy himself. *Something was terribly wrong!*

As Radhanath looked at Sara, she looked back at him blankly, licking her lips. *It must be the honey!* thought Radhanath with rising panic. Something in the honey had clearly affected them both. It seemed to have impacted Sara, who had consumed more of it, worse than him. Radhanath's eyes spun around wildly. It was then that his eyes fixated on a cluster of trees, teeming with magenta blooms. In a flash, he knew it was those rhododendrons, which grew so extensively in this region, that was to blame. He had once heard that the Gurung people favor honey made from the rhododendron or *buransh* flowers because of its hallucinogenic properties. In many ways, its effect is similar to consuming large amounts of alcohol. Radhanath's heart sank as he made the connection.

Sara was not able to walk. She seemed too far gone to recover anytime soon. It was clearly up to Radhanath now to come up with a solution. For a moment, he wondered if he should carry Sara to the horse. And then attempt to walk the horse with Sara back to the camp. But the light was about to go.

He remembered that the trail became precipitously narrow in certain places. Radhanath concluded that in her current state, it could be more dangerous to go back than stay put. They needed to find some safe place to shelter for the night. He decided to get Sara to safety, before attempting to retrieve the rifles from their horses. Radhanath looked around for the closest tree they could easily climb.

He finally chose a sprawling oak. Picking Sara up in his arms, he tried to quickly get them to the tree. Even though it was not warm, Sara's face was drenched in sweat. By this time, the winds that seem to start right after sunset in this region were generating loud rustling noises. This combined with the sight of waves on the surface of the grass began to wreak havoc in Radhanath's imagination. With each step, he kept looking back, thinking some wild beast hidden by the tall grass was tracking them.

The mere quarter of the mile they had to traverse to reach the tree Radhanath had selected seemed impossibly far. His heart thumped from fear and exhaustion, beginning to succumb to the physiological impact of the honey himself. Once they got to the tree, Radhanath put Sara's feet on the ground as gently as he could, trying to get her to lean against the tree. Sara could barely stand by herself. She tried to say something but instead retched violently. Radhanath waited a while, hoping Sara would recover enough strength for the climb.

As he waited, Radhanath noticed the light was starting to go fast. He realized he won't have time to retrieve their firearms after all. Urgently, he whispered to Sara, "You have to help me. The sun will set in no time. We need to get off the ground before the light has gone."

Radhanath thought he was finally able to pierce through to Sara. She tried to use Radhanath's help to scramble up the tree. He felt sorry to see her struggling so hard. After a while, Radhanath got Sara high enough to sit in a cavity formed by the forking of two branches. He sat himself down next to her as best as he could. Comfortable or not, they were finally off the ground.

Radhanath rested a moment looking at the distant mountains through a veil of trees, glowing pink in the light of the setting sun. He couldn't believe how fast their situation had deteriorated. He turned to look at Sara, slumped against the tree, with her eyes closed and totally wiped out from the climb.

Abruptly, a strong gust of wind shook the tree. It did not last. Shortly after, there was another one just like before. They seemed to come and go and soon grew more frequent. Within the next fifteen minutes or so, as the last of the daylight went and a brilliant moon lit the sky, a rough, cold, gale started. With their tree shaking almost continuously now, Radhanath fretted that Sara may fall off the tree. He relocated himself to be able to hold Sara securely in his arms. Her eyes were still shut; her face turned at an angle from him. Despite their predicament, as Sara's soft body rose and fell against Radhanath, waves of sweet pain seemed to wash over him. Radhanath watched the wind play with the strands of Sara's hair. He watched the moonlight kiss the exposed portions of her skin. As he observed her face, it struck him that he couldn't bear if anything were to happen to Sara Langley.

Part 2

Chapter Six

31st March 1857

About a year had passed since the news of Mount Everest had first come out. On that warm, late spring afternoon, Lawrence Cockerel, Park Street *thana*'s police chief, sat in a horse-drawn, four-wheeled coupe trotting down the Barrackpore Trunk Road (BT Road). His cart passed open marshes bordered by groves of coconut and palm, overgrown forests of mango and jackfruit trees, and occasional swathes of green paddy with ox tilling the fields. Lawrence was on his way to Barrackpore, a township about twelve miles upriver from Calcutta – home to one of the largest and oldest military barracks in the country – from which the town gets its name. Of those employed at Barrackpore cantonment, the British soldiers lived on premise and the native sepoys, right outside its walls, in the Sepai Para neighborhood (including Lawrence's good friend Pannalal who was currently part of the 34th Bengal Infantry). Following the Governor General Lord Wellesley's grand country home, it had become fashionable for officers of the East India Company to erect vacation homes in Barrackpore. Over time, they also added a menagerie, an aviary, a theatre, and a beautiful park to the township, earning Barrackpore the affectionate nickname "Little Calcutta" among its European residents.

This afternoon, Lawrence was thinking about a disconcerting incident vis-à-vis the 34th Bengal Infantry that was currently posted at Barrackpore. Two days ago, a young sepoy by the name Mongol Pandey assaulted the British officer Baugh in broad daylight. None of the other sepoys present at the time bothered to intervene. When Officer Hearsey arrived on scene and attempted to rescue Officer Baugh, he was shocked to find the sepoys unresponsive to his orders. He had to threaten them with guns to get their cooperation, a piece of news that worried Lawrence Cockerel.

After two months on an official assignment at the Madras presidency in South India, Lawrence had returned to Calcutta just a few weeks ago. On his return, he was appalled to learn about the unrest at Dumdum, the British cantonment nearest to Calcutta and at Berhampur, another British cantonment about two hundred kilometers to the north of Barrackpore. The Hindu sepoys, who held the cow sacred, and the Muslim sepoys, who abhorred pigs, had both been deeply offended by the introduction of the Enfield rifle cartridges, containing grease made from cow and pig fat. As a people who held religion very close, the sepoys were horrified by the suggestion that they must touch the cartridge with their mouths to bite off its head before use. Then when Lawrence heard about the Mongol Pandey incident, he couldn't expunge the feeling that more trouble was coming. He had contacted the cantonment board, who recommended he go to the officers' meeting to obtain a first-hand feel of the situation.

The inspector sat brooding, lulled by the gentle swaying of the carriage going down BT Road. Pannalal had told him that the sepoys suspected the British intended to convert them to Christianity. They would likely interpret the new cartridge as further evidence to support that theory. He remembered warning Stuart how deeply the Indians cared about their religion. Sensing they were beginning to slow down, Lawrence stuck his head out the window to his left and saw that they were approaching a large, white, concrete tower standing by the side of the road. *That would explain it*, thought Lawrence. The seventy-feet, four-level tower built by the GTSI six miles outside of Calcutta at Sukhchar was currently in use. To ensure that measurements made on sensitive equipment inside the tower are not impacted by vibrations from traffic, passing vehicles were required to go at reduced speed. As he passed, Lawrence eyed the square holes cut into its thick walls. Telescope muzzles attached to the theodolites they housed inside these towers could sometimes be seen nestling in those places.

As Lawrence's carriage entered the limits of Barrackpore, he began to see fine English boats marooned along the Hooghly riverfront, next to a group of modest dinghies. They went past the extensive country homes belonging to the officers of the East India Company, with their bougainvillea draperies and manicured lawns. Finally, going along coconut and palm-lined avenues inside the military cantonment, his *tanga* stopped next to a red brick building that housed the barrack's main canteen, which was where the meeting was to happen.

At the meeting, with a glass of water, Lawrence sat in one corner and noticed that most of the officers were in an informal mood. They seemed to believe that they were here to discuss a minor disturbance. They were treating the Mongol Pandey incident as an isolated matter, unconnected to the sepoy unrest at Dumdum or Berhampur. The officers seemed convinced that the root cause for the sepoy unrest had been resolved, and that the adjustments introduced to the Enfield cartridge workflow eliminating the use of cow and pig fat had adequately dealt with that problem. Baugh, the British Officer Mongol had attacked, was at the meeting with his injured arm in a cast slung over his shoulder. He felt Mongol had gone rogue under the influence of *bhang* and jovially recommended they ought to fine sepoys caught drunk anywhere near the cantonment.

After listening to various accounts, Lawrence realized everyone was taking a rather blasé view of the situation, including General Hearsey. Lawrence decided to ask, "If the matter was indeed no more serious than the foolish behavior of one drunk man, how can you explain that the rest of the sepoys did nothing? Why didn't those other soldiers attempt to either restrain Pandey or rescue Officer Baugh?"

Casually shrugging off that objection, Hearsey responded, "Ah these native sepoys, they have to be given strict orders for everything!"

Lawrence refrained from retorting that strict should not mean needing to threaten at gunpoint.

Hearsey continued, "You have to understand that the natives love drama. I have no doubt they were mesmerized by the sheer spectacle of a sepoy attacking an officer!" In a more serious tone, he added, "What this has done though is give us an opportunity to send a strong warning. We will not tolerate any indiscipline, any disloyalty. Mongol Pandey will hang to his death. His voyeuristic pals will also pay. Every last sepoy from the 34th battalion have been disarmed regardless of whether or not they were present. We're teaching them a lesson they won't soon forget."

Inspector Cockerel stared at Hearsey with disbelief. The word "disarmed" had stung him like a whiplash. From his association with sepoys, Lawrence understood that the sepoys knew no bigger insult, no bigger injury, than to be asked to yield their firearm. Lawrence regretted the lack of contact he had had with Pannalal over the past few months. Between him working at the Madras Presidency and Pannalal planning a pilgrimage to Haridwar in North India, the two had lost connection. As Pannalal's face rose before his eyes, Lawrence thought, *Pannalal must have returned from his pilgrimage. As part of the 34th Bengal Infantry, he had doubtlessly received these same orders.* Lawrence regretted that now, of all times, he had lost touch with his friend.

Lawrence stepped out of the canteen, resolved to go find Pannalal. He had decided to hold his tongue at the meeting, having sensed that this audience had already made up their minds and would not take kindly to his interference. He walked across the bridge connecting the cantonment to Sepai Para, straddling the somewhat putrid channel of water that separated the two worlds. On the native side where the sepoys lived, the scenery changed rapidly. The roads grew narrow, meandering tortuously through clumps of dingy, thatched-roof houses. *Saris* and *kurtas* stretched out on jute strings to air-dry blew in the breeze. Whatever else, the place did not lack signs of life. Ducks, chickens, dogs, and children walked about. Cows and goats, tied to stakes in the ground, sat looking bored, shooing flies with their tails. Native women went about their day's chores: peeling vegetables, running behind children, and washing utensils. Lawrence could feel their eyes following him. He noted that the courtyard charpoys, where the menfolk should be relaxing with a hookah this time of the day, were all empty. The locality shops were all bolted shut. After a few turns, he came upon a young girl, barely twelve, making cakes of manure and putting them on the boundary walls to dry. Lawrence knew this was their main source of cooking fuel. Upon Lawrence asking about Pannalal, the girl curtly mentioned that Pannalal was gone to attend a funeral. A slightly amused Lawrence understood that the little girl was channeling the current anger among the native sepoy community toward the British, in her demeanor. Unfazed, he probed and extracted directions to the crematory from her.

It was about a mile and a half's walk for Lawrence to the crematory on the Hooghly Riverfront. As he got close, he could see smoke rising from melancholy pyres still burning. Orange clad priests were performing the rites of passage for the dead. *It is hot here*, he thought, wiping his forehead with a kerchief. Looking for Pannalal, Lawrence scanned the faces of the mourners. His eyes were drawn to a largish crowd where he soon located Pannalal standing vacantly near the pyre. Men were layering wood on the sheet-wrapped dead body. From the strength of the crowd, Lawrence surmised the menfolk missing from Sepai Para were all here at the funeral.

The moment Pannalal's eyes fell on Lawrence, they lighted with happy surprise. But only momentarily. A complicated stiffness soon darkened his gaze. Lawrence came and stood next to Pannalal. After waiting silently for a while, Lawrence whispered, "Did you know him well, that man you are here to cremate?"

After a pause, Pannalal responded, "Not well, just in passing."

Pointing to the dead man Raghu, Pannalal said, "By the time the doctor arrived, Raghu's spasms had become violent. He broke his own teeth by the force of his jaws grinding together. Then the spasms got worse." After a pause, he said, "Have you ever heard a man's bones breaking? I don't think I will ever forget the terror I saw on his face!"

Lawrence realized Pannalal was re-living the horrors of the dead man's final moments. Having grown up in India, Lawrence knew how a fate worse than death waited for those who succumbed to tetanus. Unfortunately, it was more common among the natives who were in the habit of walking barefoot, cutting and scraping themselves fairly often.

Turning to Lawrence, Pannalal said, "What are you doing here? Have they called you up to discuss the Mongol Pandey situation?"

Caught off guard by the abrupt change of topics, Lawrence started to say, "No, I came by myself!" Without letting him finish, Pannalal exclaimed, "Can you believe what they did? The entire native taskforce of the 34th has been disarmed!"

Lawrence wasn't sure how he should respond. Sensing Pannalal was waiting for him to say something, he finally, rather lamely, offered, "When Baugh was attacked, the rest of the sepoys did not intervene. The bosses are questioning everyone's loyalty."

"I wasn't even there!" snapped Pannalal. "Do you know how many sepoys were actually present compared to how many you have in the 34th battalion? Negligible!" Pannalal continued, "What reward do the rest of us get for our loyalty? With one callous stroke of a pen, we are the same – all guilty! My years as a sepoy were worth nothing!"

Lawrence wished there was something he could do for Pannalal who was his first playmate and an elder brother figure in the days when Pannalal's mother tended to Lawrence. However, the inspector felt powerless in the current situation.

Absorbed by their conversation, Lawrence hadn't been paying attention to his surroundings. He had been ignoring a gradual rise of the usual sounds of conch shells, ritual bells, and people's voices. Now startled by loud ululation, Lawrence turned to look. Under the low branches of a sprawling banyan tree at a little distance from them, a young girl in a red *Benarasi* sari had come into view. She was walking toward them with a sizable crowd in her wake, the womenfolk ululating. As she neared, the words with which the crowds were exhorting her, suddenly got through to Lawrence, "Hail *Ma Sati* Nalini!"

Lawrence's confusion cleared in an instant. He knew what he was witnessing, and a cold chill went down his spine. Aided and abetted by the crowds, Nalini, the dead man's widow was aiming to burn on the funeral pyre with her husband and earn eternal glory as *Sati*. In keeping with the *Sati* tradition, she had worn her bridal *Benarasi* sari tonight. British administration had banned the practice of *Sati* in Bengal over twenty-five years ago. But truth be told, it still happened, particularly in some of its interior pockets. Disregarding the law of the land, these people were about to observe *Sati*, in plain view of Officer Cockerel, unless he could do something to prevent it. Or could he?

Lawrence immediately saw that Pannalal's eyes did not deny his awareness of what was happening. However, they held two other things that disheartened Lawrence – challenge and resolve. Pannalal's lips had curved into a sneer. Agitated, Lawrence almost pleaded, "*Sati* is illegal. You can't let this happen. You are a man of law."

As if on cue, Pannalal spat out, "Not anymore, Cockerel sahib! You forget, I am a disarmed sepoy!" His voice quivering with anger, he continued, "What do you know of it? Who are you to make laws about things you do not understand; that you never cared to understand?" Pannalal stopped, and then muttered to himself, "The *Sati* will find her place in heaven. There is nothing to keep her here."

The resigned finality in Pannalal's tone rattled Lawrence. He could not believe Pannalal was saying this. Turning back to look toward the pyre, Lawrence found the widow getting ready to mount it. A man with a torch stood next to her, preparing to set the pyre aflame.

Lawrence roared, "Stop!"

As the clamor around him quietened, he said, "This is illegal. I am a policeman. I will arrest anybody that does not disperse immediately."

Lawrence started to walk toward the girl intending to sacrifice herself. Hoping his bluster will deter the people, Lawrence spoke in a rough voice, "And I will take this woman into custody to keep her safe until her husband's body has been fully cremated."

Feeling a restraining hand on his back, Lawrence turned to find that Pannalal had come up behind him. Shrugging Pannalal's hand off his shoulder, as he attempted to continue, he found a bunch of well-built men had materialized to block his progress. Pannalal came and stood directly facing him once more, with a cold warning now flashing in his eyes. Lawrence, drenched in torrents of sweat, stood paralyzed. The drums, bells, conch shell, and ululation had resumed and soon reached a crescendo around them. Lawrence watched as the young woman climbed on the pyre, and then the man with the torch set fire to it. Amidst roars of "Hail *Ma Sati* Nalini!", saffron tongues of flame leapt up to engulf the woman.

Time seemed to stop for Lawrence. In her final moments, the girl turned to gaze directly at the white man, her eyes full of scorn. Lawrence Cockerel, who thought he knew his Calcutta, stood witness to the surreal drama unfolding, reeling with disbelief and impotence.

Chapter Seven

14th April 1857

Radhanath exited the GTSI tower at Sukhchar, the same one that Lawrence Cockerel had gone by a few weeks ago. He had spent his day recalibrating the theodolite inside the tower. Thirty years since the Trigonometric Survey had originally built the tower in George Everest's time, Surveyor General Waugh had had it reopened to repeat measurements for their work on the Calcutta Longitudinal. With that assignment starting to pick up, Radhanath was at the tower more regularly these days. Radhanath nodded at the guards standing next to the tower. Shrouded in semi-darkness, BT Road looked deserted at the moment. Tiredly wiping the sweat off his forehead, Radhanath watched a faint light some distance away on the opposite side of the road. He knew the light was from the shack next to the *tanga* stand, that sold betel leaves and smoke to *tanga* drivers. In the low light, it was hard to tell if there were *tangas* waiting at the stand; he needed one to take him home. After several weeks in his rental at Beniapukur near GTSI's Wood Street office, tonight, Radhanath was returning to the villa he had built for himself a couple years ago, in the French colony at Chandannagar. He planned to take the *tanga* up to Barrackpore and from there, ferry home across the Hooghly River.

As Radhanath started walking toward the *tanga* stand, a commotion from the direction of the Hooghly River, which flowed parallel to the BT Road, came to his ear. Wondering what it was, Radhanath was suddenly reminded that they had the Charak festival this time of the year. The natives celebrated Charak with a big riverfront fair, not fifteen minutes from where he stood. Charak was particularly popular among the lower caste Hindus and a unique experience. There are few occasions where one will find men rolling on beds of thorn or walking on bare nails of their own volition. Torn and bloodied, the performers at Charak strove to appease the gods with their suffering. The most spectacular act had the performers hang themselves from rods, with huge iron hooks running through the skin of their back. These rods were attached to a central pole, fanning out in all directions like a merry-go-round. Men on the ground rotated the central pole by pushing on a rod attached perpendicularly to the pole. This allowed those suspended mid-air, to revolve around the central axis. Despite their bleeding backs, no one uttered a single cry in a show of extraordinary forbearance.

Radhanath debated whether he should go and sit by the riverfront for a while before starting his long journey home. It had taken him much longer than he expected to get through the instrument calibration. He was stiff and exhausted from having to sit on a wooden stool and make careful measurements all day. The thought of watching the festivities and eating some freshly made *jeelipis,* sure to be sold at the fair, tempted him. Giving in, Radhanath pivoted toward the riverfront.

A year had passed since *Raja* Uday Singh's *shikar* party and that fateful night Radhanath spent perched on a treetop, sickened by wild honey, while holding a semi-conscious Sara in his arms. Notwithstanding the passage of time, Radhanath discovered that he remembered the experience in vivid details, as if it happened yesterday. He had spent the night without a wink of sleep. His fingers had grown numb from cold. His mind had run in endless cycles worrying about the winds pushing them off the tree and the possibility of predators hiding in the darkness below them. This had gone on until the winds let up at sunrise, and he was finally able to catch a few hours of exhausted sleep.

When Radhanath woke next morning, he found Sara's tired eyes resting on him. She had moved such that she now sat with her back leaning against a branch facing him. For a while, he had stared at her in confusion. As it all started to come back, a shadow of concern darkened his face. *How was Sara feeling? Had she fully recovered yet?* Sara recognized his silent questions and inclined her head slightly to reassure him. She then asked, "What happened?"

Radhanath recounted the events of that evening after which both fell silent. Allowing Sara to rest a little longer, Radhanath went to fetch their horses. Things certainly looked different in the morning; the bird songs and the fragrant, dew-fresh air gave him confidence. Relieved to find their animals where he left them, Radhanath untied one of the horses and led it back to the tree where they had sheltered the night. With Sara still groggy from her experience, there was some back and forth while helping her down the tree and getting her to mount the horse. Radhanath had chosen not to ride, opting instead to cautiously walk the horse Sara sat on, back to the camp.

That was the last time Sara and Radhanath saw each other on that trip. That night, the reality of holding Sara Langley in his arms, left Radhanath astonished by the depth of emotion it stirred in him. He couldn't believe he could feel so tenderly in such a short time or that he could feel this way for a woman at all. However, painfully aware of the insurmountable differences in their age, background, and importantly, race, any sort of future together seemed absurd to him. When Dubois came the day after to tell Radhanath that Sara was doing fine, Radhanath decided his best recourse now was to distance himself. Soon after, without saying goodbye to Sara, Radhanath had left for

Calcutta. Chandrakanta had hung back until the end, enjoying his time with Nana sahib and his associates.

Darkness had fallen by the time Radhanath reached the Hooghly Riverfront at Sukhchar. Indeed, he had correctly deduced the source of the commotion; Charak celebrations were in full swing. Numerous torches on tall poles lit the fairground. A lot of people had come from near and far. Families held each other's hands, to prevent getting separated. Several stalls were selling a great variety of deep-fried foods. Hungry after his long day, Radhanath bought *jeelipis* from a stall frying them fresh. Chomping on the crisp sweets, he meandered along the fairground. Unrestrained by the purdah, the lower caste women looked particularly vibrant wearing gawdy jewelry and flowers in their hair. They laughed and chattered freely with their menfolk and children. Many engaged in spirited bargaining, huddled around stalls that sold everything from food to toys to clothing to handicrafts. Radhanath noticed a few silk *dhuti-panjabi* clad *babus* out for revelry, probably accompanied by prostitutes. Despite the muggy heat of the evening, Radhanath was enjoying himself, breathing the moist, smoky air, touched by the infectious enthusiasm of the people.

Finally, Radhanath reached the central attraction of the fair, the Charak pole. Fascinated, he stood looking at the men hanging by the skin of their backs, revolving around the central pole. Radhanath had long wondered how these men coped with the pain. Meanwhile, a character had creeped close to him. Startled by the stranger, Radhanath was about to express his irritation, when noticing a thin iron rod pierced though the intruder's outstretched tongue, he gawked at the man. Fully aware of having rattled Radhanath, the man's eyes shone with laughter. He continued to flaunt what he had in his mouth, loving the shock on people's faces. That's when a new commotion erupted to Radhanath's right.

Several heavily made-up figures in elaborate costumes had appeared on the scene. Radhanath recognized the new arrivals as the *Shong*, peripatetic actors that performed open-air sketches, giving vent to public sentiment. The astonishing thing about them tonight was their height. The men had balanced themselves on pairs of stilts, lifting them ten to twelve feet off the ground. While mounted thus, they maneuvered the stilts like walking sticks in their hands. Dacoits of Bengal were known to be expert stilt walkers in those days, a skill that allowed them to swiftly cover large distances when on the run. Tonight, the *Shong*'s clever use of the stilts had served to elevate them, as if on a moving stage, enabling everyone to observe from near and far. The actors on these stilts, with their whitewashed faces and tattered western clothes, let go of the stilts completely from time to time and pretended to be holding a gun. It was not hard to guess that their act aimed to lampoon British officers.

As Radhanath neared the *Shongs*, he picked up fragments of the dialogue, which were in the pure, classical form of Bengali. The colloquial, spoken version sounded very different from the written. To the native ear more accustomed to the colloquial form, speaking in the pure written version, as many of the British typically did, provided opportunity for caricature. Radhanath saw that the *Shong*'s act tonight was an instant hit. They had the crowd rolling on the ground with laughter. Briefly, he wondered if their reaction was somehow colored by the recent execution of sepoy Mongol Pandey at the Barrackpore cantonment, an incident that was reported to have fanned significant anti-British sentiment.

Bypassing the *Shongs*, Radhanath finally came up to the riverfront, allowing his eyes to rest on the mysteriously glinting waters of the Hooghly River. His eyes were drawn to the pools of light from the lanterns on the boats floating upriver, ferrying passengers who were enjoying the evening air. Radhanath spotted a small fleet anchored on the bank, available for hire. Suddenly feeling tired of the crowd, Radhanath wished for a boat ride himself. With that thought, he walked down toward one of the vessels. The boatman smiled at Radhanath and asked if he was on his own. The question was not unusual because most boats catered to *babus* who brought prostitutes aboard with them. With a curt affirming nod, Radhanath got on the boat, walking straight to the middle where passenger seating was located. The boat rocked a little as the boatman untied it from its anchor, before starting to drift away.

The moist river air refreshed Radhanath. He sat enjoying the gentle rolling motion of the boat while looking back at the revelers on the bank. From this distance, those hanging midair by the skin of their backs around the Charak pole looked like giant flies. Radhanath continued to savor the breeze on his skin, this time closing his eyes and tuning out the distractions. When he opened his eyes again, the lantern that hung from the ceiling of the boat seemed too bright to him. Radhanath asked the boatman to reduce the flame. He decided to stretch his legs out and lie on his back for a bit. Resting his head on his hands, his eyes sought the stars blossomed prominently against a pitch-dark sky. He stared without being conscious of thinking about anything, letting his mind be lulled by the rhythmic beating of the oars against the water.

Radhanath had observed that over this last year, when he was alone, his thoughts would stray to Sara Langley. It happened tonight again. Radhanath had decided to remove himself from anywhere near Sara rather abruptly. He had wanted to avoid getting sucked into the idea of a relationship that he thought had no future. Over the last year though, Radhanath realized, near her or not, he had unwittingly carried two things back from that *shikar* party in his heart – her smile and the way she had looked at him in their first encounter. The look that hinted at an unprejudiced, aware mind, capable of appreciating the nuanced complexities of life. The force of his conviction astonished him. It also disheartened him because his reasons to distance himself from Sara could never change.

The boatman, in no particular hurry, allowed the boat to languish mid-river. He was feeling pleased because his customer had neglected to settle on a rate before he boarded. This left the boatman free to name any price he liked. Radhanath could complain, but he would still have to pay up. The boatman sat smoking a native *beedi* contentedly, idly watching the crowds on the fairground.

Radhanath's thoughts drifted to his work. Over the years, he had toyed with the idea of teaching at a college. Of late, he thought about it more often. He felt he had gotten all he had wanted from GTSI, and it was time for him to move on. Meanwhile, the official seal on renaming Peak XV as Mount Everest had not been issued yet. Waugh was lobbying hard for it these days. Radhanath's thoughts jumped to Francois Dubois, who had visited their Woods Street office in Calcutta soon after the hunting party. While returning the telescopic gauge that he had borrowed to Radhanath, Dubois mentioned that he had accepted a year's appointment on *Raja* Uday Singh's staff at Jainagar. His job, in addition to maintenance of the telescope he had installed, would be to help the monarch discover various astronomical wonders of the night sky. Noting Dubois reticent on the subject of Sara Langley, Radhanath didn't press him much beyond the demands of politeness.

A burst of firecrackers made Radhanath turn his head toward the bank. He watched its red and gold fill the sky and followed the path of the sparkles until they melted into the darkness. Suddenly he thought of Chandrakanta, who he hadn't seen in a while. The few times they met over last year, Radhanath had noticed changes in his socially conscious friend. Always nationalist leaning, he somehow seemed more so – a development Radhanath linked to Chandrakanta's growing friendship with Nana sahib. From the moment Radhanath saw Nana sahib at the *shikar* party last year, he had sensed a certain ideological resonance between the two. When Radhanath learned that Chandrakanta was going North frequently these days, he suspected Chandrakanta was in touch with Nana sahib on these trips.

At this point, a very loud roar that rose from the direction of the fairground, shook Radhanath out of his contemplation. Sitting up, he squinted that way, trying to understand what was happening. Waves upon waves of cheering filled the air. Radhanath couldn't fathom the cause of the excitement. He noticed the boats on the river were beginning to turn around, in a sudden hurry to get to the bank. His own boat also started to turn causing Radhanath to look toward his boatman with annoyance. The man had simply not considered it necessary to take Radhanath's permission. Not wanting to go back yet, Radhanath questioned why the boatman was turning around. The man paid no heed to his question, driven by his own strong curiosity to find out what was happening. In the meantime, the roaring from the crowd continued to swell.

When the boat finally arrived at the *ghat*, Radhanath had no choice but to get off along with the boatman. He gathered that the hullabaloo was all about a dozen native sepoys' sudden appearance on the fairground. These were sepoys of the 34th Bengal Infantry who had been expelled in the wake of the Mongol Pandey incident. They had come to the carnival to vent their frustration against the British. Protesting the orders to relinquish their guns (arms that the British had once put in their hands), they had arrived fully armed with traditional weapons, daggers, and swords and dressed in red coats (their colors in the British army before they were sacked). The sepoys were thoroughly enjoying their non-verbal interaction with the masses, lapping up their frenzied approval. Everyone present tonight was united in their animosity toward the British. Radhanath saw that the *Shongs,* who were lampooning the British earlier, had gotten off their stilts. They had approached the redcoats to add to their interplay. *The Shongs looked rather odd from the ground level.* Suddenly, there was some discussion among the redcoats and the *Shongs*, and everybody started walking toward the Charak pole, the hooting and cheering crowd in tow. Feeling curious, Radhanath also followed them.

When they reached the Charak pole, the *Shongs* had iron hooks pierced through their Western style shirts like the Charak performers and hung themselves from the rods fanning out from the pole. As the native redcoats pushing the horizontal rod attached to the pole near the ground increased the speed of its revolution, the *Shongs* contorted their faces, feigning pain, screaming to be relieved in classical Bengali. Radhanath understood that this was meant to be a vicarious punishment of the British. The sepoy community clearly couldn't forget or forgive their recent humiliation. In fact, Mongol's execution had united the natives against the administration. As an ecstatic audience celebrated the performance, Radhanath decided he was done here tonight.

Remembering he hadn't paid the boatman yet, Radhanath looked around, wondering how to locate the man in this crowd. Fortunately, he spotted the man staring wide eyed at the events, seeming to have forgotten about the money owed to him. The man looked very surprised when Radhanath tapped him on his shoulders. Radhanath held out an amount about twice the standard fare. The boatman took the money and tucked it away wordlessly. Radhanath waited a moment to see if he intended to demand more. Finding the man neither thanking him nor protesting the amount, in fact returning promptly to stare at what was happening with the *Shong*, Radhanath turned away. He started a brisk walk toward the *tanga* stand near the tower, hoping to hire one for the first leg of his journey to take him home to Chandannagar.

Chapter Eight

As far back as he can remember, *zamindar* Chandrakanta Raychaudhuri had lived with the uncomfortable sensation of being the odd one out. At first, this was because of his own dark complexion, a conspicuous oddity among the pale Raychaudhuri clan. Both his family's and the Indian society's widespread fascination for fairness upset the sensitive child. Father Surjyokanta did not help matters with his obsession with European society – always found at their balls, their games, and their taverns – far from the parochial environment of his family home. Surjyokanta's purdah-secluded wife Sunayani, the *rani* of Dhanulia, had long resigned to the idea that her Westernized husband did not belong in her world. She did not object, her fate not uncommon for women from *zamindar* families. However, for Chandrakanta, his father's absences festered like a wound. He grew up believing that his father disliked him because he was dark. Unable to feel like he belonged with his kin, this was Chandrakanta's first taste of a crisis of identity.

At seven, Surjyokanta got his son admitted to the legendary Hindu school, established by Indians to give their children quality English education. In an environment with many British teachers, Chandrakanta got his first exposure to the Western world through their literature, science, and philosophy. Hindu School's charismatic teacher Henry Vivian Derozio fired up his young mind with progressive ideas. However, Chandrakanta's exposure to the West created a new crisis of identity for him. He found it hard to straddle the ever-widening chasm between the Westernized world he experienced at school and the native world he experienced in his home environment with a large extended family living under one roof. He tried to share his new world with his beloved mother by reading her his favorite English poetry, translating each line patiently, but he couldn't get her interested. He grew aware that these two worlds didn't speak to each other. As Western ideologies shaped him, he struggled to stay connected to his native roots. At the same time, he struggled to feel integrated with the West. For example, Chandrakanta's interaction with the traditionally stiff-upper-lipped British teachers at his school used to intimidate him. His boyhood friend Radhanath Sikdar would remind him to keep focus on the subjects they were learning and ignore all else. Radhanath said they weren't that familiar with the English and therefore didn't necessarily understand their ways. This never satisfied Chandrakanta. With a growing awareness of the European milieu, he wanted to feel comfortable around them. The unresolved question of where he belonged, that started with his brown body sticking out like a sore thumb among his pale family, resurfaced inside him as a much larger question.

Things took a radical turn for Chandrakanta when he turned twenty-three, and his mother fell violently ill. When the doctors declared that the *rani* of Dhanulia wasn't for long now, Sunayani extended badly shaking hands holding an age-yellowed parchment toward her son. It referred to an incident that happened before Chandrakanta was born. Apparently, she had written it a while back in anticipation of this day! At nineteen, Sunayani's palanquin was ambushed by dacoits, but she managed to slip away and was eventually rescued by a group of ascetics who found her stranded in a jungle.

Chandrakanta had heard the story many times. In Sunayani's note to him, Chandrakanta sat reading a bewildering alternate version!

On that fateful journey, the headman of Sunayani's entourage had joined forces with a group of respectable-looking merchants, hoping for safety in numbers on the isolated, robber-infested roads they were passing. It turned out these were no ordinary merchants. They were *thugees* who were waiting for the gold laden Raychaudhuri *zamindar*'s wife on the road that day. As the party began walking together, peeking through the curtains of her palanquin, young Sunayani's eyes met those of a dark-skinned, well-built, curly haired bloke, walking with them. In course of time, the palpable chemistry between the two had the young girl come alive with feelings she had never experienced before. Sunayani had written: "It was *thugee* Gokul who saved my life that day! Betraying his own clansmen, he smuggled me out of their reach and hid me in Burir Jungle. I spent the most nerve-racking moments of my life that night, in that godforsaken, abandoned castle where he left me to wait. When I had almost given up hope of his return, he did, bleeding profusely from a knife wound on his arm. He told me he got that while fighting my men. He also told me that my men had all been murdered by his clansmen. To be honest, I couldn't think beyond the fact that I was alive, and that Gokul had come back for me. That murderer showed me tenderness that no one else had up to that point in my life and certainly not my husband. Afterward, my son, on the bare grounds of that decrepit castle, you were conceived. Yes, *thugee* Gokul is your real father. You may choose to think of this as a betrayal. But I refuse to feel ashamed for what happened. Do rest assured, no other soul knows the secret of your birth, not even Gokul."

Holding his mother's note, Chandrakanta sat staring absently at his own dark skin. *Finally, it all made sense.* His alienation from the Raychaudhuris was real; he was his mother's bastard with no relation to them. Chandrakanta's mind drifted to Gokul. *How could a thugee win his mother's affections? Was the man alive?* He didn't get the chance to ask Sunayani any further questions.

The answer however did come, eleven days after Sunayani passed away. That morning, a shaven-headed, *kacha*-clad Chandrakanta had been preoccupied with his mother's *Shradh*, Hindu rites of passage. The usually deserted *rajbari* was overflowing with guests, who had come to attend the *Shradh* luncheon. Among the poor enjoying a free meal, sat a man, eating *pulao* with his hands. As he licked his fingers, he eyed the *zamindar*'s son. Briefly, he tried to remember the woman Chandrakanta's mother was. Gokul had stayed away for over two decades as he believed the *zamindar*'s wife was beyond his league. Somehow, he also fretted that if they met a second time, she might give him away. Upon hearing that the Raychaudhuri *zamindar*'s wife had died, he had come with the throngs of the poor. Perhaps, in his mind, he had come to see his lover off. Was he feeling emboldened to think about this bit of his past now that Sunayani was no longer a threat? If asked, he wouldn't be able to exactly tell.

Gokul passed his left hand over the ugly scar that ran along his right arm. It was a knife wound one of Sunayani's men had inflicted. He remembered how Sunayani had rushed to bandage his wound with cloth torn from the ends of her sari. After depositing Sunayani at an old, dilapidated castle that he was familiar with, Gokul had returned to their camp and found that their absence had not been noticed yet. The men were preparing for a feast on their last night together, and the *thugees* waited for Sunayani's men to become sufficiently drunk and unguarded. When the time came, Gokul played along with his clansmen, his own kerchief tightening remorselessly around the necks of Sunayani's men. Gokul remembered how he had pretended to be amazed when they discovered her gone. The *thugees* had wanted to go looking for her right then. That was until they found the gold that cunning Gokul had instructed Sunayani to leave behind. With the gold in their hand, the thuggees had voted to wait until morning, reasoning that Sunayani was unlikely to get far, or even survive the night in the jungle. Gokul had wandered off, insisting he would go looking himself. Later, it was Gokul who escorted Sunayani to the outskirts of her family's estate.

Chandrakanta went to stand at one corner of the verandah, finally done with the day's proceedings. His mother was often found at this spot, feeding grains to the peacocks that roamed free on their estate. Idly, Chandrakanta stood reflecting on his mother's explosive secret.

"*Katta*!" Chandrakanta was startled out of his reverie by Gokul, who, after eyeing him for a while had decided to come talk to him, addressing him as *Katta* to show respect. As father looked upon the son who he never knew he had, Chandrakanta saw a dark-skinned man holding his hands in a *namaskar*, a long scar running down his right arm. Chandrakanta remembered he had seen this man before, working with the natives alongside Calcutta's Reverend Stuart. As the *zamindar*'s son waited for the man to speak, he also remembered what he had heard of the Reverend's efforts to push Christianity among his constituents.

"Your mother no more, eh?" spoke Gokul gently. Nodding politely, Chandrakanta inquired whether the man had eaten well.

"Yes, *katta*!" responded Gokul and then, "God will reward your generosity." Chandrakanta stood silently with a noncommittal smile on his face.

Encouraged, Gokul mentioned, "*Katta*, I work for the Christian priest, Reverend Stuart. I help him distribute milk free of charge to the poor. It is such a joy to see the happiness on people's faces when we feed them."

Nodding in agreement, Chandrakanta was about to turn away when Gokul held him back with a hasty request. Reverend Stuart was going to deliver a lecture this Saturday at the open space outside Burir Jungle. Stuart's trusted sentinel had suddenly thought of inviting Chandrakanta to the gathering. A lot of Chandrakanta's tenants were coming. What did Chandrakanta think of coming there himself? It was the mention of Burir Jungle where he had been conceived according to his mother's note, that caught Chandrakanta's attention.

The observant Gokul did not fail to notice Chandrakanta's sudden attentiveness. "Do come, *katta*, you will like it!" Gokul repeated his earnest invitation. "And ask for Gokul once you get there," he said pointing to himself, "I can introduce you to the Reverend sahib!"

"What did you say your name was again?" asked Chandrakanta, his brows furrowed with disbelief.

"I have a Christian name, Gary, but my friends, they call me Gokul. You *katta*, you can call me what you like," he preened. Chandrakanta stood looking at the man in front of him. *It was simply a coincidence, it really was,* he said to himself. Chandrakanta remembered the gash he had seen on this man's arm moments ago. *Was that the wound Sunayani mentioned?*

Gokul stood hesitantly now, wearing an ingratiating smile on his face. He was wondering if he should go or stay, nervously rubbing his hands together and eyeing Chandrakanta. He was intrigued by the manner in which Chandrakanta was looking at him. Feeling a bit pressured by the silence between them, Gokul said, "*Katta*, you know, I had once seen your mother. A very long time ago."

"Really?" asked Chandrakanta, waiting for the man to elaborate.

Shifting uneasily on his feet, Gokul continued, "Remember the year the *thugees* attacked her palanquin? It was huge news. I came to the feast your grandfather had organized to celebrate your mother's miraculous survival."

Chandrakanta looked at Gokul in silence, the word *thugee* jumping out at him. They did celebrate his mother's return, but his mother had reported attack by ordinary dacoits, no *thugee,* perhaps to keep her paramour safe.

"Your grandfather had declared her the incarnation of goddess Durga! And why not? Who but a true goddess could thwart the *thugees* and survive such a dangerous jungle!" Gokul paused, looking at Chandrakanta, a smug expression brightening his face.

Chandrakanta pondered the implication of this man's knowledge. And then, a paralyzing helplessness washed over him. The man that stood at a stone's throw from him was perhaps his real father – that lowlife, mass murderer Gokul. The repugnant circumstances of his birth notwithstanding, it was Gokul's blood that ran in his veins. Despite the difference in their social standing and body language, Chandrakanta noted his own physical similarities with Gokul: dark skin, body build, and curly hair. He silently acknowledged the complicated emotion this monster stirred inside him.

...

"Achha bolunto, how can I marry a man I have never even met, let alone felt affection for?" Swati Ray's voice played in Chandrakanta's ears as he sat sipping Turkish coffee late that afternoon, watching the speaker exit Basir Ali's Kebob Masala, a modest and unpretentious, one-of-a-kind eatery next to Portman Square in London. After his mother's passing, Chandrakanta had felt a strong urge to get away from his Dhanulia home. The twenty-three-year-old then decided it was time for him to explore the West that had always attracted him, even though he wasn't sure of his footing among them yet. Soon after, Chandrakanta had left the shores of Calcutta in 1838. It was now six months to the day that he set foot in England.

Today was the first time Chandrakanta had chatted with Miss Swati Ray, even though she lived at Mrs. MacDonald's Boarding House on Aldersgate, where Chandrakanta was also a lodger for the last several months. He had seen Miss Ray with her parents, heard they were from Calcutta from their ever-chatty, middle-aged proprietress but chosen to remain distant. However, this afternoon, Chandrakanta was not feeling his usual self. And so, when Miss Ray appeared at Basir's Coffee Shop, in a simple yet elegant gown and her hair in a thick braid falling over her shoulder, he had impulsively stood up and pulled out a chair for her. Not unsurprised by the gesture, she had nevertheless come over to join him. Chandrakanta learned their family had been on travels across Europe for the past several years. He was most impressed to learn Miss Ray occupied herself translating French poetry into English. Time passed quickly for Chandrakanta since opportunity for one-on-one conversation with a sophisticated Bengali lady was rare in the purdah culture where he came from; his interactions with the opposite sex back home was limited to either prostitutes or family. Chandrakanta's hunch, that Swati was about the same age as him, was confirmed when at one point she said, "My family in India are angry with me, pity me, even ostracize me because I am twenty-two and not married yet. I have refused to marry my so-called betrothed!" With a sincere, pained look, she had then asked, "*Achha bolunto*, how can I marry a man I have never even met, let alone felt affection for?"

After Swati was gone, Chandrakanta continued nursing his coffee and reflected on their conversation. When she spoke of her challenge in finding a life partner, Chandrakanta could immediately empathize. He was nineteen when his family had brought him a ten-year-old stranger to marry, which of course, he had declined straightaway.

Outside the windows of Basir's shop, Chandrakanta's eyes fell on a typical London scene, its roads and buildings cloaked in veils of mist. Nevertheless, smartly dressed men and women could be seen walking with their hats, umbrellas, and briefcases. Chandrakanta's eyes were drawn to an elegantly dressed young woman getting off a hansom cab, her décolleté neckline accentuating her charms. London's women, unfettered by the purdah, had mesmerized Chandrakanta from day one. In the mellow light of the evening, he saw a lamplighter walking with his ladder, bringing the golden orbs to life one by one. Chandrakanta spotted passersby with kerchiefs pressed to their nose. It had taken him several weeks to get used to the city's horrendous stink himself. Just then, a horse-drawn omnibus came into view and armies of dirt-streaked children ran in its wake, removing manure faster than it could accumulate. When he had first come to London, the white emaciated faces of the poor, including the beggars all over the city, had been a huge shock to him. He had found it hard to reconcile these destitute souls with his image of the British as powerful colonials.

Finishing up the last of his coffee, Chandrakanta found the heaviness he had been fighting earlier this afternoon, returning to him. In fact, his enthusiasm for the West had reached an all-time low. When he arrived, Chandrakanta had tried hard to embed himself into London's cultural scene by attending plays, recitals, and literary salons all over the city. He faced no great culture shock or language problems, thanks to his Hindu School education. Nevertheless, everywhere he went, he found himself feeling left out of the conversation. If he happened to initiate one, he found the person shy away from him. Behind the facade of politeness with which he was received, he discerned cold curiosity, or circumspection, and sometimes also condescension. A few weeks ago, his landlady, Mrs. MacDonald had invited Chandrakanta to attend an opera at the famed Covent Gardens. During recess, when she introduced him to her friends, Chandrakanta had a feeling of déjà vu, watching the curtain fall on the faces of Mrs. MacDonald's friends. When someone brought up kite fighting, Chandrakanta had become excited and tried to share his own experience. But he shut up soon enough, realizing that they had brought it up simply to tell each other they were people of the world. However, they believed they knew all that there was to know about something as trivial as kite fighting; they had no interest in his perspective on the subject.

On their way out from Covent Gardens, Mrs. MacDonald had introduced Chandrakanta to Gladstone, proprietor of a monthly called *The Orient*. To Chandrakanta's surprise, upon learning that he was from Calcutta, Gladstone had enthusiastically exclaimed, "Hah, you are from James Princep's city!" An embarrassed Chandrakanta had to admit that he didn't know what James Princep had done. With a patronizing smile, Gladstone had explained how the long-forgotten edicts of the Indian king Ashoka had recently come to light. James Princep of the Asiatic Society had deciphered the writing on them. In doing so, he had uncovered details of India's history from around the time of the Buddha, almost two thousand years ago. Upon learning that Chandrakanta knew Sanskrit, Gladstone had offered him a job as his secretary, on the spot. However, after starting his work, it did not take Chandrakanta long to understand that Gladstone's love of India was purely intellectual, the attraction of one called upon to solve a puzzle. Gladstone cared nothing about Indians.

Getting ready to leave, as Chandrakanta sat counting the coins to offer as *baksheesh* for his waiter, a sarcastic "hmph!" escaped him, remembering Gladstone profess, *Karna and Arjuna from the Indian epic Mahabharata were like family to him!*

That's when Chandrakanta's eyes fell on Basir. The stocky, elderly proprietor of Kebob Masala was coming toward him with a tray, most probably carrying something complimentary from the kitchen especially for Chandrakanta. Settling back in his seat, Chandrakanta watched Basir approach, feeling heartened that the man had made a habit of this sweet gesture and done it almost every time Chandrakanta visited. Basir's warm smile deepened the laugh lines around his eyes. Having left his fishing village in Khulna at seventeen, he has lived off the streets of London for more than four decades now. As Basir put the tray on the table, Chandrakanta surprised himself with the words that came out of him, "Basir, I am going home!"

Frowning slightly, Basir looked down at the steaming meat pie on the tray he had brought and then up to Chandrakanta's face, asking, "Should I pack this for you then?"

"No, no, I meant I am returning home to Calcutta!" Chandrakanta corrected. Basir's eyes showed surprise and then sadness. He had grown rather attached to his young Bengali patron.

Chandrakanta was definitely feeling vulnerable this evening, for he next asked, "Basir, do you never think of returning to your home?"

The veteran looked piercingly at Chandrakanta. Then with a chuckle, he responded, "My home? Right here is my home! I have lived here longer than anywhere else…"

Chandrakanta interrupted, "I mean your home in Khulna. I loved how you spoke of stealing wolf pups from their den with your bare hands in your village. How your grandmother pointed to the eerie marsh lights and told you of fiery monsters that lived there…"

Basir had listened with an impassive face. Now, with his eyes abruptly flashing, he butted in, "Don't fool yourself, Chandrakanta! People like you and me, we don't have a home!" He had spoken in perfectly British accented English. Then Basir had walked away from the table, leaving the meat-pie for Chandrakanta to eat alone.

Soon after this, Chandrakanta returned to India.

When Basir said *people like you and me,* despite the differences in their social standing, level of education, and religion, Chandrakanta had no difficulty understanding what he meant. In straddling the two different cultures, they had each found themselves treated as outsiders – by both the English and their birth community of people. In this sense, a home, where one is accepted and understood, had forever eluded them. Chandrakanta got a taste of this when he found it hard to reconcile between his Westernized world in school and the native world from which he came. Over the years, despite no lack of affection between them, he found himself growing distanced from his mother because she lacked the wherewithal to appreciate who he was becoming in his head. In London, he finally realized, not only was he not accepted by the British, but that they had neither interest nor awareness of the isolating aspect of a cross-cultural experience. Ironically, of all Indians, it was people like him, who were a direct product of the experiment the British started with their colonization, who were best equipped to understand the West.

When his father passed away shortly after his return to India, alongside assuming responsibility for the Raychaudhuri estates, Chandrakanta worked to raise awareness of the Western society among those he had the power to influence. He promoted Western literature by commissioning translations of his favorite pieces into Bengali. He also commissioned translation of Sanskrit literature into Bengali to foster appreciation of their indigenous roots. After acquiring an iron press, he started a monthly magazine with recruits from his own Hindu school. He got in touch with Swati Ray, and the two worked side by side on various projects. Unfortunately, two years down the line, Swati died of tuberculosis. Her companionship had given Chandrakanta a sense of peace for a short time in life.

Over the years, Chandrakanta grew convinced that British rule in India was superfluous and doomed to fail. Regardless of the infrastructure the English built and the social reforms they instituted, their implementation showed they did not understand the Indian people. They refused to engage with Indians beyond a superficial level. However, they insisted on expansion, systematically taking control from previously sovereign states. After the British annexed Punjab, Burma, and then Nagpur, Chandrakanta found his friends from royal families constantly fretting over who will be next. It was at this time that Chandrakanta met Peshwa Baji Rao's charismatic son Nana sahib at a wedding reception hosted by the Maharaja of Bajragarh. Chandrakanta had instantly liked Nana sahib. In the younger Nana sahib, he saw what he thought he lacked in himself – that recklessness to flirt with danger that never came as easily to him. Nana sahib had said, "Indians need the opportunity to think for themselves, make their own decisions." Chandrakanta couldn't agree more. *How was that ever going to happen if the British always insisted on having the last word, about India and Indians?*

Chapter Nine

18th May 1857

Andrew Waugh and Radhanath Sikdar emerged from GTSI's Calcutta office on Wood Street. The contrast between the *punkah*-cooled interiors of their office and the street, brought a look of exasperation to Waugh's face. Radhanath responded by sadly shaking his head. The two started walking, Radhanath intending to lead them to a Portuguese tavern about ten minutes away. Surveyor General Waugh was visiting from Dehradun. An official letter from the Asiatic Society had arrived by the morning's post today. Responding to Waugh's recommendation on naming Peak XV as Mount Everest with stiff objections, the Asiatic Society had cited GTSI's long-standing practice to adopt local names for landmarks. Why should they make an exception this time? Wanting to discuss the matter with his Chief Mathematician, Waugh had come to see Radhanath in the office next to his. As it was close to noon, Radhanath had proposed they continue talking over lunch. Radhanath suggested the tavern Evora which he frequented. In fact, he had dined there last night.

Evora has been a fixture in this area for the past thirty years now, ever since the half-Indian Alfonso sahib of Portuguese descent set up shop when Park Street was just beginning to hum. It was hard to miss, occupying a large square at the corner of Theater Road and Loudoun Street. Rows of cute curtains flying along its street-side windows beckoned passersby for a drink. One can see a reasonable sized crowd inside Evora at all hours of the day. A foyer, where guests deposit their bags and umbrellas, led to a well-lit interior, with ornate bell jar lanterns set against bright turquoise walls. Portraits of Alfonso sahib's family hung in gilded frames behind the cash counter, the most prominent of them being that of his great-great-grandfather from the city of Evora in Portugal (the first of his ancestors to have come to India). Right next to it, sat the portrait of his own Bengali mother. Traditional garlands of chili, garlic, and onions were seen hanging from the ceiling. The well-run restaurant boasted spotless, comfortably upholstered furniture and a tasty selection of European and Indian dishes, most with a delightful Portuguese twist. Evora was also known to host live performances in the evenings, bringing a mix of timeless European music to their clients. The atmosphere was semi-formal, welcoming well-to-do diners of all races. European attire was not strictly necessary; appropriately attired Eastern ladies and gentlemen were welcome on their premises. Although they left the final decision of who to admit somewhat subjective, it seemed to work, and no one had ever complained. A usually dapper, sufficiently polished Radhanath, more than fit with their clientele.

Radhanath and Waugh passed sprawling bungalows, ubiquitous in the predominantly British neighborhood they were going through on their way to Evora. The light breeze that had started to blow made their walk pleasant despite the relentless glare of the sun. Radhanath eyed a cluster of natives: *ayahs, saishes*, and *khansamas*, who were standing under a banyan tree on the corner of the street and possibly discussing the day's activities at the various households they serviced around here. A pastor in white cassocks walked by, a common sight in this area not twenty minutes from the St. Paul's Church of Calcutta. Waugh was busy explaining that Everest's name, being synonymous to that of the Trigonometric Survey, was therefore an obvious choice for naming the highest peak.

About to enter Evora, Radhanath looked at his boss askance and said, "How about we call it Mount Sikdar? After all, you were buried under a tsunami of data, and if it weren't for me, we may not have found this result." Taken aback, Waugh stared at Radhanath's poker face. He looked decidedly relieved when he noticed the glint in Radhanath's eyes. *Rady was trying to be funny!*

On a serious note, Radhanath said, "Well sir, you know my opinion of Everest's contributions. Colonel Lambton may have started this organization, but it was Everest's leadership that helped it reach its full potential. There's no doubt in my mind that George Everest deserves to be honored. However," he paused, before continuing, "as the Asiatic Society said, in the past, the indigenous names have been retained for the mountain peaks we measured. Mount Annapurna, Mount Kanchenjunga, there are many examples. How will you convince them to make an exception?"

At this point, both fell silent as they entered Evora. The Anglo-Indian doorman knew Radhanath because he was a regular customer. Radhanath found him bowing a tad stiffly as he held the door open this afternoon. His reception immediately reminded Radhanath of the disquiet he had sensed when he was dining here last evening, an uneasiness he had forgotten all about until this moment. Radhanath had heard strange rumors circulating at Evora – reports of skirmishes breaking out in the North between the natives and the British. Because he hadn't heard anything remotely related to this in the prior weeks at the native bazaars, *tanga* stands, or ferry stations, he speculated that the native sections in Bengal were largely unaware of this development, true or otherwise.

As Radhanath waited at the foyer alongside Waugh to be shown to their table, he observed a certain difference in Evora's ambiance between yesterday and today. Last night, the Europeans chatting among themselves had seemed relaxed. Perhaps they hadn't taken the rumors doing the rounds seriously yet. They looked more jittery today; their disapproving eyes surreptitiously darting to the native faces around them.

There has been an uptick in rumor mongering lately, thought Radhanath. Random whispers found quick foothold in public imagination and spread like wildfire. Just a few days ago, everybody was talking about a Sunday when the dead were going to rise. Though it was obviously superstitious nonsense, it seemed to affect people, making them antsy.

Perhaps Alfonso was busy right then. A young Armenian woman Radhanath hadn't seen before came to lead them to their table. As they followed, Radhanath had the distinct feeling of eyes burning holes in the back of their heads, while also pretending not to look. Once settled at their table, Radhanath asked for scotch eggs and beef stew. Waugh ordered scotch eggs with lamb vindaloo, a Goan recipe he loved. As they waited for their meals to arrive, Waugh and Radhanath looked at each other across the table wondering what to do next. Both had become unavoidably conscious that they were somehow the topic of the low whispers around the room. They were the only guests with both white and native persons at the same table. In the current atmosphere, the idea of a white man breaking bread with one of the natives may seem especially odd. The looks they were receiving reaffirmed Radhanath's intuition that things had changed between last night and this morning.

Unable to ignore the overwrought atmosphere any longer and unsure of how much Radhanath knew about the situation, Waugh decided to directly address the rumors. "You've heard, I presume?"

Radhanath answered without meeting Waugh's gaze, "Yes. When I was here yesterday, I heard the sepoys have clashed with the British in Meerut."

Waugh nodded and said, "My neighbor told me they have information on disturbances in Delhi as well. And not just the sepoys. The princely states seem to have joined hands with them. They're in this together. I am not sure who or where this information is coming from. It's hard to tell what is true."

Radhanath said, "Last I heard, Dubois was working in Jainagar for Uday Singh. That's not too far from Meerut."

Picking up on the implications of what Radhanath was trying to say, Waugh responded, "I do believe you're right. If memory serves, Dubois' engagement at Jainagar was for a year. Heaven forbid, he may have found himself squarely in the middle of all this."

Waugh noted Radhanath had fallen abruptly silent. As a matter of fact, Radhanath had become distracted by thoughts of Sara Langley. Last evening, upon hearing of trouble brewing in Meerut, his thoughts had flown to the lady living in Jainagar as far as he knew. For a moment, he felt sorry for not having kept in touch. But then he rationalized, these were probably just rumors, not true. Besides, there was never any commitment between them to give him a right to know what was happening in her life. Waugh's words caused Radhanath to feel anxious for Sara once more.

Their scotch eggs, served faster than most other entrées, arrived, and the two dug in. "So, what does Everest think of this proposal to name Peak XV after him? How is he, do you know?" asked Radhanath.

Assuming Radhanath didn't want to speculate on the rumors anymore, Waugh gladly switched back to discussing Everest. Jovially, he answered the last question first, "Life assuredly becomes interesting if you marry a twenty-three-year-old at fifty-six! I hope he is happy." The disparity in age between Everest and his current wife was common knowledge at GTSI. Waugh had brought it up to share a good-natured laugh on an old joke. However, for once, alongside the amusement he expected to see, Waugh noted the flash of an unfamiliar emotion on Radhanath's face. Watchfully, Waugh continued, "Everest has written that he does not care whether or not we use his name. See, it's a matter for people like you and me to decide – the ones who know of his enormous contribution and would like to see it remembered."

An image of the inimitable, tyrannical taskmaster that George Everest was, came to Radhanath's mind. Almost everyone who ever crossed paths with him had faced the wrath of the man. People remembered him with more deference than love. The one exception perhaps was Radhanath himself, who remembered Everest fondly and whose own mathematical genius had endeared him to Everest. Turning to Waugh, Radhanath said, "As far as I am concerned, I have no objections to naming Peak XV after George Everest."

Waugh looked visibly relieved. He was glad to have GTSI's star mathematician's endorsement on this matter. It could prove useful in convincing the Asiatic Society.

Waugh looked at Radhanath with a weak smile dawning on his face, "You know, I did try to get a local name. But it was hard to find a definitive name to use. If this was not such an important landmark, we might have tried to be more creative. Under the circumstances, I think we are making the right decision."

Radhanath and Waugh's conversation was interrupted by the sound of raised voices. An altercation had erupted at one of the tables. The two craned their necks to observe a British man towering over three Indians seated at a table near the window, pointing threateningly at them. He was saying, "British women are committing suicide to save themselves from the bloody natives in Delhi!" Through gritted teeth, the man continued, "You… we allow you to sit here and breathe because those rumors have not been confirmed yet. If there's a shred of truth to this, then upon my honor, …"

One of the men at the table rose up and standing nose to nose with the British man returned fire, "Don't talk to me of honor. Allow me to refresh your memory. You are here because your Robert Clive bribed nawab Siraj-ud-Daulla's minister to commit treason. You think you are allowing me to breathe? I have more people living on my estates than the total British population in India right now. For all your firearms, you are ridiculously outnumbered. You wouldn't be here but for the mercy we show you, sir!"

Hastily running to the table, Alfonso intervened, “Sirs, I must respectfully ask the both of you to take a step back. You cannot talk like this here. Evora is open to everyone!”

A native man’s voice now rang out loud, “If you gave your sepoys the trust and respect that they deserve, you wouldn’t have to worry about your necks right now.”

Alfonso turned toward the man who had spoken, his eyes flashing. “Do not, I beg you sir, force my hand. All guests are required to remain respectful inside Evora. We reserve the right to evict any disruptors, native or European.”

Conversation between Waugh and Radhanath did not progress much further that afternoon. Completing their lunch, the two departed the diner.

29th May 1857

Several days after that lunch, Radhanath had decided to take a day off, exhausted from the overtime he was needing to toil at work. It was timely, because the leave he had accumulated was also set to expire. After pouring incessantly throughout the day, the rains had paused toward early evening. Though the overcast skies made Radhanath melancholic, Calcutta was relishing the showers after the intense heat spell stewing the city for the past several days.

Through the open window of his room at his Beniapukur rental, Radhanath, propped against a pillow on his bed, sat watching the fast-falling dusk outside. He was feeling anxious. From the scattered news trickling in from the North, the fact that a sepoy mutiny against the British had broken out had become impossible to ignore. It was clear that the princely states were complicit, but no one knew exact details yet. Learning of the aristocracy’s involvement, Radhanath’s mind had flown to Chandrakanta’s British-bashing friend Nana sahib. Radhanath’s gut said that Nana sahib would have known of any organized efforts to revolt against the British. A couple days ago, when a troubled Radhanath had gone to see Chandrakanta, he learned his friend was out of station with no expected date of return.

Eyeing the remaining cloud cover on what he could see of the sky through his window, Radhanath tried to guess if the rains were really done for the day. *Probably yes*, he optimistically concluded. He remembered how it was raining so hard this morning that everything had looked white through this same window. His eyes next fell upon Haru's convenience store, visible from his bed. Haru had lit a *kupi* lamp in preparation for the evening. In the little yellow glow of its naked flame, Radhanath could see the dingy shelves of Haru's shop, packed with all kinds of things. One or two customers had started to trickle to the shop with the rains stopped for the moment. The neighborhood children had also emerged, intent upon floating their paper boats in the various puddles on the street.

Radhanath hadn't eaten much of anything throughout the day, feeling lethargic to get up and cook for himself. Beginning to feel hungry now, he wondered if the small native hotel near his house was open at this time. He doubted it, given the weather. He decided he was going to take a brisk walk up to Evora and grab dinner there. The walk was certain to refresh him. Additionally, he'd have the chance to learn the latest on what was happening in the North.

Stepping outside in his gumboots, Radhanath started walking, carefully skirting the muddy patches and overflowing puddles. As he passed by Haru's shop, he saw the number of customers had grown, with a bunch of regulars huddled together on a wooden bench, smoking *beedi*. Although Radhanath had hoped it wouldn't rain again, he had come prepared with a large, black umbrella. So, when it started to drizzle, he continued walking. After several waterlogged alleys, Radhanath finally got on to the Lower Circular Road. From that point, his progress was relatively straightforward on the wider, better drained roads in the whiter neighborhood of the city. In about twenty minutes, Radhanath reached his destination.

As Radhanath entered Evora tonight, the first time since that lunch with Waugh, he found the Anglo-Indian doorman curtly move his head away. With his heart thumping loudly, Radhanath entered the dining space. All the tables fell silent. Radhanath immediately sensed there wasn't a second native face here tonight. Then, his wary eyes stopped at a table not twenty feet away. There, along with Andrew Waugh, sat Francois Dubois and Sara Langley! Gripped by inexplicable numbness for a few moments, Radhanath stared at the face never too far from his mind. Sara looked very different absent of her arresting vitality, her color frightfully pale and her hair limp and damp, left hanging loose around her face. Next to her sat a gaunt and grim-looking Dubois. Steam rose from the bowls of hot soup sitting in front of them. Waugh was nursing a shot of whiskey. Nodding to Alfonso who was on his way to show him to a table, Radhanath advanced toward where the three were seated.

As Radhanath neared, Waugh gestured to him to join them. After Radhanath sat down, Waugh looked at him for a few moments without saying anything.

Finally, began Waugh, "The North is up against the British, Rady. The revolt broke out first in Meerut on the 10th of May. The princely states and the sepoys are in this together, as the rumors had it, mercilessly butchering British civilians. Yesterday afternoon, a group of Europeans, mainly French, arrived from Jainagar. Our friends came with that group." Calcutta would be an obvious choice in these circumstances: far enough to avoid the heat of the rebellion, safe for Europeans being a British hub, and accessible within a few days of travel.

"They have been through hell," Waugh continued. "Dubois says Uday Singh smuggled them out of Jainagar as a personal favor to him. They have mostly been at the mercy of those natives still loyal to the Raj, who helped them make it to Calcutta alive. When they got here yesterday, Dubois asked Inspector Cockerel of Park Street *thana* to see me. They're staying at my house for now. I thought this place might cheer them up."

Dubois turned to Radhanath and said, "*Raja* Uday Singh's entire native army has turned against the British. He barely managed to get us out."

Waugh added, "On the way, they had taken refuge at a British judge's house. The natives, unaware of their presence, dragged the judge out and beheaded him, as Dubois' group watched hidden from the cow shed. The hooligans then rejoiced down the street with the judge's head impaled on a pole."

Abruptly, Sara spoke up, startling Radhanath. "The females in this convoy from Jainagar carried poison. We were ready to die before we let them touch us."

Radhanath thought she had aged years from the horror of her experience. His heart went out for the poor girl. He gently said, "Not all Indians are after English blood, you know? You are safe here." He noted Sara's eyes lost focus before he finished speaking.

By now, the rains had started in earnest again, accompanied by lightning and thunder, visible through the glass panels of Evora's windows. Sara's unseeing eyes had sapped Radhanath of the strength to continue talking. As he watched her mechanically eating her soup without any sign of pleasure, Radhanath thought of Chandrakanta. *Had he known about this?* And then he thought, *was it only a matter of time before Calcutta succumbed to this chaos? Perhaps it was all scripted already and the actors waiting in the wings!*

As Radhanath turned to Waugh with a question, he found the General watching him with narrowed eyes. Momentarily deterred, Radhanath lowered his head and then looked up again with the question, "Did you say they are put up at your house?"

"For now," Waugh responded. "Reverend Stuart has arranged to accommodate the others that came with Dubois and Miss Langley at his church. We can expect that more people escaping the North will make a beeline for Calcutta in the coming days. Everyone seems to think Calcutta is the one place where the English are safe. However, I told the inspector that it would be foolish to expect Calcutta to remain entirely peaceful. We have to remain on alert."

Just as he had a little while ago, Waugh was looking piercingly at Radhanath as he spoke. "Any thoughts on that, Rady?" he asked finally.

Radhanath said nothing, only shook his head in denial.

Chapter Ten

As the rebellion in Northern India spread over the next few weeks, the beleaguered British fleeing persecution stumbled toward Calcutta. The city opened the doors to its churches and school buildings to accommodate them. Reverend Stuart's church grew crowded. The refugees, bruised in body and soul, laid on hastily made beds and were glad to have the comfort of a clean sheet to lie on at last. Their long and arduous journey under a blistering North Indian sun had been a rude awakening. They had traded possessions precious to them, sometimes the last of what they owned, to arrange for safe passage. Many had no tears left to cry. They stared listlessly at their tuberose-wrapped Lord's face, remembering the faces of friends and families they had watched getting slaughtered, and others they had watched dying of sickness and starvation. As their stories traveled through word of mouth, they grew fraught with inaccuracies and exaggerations. To the British, they became tales of betrayal they found hard to fathom. European Calcutta held its breath wondering about their own fate. British forces from all over India were being diverted to the North to curb the uprising. Calcutta was left to fend for itself since it was considered a relatively lower threat. While not everyone agreed on this approach, factions within Calcutta's administration struggled to admit they might need protection. The British had transformed Calcutta from a fishing village to the second largest city of their empire. They found it hard to accept that they could be at risk in their Indian heartland.

The reality was, even the most optimistic of the British understood they could not remain complacent; there wasn't enough reason for Calcutta not to turn against them. The government organized town hall meetings with the natives to pledge friendship and inspire confidence in the administration. However, underneath all that, speculation on what the natives were plotting raged unabated. There'd be sudden waves of false rumors claiming blood-thirsty rebels were marching toward English neighborhoods. In the English imagination, they conjured terrifying images of drunk and reckless sepoys, brandishing swords and daggers. In the ensuing curfews, armed sentries swiftly cordoned off the white majority areas of the city, cutting off all access. If caught on the wrong side at such times, the natives ran a clear risk of getting shot. Therefore, they were forced to wait these curfews out in hiding, while friends and families endured terrible anxiety from not knowing what to expect. The heretofore tolerant city experienced an unprecedented escalation in interracial friction.

Europeans started to carry firearms around for personal protection. Armed convoys of British civilians started a nightly patrol of the neighborhoods. These vigilantes typically caught stray vagrants and amateur arsonists loitering the streets. The one thing that bewildered them were the jokers and pranksters that ended up in their nets – native men, who seemed to thrive in this disorienting environment and eager to fuel the confusion. Meanwhile, Inspector Cockerel couldn't help but view the burgeoning vigilante culture with concern. He feared panic, or the need for revenge, would sooner or later get the better of these men. His own resilience came from his intimacy with native men and women. A native *ayah* had loved him like a son; Pannalal was like a brother to him.

There was also Shashibala. This was the girl Lawrence first saw at Botu *babu*'s *khemta*, and then stumbled upon at a disreputable establishment in Chatawalapara in Central Calcutta a few months after he first met her. The inspector had kept in touch. And though he noticed a strange, unfeeling deadness about Shashi, there was something raw and honest about her that kept him interested. When a glum-faced Lawrence had gone to see her a few days after the *Sati* he had been unable to prevent, bereft of social pretenses, the girl had blandly said, "Sahib, it's not as if a widow's life is infinitely better if she escapes those flames. The in-laws reject her. The parents reject her. She has no legal rights to her husband's property. She has no skills to support herself. Where is she to go? Noor Bibi at our brothel says, many end up in places like ours in the end." Then, with slight amusement glinting in her eyes she had added, "And it's not just us natives, sahib. In the gullies of Calcutta, there is no dearth of penniless British widows seeking to prostitute themselves." Lawrence hadn't immediately found words to respond to her comment that evening.

Lawrence felt the weight of his responsibility all too keenly these days. He knew the implications of making a mistake were too terrible to contemplate. However, with the chatter on his spy networks going through the roofs, Lawrence struggled to separate fact from fiction. At the time, Wajid Ali, the ex-king of the North-Indian state of Oudh, was stationed at Metiabruz in Calcutta. Wajid Ali's friend, the Maharaja of Gwalior, had invited the entire European community to gather outside the city for fireworks at the Botanical Gardens. A few days after this, Lawrence was appalled to stumble upon evidence to suggest that this had likely been a ploy to draw the British away from Fort William; *the natives, with help from native workforce inside Fort William, had planned to attempt a coup!* If it wasn't for one of Bengal's notorious *Kalboishakhi* storms, that forced a cancellation, the British may have been within a hair's breadth of losing Fort William! Lawrence fumed with frustration knowing that he didn't have evidence strong enough to put the main instigators, especially Wajid Ali's close companion, the slippery *Nawab* Ali Nukhi Khan, behind bars yet.

Then Calcutta woke to the news of rebels in the North having marched to Kanpur, a city about five hundred kilometers to the west of Delhi. There, thousands of them had surrounded Major General Wheeler's entire garrison of three hundred military men, along with their families, who had taken refuge in an open, tree-less compound with scant building cover at the southern end of the city. These men and women had apparently been under constant bombardment ever since. It was rumored they were beginning to run out of food, water, and medical supplies, implying an imminent surrender to the rebels. With only a handful of the wire posts still functioning, news from the region was spotty at best. However, it was becoming increasingly clear that the character who led the siege was well-known to the British. It was Peshwa Baji Rao's adopted son, Nana sahib of Bithoor, who used to be a darling in India's European circle. Multiple reports claimed that Nana sahib had given General Wheeler an understanding that he was coming to help but then joined hands with the rebels instead. The British condemned Nana sahib's actions as a classic example of Asiatic cunning in their inner circles. However, the more notorious Nana sahib became among the British, the more popular he grew among the natives, who saw his actions as those of a consummate politician.

The Kanpur Siege took its toll on Lawrence more than any other development to this point in the mutiny. Reverend Stuart's daughter Emily was the one love of Lawrence's life. As her husband worked for General Wheeler, Emily was now stranded at the mercy of the rebels. That knowledge, somehow, suddenly pushed Lawrence to the brink of his endurance. Not even that evening when he had found himself powerless to stop a young woman from being burned alive on the banks of the Hooghly River had he doubted his understanding of the natives as much as he now did. *Had he been blind about Pannalal and every one of those natives he trusted?* Lawrence struggled to hold on to tenuous optimism that General Wheeler, a pro-native, experienced leader, would know how to ensure the safety of his garrison. He realized it would be a while before reinforcements came to the gates of Kanpur; in the meantime, it was down to General Wheeler's diplomacy and the bravery of his men. Lawrence asked each refugee that arrived from that part of the North about Emily and her family, but he wasn't able to learn anything significant.

Waves of terror rocked Calcutta as the 23rd of June loomed on the horizon. The date was the hundred-year anniversary of the Battle of Plassey that marks the dawn of British rule in India. They said a showdown was coming. Lawrence worked furiously, trying to find concrete evidence of malintent. His gut told him that Calcutta could not remain untouched by the current mood of the country. As he followed each lead that came to his hands, he sometimes wondered if one of them would lead him to Pannalal, his one-time trusted friend. Lawrence had a warrant out in Pannalal's name ever since the *Sati* Pannalal refused to help him prevent. Lawrence realized that the disillusioned Pannalal, a man who lived by his beliefs, would now wholeheartedly support the cause of the rebels. He wondered if Pannalal had gone North to join them. *Or was he in Calcutta right now, plotting carnages for the 23rd of June?*

Chapter Eleven

In her room at a brothel in Central Calcutta where she lived these days, young Shashibala lay in fitful half-sleep, a bangle clad arm resting on her head. One of her parted legs was thrown over an oversized, embroidered bolster pillow that occupied quite a bit of her bed. Shashibala lay breathing through her mouth, held slightly open, tired from the hectic *mujara* she had performed in Calcutta's predominantly native Colootolla neighborhood last night. A sun-washed scene from the courtyard of a house she used to know in Colootolla came to her mind. She saw a gold bedecked, young woman, clad in a dazzling red *Benarasi* sari, walking toward a crowd fallen silent. A dead body lay on the ground before her, covered in a white sheet, not turned cold yet. Years ago, another wife of the same Colootolla's Dutta family had come out dressed like this and honored the family by becoming a *Sati*. Everyone knew, this one could never equal their revered *Ma* Pronoti, who had willingly embraced the flames of the funeral pyre with her husband. This was a wayward, free-spirited teenager, who had spent every day of the past year of her married life, incessantly lectured on how a Dutta family wife should behave – how she should walk, talk, and not eat before the rest of the family is done with their meal – while always wearing a stifling *ghomta* on her face.

Besides, the red-faced sahibs had banned *Sati* from Bengal these days. *What was this woman doing in a bridal red Benarasi, when she should be donning the mournful white of Hindu widowhood instead?* The woman stood moodily next to her dead husband, closely watched by her in-laws who were curious to see what she would do next.

The parrot hanging right outside Shashibala's half-open door profanely shrieked "*banchot*", interrupting her muddled reflections. The woman in front of the dead body she had been dreaming of was herself, the day she had become a widow, just a year into her marriage to the Duttas of Colootolla. Now jarred fully awake, Shashibala raised her head to figure what had disturbed her feathered friend. Catching sight of Rakhal, the proprietor of their brothel passing by her room, Shashibala turned to the bird with a knowing smile on her face. *Yes,* Shashibala agreed with the colorful word the parrot had chosen. She gently lay her head back on the bed. Like the rest of the girls at their brothel, Shashibala hated Rakhal, especially for bullying them to get tested for venereal disease. He wanted his girls cleared, so his brothel could become licensed with the East India Company as an official supplier of women. The girls were mutinous because as licensed prostitutes, they will only be allowed to cater to British soldiers – a scary thought for women who spoke little English. They didn't want to give up their regular, native clients.

As the warm morning began to coat her poor body in sweat, Shashibala picked up her ivory hand-fan and twirled it absentmindedly. Shashibala knew she would be permitted to keep her *gora*, Park Street *thana*'s Inspector Cockerel. *Sahib had refused to kiss the Shashibala that night!* Although Lawrence disappeared before her event completed, he had showed up at her doorstep soon after by accident, then became one of her regular clients. Shashibala's thoughts drifted to the possibility of getting diagnosed with disease herself. *What happens then?* She would become useless to Rakhal. Turning her head to look through her open doorway, Shashibala eyed a soot-blackened room on the second floor of the wing opposite hers. Just a week ago the middle-aged prostitute Bishnupriya, who was rapidly losing clients, had burned to death in that room. They said she committed suicide, but nobody put it past Rakhal to orchestrate the murder so he could reclaim her space.

Death didn't affect her much – discovered Shashibala unexpectedly, one fateful morning a few years back. That day, as a Dutta family wife, she had been standing mutely by her potbellied husband, thirty years older to her seventeen, a round-bottomed brass container of water in hand. The husband, who never bothered with conversation, was intent on swallowing one *pantua* after another, which was his breakfast routine. Suddenly, he had started to choke on the sticky sweetmeat. Shashibala had stared at the man unable to breathe, doing nothing to aid him, not even getting him the water that she supposedly held for him. All that flashed in her mind just then was his unpleasant nakedness when he pawed her nubile young body each night in bed. Then, after he died right before her eyes, Shashibala had stood vacantly wondering about what just happened. *What exactly was expected of her next?* Her husband's presence had been little more than a disgusting imposition on Shashibala's life. It occurred to her that she would no longer be obligated to carry a child now that this man was dead.

A waft of wind brought the smell of dried vomit from a drunk brothel visitor, who failed to keep it in two nights ago; it was still stuck to the window of Shashibala's room. Grimacing, she kept her hand-fan down, then rubbed the remnants of sleep from her eyes before sitting up on the bed. Intent upon looking in the mirror, Shashibala stumbled to the carved teakwood dressing table, a luxury she could ill afford but had nonetheless indulged in. As she tucked a lock of hair behind the ears, sounds of harmonium, *tabla*, and ankle bells floated up to her; the novices in their building were starting their morning practice sessions.

Absentmindedly, Shashibala reflected on a time not that long ago when she wasn't a Dutta family wife yet. Attracted by these same sounds of ankle bells, a carefree Shashibala had peered into this building from the narrow alley by the side of the building where she was standing that day. She had come to town with her good-looking, mild-mannered, childhood playmate Kanai, with whom she often went secretly gallivanting – climbing mango or guava trees, swimming in ponds, or escaping to Tiretti Bazaar in Central Calcutta to eat spicy Chinese food. They had come to Chatawalapara, one of those Calcutta neighborhoods whose multicultural environment Shashibala liked, despite knowing women of questionable character lived there. Shashibala had twisted Kanai's arms to share a puff of his scented cheroot with her, and the two had come to this shaded alley, so Shashibala could try it concealed from prying eyes. Drawn by the sounds of the tabla and ankle bells, Shashibala had looked inside the room, becoming transfixed, fascinated by the jerky, pelvic movements of the girls practicing *khemta* that day.

"What is this?" she had whispered, breathless.

An agitated Kanai had curtly responded, "It's *khemta*. Let's go!"

The *ghomta* had slipped from Shashibala's head, baring her face. Spellbound, she watched the tabla player who was energetically moving his head to the tabla beats. When the blue-eyed, tan skinned tabla player's eyes finally fell upon the damsel, the man had winked at her, making Shashibala blush. Noor-Bibi, the middle-aged, kind-looking *khemta* dance teacher, had invited Shashibala and Kanai inside. Finding nothing wrong with watching women dance, Shashibala had dragged the reluctant Kanai along. Ever since, Shashibala would come here from time to time to watch the *khemta* class in progress. Whenever they came, Noor Bibi fed them delicious betel leaf wraps that melted on their tongue with delectable sweetness.

When rumor that Shashibala was seen in a shady neighborhood reached her parents, flabbergasted, they locked her up, cutting her off completely from all her friends. Restless in the loneliness of her confines, when Shashibala learned that Kanai was leaving Calcutta and not expected back anytime soon, for the first time in her life, she had felt truly broken. Within weeks thereafter,

Shashibala had been married into Colootolla's Dutta family of oil merchants – to a man about three times her age.

Standing in front of her carved teakwood mirror, a misfit at their dingy brothel, Shashibala opened a drawer to finger a piece of jewelry she had worn that morning of her husband's death. The images that had stolen upon her in her half-sleep earlier today, had unexpectedly tugged at those memories she usually kept boxed away. Hearing of her husband's death, her in-laws had rushed in. Then, as dry-eyed, *ghomta*-clad Shashibala stood inanimately in their presence, they had blubbered on, offering the girl relentless counsel. Piercing the fog that settled around her brain, Shashibala had heard them mention their venerated daughter-in-law, who had honored the family by jumping into the funeral pyre with her dead husband – the *Sati* Pronoti – who, in their eyes, Shashibala could never match. Even on a day like this, they had found reason to compare the two. They were lamenting that with *Sati* made illegal these days, poor Shashibala had lost the opportunity to earn glory like Pronoti. Abruptly, Shashibala had started to walk toward her room, leaving the family staring at her back in open-mouthed puzzlement.

To this day, Shashibala relishes the look on their faces when she had re-emerged dressed like a bride, ala their beloved *Sati* Pronoti. She had walked toward where her husband's dead body lay on the ground, covered in white sheet, not turned cold yet. As the crowd watched her in pin drop silence, a barefaced Shashibala addressed her in-laws for the first time to their face, "You! Let me tell you, I am no Pronoti. And you Duttas are the scum of the world. I have not been happy a single day as part of your sick family! I am going to leave. I will probably live in disrepute. But whoring is better than the life you give your women in this house."

Shashibala had stepped outside on Colootolla Street that morning, becoming a *kulota*, a woman who has egregiously shamed her family. She had gone straight to Noor-Bibi in Chatawalapara, a place she used to visit with childhood friend Kanai before marriage; the one place she knew might give her shelter yet. Noor-Bibi had taken the girl in, training her to survive by the only means she knew, *khemta,* in which Shashibala showed great aptitude, rapidly surpassing all her other pupils. Young Shashi had the body, the age, the intelligence, and the oomph, and it won her many admirers. It hadn't taken her long to realize that prostitution was unavoidable in her circumstances. So, she had done it one day and never looked back since then.

Chapter Twelve

As night cloaked the city, Calcutta's stomach twisted in knots, her imagination brimming with horrors that could transpire under the cover of darkness. Against this backdrop of mistrust and intrigue, bathed in warm candlelight, the cheerful interiors of Evora stood like an island tempting the passersby, promising escape, and excitement. Evora's proprietor, the half-Bengali Alfonso could be seen talking to his guests, smoothly transitioning between Bengali, Portuguese, and English. When word of the mutiny had initially reached Calcutta, Evora's numbers of native clients had dropped. However, things were normalizing. Evora seemed committed to keep its doors open to both native and European clients.

Sara Langley was currently living near Park Street in rooms she had rented within a few days of coming to Calcutta. Earlier this year, eager to see more of India, Sara had chosen not to return with her uncle to England. However, when the mutiny broke, her plans were upended. Currently, she was living her days in a sort of limbo, roiled by uncertainty. She kept busy volunteering at a shelter in Calcutta, helping refugees from the North. However, regardless of having regained her physical strength, harrowing memories of fleeing the mutineers continued to haunt her days – especially the brutal beheading of the judge she had witnessed. With the city rife with rumors, the days leading up to the 23rd of June, the hundred-year anniversary of the Battle of Plassey, had been nerve-racking for Sara Langley. All of European Calcutta had heaved a quiet sigh, after the anniversary passed without any major incident.

7th July 1857

Sara had fallen into a habit of coming to Evora, usually with Dubois, as of late. They had done so today, although earlier than usual. They chose to come early because for one, Sara had hoped to avoid the crowds. She had noticed that the later it got, the more strained the looks between Evora's Indian and European clients became. Evora then felt like a microcosm of greater India: its guests rocked by the same emotions as those at large in the country. The unfriendly atmosphere made Sara anxious. The other consideration was a desire to avoid Dubois' native friends. On previous occasions, Sara hadn't appreciated being left alone while Dubois was pulled away into conversations with strangers. Sara was always surprised by how many natives Dubois seemed to know. The last time that they were here, while a miffed Sara sat waiting for Dubois to return to their table, her eyes had met those of the inspector who registered their names as refugees when they first arrived in Calcutta. Sara was relieved when Inspector Cockerel graciously came over, offering to keep her company until Dubois got back. Lawrence Cockerel mentioned that these days his constables monitored hotspots of European activity throughout the city, keeping an eye out for trouble. Because of a staff shortage, it had fallen on him to cover Evora tonight. Sara found the inspector to be an engaging man. She was in fact pleasantly surprised when, despite the uncertainty of the times, Lawrence spoke about his sense of belonging with the Indian people.

That evening, while watching Dubois laugh unreservedly at something the Indian gentleman he was with must have said, Lawrence made an observation.

Thinking out loud as he twirled the glass of wine he held, Lawrence said, "Miss Langley, I've noticed Mr. Dubois is very comfortable around the natives. I like that. I am like that too."

He then added, "Although unlike Mr. Dubois, I have never been as comfortable with the aristocratic type he seems to admire. I get more from being with ordinary, everyday Indians."

On that day, Lawrence's comment had made Sara think of one particular native man, who was the final reason why she had chosen to get here early tonight. Ever since Sara first ran into Radhanath Sikdar at this tavern on the day after she arrived in Calcutta, she had seen him several other times at the restaurant. He was usually done with his dinner and on his way out just as Sara and Dubois were arriving. It would make Sara wonder, *had they caught him earlier, would Radhanath perhaps engage in a longer conversation?* Sara had been puzzled by Radhanath's abrupt departure from the *shikar* party last year. When she met him again in Calcutta, she found the mutiny-related trauma of her circumstances had not been able to diminish her interest in this oriental gentleman. Not finding Radhanath upon arrival earlier this evening, Sara was conscious of feeling a rush of disappointment.

Seated opposite Sara just then was Dubois browsing the day's edition of the *India Chronicles*. Having ordered their dinners already, the two sat nursing their drinks while soulful *fado* songs by the graceful Signora Pereira made the air hum. Resting her elbows on the table with her chin cupped in one hand, Sara was listening to the hauntingly beautiful performance when feeling eyes on herself, she turned to look at Dubois. Aware that the bertha neckline of her gown flattered her delicate collarbone, Sara's lips curled into a smile. Returning her smile, Dubois turned his eyes to the stage. Sara's thoughts stayed with the Frenchman in whose company she had begun to feel quite at ease these days.

With Dubois spending a lot of time in Jainagar over the last year, the two had indeed grown closer, a development Sara had not resisted. They took long horse rides together, went on picnics, and spent nights stargazing. Dubois seemed to have deep knowledge of India's history, and Sara liked his telling her stories about them. When the mutiny broke, Sara simply could not imagine what she would have done, had it not been for Dubois. The man had orchestrated getting her out and bringing her to Calcutta. In a sense, Sara felt she owed her life to Dubois. However, Sara was regrettably conscious of things somehow being too easy between them. With that thought, her mind would slip to the hunting party, where she had experienced a distinctly different flavor of male company she found stimulating.

With Radhanath, Sara felt a heightened awareness of her own body, a pleasant tension, which was exciting. He made her feel both uncomfortable and hopeful, buoyed with the promise of something she didn't quite understand. She was astonished by how easily she could recall the details of his person and caught herself thinking of their various encounters from time to time. Thoughts of the day, when he had abruptly dismounted from his horse upon seeing her, invariably made her smile. Recalling the time when she'd woken up in his arms on a treetop, made her self-conscious with a feeling she refused to name. She could, of course, hardly forget that exquisite dusk when he had looked her in the eye, without guile or arrogance, claiming to have discovered the tallest point on Earth. Since meeting him in Calcutta again, Sara became conscious that the effect he had on her had lost none of its potency. She loved that sense of being pushed to the brink when she was with him.

Her thoughts were interrupted with Dubois' voice booming above the background, calling out, "Reverend Stuart!"

The singer was taking a break just then. Sara saw the Christian Pastor William Stuart talking to Alfonso near the entrance. She knew the pastor from her work at the shelter; besides, the European community in India was pretty close knit. Everyone knew everyone. Stuart raised his hand in greeting, indicating to Dubois that he had seen them. Finishing up his conversation, the Reverend walked towards their table. As they exchanged greetings, Dubois inquired if Stuart was on his own, in which case, they could all dine together. Stuart said he would be glad for their company. With none of the four-seaters available, the staff moved the three to a six-seater table.

After the girl, who helped them, left with Stuart's orders for a plate of *reshmi kebob*, the pastor eyed the crowd inside the restaurant askance. "It looks peaceful now," he murmured, and then added, "if it would only stay like this!"

"How do you mean?" asked Sara with some surprise.

"According to my sources, there is a chance of trouble tonight," confided the pastor.

Her voice betraying alarm, Sara immediately inquired, "What's going to happen?"

Stuart sat silently debating with himself. Then, lowering his voice so none other than those at his table could hear, he began, "You know, being a man of God, perhaps I should focus on the church and leave matters of state to other people. But these are no ordinary times. I work with many natives, good Christians who have found their true God with my counsel. And some of these," he hesitated a moment looking for a word and then continued, "*friends,* bring me news. Especially now, about possible conspiracies to harm the British. It has come to my ears that Evora may be attacked by goons tonight. They're calling themselves freedom fighters, working for that imposter Bahadur Shah Zafar they have installed on the throne of Delhi! I was telling Alfonso to stay alert. If they come, they'll be intending to massacre British souls they find inside the restaurant."

The European community in Calcutta had noticed Reverend Stuart's aggravated state of paranoia since the Kanpur Siege. It was perhaps understandable, with his son-in-law being part of General Wheeler's garrison at Kanpur and his daughter's entire family trapped there. As far as they knew, no news of his daughter Emily's exact situation had made its way to Stuart yet. Sara now spoke as the voice of reason, "Reverend, there are many Indians who come here. They enjoy being at Evora as much as we Europeans do. I imagine they will resist if the mob storms in."

With a wry smile Stuart said, "I'd have to say you're being rather naïve, Miss Langley. The Indians who come to Evora are the upper class, the exact people who are leading the mutiny in the North. The native guests here are more likely to join hands with our assailants."

Although he said sources, Stuart predominantly relied on Gokul for information. The man had a knack for eavesdropping, a habit honed during his time as a *thugee* when he was charged to gather intel on who was traveling with a lot of money and whose disappearance would go unnoticed. Instigated by Stuart, Gokul's old skills had found new, unexpected use. Gokul became Stuart's eyes and ears, bringing suspicious chatter he heard to the Reverend's attention. Recently, Stuart had decided to share Gokul's history with Lawrence and convinced the inspector to occasionally meet the man to get a download of the same intel. While Lawrence himself was skeptical of what he heard, he understood the distraught father's tendency to take Gokul seriously. However, Lawrence was annoyed that Stuart wouldn't content himself with Gokul simply passing the information to Lawrence. For example, Stuart had taken it upon himself to come down to Evora tonight, to warn Alfonso.

Dubois and Sara were still digesting Stuart's news, weighing it against the Reverend's state of mind when he further grumbled, "I sent my man to Inspector Cockerel to give him this same information, but he treats it all as a false alarm. I hope he doesn't end up paying a price for the cavalier attitude he takes."

For a while everyone sat in silence. Then, Dubois attempted to lighten the atmosphere saying, "*Pardon* Reverend, I am with the inspector on this. Why let this hypothetical thought disturb your peace of mind? Let us enjoy the evening, shall we?" Stuart was getting ready to hotly counter Dubois when they were distracted by some people nearing their table.

"Hello Ms. Langley, Dubois!" Nodded the tall, dark-skinned, Indian man, flanked by Surveyor General Andrew Waugh on his right. Sara stared at Radhanath for a few moments feeling at a loss for words. She recovered as she heard Waugh speaking.

"And this…" Waugh began introducing Radhanath to the Reverend, "is a senior officer on my team, Mr. Sikdar." Turning to Stuart he completed, "Reverend Stuart of the People's Church."

As they shook hands, Stuart invited the two new arrivals to join them at their table, large enough for the five. As Radhanath and Waugh settled in, Stuart eyed Radhanath with distinct curiosity. He started the conversation with, "Tell me Mr. Sikdar, isn't it rather unusual for a native man to be part of a scientific mission? I am curious how that happened."

Before Radhanath could respond, Sara Langley said, "With your permission Rady, might I add," turning to Stuart she continued, "not only is he a member of their team, but he made seminal contributions to calculate the height of Mount Everest, which was all over the papers last year." Everyone, especially Dubois, looked at Sara, surprised by her spontaneous compliment.

Stuart graciously commended Radhanath, not forgetting to include Waugh in his appreciation of the strides the GTSI were making to advance the cause of science. And then turning toward Radhanath once again, Stuart said, "At least you are channeling your energies constructively and not engaging in hooliganism like what is happening in the North!"

Radhanath stared at the pastor. He was surprised by how easily the Reverend had made what struck him as a distinctly inappropriate statement. Like the others at their table, had Radhanath known how Stuart's daughter was caught up in the middle of all this right now, of a father's constant worry that her and her family may be dead at the hands of those he called hooligans, he might have been more willing to overlook Stuart's comment.

Before he could react though, Waugh smoothly interjected, "Have you heard any further of your daughter, Reverend?" As Stuart shook his head from side to side, Waugh turned to Radhanath and explained, "The Reverend's daughter and her family are caught up in the siege at Kanpur. He has had no news in weeks."

After a pause, the Reverend said, "The last I heard is that the entrenchment where they are stationed is completely surrounded by the rebels. They are expecting Colonels Havelock and Neill to get there by the end of the month. I worry how they will hold up with food and water getting scarcer by the day." Toward the end, his voice broke. Taking a moment to compose himself, Stuart spat hatefully, "I cannot imagine a man more vicious than that Dhondu Pant! They call him Nana sahib! After fraternizing with us at hunting parties and fetes ad infinitum, despite the army paid for by the British left at his disposal, this is how he repays us. I am sorry to say Mr. Sikdar, the natives have no honor. Nana sahib gallivants to Kanpur on the pretext of helping the British under siege. And then he shows his true colors by joining the rebels." Stuart stopped talking as Alfonso came to take dinner orders for the two new guests.

When Waugh good-naturedly inquired why the Goan vindaloo he loved was missing from the menu, Alfonso admitted that his native cook had become indisposed; he was working to get it back on there soon. After confirming that Radhanath and Waugh wanted their usual scotch eggs and kebabs, Alfonso turned toward Dubois and Sara to inquire what they thought of the *fados* tonight. Both expressed strong approval. Alfonso informed the newcomers that Mrs. Pereira was going to start another round soon.

After Alfonso left the table, Dubois turned to Radhanath and said, "Rady, I seem to remember seeing you with Nana sahib at the dinner at Uday Singh's *shikar* party. Weren't you with him almost the whole time that evening?"

Everyone turned to look at Radhanath. A flicker of amusement crossed Radhanath's usually composed face. Radhanath had guessed that the new grumpiness in Dubois' manner was a result of Miss Langley's earlier compliments to him.

"Yes Dubois, you remember correctly!" he finally retorted. "Nana sahib and I spoke as two gentlemen may speak in a social setting. If you're asking whether I had inklings of his plan related to the mutiny, then no, I did not. Not then, not now."

Without skipping a beat, Radhanath next looked piercingly at Dubois and asked, "You've been pretty tight with *Raja* Uday Singh yourself, haven't you? With Jainagar up in arms, I heard they're saying Uday Singh had a hand in it. So, tell me, Frenchman, should we assume you knew something of this and staged a timely exit?" Inscrutably, Radhanath watched Dubois's face flush with discomfort.

There was an awkward pause, with Sara looking disconcertedly at Radhanath. Then a faint smile bloomed on her face. *Rady was teasing Dubois.* Responding to Radhanath's play on the French-English angle, Sara broke into a soft chuckle, joined by the others. The Frenchman produced a tight smile. Taking his spectacles off, Stuart started to wipe them and said, "That was a good one, Mr. Sikdar. This rebellion has destroyed my peace of mind. I thank you for your humor."

Though Radhanath had responded lightheartedly when Nana sahib's association with the mutiny came up, the color of his mind darkened with unease. As on previous occasions, he was worried about Chandrakanta growing too close to Nana sahib. Radhanath did not put it past his friend to have become personally embroiled in this uprising.

That's when both Stuart and Sara started to speak at the same time. The Reverend stopped, indicating the lady should go first. When the *shikar* party first came up earlier this evening, Sara had wanted to ask why Radhanath disappeared last year without bothering to say goodbye. However, now, Sara asked, "How is your friend Chun-dra…?" She struggled to exactly recall the name.

At this point, their food arrived. To avoid the waiter standing at their table, Radhanath had leaned sideways on his chair maintaining eye contact with Sara,

"I haven't seen much of Chandrakanta recently, Miss Langley. I have been commuting from Chandannagar myself. And he has been out on travel." Radhanath noticed Sara break into a little smile unable to contain her amusement at the odd angle in which they were talking. Her smile caused Radhanath a wave of pleasurable pain, a feeling he had had before, when thoughts of the sweet Sara stole upon him.

The waiter had finished serving Dubois and Sara their *bhetki* casseroles and Stuart his *reshmi kebob*. Waugh and Radhanath's *kebob* orders weren't ready. The waiter laid out scotch eggs to get them started. Sounds of clapping from the dais indicated that the *fado* artist was taking stage again. With a knife and fork poised on his food, Radhanath turned to the Reverend and asked, "Am I making a mistake, or were you about to say something to me right before the food got here?"

Stuart hadn't met another native man quite like Radhanath Sikdar. He was a bit startled at being hurled the direct question. He sat quietly for a moment thinking before responding, "Right. I was going to ask what your stance is, on this rebellion? The Indians want to overthrow the yoke of foreign rule. How do you feel about it as an Indian?"

The abrupt question caused Radhanath to stop eating. With the table falling eerily silent, Radhanath laid down his knife and fork in the manner of one preparing to do something seriously. Wordlessly, he looked at Andrew Waugh for a moment. Then facing forward again, he began, "The incident I am about to relay happened before General Waugh's time at the GTSI. Everest was Surveyor General then. And I was more than twenty years younger!" He looked at Sara with a regretful smile that softened his face.

"We were doing some work on a stretch of the Sal forests near Mussoorie. With GTSI's Dehradun site undergoing renovations, Everest had turned his property at Hathipaon near Mussoorie into a temporary office. A large number of tents and sheds constructed around his house accommodated both GTSI's personnel and equipment. That day, Everest was out of town. A magistrate named Vansittart had arrived in Mussoorie by the morning train. Iron chains we use for land survey were coming for us from Calcutta on that same train. Our men, coolies in the GTSI's employ, had gone to the station to collect the chains. When Vansittart saw these men, he coolly ordered them to abandon their task and ferry his luggage up the hills to his guesthouse instead. I was later told that he had even threatened to whip those who hesitated to fall in line before he left."

"With no sign of the men and rainclouds looming on the skies, I worried we were going to run out of time. Everest was expecting us to be done by the end of the day. When I finally went down to the station looking for our men, I met them en route and learned what had happened. Under my instruction, they dumped everything at Everest's house and got started on our work."

"The next morning, the magistrate and another British fellow showed up at Everest's house amidst pouring rain. Everest hadn't returned yet. I told them, we were running a tight timeline, and our coolies had acted on my instruction. While the magistrate's eyes turned to steel, his companion did not bother refraining from swearing at me, using a racial slur, no less. They left, threatening to make me pay."

"To GTSI's credit, in all my years of service, that was the only time I had ever faced a racially colored remark from a British officer at work. However, that wasn't the worst part for me. The worst came when I learned that the magistrate had complained about me to Everest. And Everest," paused Radhanath for a moment, "utterly failed to defend my actions. He made no objections to the court order that fined me half a month's salary. He allowed me to be punished for doing my job, while that man Vansittart got away with bad behavior. My word against a white man's wasn't worth enough. I felt the full weight of the difference between our races that day."

Silence fell at their table after Radhanath stopped talking. Waugh shifted uncomfortably in his seat. Sara noticed, although melancholic, there was a luminous sheen in Radhanath's eyes in that moment. His inspiration for life seemed to come from someplace deep within. With a gentle exhalation, Radhanath resumed, “That said, I have been with the GTSI for over two decades now, and worked alongside the likes of George Everest. I have been enriched by this environment, solving problems big and small, mathematical and practical, working as peers most of the time, thinking nothing of the difference between us. Earlier in my life, I was educated at the Hindu School under firebrand teachers like Mr. Derozio, to whom I owe my love for English literature. My mathematics teacher, Mr. Tytler’s recommendation got me my first job at GTSI. I could go on…” Turning toward Stuart with his eyes squinting subtle cynicism, Radhanath concluded, “I’d be a bit of a misfit among your mutineers, Reverend.”

Stuart had been sitting like a statue all this while. He didn’t immediately respond to Radhanath. In fact, for a few moments nobody said anything. Then Stuart spoke, sidestepping all Radhanath had said, “But then what in the world makes India’s nobility who pretend to be so tight with us, so darn unhappy! I don’t understand what could possibly justify their slaughtering innocent British lives, do you?”

Radhanath said nothing. Dubois piped up, “Look here, Reverend. India’s nobility may have joined hands with the British simply as a matter of politics. You have no real bonding to speak of, with them. Besides, Rady here is a man of science; if his mathematics is right, then it is right. He doesn’t care what the British thinks of it. But the nobility in India? The British want to micromanage them. Suddenly, everything they do must be ratified by the British. Do you think they like that? You cannot pass laws to gain control, and then expect people to pretend you’re doing it for their benefit.” Dubois’s face had twisted into a scornful smile.

Abruptly, their table was distracted by a loud bell coming from the cash counter near the entrance. They saw Alfonso standing next to Officer Cockerel who had presumably just arrived. Alfonso was ringing the bell to grab his customers’ attention. “Ladies and gentlemen,” he began as a hush fell inside the room. "I am sorry to be the bearer of grave news. Inspector Cockerel has brought copies of the dispatch that came into Fort William, received from the British outpost at Dehradun earlier this evening. They are reporting large numbers of General Wheeler's garrison dead at the Satichura Ghat near Kanpur. While I offer my deepest condolences to the friends and families of those directly impacted, I beg everyone to remain calm, be strong, and be patient. Inspector Cockerel says a Calcutta-wide curfew is set to start shortly. We will be closing within the next half hour. You can come up here and talk to the inspector to get more information." As Alfonso finished, the four saw Stuart's face turned ashen. Waugh promptly rose from his seat, offering to go find out more from Lawrence Cockerel.

Lawrence stood in the midst of the crowd inundated by questions, struggling to convey the details. Time seemed to have run out for General Wheeler and his men at the fort of Kanpur. At the end of three weeks, their food and water reserves were completely depleted. The poor sanitation at the fort had led to an outbreak of the dreaded cholera. On the 27th of June, General Wheeler had attempted to negotiate, accepting Nana sahib's offer of safe passage to the nearest British outpost at Allahabad, in lieu of surrendering Kanpur to the natives. At Satichura Ghat, boats stood waiting to ferry the English, but it wasn't easy to set sail on the unusually dry riverbed. Then, a shot out of the blue hit a pile of ammunition on one of the English boats, setting it on fire. Almost simultaneously, natives from the riverbank were seen jumping into the shallow waters to attack the British. A bloody butchery ensued, and before they knew, most of the British men were dead. Those that escaped from the Satichura Ghat were pursued by the rebels. The news ultimately got out from the handful that made it alive to the British loyalist *Raja* Dirigibijah Singh's estates, several miles away. It is believed that the British women and children who survived that day at the Satichura Ghat have been taken into custody by Nana sahib's men. They are being held at a barn, called Bibighar, as hostages.

Waugh relayed the facts he gathered from Lawrence. With most of the males in General Wheeler's garrison presumed dead, it was hard for the group to not conclude that Emily's husband had met that same fate. There was a reasonable chance that Emily and her son had survived and were being held at Bibighar. A shell-shocked Stuart stood up and bade everyone a hasty farewell. They watched him hurrying toward Inspector Cockerel, still surrounded by anxious men and women looking for information.

On the days Calcutta received news of setbacks in regard to the mutiny, the authorities feared that it could embolden the local goons. Therefore, they took extra precaution. There was enhanced police presence on the streets. They recruited armed volunteers to patrol with them. Of late, the authorities also encouraged British families to get on boats and sail upriver on the Hooghly River. The boats were difficult to approach without detection, making it easier to protect the people on it.

That night, Sara sat stiffly with several others on a boat floating on the Hooghly River. The wind was pretty strong, causing the passengers to nervously grip the hull. Several boats like theirs stood around them, all waiting for dawn. As the wails and sniffles of those that feared their loved ones dead at Satichura receded, Sara eyed the armed men on guard duty, their pipes or cigars glowing eerily in the dark. The bigger boats had been fitted with cannons which sat aimed toward Calcutta. Sara's eyes scanned the silhouette of the city. Dubois was still out there. He had promised to join them after he was done with some personal errand, reluctantly accepting the guard duty the British had forced upon him. With the day's horror beginning to take its toll, Sara leaned back against the boat and looked for solace in the starlit skies.

She may have dozed off briefly. In the next moment, she discovered their boat was under attack! Tall, dark men wearing high-necked jackets and turbans were leaping aboard, their swords shining in the moonlight, some dripping blood. The chilling laughter on their faces paralyzed her. Suddenly, a familiar face came into view. Radhanath Sikdar stood next to the beheaded body of a

British woman, a bloody sword in his hand. Sara stared at Radhanath, transfixed. Radhanath drew close, holding her gaze, his intense eyes starting to soften. Sara stood up to go toward him, as if he had commanded her to do so by hypnosis. In that instant, a warm spray hit her face. As Sara attempted to wipe the spray off her face, she looked down and saw blood on her hand. Someone had beheaded a British man next to her, causing the blood from his severed arteries to spurt on her face.

A sudden jerky movement of their boat caused Sara to sit up, wide awake. She realized she had been dreaming. The wetness she had felt was really just water that the rough wind had sprayed on her face. Sara found Dubois seated next to her. Realizing Sara was awake, he leaned towards her, whispering, "I came about half an hour ago. You were sleeping so soundly that I hadn't the heart to disturb you." Pointing to the gun-toting guards, Dubois said, "They told me that my turn to watch starts at three a.m."

After the nightmare she had just been through, Sara felt a strange peace engulf her as she saw the Frenchman's familiar face. Swallowing to compose herself and telling Dubois nothing of her dream, Sara gently laid her head on his shoulders. Looking at the stars, she raised her hand pointing to one, "Let me see what I remember of what you've taught me, Francois. That one there is…" Sara forgot the mutiny, the massacre at Satichura, and became lost among the stars, slipping into a familiar habit from her Jainagar days.

Chapter Thirteen

23rd July 1857

As the pair of horses pulling his *tanga gari* trotted down BT Road, Chandrakanta wiped beads of sweat from his forehead for the umpteenth time this afternoon. With no rain over the last two days, the temperature was starting to soar again. When his eyes fell on the GTSI tower at Sukhchar coming up ahead, he turned his face away. The stately tower built by the British was at odds with the errand he was running this afternoon, which was to meet the disarmed sepoys of the 34th Bengal Infantry at the Barrackpore cantonment. As the *tanga* passed the tower, Chandrakanta's eyes flitted to it, and he was reminded of Radhanath who talked fondly of the hours he spent working in that place.

With the horrors at Kanpur shaking the very foundations of British rule in India, Chandrakanta was convinced that now, more than ever, the time was ripe for India to seek her freedom. Regardless of the human cost, with the Indians up North doing their part, he felt it behooved those in Calcutta to seize this moment. As the events at Kanpur pushed the name of his friend Nana sahib into prominence, Chandrakanta plotted how his own Calcutta could play a bigger role in this rebellion.

In the days immediately following the news of the Kanpur and Satichura massacres reaching Calcutta, a charged-up Chandrakanta had orchestrated a clandestine meeting with the sepoys stationed at the Dumdum cantonment. He chose Dumdum because it was the cantonment closest to Fort William, the heart of British stronghold in Calcutta. The fact that, even before Mongol Pandey attacked the British officer at Barrackpore, it was here at the Dumdum School of Musketry, where sepoys from the Bengal army had resisted the British for the first time – by refusing to use the controversial Enfield rifle cartridges – that gave Chandrakanta hope they would be amenable to what he had to say to organize an attack on Fort William.

At their meeting, Chandrakanta found the Dumdum sepoys deeply embroiled in a quandary over the use of the new cartridges. The idea that the cartridges contained cow and pig fat continued to dominate their imagination. To appease their fears, their bosses had tried instituting new protocols, where they would not necessarily have to bite the cartridges. However, riddled by rumors at this point, the sepoys loathed to even touch the cartridges, suspecting everything as a ruse to defile the chastity of their caste. Chandrakanta couldn't get the men at Dumdum interested in much else.

A dejected Chandrakanta was wondering what to do next, when an unexpected break came from Nar Narayan, the *zamindar* of Budgebudge, an estate thirty kilometers to the south of Calcutta. Nar Narayan, a long-time Raychaudhuri family friend, was well-known to Chandrakanta. One day, when the two ran into each other at a family function, Chandrakanta started to lament about Bengal's lack of participation in the mutiny. He talked of his disappointment with the sepoys at Dumdum. It was then that Nar Narayan revealed that he knew a bunch of ex-sepoys who would likely be more willing to listen to Chandrakanta's proposal.

The British had disarmed and disbanded the 34th Bengal Infantry soon after the Mongol Pandey incident, turning the sepoys loose without work or money. An astonished Chandrakanta learned that Nar Narayan had literally salvaged around four hundred of these men by employing them on his estates. Nar Narayan suggested that these men, with an axe to grind against the British, could be persuaded to mutiny. At the same time, he warned that all he could do was request the men to come to the initial discussion; Nar Narayan was clear that while he was willing to be a messenger, he was not going to force his men to help.

The idea instantly appealed to Chandrakanta, who had heard vague rumors about the disbanding of the soldiers. But because the British actively suppressed news of this incident, the possibility of going after these men hadn't occurred to him. The two discussed that Chandrakanta should talk directly to these men. If he could build that core group of support, more sepoys may spontaneously join his movement. Instead of Budgebudge where Nar Narayan's sepoys now lived, Chandrakanta asked if Nar Narayan could organize the meeting at Sepai Para in Barrackpore. *The disbanded men knew the current sepoys. If they held the meeting in Barrackpore, there could potentially be participation from both groups.* Since getting support from the current sepoys would be crucial to his success, he was keen on this arrangement. Nar Narayan agreed. It was to this meeting that Chandrakanta was going this evening. He drummed his fingers on the upholstered seat by his side, wishing the *tanga* would go faster.

When Chandrakanta's *tanga* stopped at the edge of Sepai Para in Barrackpore, he went up to the nearby butcher's shop per his plan with Nar Narayan. Two *lungi*-clad men emerged to escort him to the clandestine meeting location. Chandrakanta was led up the tortuous alleys lined by dingy houses, passing old men on charpoys smoking or cleaning their rifles. Chickens, ducks, goats, and children kept getting in his way. The women pulled their *ghomta,* hastily covering their face as soon as they caught sight of an outsider in their midst. Chandrakanta noted several shops on his way, but all were bolted shut at this late afternoon hour. Soon, they entered a lane so narrow that Chandrakanta had to turn his body sideways to make progress. Feeling cold from the sudden lack of sun, Chandrakanta looked up to see the sky had become nothing more than a meandering blue river. About ten minutes later, they emerged into an enclosure. As Chandrakanta's eyes adjusted to the increased light, he found roughly two dozen inquisitive pairs of eyes watching him, dark coverings hiding the rest of their face.

A man stepped forward, removing the mask from his face, then introduced himself as Pannalal Chettri. This was the same man that had been Inspector Cockerel's buddy, until recently. After being fired from service in the wake of the Mongol Pandey incident, Pannalal had hung back at Sepai Para despite orders to get out of the area. But then, having obstructed Lawrence's efforts to stop the *Sati* on the banks of the Hooghly River, he fled, seeking refuge with Nar Narayan. In his days on Nar Narayan's estates, Pannalal had eagerly followed the developments happening up North. When Pannalal learned of Chandrakanta's ambitions, he felt curious and eager to meet the man. However, when he finally saw Chandrakanta, Pannalal was left unimpressed. His expression may have given away some of his disappointment because Chandrakanta had the distinct feeling of being passed over by this unremarkable looking, working-class fellow – a reception that the *zamindar* did not take kindly.

As the men uncovered their face, Pannalal introduced them. Most were part of the disbanded group. Chandrakanta was heartened to see an elderly man, by the name Moidul, who said he was part of the current regiment at Barrackpore. Unlike other presidencies, seniority in years implied a higher rank within the Bengal Presidency. A high-ranking officer was likely to wield a good amount of influence.

Chandrakanta began his discussion sympathizing with the predicament of the disbanded men, praising their erstwhile compatriot Mongol Pandey. His voice warmed with enthusiasm as he referenced what was happening up north. He brought up the Kanpur Siege where Nana sahib had got the British by their balls. “Brothers,” he addressed them. “Those of you working for Nar Narayan now, are no small number. I believe you are a total of four hundred men, correct?” Looking around to include the others, he said, “If in addition, we can recruit those of you currently employed at the cantonment, your numbers will become formidable. There’s not that many British guns in Calcutta at this time. All their troops are busy fighting the mutineers in the North. At this time of crisis, we have a good chance to defeat the English if we work together. We can repeat Kanpur right here at Calcutta. Shall we take Fort William? What do you say?”

Instead of the cheers he hoped for, Chandrakanta watched Pannalal and Moidul exchange smiles in response to his impassioned appeal. From their restlessness, he had sensed he wasn’t connecting with his audience, especially Pannalal. He eyed them now, feeling both flustered and out of depth.

With a sigh, Pannalal said, “Weeks before the Mongol Pandey incident, some of the sepoys had proposed the same thing Chandrakanta-*ji* – murder the officers at the cantonment and then march to Calcutta to oust the rest of them. They had put out a call for all to join hands; however, few showed up. Many did not believe that it could be done. You may perceive the Mongol Pandey incident as an isolated act, but it was not. A lot of repressed energy and frustration had been brewing among the sepoys. Even then, not all unanimously responded to the call when it came. I don’t see any reason why that would change today. In order to do this, we need a leader that men will stand behind, one who can inspire their confidence.”

The sepoy’s implication that he was no grand leader frustrated Chandrakanta. *Pannalal was being pessimistic, intent on discrediting his plans!*

“Were you among the naysayers when your original plan was made?” a gruff Chandrakanta challenged.

Pannalal's face hardened with antagonism. "I felt our sepoys' half-cooked plans were doomed to fail," he retorted. After a pause, Pannalal added, "Besides, I wasn't ready to murder the British I had worked with for most of my life, not back then."

"And you call yourself a hot-blooded Indian?" Chandrakanta lashed out readily. Attempting to exclude Pannalal from further conversation, he looked toward the others and asked, "Perhaps it's time to hear what the others think."

Everybody started to speak at once. Although some seemed unhappy at an upper-class outsider's treatment of a fellow they trusted, Chandrakanta was pleased to see that he had been able to stir up commotion against Pannalal among the youngsters. They grew unruly as their voices rose in strength.

"Yes, Haldu, you speak. Pannalal was sitting on his ass that last time."

Another from the back of the crowd offered, "With him so close to the Cockerels, isn't it natural for Pannalal to resist a rebellion?"

As the noise around them grew, Chandrakanta and Pannalal looked at each other; Chandrakanta enjoyed the scowl on Pannalal's face.

Seizing the floor with his voice booming above the rest, Moidul, the senior officer who had been silent up to this point, said, "Stop! Before you question Pannalal's patriotism, let me remind you that Pannalal is the son of a man who lost his life to a British bullet!" A hush fell among the men who didn't know this despite having known Pannalal for some time. "When I look at Pannalal, I can see his father in him," added Moidul softly.

Casting a quick warning look at Chandrakanta, Moidul turned his face back to the gathering. "The younger among you may not know about this. It happened back in 1824, when I had just started service at the Barrackpore cantonment. The sepoys had received orders to march all the way to Burma border for the Anglo-Burma wars. The authorities had callously announced that the sepoys need to carry their own luggage on foot on this long journey. Pannalal's father, Chunilal Chettri, lodged a formal complaint against the directive, requesting funds to hire cow carts be sanctioned. About two hundred others stood with him, refusing to pack up and move, demanding the authorities reconsider what was an obviously irresponsible suggestion. When General Paget who was overseeing the matter heard about it, he ridiculed the poor sepoys, recommending they pay for the cow carts from their own pockets. You would not believe what Paget did next! I had stepped away for a half hour. I came back to find the General had ordered his men to open fire on these peacefully protesting sepoys in a senseless killing spree! Over one hundred and fifty lost their lives that day; my friend Chunilal was among them. Later, we had found that the sepoys hadn't even loaded their guns!"

Here, Moidul paused his narrative. Chandrakanta observed the people who were listening closely to Moidul's tale. He felt frustrated that this man's narrative from thirty years ago, important in its own right, seemed to have derailed his meeting. Nevertheless, Chandrakanta understood, this was not the moment to try to reorient the discussion.

Moidul gazed from Chandrakanta to the sepoys, then continued in a whisper, "What an irony! Chunilal had sent his wife to serve as *ayah* to his beloved squadron lead's household, when his squadron lead's wife passed away, leaving a day-old newborn. Chunilal was loyal to them all his years, always praising the British for their mastery of the art of warfare. And then he dies at their hand, on the whims of a bizarre, irresponsible officer. After the massacre, Paget claimed, he had attempted to hold some sort of dialogue, talking directly to the sepoys, demanding they lay down their weapons if they wanted to negotiate. Rest assured, no one had understood him as per usual. His broken Hindi was a matter of amusement among the sepoys. Half the time they couldn't follow him, and it was known to have caused utter chaos on battlefields. When the sepoys did not respond, the foolish General should have known it was because he hadn't managed to communicate his message. Instead, he retaliated by opening fire. With a bullet wound in his stomach, Chunilal had lived for a day and half after. I was there when young Pannalal reached his father's deathbed. I still remember his last words – Hindi *bujhini*!

– telling his son, he hadn't understood General Paget's Hindi in the crucial moments!"

As the sepoys stood in pin drop silence absorbing the powerful tale, Moidul turned to Pannalal and said, "Those of us who knew Chunilal, knew him to be a good man, a brave soldier, a loving father."

Pannalal, who had been listening with his head bent, now raised his head. His eyes burned with fury, as he burst with the words, "Chunilal was a fool! Not just him, but I have paid dearly for his naïve points of view. He taught me never to hate a man just because he is a foreigner. In spite of everything, I became a sepoy following in his footsteps. And after thirty years of loyal service, they casually kick me out without bothering to ascertain if I am guilty." Pannalal's lips trembled with emotion.

"How dare they ask me to lay down my weapon?" Shaking his head disgustedly, Pannalal said, "When they took my gun, my whole life appeared to be a farce. What is a sepoy without his firearm?" Turning fierce eyes to Chandrakanta, he added, "If only I could show you how much I am burning inside to destroy the last one of them, Chandrakanta-*ji*!"

Controlling himself, Pannalal reiterated his earlier sentiment, "With all due respect, you are no Nana sahib. I am a practical man. You are not going to repeat the Kanpur Siege at Fort William. We need a man with substantial charisma to unite and rouse the sepoys. Without that, if we attempt this, we will all be marching to our deaths."

Dusk had fallen by the time Chandrakanta started walking toward where his *tanga* was waiting, escorted by the same men who had shown him the way earlier. In his heart, he knew he had completely blown the meeting. Although some men had jumped at the bone he threw at them to raise doubts about Pannalal, in the course of the meeting Chandrakanta had realized that the sepoys here largely favored Pannalal, viewing him as a level-headed, responsible person. Putting his own instinctive antagonism toward Pannalal in the open had misfired, especially in light of the man's poignant history.

They were retracing the path they had taken earlier, mused Chandrakanta. Women had gathered around coal-fire earthen ovens in their courtyard, cooking evening meals for the family. Sepoys in *fatua* and *lungi* were relaxing in small clusters around the street side shops selling deep-fried fast food. Feeling burdened by the futility of his efforts today, Chandrakanta increased his pace to get back to his ride. When they reached his *tanga*, he turned to thank his guides, bidding them farewell. As he boarded, Chandrakanta was startled by the roar of tigers and was reminded of Lord Wellesley's gift to the people – Barrackpore had a well-stocked menagerie not too far from where he stood. *It was probably feeding time for the animals, which had excited them.* With his *tanga* starting back for Calcutta, a tired Chandrakanta slumped back on his seat.

In the dying light of the day, from his vantage under a tree, a man in his early sixties had just spotted Chandrakanta walking toward his *tanga*. Chandrakanta remained completely unaware of the man, who was none other than his mother's paramour Gokul.

Ever since the Mongol Pandey incident, Reverend Stuart believed something was just waiting to happen at the Barrackpore cantonment. The Satichura Ghat Massacre made him more nervous than ever. The paranoid Reverend had instructed Gokul to set himself up around the Sepai Para area and collect information. This, Gokul did very effectively because he had the nose for it. Besides, when he chose, he could become so innocuous as to be invisible. The sight of Chandrakanta in these parts thoroughly surprised Gokul. Though he had never spoken to Chandrakanta after that day at Sunayani's *Shradh* some twenty years ago now, he saw the rich man from time to time, typically at philanthropic events, such as food or cloth distribution to the poor. *What could zamindar Chandrakanta want from this god-forsaken neighborhood?* wondered Gokul. He was going to ask around. His instincts said Chandrakanta was going to be back.

The evening's excitement had riled Chandrakanta up. As the *tanga* breezed along BT Road toward Calcutta, the air on his skin acted like a balm soothing him body and soul. The disappointment that had colored his mind over the last hour began to dissipate, and he objectively reflected on the events of this evening. Moidul and Pannalal had both played their parts in derailing the meeting tonight, but Chandrakanta hadn't been able to connect with the sepoys from the very beginning. When Chandrakanta was telling what was happening in the North, there was a blank look on the sepoys. In contrast, they had listened to Moidul and Pannalal with rapt attention. Where Chandrakanta's factual statements had fallen flat, Moidul and Pannalal's emotionally charged personal narratives had touched a chord. Chandrakanta realized he had to master the art of appealing to the heart to communicate effectively with the sepoys.

Rocked gently by the rhythmic movement of the horses, the emotionally exhausted Chandrakanta leaned back into the seat of his carriage with his head resting against the window. After a while, he noticed a reddish-yellow light high-up on the horizon. He assumed it was coming from the GTSI tower, which meant they were nearing Sukhchar. Chandrakanta's thoughts returned to Radhanath a second time that day. He hadn't seen his friend in a while. Vaguely, he recalled his servants reporting that Radhanath had stopped by his house when Chandrakanta was out of station a few days ago. Idly, he wondered if Radhanath was in Calcutta tonight. On the spot, he decided he was going to swing by Radhanath's rental house to check on his friend. The thought improved his mood. And with that came the conviction that there was no reason to feel quite so disheartened with the outcome of tonight's meeting. He resolved to meet Pannalal and the others soon again.

When Chandrakanta alighted from his *tanga* in front of Radhanath's one-story rental house on Beniapukur Street, he found it entirely cloaked in darkness. He assumed Radhanath was not home and felt disappointed. To be absolutely certain, he tried the front door, and, to his surprise, the door was not locked. He pushed the door open and entered the narrow passage that opened into a tiny courtyard. After calling Radhanath by name several times, he didn't get any response. Radhanath's bedroom and study were on one side of the courtyard and his kitchen and bathroom on the other. The door to the study was closed, but the door to his bedroom seemed slightly ajar. In the faint light of the evening, Chandrakanta suddenly grew alert, wondering if someone had broken in. Then, detecting a weak sound of groaning coming from the direction of the bedroom, Chandrakanta hurried inside, extracting a matchbox from his pocket to strike a flame. He could barely make out the shape of a man lying on the bed before the light of the rapidly burning stick was gone. Lighting a fresh matchstick, Chandrakanta moved his eyes swiftly around the room to locate a candle. He found one on the desk next to the bed. In the meantime, the man lying face down groaned one more time, perhaps aware of the presence of someone in the room. While holding the candle, Chandrakanta went close to the bed. He found Radhanath fully dressed in his office clothes, almost unconscious. Touching his friend's forehead, he found it was burning with fever. Feeling the touch of cool hands on his forehead, a weak "ummm" emerged from Radhanath's parched lips.

Chapter Fourteen

Radhanath battled death for the next two weeks. As his fever soared, he lay barely conscious, shivering under layers of blankets. Chandrakanta had arranged for his servants and his family *kobirej* Sidhu to take care of Radhanath. He personally came to check on his friend as often as possible. Old Sidhu used his traditional techniques, administering camphor to make the patient sweat and having the attendants sponge the patient's body to drive the temperature down. However, when he palpated Radhanath's spleen each morning, Sidhu's white brows furrowed with concern; his patient wasn't responding too well. Putting ego aside, the old man finally asked Chandrakanta to get another opinion. When Dr. Benson made his house call, he carefully examined Radhanath and diagnosed the dreaded malaria. Pointing to the wild overgrowth bordering the courtyard next to Radhanath's kitchen, Dr. Benson explained, malaria is caused by mal- (bad), -aria (air), or noxious vapors that rise from the ground. With the overgrowth, he conjectured that these vapors had become trapped and concentrated. Dr. Benson put Radhanath on a regiment of quinine, plus daily bloodletting. Chandrakanta's servants continued to look after Radhanath – giving him his medicines, bleeding him, and applying cold compress to his head. Slowly but surely, Radhanath started to regain his strength.

…

8th August 1857

Late that morning, propped against pillows to his back, Radhanath was sitting up on his bed for the first time since his illness. It had rained the night before, bringing much-needed relief. Sunlight poured in from the roadside window next to his bed. Bottles of quinine and herbal potions lined the table on the opposite wall. Radhanath was staring out through the window when Chandrakanta entered his room. Smiling warmly at the sight of Radhanath sitting upright, Chandrakanta came toward his friend.

Reaching for one of Radhanath's hands, Chandrakanta held it in his and asked, "My dear friend, how are you feeling today?"

Spontaneously placing his other hand on his friend's, Radhanath emotionally responded, "I cannot repay what you have done for me in this life, Chandrakanta. If it wasn't for you, I'd be dead."

As he looked at his friend's face, the sigh that escaped Chandrakanta was a mixture of satisfaction and relief. After describing how he had found a burning hot, semi-conscious Radhanath lying in the dark, Chandrakanta requested Radhanath to tell him exactly what had happened. Radhanath recounted the last he remembered was feeling sick at work and hiring a *tanga* to get home. The rest had gone blank for him. It was fortunate that Chandrakanta had stopped by that day. Nodding in agreement, Chandrakanta reminded his workaholic friend to take things easy for a few days now.

As Chandrakanta stood saying this and that, Radhanath detected a certain hesitation in his manner. With his usual directness, Radhanath asked. "Is there something you want to tell me?"

Chandrakanta took a moment before responding, his gaze faintly annoyed, a wry smile twisting his lips, "I heard you mumble the name Sara when you were very sick. Wasn't Sara Langley the girl you were stranded with at the *shikar* last year?"

Radhanath was caught totally off his guard, evident from his inability to say anything for the next few moments. He finally responded by sitting up, looking down at his hands. "Yes," he conceded softly.

Chandrakanta said, "She is in Calcutta then? I thought I recognized Miss Langley on the street a few days back. I had wondered if she'd arrived with the hordes fleeing the North."

Radhanath's eyes shot up to look at Chandrakanta, picking up an abrupt unfriendliness in his tone. Biting his lower lip, Chandrakanta asked, "Have you been in touch with her all this time?"

It was a decidedly personal question, though not unusual between two such close friends. Abruptly though, an unforgiving look came over him and Chandrakanta exclaimed, "Actually, don't answer that. At another time, I might have wanted to understand what a brown man in his forties imagines he might have in common with a British girl half his age. But…"

Chandrakanta shrugged, "After what has happened between the English and the Indians, the idea of anything between the two of you is so absurd that it is laughable!"

Radhanath became very still, watching Chandrakanta, and realized something significant has transpired in the time he had been sick. He waited for Chandrakanta to elaborate. After several moments of tense silence, Chandrakanta said, "You know about Satichura Ghat?" Radhanath nodded to confirm.

"Well, within weeks of women and children from Satichura transferring to Bibighar under native guard, Colonels Havelock and Neill led British relief forces to Kanpur and dealt grave blows to the native battalions. Last Saturday we received unconfirmed news that reacting to those defeats, Nana sahib sent orders to execute the women and children they were holding prisoner at Bibighar."

Giving Radhanath a sharp, defensive look, Chandrakanta insisted, "I do not believe Nana sahib did anything like that."

After a brief pause, Chandrakanta continued, "However, this much is clear that an order did come, instructing the sepoys to execute the prisoners. We heard that when the sepoys opened fire, the screams of terror from the prisoners gave them pause; the ask to murder the defenseless weighed heavily on their conscience. In this state of confusion, we have reports of a Khanum Bibi, a well-known prostitute from the area, showing up on scene. Learning of the sepoys' procrastination, she ridiculed them for cowardice and took it upon herself to hire butchers to complete the job. They say she stormed Bibighar with her entourage. They hacked the prisoners with meat cleavers and accumulated their severed body parts in a drywell on the property. After defeating the forces at Kanpur, Colonel Neill and his men arrived at Bibighar hoping to rescue these prisoners, but all they found were hairs and clothes of British women and children flying in the wind. They discovered the floor of Bibighar flooded, ankle-deep in human blood. The dry well on the courtyard was packed with mangled human bodies, a few still alive, buried beneath corpses."

Silence reigned in the room as the horror of Chandrakanta's tale sank in.

"How is the British reacting to this?" muttered Radhanath.

"Whoever Neill and his men could find thereabout, they went after ruthlessly. Those captured were flogged mercilessly and hanged on the spot. There are reports that before the killing, Neill forced beef down the throat of Hindus and pork down the throat of Muslims. Driven insane with hatred, he has made every high-caste native he could find lick blood off the floor at Bibighar."

Chandrakanta stopped talking, feeling exhausted from the tirade of gory details that seemed to have poured out from him with a force of its own.

Stretching his lips in a painful smile, he moved away from Radhanath's bed to stand by the open window in the room. Outside, a peaceful Calcutta morning was in progress. Birds chirped; people were up and about with their usual business. Freshly washed by the rains last night, the fig tree behind Haru's convenience store sparkled in the innocent light of the morning. Chandrakanta stared at a leafy branch hanging low on the roof of Haru's shop, needlessly trying to locate an insistently cawing crow hidden somewhere in its depths. A man carrying earthen pots of locally made sweet yoghurt appeared on the road, "Anyone want *doi*?" he called in his singsong voice, drawing out a handful of children. Chandrakanta let his eyes wander, hoping to draw solace from these sights of normalcy. After a while, he turned to face Radhanath who sat stiffly on his bed, his arms hugging his knees, his face resting on them.

"Is that all?" Radhanath questioned without looking at Chandrakanta, fearing he hadn't heard the worst of it yet.

From his stand near the window, unconsciously maintaining a distance between himself and Radhanath, Chandrakanta picked up the threads of his terrible tale, "Of course, it doesn't end there. Colonel Neill's soldiers fanned out combing the native localities near Bibighar, going after every native they could remotely connect to this. Word on this is being heavily suppressed. We only know what we are hearing from stragglers and night-runners and from what I am able to gather from my contacts within the British quarter. There is no apparent end in sight. If anyone dares to protest, they are openly flogged, and if they merely suspect anyone of being complicit, they are taking action. There's no trial. There's no pretense of justice. The highways of Kanpur are lined with rotting bodies of the dead hanging from trees, feasted upon by animals. There was a recent story about hundreds of villagers protesting the atrocities. They were forced inside huts to which the British soldiers then set fire. Those who tried to escape were shot dead. The native death toll is going through the roof, and nobody is counting."

At this point, there was a knock on the door to the bedroom. Chandrakanta was surprised to see one of his own servants appear, apparently sent over by his *Dewan* to summon him back to his estate. To the *zamindar*'s irritation, the errand boy couldn't explain the reason. After asking the boy to wait outside, Chandrakanta walked toward Radhanath's bed. Looking directly at his friend he said, "Radhanath, the massacres at Satichura, and now at Bibighar, have brought out the chasm between the English and the Indians. Only a fool will turn a blind eye to this. These two races were never meant to be together. They have no respect for each other, let alone affection."

The last words Chandrakanta spoke were an obvious reference to Radhanath's nursing feelings for the British girl. Making his disapproval explicit now, Chandrakanta continued, "It is one thing to think of the absurd in delirium, quite another to continue to entertain any idiotic obsession with Sara Langley in your sane mind. If someone as bright as you cannot see exactly how preposterous this is, I can only conclude that you are losing your mind."

Radhanath sat stone faced. After a silence that Radhanath did not break, a disappointed Chandrakanta, who was hoping for a response, turned to leave, starting to walk toward the door. And then he heard Radhanath asking, "Have they taken Nana sahib into custody yet?"

Chandrakanta spun around, his eyes glittering. Closing the gap between them in two long strides, he growled in a low voice within inches of Radhanath's face, "How dare you say such a thing!"

This was his friend lashing out at him for Sara Langley. For a few moments the two stared at each other.

"No, Nana sahib has not been found," said Chandrakanta through clenched teeth before he straightened.

"No one has heard from or seen him since the Bibighar incident. Of course, regardless of his culpability, he has been labeled a highly dangerous criminal by the English, the epitome of fairness!" spat Chandrakanta, his sarcastic emphasis on English fairness not lost on Radhanath either.

After a pause, Chandrakanta spoke with quiet conviction, "I do not believe Nana sahib gave orders to kill the women and children at Bibighar. Someone foolish orchestrated this. And it has given that animal, Colonel Neill, the license to murder, pilfer, and gratify his racial hatred."

That said, Chandrakanta turned and left the room without waiting for Radhanath to respond.

...

Radhanath slid down on his bed to lay himself flat on his back, a strange deadness smothering his heart. Since the start of the mutiny, many stories of both Indian and British atrocities have come to his ear – but none so devastating as these last events. Listlessly Radhanath's eyes wandered around his room, the ceiling, and his almirah until his eyes came to rest on the table. He eyed the bottles of quinine that Dr Benson had prescribed and the herbal potions that *kobirej* Sidhu had mandated for him. A blood-stained container where he was being bled stood to the side. Radhanath felt strange, realizing while they had battled to keep him alive, so many lives were being lost to senseless massacre.

Suddenly, hearing voices on the street, Radhanath struggled to sit up again to look outside. He leaned on his arms for support. After staring for a while at the urchins creating a commotion in front of Haru's convenience store, Radhanath saw Haru emerge on the street, dangling a largish dead-looking animal. He guessed it was a rat that Haru must have caught inside his shop. Rodent infestation was nothing new for convenience stores. The street kids cheered Haru on, following behind him, some even breaking into a dance. Haru hurled the dead rat into an overgrowth on the other side of the road. Immediately, several crows emerged from the fig tree behind Haru's shop and flew in that direction. One lifted the heavy feast in its beak and brought it back in view on the road. Within minutes, they had torn the animal apart, spilling its guts. The children were shouting, chasing the crows that dragged the bloody carcass behind them.

Radhanath laid himself back on the bed. The morning's exertion was beginning to take its toll on his fever weary constitution, both physically and emotionally. Gradually, his eyes drooped, and his thoughts became tangled with sleep. In that groggy state, Radhanath remembered Chandrakanta mentioning that he had called out Sara's name when he was delirious with fever. Of all the sinister things he had heard this morning, it was the thought of having done that, that came to him now. And just before he succumbed to sleep, he felt an unreasonable annoyance that Chandrakanta had tried to discuss it directly with him. *Chandrakanta should've let it be.*

…

Chandrakanta tapped his feet impatiently as his *tanga* navigated the tortuous lanes of Calcutta's native neighborhoods, aiming to go toward Dhanulia where he lived. The *zamindar* did not appreciate having his schedule disrupted by his *Dewan* summoning him back to the house like this.

As the *tanga* trotted on, disappointment in his friend welled up inside Chandrakanta. *When will Radhanath wake up to the realities of the Raj!* His blood boiled at the thought of Radhanath harboring romantic feelings for a British woman. *How could he not see that he will never be one of them; that she will, sooner or later, go against him*, Chandrakanta grumbled to himself. As far as Chandrakanta was concerned, any romantic entanglement between the two was completely unreal.

Tired of feeling resentful, Chandrakanta tried to conjure some positive thoughts, turning his mind to what had been happening on the Barrackpore front. He had visited Sepai Para several times in the past few weeks. Having blown the initial meeting, he had forced himself to become more careful around Pannalal, and it worked. Their discussions had grown more constructive. Moidul Ahmad's story of the 1824 Massacres involving Pannalal's father turned out timely. That and the Mongol Pandey incident were now hot topics among the sepoys, fanning anti-British outrage just as Chandrakanta had hoped. Chandrakanta also discovered that he had a tool he hadn't quite appreciated. Being a well-connected person, he was able to offer key information on what was happening in the North, and that was an important hook to draw the crowds. Nana sahib frequently came up in their discussion. The British loudly publicized the atrocities spearheaded by Nana sahib and his associates at Satichura and Bibighar, pushing to delegitimize India's bid for freedom. *But nothing could tarnish the image of Nana sahib for the sepoys!* They saw him as an unpredictable, ruthless strategist and, most importantly, someone who knew how to fight the British. Even if Nana sahib was defeated and absconding for the moment, he was an inspiration. *And, who knew what he was plotting right then?* Meanwhile, to keep the sepoys stoked for rebellion, a resolute Chandrakanta fed them the horrors the British were perpetrating to avenge the mutiny. Chandrakanta was glad to see a change in Pannalal. The last time Chandrakanta visited, the man had looked optimistic and had even started taking personal initiative to talk to those he could influence.

Chandrakanta, however, was cautiously optimistic. No matter how well they planned, one could hardly predict the course of events once an uprising was set in motion. People, prone to impulsive outbursts, could trip up the best laid plans. That's what happened at Satichura and perhaps also at Bibighar. Then there was interference from the desperadoes to consider, whose looting and pilfering could taint the entire undertaking. *How were they going to maintain control?* That was the worry that dominated Chandrakanta's thoughts these days. Looking outside as his *tanga* slowed, Chandrakanta found they were entering the boundary walls of his Dhanulia estate. He was home.

Passing one of their resident peacocks, Chandrakanta entered the *rajbari* and headed straight for the *Dewan*'s office. The thin, energetic young man, a recent recruit, informed him that a European man had appeared at their house requesting to see Chandrakanta as a matter of urgency. The stranger had refused to divulge his exact reasons which is why the *Dewan* couldn't give any information to the errand boy he sent. The man had assured the *Dewan* that Chandrakanta would thank him for acting as he did. Chandrakanta exhaled disappointedly. The young *Dewan* had probably been overwhelmed by the unusual honor of a white man's visit. After all, he did not often interact with Europeans. The nationalist-leaning Chandrakanta had dismissed the last of the European employees from his father's time. As of late, Chandrakanta had stopped going to Western restaurants, wearing Western clothes, and limited the use of Western products. The hardest had been giving up foreign liquor, but he had become a teetotaler these days. Learning that this guest was waiting in the living room, Chandrakanta went to find him. He could not have guessed the identity of the man waiting for him, not in his wildest dream.

Radhanath's colleague who had invited him to *Raja* Uday Singh's hunting party almost a year ago – Francois Dubois – sat in the Raychaudhuri living room. As Chandrakanta stood wide-eyed at the door, Dubois rose quickly and came closer.

"Remember me?" asked Dubois, as he shook the hand Chandrakanta had mechanically extended.

As the two made their way into the room, Chandrakanta watched Dubois turn cautious eyes around to make sure they were alone. Then, leaning close to Chandrakanta, Dubois said, "I have Nana sahib in Chandannagar right now. He wants to see you. How quickly can you come with me?"

Chapter Fifteen

8th August 1857

In Lawrence's office at the Park Street police station, Gokul had just shown Lawrence how it was done. Imitating the process, Lawrence put a white kerchief around Gokul's neck. Although the noose sat loose, Gokul thought he felt a twinge at the back of his neck where the inspector's cold knuckles grazed his skin. Unable to bear the tension of wearing a noose with its ends in the inspector's hands, Gokul attempted to sneak a glance at Lawrence. That's when, Lawrence's fingers moved at lightning speed, causing a sharp, shooting pain down Gokul's neck. Panicking, Gokul tried and failed to move away, instantly regretting having submitted to the inspector's bizarre request to practice on him. By now, Lawrence was pulling on the ends of the noose with all his might. He watched Gokul's eyes starting to bulge. And thoughts of finishing off the low life he considered Gokul to be, here and now, danced insidiously inside him. Lawrence wondered how people would react if they saw him now. Anyone at the police station could walk in on them, including the *punkahwallah*. It was the thought of Reverend Stuart that finally made

Lawrence slacken the noose. Immediately, Gokul started to cough, gasping for breath.

Urged by Reverend Stuart, Gokul had started to stop by Park Street *thana* from time to time, to report on what he was hearing on the streets. Earlier today, Gokul went to Stuart's, but the Reverend wasn't home. Deciding to check back later, Gokul had come over to the *thana*, where he found a somewhat red-eyed, disheveled inspector smoking a cheroot, taking swigs from a near-empty bottle of brandy. Lawrence was gazing intently at the portrait of an English girl in a burgundy dress on his desk. Painted several years ago, the portrait was that of Reverend Stuart's daughter Emily, when she was about fifteen, on her first trip to Shimla. Way back, when he was courting her for a brief period, Emily had given this to Lawrence as a keepsake. That was before she met the colonel in General Wheeler's garrison who she eventually married. Lawrence and Emily had remained friends, and Emily used to tease the sentimental Lawrence for never returning her portrait.

Emily's entire family had perished at the Kanpur siege. Her husband died in crossfire at Satichura Ghat. She and her seven-year-old were slaughtered a few days after, at Bibighar. When Colonel Neill finally ended the fight, the English began to tally their missing and dead. Lawrence pieced together what Emily went through in her final days. The images of Emily and her child's mangled bodies weighed on his conscience. Consumed by bitterness for his loyalty to the natives who were responsible for Emily's fate, Lawrence kept her picture displayed on his table, as a constant reminder for himself.

Slouching at his desk this morning, Lawrence was moodily nursing his brandy when Gokul entered through the front door to his office. The man's obsequious greeting caused a helpless wave of irritation in the inspector. With Satichura and Bibighar Massacres destroying the last of Lawrence's fellow feeling with the natives, the mistrust he always felt for Gokul had amplified. The inspector had little faith in the intelligence Gokul provided, tolerating the man only because Stuart insisted.

When Gokul stood across from Lawrence this morning, the inebriated inspector sat looking at him expressionlessly, observing the scar that ran along Gokul's right arm with singular attention. Gokul usually attempted some sort of chitchat before getting down to business. Not knowing what to make of Lawrence today, Gokul found himself rambling more nonsense than usual. He complained that his spotted goat had not produced milk for the last two days. Lawrence normally tolerated Gokul's ludicrous gossip with a patronizing smile. Today he didn't look amused. Faltering to a pause, Gokul cleared his throat and attempted to speak out the message he was here to convey.

When Gokul got to the part suggesting unusual excitement among the sepoys of Barrackpore cantonment, Lawrence, who had been uncommunicative so far, began to nod his head. He seemed to agree that his sources had picked up chatter in a similar vein. As soon as Gokul paused, Lawrence used the silence to thank him for his report, effectively cutting off anything else Gokul had intended to say. In his mind, Lawrence has already dismissed Gokul's information since the idea of discontent brewing at the Barrackpore cantonment was nothing new to him. It had been a constant ever since the Mongol Pandey incident. It had not led to anything concrete in the past. He had become especially impervious because his chain of command refused to do much beyond declaring a curfew. It was hardly practical to have a curfew every day.

Gokul stood wondering what to do, having failed to get out much of what he had painfully collected over the last week. He hadn't managed to tell Lawrence several things that felt suspicious to him: first, that the disbanded soldiers had begun showing up for no apparent reason; second, that Dhanulia's *zamindar* Chandrakanta Raychaudhuri was spotted in Sepai Para; and third, that everybody was suddenly talking about the 1824 Massacre. Abruptly springing to his feet, Lawrence hollered to the *punkahwallah* outside his office to take his break. He also asked the man to shut the door to his office on his way out. The *punkahwallah* promptly did as asked, intimidated by the boorish mood Lawrence seemed to be in. Meanwhile, nearing Gokul with a chilling smile on his face, Lawrence had asked if Gokul would show him how the *thugee* killed their quarry. Lawrence's manner had spooked Gokul from the start today, but this last question stumped him into shocked silence. Lawrence patted Gokul on his back, saying he knew all about him from Reverend Stuart. He assured Gokul that while under the Reverend's protection, Gokul had nothing to worry about. Lawrence was only asking out of curiosity.

Gingerly, Gokul had taken the kerchief Lawrence produced from his pockets. While examining it by turning it around and feeling its texture, he expressed dissatisfaction that the material was different from what *thugees* used; nevertheless, he was going to make an attempt, since the length looked adequate. Once he got started, Gokul's diffidence seemed to abate. He tied a large knot at one end of the kerchief, weighting it with a piece of silver he brought out wordlessly from his *fatua* pocket. Next, his eyes moved quickly around the room. Then without any warning, he flicked the kerchief such that it flew across the room, swirling itself around the pole of a coat hanger that stood to one side. It was only when the silver in the kerchief hit the pole with a sharp thwack that Lawrence realized what had happened. "If that were a man's neck, it would be broken!" remarked Gokul.

Retrieving the kerchief, he brought it to Lawrence, holding one end in each hand. "From close quarters," he made a swift motion to show how the kerchief is slipped around the victim's neck. "Go like this" he whispered, his knuckles moving in a masterful, sharp twist. "When done right, the victim doesn't get a chance to move or make a sound. His companion next to him will not know he's dead. It takes a lot of practice!"

Lawrence asked for the kerchief back from Gokul. Wielding it just as Gokul showed, Lawrence said, that depends, implying it wouldn't take him long to master the technique. With a mean smile, he suggested Gokul let Lawrence practice on him. Watching the look on Gokul's face with amusement,

Lawrence asked if Gokul thought Lawrence wanted to kill him. Put on the spot, Gokul couldn't find the words to resist the inspector.

Feverishly rubbing his neck where the noose was squeezing him moments ago, Gokul coughed and gasped for breath. *Had Lawrence sahib lost his mind?* The very next moment he stumbled out of Lawrence's office with unsteady steps. After this bizarre encounter, Gokul did not feel up to going to Stuart's house as he had originally planned. The Reverend's insistence, that he be told everything Gokul told Lawrence, would have to wait. As he hurried down Park Street, for the first time in his life, Gokul felt an uneasy suspicion in his heart about the Reverend. *Stuart and Lawrence understood each other. But did Gokul understand the Reverend? Would Stuart do a thing if Lawrence had killed him today?* Gokul's mind escaped twenty years back when he had snitched on fellow *thugees* to curry favor with his new Christian friends. His sudden and surreal encounter with Lawrence had brought on a thought that surprised him – that he understood little of the English he worked for these days.

Gokul grew impatient, feeling at odds with such thoughts. He increased his speed to get to Chowrungee, eager to be rid of these unfamiliar, useless misgivings. He had developed a splitting headache by this time. He decided to return to the sepoys in Barrackpore, among whom he was staying these days. He was going to dig deeper and look for concrete details of a plan. In about a week's time, fortified with the additional evidence, Gokul resolved to go and see Stuart. He promised himself that he will complain to Stuart about Lawrence's behavior then. But not today. Gokul felt unable to muster the nerve to deal with yet another British person today. The thought of being among the natives seemed to calm him. The irony of how he was resolved to spy on the very natives he was more comfortable with, was completely lost on Gokul.

…

After Gokul fled from his room, Lawrence sat down at his table continuing to drink. He was sweating from his exertions in the past few minutes. *Why wasn't the punkahwallah back from his break?* he wondered with irritation. The old Lawrence would be hard-pressed to believe how precipitously the value of native lives had dropped for the present-day Lawrence. In the wake of the massacres, Lawrence's need for vengeance had driven him where his conscience would never allow him before. Lawrence had finally joined hands with the vigilantes flourishing under the cover of darkness; the same vigilantes Lawrence had vocally denounced in the past.

The day had not been going too smoothly for the inspector. A few hours before Gokul arrived, Lawrence had been to Bishwambhar's liquor store for a late afternoon fix of *bhang*. His Saturday habit had fallen away ever since he broke with Pannalal. Bishwambhar wasn't in at that moment, leaving his brother-in-law, Madan, in charge. The shop was relatively empty, still early in the day. Lawrence drank his glass and smoked his preferred flavor of hookah before he appeared at the front of the shop to pay. As per his habit, he left a little extra as *baksheesh* with the cashier. The new manager, Madan, didn't know Lawrence's habits. Since tipping was not common among Bishwambhar's customers, Madan held the extra cash back for Lawrence with a broad smile.

Making sure the other guests heard his words spoken in good humor, Madan added, "Sahib is too drunk to count his cash now. Soon as he sobers, he will be back to snatch it."

The natives who heard Madan broke into an amused guffaw causing Lawrence's volatile temper to flare up. With one hand, he retrieved the money Madan held for him; with his other, he grabbed the pint-sized man by his neck, throwing him against the wall, shocking everyone. Madan's body slid down, crumpling to a heap on the floor. It was not hard to see the streak of blood on the wall where Madan's head had struck. Lawrence stormed out from the scene, ignoring whatever may have happened.

Couped up in his Park Street office, Lawrence sat sweating profusely with no sight of his *punkahwallah* yet. The multiple drinks weren't helping. Checking his pocket watch, Lawrence realized his wretched day was finally done. He decided he needed the nubile Shashibala's company to calm him tonight. While the massacres had made it hard for him to relate kindly to the natives, Lawrence was surprised by how his feelings for Shashibala had not changed. In fact, Shashibala's heartless aloofness fascinated the inspector. She didn't seem to give two hoots about who ruled – native, English, or anyone else. She was clearly desensitized to who or how many died. In her betel-leaf-juice-stained raucous laughter and her unwavering zest for life, Lawrence sensed a different kind of rebellion. She seemed convinced that things could never change for her, no matter where India's politics headed. She had denounced the very society that denounced her. Lawrence saw her as utterly alone – without a race, a country, or a people. The inspector picked up his intoxicated body and stumbled out of the police station, heading toward the alleys of the Chatawalapara brothel where Shashibala lived.

Chapter Sixteen

8th August 1857

When Dubois got on a boat to cross the Hooghly River after a quiet *tanga* ride from Calcutta to Barrackpore, Chandrakanta followed him without questions. Chandrakanta had not kept in touch with Dubois since the *shikar* party. So, he was shocked to find Dubois waiting in his living room. And even more so, by Dubois' invitation to come with him to meet the principal accused for the massacres at Bibighar and Satichura – Nana sahib – a man with an astronomical ten thousand pounds worth of bounty on his head! Ever since they set out, beyond briefly explaining that Jainagar's *Raja* Uday Singh had personally asked Dubois to orchestrate a safe passage for Nana sahib, the Frenchman remained tightlipped. Chandrakanta struggled to understand the true connection between Dubois and Nana sahib. Dubois' taciturn manner led him to suspect that the Frenchman had somehow been dragged into all of this. He may not have been comfortable defying the British to this extent. However, mused Chandrakanta, Uday Singh had been wise in getting word out to a foreigner that nobody was watching.

As the boat sidled along the placid river, a late afternoon sun squinted at them. The gentle river breeze had made the normally impossible heat slightly more bearable. Thoughts that he usually kept at bay, his qualms about how much Nana sahib was actually to blame for the massacres, crept inside Chandrakanta. Though he had defended Nana sahib in front of Radhanath, he did wonder about what happened sometimes. Interspersed with those thoughts, another interesting consideration vied for his attention. Nana sahib's being here had presented Chandrakanta with a unique opportunity. Like the rest of India, the sepoys in Bengal were excited by Nana sahib's notoriety. Chandrakanta's efforts to unite them in rebellion was not a hundred percent successful yet. If at this juncture, he could get the charismatic Nana sahib to speak to them, it could rally those still sitting on the fence. Chandrakanta had grown impatient as of late, concerned that he might lose those he had in his camp in the time that it took to convince those who weren't with him yet.

As the boat approached Chandannagar's magnificent Strand promenade, elegant examples of French architecture came into view. Back in the mid-1700s, the French East India Company's Chandannagar hosted up to one lakh citizens, at a time when British Calcutta was but a poor cousin downriver to the South. Then, England's Robert Clive entered the scene to challenge the French. Anglo-French battle cries sounded on the banks of the Hooghly River, far from Europe. After extensive wars, it was in 1816 that Chandannagar was finally, permanently restored to the French.

As their boat prepared to dock, Chandrakanta looked at Dubois askance. Headed into French territory and led by a Frenchman, Chandrakanta wondered, *was Dubois acting alone, or was the French administration in India helping him?* Dubois had offered nothing illuminating yet. Asking the boatman to wait, the two boarded another *tanga,* which after countless turns through a maze of houses, stopped in front of a run-down *haveli*. Chandrakanta was sweating badly as he followed Dubois in. The Dhanulia *zamindar* was an important man and did not lack enemies. After leading Chandrakanta down a dirty hallway for some time, Dubois came to a halt in front of a door. Then he knocked, and someone from inside the room asked for his name. As Dubois whispered it hoarsely, the door opened, and after entering the room, Chandrakanta saw two occupants.

As Nana sahib rose to greet them, Chandrakanta looked at the man, whose personal courage and dreams for India's emancipation, Chandrakanta had grown to admire over the last year that they got to know each other better. Nana sahib surprised him. Chandrakanta had imagined the hunted Nana sahib would be subdued. Instead, Nana sahib's eyes shone with fire brighter than ever. As his thickly bearded face broke into a warm smile, Chandrakanta felt electrified by this fearless, charismatic man, who will doubtlessly go down in history as one of the linchpins of the mutiny.

"Chandrakanta-*ji*, thank you for coming!" Nana sahib said.

Turning to the other man who was in the room with him, Nana sahib introduced *Nawab* Ali Nukhi Khan, companion to the erstwhile king of Oudh, Wajid Ali, the same character that Lawrence Cockerel had suspected of plotting to overthrow the British at Fort William. Nana sahib acknowledged the risk all the good men around him were taking by giving him refuge. Chandrakanta learned that Uday Singh had reached out to Wajid Ali, who then selected this house in the French territory of Chandannagar as a safe place to hold Nana sahib, at least for a few days. At this point, their plan was to smuggle Nana sahib across the border to the French stronghold in Burma, sometime tomorrow evening.

Nana sahib said, "The rebellion in the North is losing steam. The British have reclaimed Kanpur, but Delhi is ours for the time being. The question is, for how long? We will need reinforcements. Wajid Ali has arranged for me to meet his good friend, the French mercenary, General D'Orgoni, who is currently in Burma. D'Orgoni has a sizable, well-trained army. If we can make it worth his while, he will help. And we can turn the tide in our favor yet."

Looking straight at Chandrakanta, Nana sahib gravely asserted, "Chandrakanta-*ji*, the cause that we both hold dear in our hearts, needs money to keep it going. Will you help? A lot rides on this fortuitous meeting with the French General. I must be able to meet the price he names."

"But of course!" Chandrakanta agreed. Looking at Nukhi Khan, he added, "Let me work with you to make arrangements for the payment."

As Nukhi Khan nodded, Nana sahib noticed Chandrakanta hesitate. And then, seeing Chandrakanta shoot a surreptitious look at Dubois, Nana sahib prodded, "Speak freely, Chandrakanta-*ji*. Monsieur Dubois is a friend."

For a moment, Chandrakanta stood with his brows furrowed in thought, wondering how to bring up what was on his mind. Looking at Nana sahib directly, he finally said, "I have some news for you. The Bengal army is ready for rebellion. They are tinder waiting for a spark."

Chandrakanta's sudden statement was met with incredulous silence in the room.

"How do you know this?" whispered Nukhi Khan.

With an air of smug satisfaction, Chandrakanta elaborated, "I've been to the Barrackpore cantonment several times over the past few weeks, meeting with the sepoys and discussing how Bengal can participate in the revolt. While there were only a handful present when Mongol Pandey attacked that British officer, the bosses had chosen to sack the entire 34th battalion. I was able to connect with around four hundred of those ex-sepoys, still smarting from their dismissals. And not just them, we found many who are currently part of the British forces interested. They have been attending our meetings pretty regularly. They were guarded at first, but as news from the North trickled in, I have seen the men change."

With the hint of a smile forming at his lips, Chandrakanta danced his brows at Nana sahib and said, "They enjoy hearing Nana sahib put the fear of God into the British. I am confident, if a call is sounded in this climate, the men will respond. We can deal the British a blow they won't soon forget, right here in Bengal!"

Nana sahib's eyes were shining with approval as he commended the developments. "That is very good, Chandrakanta-*ji*. If the Bengal army joins forces with D'Orgoni's men when he attacks Calcutta from Burma, that could be powerful."

Warily, Chandrakanta asked, "But how long will that take?"

Nana sahib responded, "I won't know until I have spoken to D'Orgoni."

Chandrakanta ran a hand over his face to give himself a moment, then firmly objected, "Nana sahib, I do not think we should wait. We need to act within the next couple of weeks. The sepoys are charged up now, and the flame may die if we delay for too long."

Nukhi Khan said, "Chandrakanta-*ji*, coordinating something like this is not simple. His highness Wajid Ali and I have attempted to organize the native workforce inside Fort William to revolt on several occasions. Every time, something or the other has foiled our plan."

Turning to Nukhi Khan impatiently, Chandrakanta said, "Khan-*ji*, forgive me, but we are talking about two very different things. I am talking about the sepoys of the British army, not the domestic help at Fort William. Here in Calcutta, we've never pitted the sepoys trained by the British against them. If we can get the sepoys on our side, we have a good chance."

Nana sahib forcefully interjected. "Do you or do you not have the sepoys? Forgive me, there is no place for *ifs*, Chandrakanta-*ji*. Failure will come with serious consequences."

Chandrakanta looked expressionlessly at Nana sahib. He admitted that though he had a fair number on his side, not everyone was on board yet. He had the four hundred. However, many of those currently on British payroll had not committed.

Looking dubious, Nana sahib said, "Chandrakanta-*ji*, you have to get them to commit before you kick off a rebellion. If people join at the eleventh-hour willy-nilly, it will fuel chaos. I have witnessed this happen at Satichura and Bibighar. The newcomers didn't have a clue of the meticulous plans we had made, and the chain of command simply became confused. Before we knew it, unknown individuals took matters into their own hands, triggering tragic events."

"Well, we have to take that risk!" Chandrakanta spoke firmly, his brow furrowed, tempering his impatience with a smile. "This time it will be different. Perhaps you can rally them around, Nana sahib. I cannot imagine a more convincing figure than the Lion of Bithoor to motivate the men. What do you say to addressing some of the sepoy leaders directly, in a secret, face-to-face meeting?"

Nana sahib looked at Chandrakanta in silence. He thought Chandrakanta had changed. There was a certain recklessness about him that was new. Sensing Chandrakanta's mind was made up already, "Very well," Nana sahib said. "I will speak to your men. If you can weaken the British here in Bengal, you make it that much easier for General D'Orgoni's army to march through here."

Turning to Nukhi Khan and Dubois, Nana sahib asked, "How can we accommodate Chandrakanta-*ji*'s request?"

Dubois piped up before Nukhi Khan could say anything, "*Impossible*! Nana sahib, you must leave here tomorrow."

Addressing Chandrakanta directly, Dubois added, "I trust you can imagine, coordinating how and where to shift Nana sahib has been a huge challenge. No one knows the complete itinerary, so that it stays secret. If the chain breaks, I cannot make alternative plans this late in the game. If there are delays, you risk jeopardizing his meeting with D'Orgoni. The General has done Wajid Ali one favor, and he may not be inclined to do another."

Dubois' tone rattled Chandrakanta. From his perspective, Uday Singh's employee should have remembered his place. "Monsieur Dubois, I am certain we are very grateful for everything you are doing." Curtly, Chandrakanta continued, “General D’Orgoni won’t be doing us any favors; he will be compensated for his efforts. As are you, I am sure!”

“*Arrêtez*!” An incensed Dubois did not let Chandrakanta finish, “I am no paid stooge!” Tilting his head toward Nana sahib, “I risked my life to save this man’s neck”, he countered, “which, by the way, I didn’t do to return Uday Singh’s generosity for sparing my life as I’ve heard some of you allege. Know this. As part of the French mission, my father and grandfather have fought on Indian soil, shoulder to shoulder with Indian leaders against the British.”

Nana sahib and Nukhi Khan looked at Dubois with surprise. Dubois continued, holding Chandrakanta’s gaze. “French generals fought the British alongside the Sultans of Mysore in the South. My grandfather, Jean Dubois, was Hyder Ali, the Sultan of Mysore’s right-hand man. And my father, Jacque Dubois, served Tipu Sultan, Hyder Ali’s son. He was in charge of ammunition in Tipu Sultan’s army during the Anglo Mysore Wars at the turn of the century.”

While Nana sahib and Nukhi Khan digested Dubois’ revelation, Chandrakanta, who was no less surprised, inquired poker-faced, “Why don’t you tell me exactly when Nana sahib is slated to leave here tomorrow?”

After a short, mutinous silence, Dubois vaguely responded, “Late in the afternoon.”

Looking unimpressed, Chandrakanta turned to Nana sahib and said, “I will go to Barrackpore right now to meet with the others. Let me see how many leaders I can gather for a meeting with you.”

Turning to Nukhi Khan, Chandrakanta requested, “Khan-*ji*, can you arrange for a secret meeting for early tomorrow morning here in Chandannagar? Say for about twenty people?” Nukhi Khan was still nodding uncertainly when Chandrakanta turned to Dubois and said, “All I ask is for Nana sahib to speak briefly to these men. These are leaders who hold sway over the sepoys and can disseminate Nana sahib’s message. After that, he is all yours, I promise.”

While the group seemed to fall in with Chandrakanta's proposal, Dubois sat feeling annoyed. Chandrakanta's manner, he felt, was dismissive toward him. Deciding to go after Chandrakanta, Dubois said, "What if you're overestimating how much sway these so-called leaders actually have? What happens if your sepoys hesitate when it's time to act?"

Irritably, Chandrakanta retorted, "Well, we are doing what we can. Do you have a better suggestion?"

Staring at Chandrakanta for a few moments, Dubois said, "I do, in fact. You need something spectacular to happen when it is time to act, so that it's an inspiring reminder for everyone to stay the course."

Turning his head to address everyone together, Dubois suggested, "What if you set fire to the GTSI tower at Sukhchar? It's at a stone's throw from the Barrackpore cantonment."

Dubois relished the looks on the faces in the room in the silence that followed his suggestion. "The tower, gentlemen, is a symbol of British pride," Dubois elaborated. "It is the tallest structure in the region. The blaze can be seen from both the cantonments at Barrackpore and Dumdum. If we can stage a blazing inferno there, it can become a larger-than-life signal to start action. It can serve to coordinate, galvanize, and even turn the hearts of the undecided."

The image conjured by Dubois's proposal was so dramatic that people forgot to react or say anything for a few moments. Dubois noted that Chandrakanta's previous nonchalance was gone. Feeling greatly pleased with the idea himself, Dubois expanded, "I can help you! It is no mean task, mind you, to set up a blaze that will go through the roof of a concrete building and will also last for long. But I'm just the man. I know a very effective way to make the flames shoot high into the sky. Because of its columnar structure, the tower will actually aid the process."

Albeit weakly, Chandrakanta protested, "Don't you work for the GTSI?"

His brows knit with impatience, Dubois shot back, "*Oui*, I work there. I also worked for *Raja* Uday Singh. And the *Raja* knew my worth unlike the Brit dogs who have done nothing to prove they value me. This is war, Chan-dru-can-ta. I will have nothing to do with the side that's just too full of themselves. My ancestors fought against the British on Indian soil. And I will help you burn that tower in a blaze no one will soon forget."

A cautiously hopeful Nukhi Khan brought up the all-important question, "Mr. Dubois, I have seen the GTSI tower at Sukhchar. It is no Qutub Minar. Are you sure it is tall enough to be seen from the Barrackpore cantonment?"

Dubois confidently responded, "Absolutely! Remember that the GTSI built it there to see across large distances. On a clear day, you can see all the way up to St. Paul's Cathedral in Calcutta."

Turning toward Chandrakanta again, Dubois saw him smiling, pretty much sold on the idea. "Dubois, we cannot afford to wait too long," warned Chandrakanta, "Especially after Nana sahib speaks to the men, we have to act soon."

Dubois said, "I get that. I'll be done with getting Nana sahib out of here in the next two days."

Chandrakanta asked, "What fuel will you need?"

Confidently, Dubois responded, "The bulk of it will be mud and hay soaked in paraffin. And we need Greek fire, a combustible quicklime-based fluid that creates a brilliant blaze. My father was fond of this concoction; he often used it in the flamethrowers he designed. However, it is a double-edged sword. It's a ridiculously dangerous substance that needs professional handling to ignite. No worries though, I can deal with that."

"Do you know how long it'll take you to get the raw materials?" continued to prod Chandrakanta.

"Most of the ingredients are readily available," responded Dubois airily.

"Perfect! Let's settle it then. I will get my men here tomorrow in the early hours to meet Nana sahib. And then, you need two days to see him off, and a couple days further, I imagine, to make your preparations. Can we pick a day sometime around the end of next week?" proposed Chandrakanta.

Nukhi Khan hastily interrupted, "You think you can make this work in just two weeks? Aren't we cutting this too close?"

Looking at Nukhi Khan, Chandrakanta solemnly said, "Khan-*ji*, this is the moment; I can feel it in my bones. If we wait too long, we will miss the boat. The sepoys are ready. They want to be a part of this historic movement."

The four decided they were going to store the raw materials initially at Barrackpore. On the day of reckoning, they were going to move it somewhere near the tower and keep it camouflaged until it was time. Once the tower was aflame, the bloodbath on the British was to start at the Barrackpore cantonment. After gaining control of the cantonment, the soldiers were going to march along BT Road toward Calcutta with the image of the towering inferno burning in their eyes. It was sure to keep them pumped and perhaps also swell their numbers. The growing uproar might even bring the Dumdum cantonment into their fold as they cross it on the way.

Chandrakanta felt electrified. However, all too aware how newcomers joining on the fly could backfire, he also felt a tad anxious. But then the desire to leverage Nana sahib's presence and the way everybody tonight was moved by Dubois' proposal, made Chandrakanta feel he couldn't afford to backtrack. Pushing his misgivings aside, he convinced himself that if the key players worked in synchrony, the greater numbers will ultimately be an advantage. It will certainly amplify the panic among the British, which could be their undoing.

Dubois now turned to Nukhi Khan and said, "Khan-*ji*, there is one thing. I have a lady friend in Calcutta who I'd like to provide protection." As Nukhi Khan looked at him curiously, Dubois mused out aloud, "Since I won't be at liberty to share too many details, it may be hard to convince her to get out of town around whichever day you pick. So, what can we do?"

Nukhi Khan suggested, “I can have friends organize a ball for the Europeans, here in Chandannagar on the day if you like. Why don’t you ask your friend to come directly to Chandannagar and meet you here? I can provide a reserved *tanga* to bring her over. After you are done at the tower, perhaps you would like to join her at the ball?”

Dubois beamed, “*Merci*! That will be great! After my part is done, I was thinking of going to Chandannagar myself.”

Nukhi Khan suggested, “We can pick her up from Evora near Park Street. Will that work?”

As Dubois nodded his head, he offered, “Have your man ask for a Miss Sara Langley then.”

Picking up on the name, Chandrakanta turned to look at Dubois. With his attention on Nukhi Khan right then, Dubois missed the look. *Poor Radhanath*, thought Chandrakanta, in light of Dubois’s singular concern for Miss Langley. And then, *poor, poor Radhanath*, he thought again, with a twinge of guilt. The GTSI that defined Radhanath’s life had come up at the center stage of their rebellion. *Well, Radhanath’s fond memories were but a small price to pay compared to what was at stake*, deemed his friend. As he sat watching Dubois, an enthusiastic party to their rebellion, he thought it ironic that whereas the Frenchman was willing to destroy the tower, his Indian friend could never be convinced to do the same.

Chapter Seventeen

21st August 1857, 6:00 PM

It had been about a week since Radhanath recovered from his terrible bout of malaria and rejoined service. He was returning from GTSI's Wood Street office that evening when it started to rain. Unwilling to get drenched so soon after his illness, Radhanath decided to seek shelter at Evora. Earlier this week, mindful that Sara Langley frequented the place, Radhanath had stopped by the restaurant on two different occasions. Their paths hadn't crossed. Radhanath hadn't enjoyed his visits either. Ever since news of the Bibighar Massacre reached Calcutta, Evora's atmosphere had grown increasingly hostile. While Evora's management continued to insist that their doors remain open to all, owner Alfonso and his European guests had grown noticeably cooler toward the natives. On his last visit, Radhanath had resolved to stop coming; a decision he would have respected, had he not found himself next to Evora just as it started to rain.

Ignoring the Anglo-Indian doorman's unsmiling face, Radhanath stood at the foyer eyeing the candlelit cheer inside. Signor Alfonso was talking to someone. Radhanath waited for either him or one of his waiters to show him to a table, vaguely hoping they do not repeat the disasters he had experienced twice in a row now. On Monday, they brought his food out very late, claiming to be short-staffed, while a hungry and tired Radhanath noted European guests arriving later than him getting served ahead. Two nights ago, Radhanath was disgusted by the grimy bowl in which his soup finally arrived. Nonetheless, he had persuaded himself to take another chance tonight, not oblivious to the possibility of seeing Sara.

As Radhanath waited at the foyer, sounds of violin wafted to him from the dais at the back of the restaurant. It wasn't Mrs. Periera, the *fado* singer's turn today. Radhanath spotted the old gentleman playing an instrument, his face creased in meditative concentration. His soulful tunes mingled with the dull thrumming of the rain. Not greatly fancying the vacant tables in the interior of the restaurant, Radhanath looked for a street-side spot. As he eyed the crowd, with some surprise he realized that he was the only native guest tonight.

At this point, Radhanath's searching eyes came to rest on a British man seated at a street-side table with no food in front of him. Radhanath wondered if the man was done, in which case that table could soon become available. Unless of course, that man had arrived recently, shortly before Radhanath himself. Suddenly, a streak of lightning drew Radhanath's eye outside to the rain-darkened, wind-swept trees, framed by the curtain-bordered windows that lined Evora's street-side walls. The contrast between the melodic, candlelit cheer inside and the desolate drama outside bemused him momentarily. When the outside went dim, his eyes got stuck on the windowpane. A solitary flame from a candle on the table next to it had given rise to multiple reflections on the glass of the pane – an infinite number, fading into the darkness. Radhanath stood absorbed by the identically flickering images. He had seen this exact phenomenon at Evora before but never quite thought about why it happened. As he continued to wait for a table, Radhanath found himself succumbing to the nerdish joy of working out the physics behind those reflections.

Vaguely conscious that Alfonso was finishing up with the guest he had been attending, Radhanath half-turned toward him. He was frustrated to see Alfonso turn in another direction. As Radhanath wondered if he was seen and ignored, or not noticed altogether, Radhanath's eyes were drawn to the same British man he had noticed earlier. The British man looked rather fidgety, seeming undecided about whether to stay. Then he stood up, and Radhanath concluded he must have been done for some time and now got tired of waiting for the rain. Lest he lose this one good spot with its street view, Radhanath beelined for the table. And in a polite attempt to stake his claim, he asked if the man was leaving.

Even in these tumultuous times, one didn't encounter naked animosity like this man projected as he turned to Radhanath. Then rudely breaking eye contact, he hurried away, spewing a bunch of unintelligible words in Radhanath's general direction in parting. Radhanath was not able to follow most of it save the words "late" and "chum". He sat sour-faced at the newly vacated table, eyeing the man collect his Mackintosh from the doorman.

The violinist had started to play a lively aria, and its rich strains soothed Radhanath's agitated nerves. Radhanath looked outside the window. The rains were beginning to let up. A few pedestrians had stepped out on the roads, taking advantage of the receding rain. Radhanath's mind drifted to Chandrakanta, who he last saw two weeks ago when Chandrakanta came to check on him. Radhanath reflected uneasily about the man that had brought him back from the jaws of death. He remembered Chandrakanta's face when he spoke of Sara Langley, deriding the very idea of anything romantic between Radhanath and that woman.

Radhanath sighed with resignation, doubting he could explain what he felt for Sara Langley to anyone at all. When Chandrakanta mentioned he had mumbled her name in sickness, he had vaguely remembered those distressing moments when he had indeed sought comfort in her memory. From the day he first laid eyes on her, the essence of who he perceived her to be had made her special to him. Radhanath had resisted his growing feelings for the lady. *Not just race, he was conscious of all manners of differences between them: cultural background, age, and life experience.* Even so, Radhanath's soul, reeling from both his recent illness and news of the horrors from the North, simply yearned for her presence.

Suddenly Radhanath registered that the rain had paused, and more people were out on the streets, with several trickling toward Evora, umbrella in hand. Feeling frustrated, he debated if he should step out given that the waiter hadn't showed up yet.

Right then, his eyes fell on the Armenian waitress coming toward his table. "What can I get you, sir?" she inquired.

Radhanath ordered a very English boiled beef with vegetables, and then asked upfront how long it would take. Giving him a watery smile, the girl hurried away without directly responding to Radhanath's question. Feeling mollified that dinner had at least been ordered at this point, Radhanath leaned back in his chair stretching his legs under the table. Then, as his gaze moved to the foyer, he felt his heart start to race.

Sara Langley, a vision in her purple-blue silk dress festooned with petite white roses, was handing her rain drenched parasol to the doorman. Apparently, she had come to Evora by herself this evening. As she turned to look inside, she spotted Radhanath almost immediately. Sensing Alfonso approach to escort her, the lady gestured to him indicating that wasn't necessary. Then she walked toward the table where Radhanath was seated, gently removing the gloves from her hands on her way.

Time stood still for Radhanath as Sara walked up to him. He watched the graceful movement of her body, her exquisite face framed by soft, golden hair falling delicately on her cheeks. He savored her expression imbued with pride, graciously tempered with strength and kindness. His own thumping heart was all that remained in his ears as she stood directly in front of him. He felt startled when that vision spoke.

"Good evening, Mr. Sikdar," she said, sounding unfamiliarly husky.

In the few seconds Radhanath delayed before he stood up to offer her a chair, he found the lady observing him with curious attention.

"Didn't you hear what I said, you swine? *Bhago*!" yelled a jarring voice from behind Sara, making the both of them jump.

Radhanath, who hadn't noticed the two men approach their table, now recognized the rude interruption had come from the person who was sitting at this table before him. Apparently, he had returned with a companion. In a flash, Radhanath connected the man's reappearance with what he had said in parting. "Chum" and "late" may have meant that he had left with the intention of returning with a companion later. Infuriated by the man's boorishness though, Radhanath loudly complained that the table was no longer available. Without looking, Radhanath could hear Alfonso pleading with the man and his companion. Alfonso appeared to have failed in his attempt to restrain the two from angling toward Radhanath's table with an obnoxious air of entitlement.

The man's companion tapped Radhanath roughly on his shoulder. Tilting his head rudely toward the door, he said, "Get the devil out of here. Now!"

Before Radhanath could react, Sara spoke up, her eyes flashing angrily, "Stop doing that, sir. Leave him alone. Leave us alone!"

Without looking at Sara, the first man, who was about as tall as Radhanath, seized Radhanath by the collar of his shirt. "Stay out of this, madam!" he rasped, "Have you forgotten what these bastards did to British women at Bibighar? How can you bear to look at this filthy pig?"

"Need I remind you of what followed?" Sara retorted. "There is no shred of decency in what Colonel Neill has done after. Any moral ascendancy the English feel has been lost by the inhuman atrocities he has committed in the name of retribution. Making the natives lick blood off the site of carnage? Hanging them without proof of guilt? Where is English justice in that, sir?"

Despite becoming transfixed by Sara's passionate outburst, the man didn't loosen his grip on Radhanath's collar. "Take your hands off me!" Radhanath's cold voice rang out like the crack of a whip.

Biting his lips doggedly, the man responded with a powerful blow that landed squarely on Radhanath's jaws. Radhanath held the corners of the table to prevent from falling to the ground. With the violin coming to an abrupt stop, a tense silence fell inside the restaurant, all eyes on the two men. Alfonso hovered anxiously in the background, at a loss at the sudden escalation of the situation. Sniggering at Radhanath's condition, one of the two men said, "Go now, while your bones are still intact, you dirty nigger."

Malaria had left him weaker than he realized, mused Radhanath, his head throbbing from the strength of the blow. And in that state of dizziness, distant memories from his final years in school flooded his mind. He saw a boxing ring, a match in progress, and an enthusiastic audience gathered around the ring. A regular at the gymnasium in his Hindu school years, Radhanath used to practice boxing with a couple of young British soldiers who had permission to use the school gymnasium alongside the students. They would challenge Radhanath to direct fights, most of which, to their utter amazement, Radhanath would handily win. As those memories flashed in Radhanath's mind, he stood breathing calmly. Sucking the blood off the small cut that had appeared on his lip, Radhanath next started to roll up the sleeves of his shirt. With effortless recollection, he launched into some footwork that looked so fancy that it drew a gasp from his audience. And in the next instant, everyone saw the man who had hit Radhanath passed out on the floor, from the lightning quick uppercut Radhanath had delivered to his chin.

Turning to Sara, Radhanath said, "Let's find a different table."

Bringing his face overbearingly close to the unconscious man's wildly surprised companion, Radhanath said, "Move!"

The man stepped back, still trying to wrap his head around what just happened.

After Sara took the chair Radhanath had pulled out for her at a newly available, street-side table, Radhanath walked to his own chair opposite hers, eyeing the crowd that had formed around the passed-out man on his way. Alfonso and others were sprinkling water on the fallen man's face, holding smelling salts to his nose.

"He'll be all right!" said Radhanath as he took his seat. Looking at Sara with a slight smile, he added, "With all the attention we drew, I trust the waiter will know where to deliver my dinner."

Sara did not immediately respond. She sat looking at Radhanath with a mixture of amusement and admiration. After a while, she said, "You pack a punch, don't you?"

Clenching and unclenching the fingers of his hand, Radhanath responded, almost a little distracted, "When I last hit a man some twenty years ago, my knuckles hadn't hurt like this."

Teasing Radhanath gently in response, Sara said, "You have rather paradoxical skills, Mr. Sikdar. I would not have believed mathematics and boxing go together. How did that happen?"

Radhanath shrugged, "It's my schooling. They made everyone take some sort of physical exercise, so I took up rowing and boxing."

"I haven't ever seen anyone black out instantly like that in my whole life, except..." Sara screwed her brows as her face seemed to brighten with signs of amusement.

However, uncharacteristically, Radhanath interrupted, "How long is that, Ms. Langley? Your whole life is what?" His narrowed eyes shone with an edgy sort of playfulness, suggesting he was aware of the somewhat improper nature of his question. It was also pleading, imploring her not to destroy the moment with any sign of impudence. Sara sat quietly, refusing to react to his delicate intimidation.

Lowering his eyes, and raising them back to her face again, Radhanath ceded, "I shouldn't have interrupted. You were saying?"

Sara sat watching Radhanath with a haughty light in her eyes before responding, "I was saying that I have never seen another person black out instantly like that in my *twenty-one* years of life." As she spoke the word twenty-one, the upper portion of her body came forward in an unconscious show of aggression.

"Mr. Sikdar, do not make the mistake of equating my twenty-one years to an insignificant experience of life. Having lost my parents early, ever since age seven I have lived with uncles and aunts, six months or less at a time, endlessly shipped to new homes. It stopped only after Uncle Dick, a family friend, took me under his wing. He was the one that gave me an education, and it is on his generosity I was able to travel to India to make a life for myself. My days here have been anything but ordinary, anything but secluded." At this point, Sara paused, looking directly at Radhanath, unflinching steel in her gaze. "I have walked endless miles in scorching sun, fleeing mutineers, feeling hunted at every step. I have bargained my clothes for bread from strangers. I have seen sickness, starvation, and exposure at the shelter where I help. All this in my twenty-one years, Mr. Sikdar."

Radhanath slammed his hands on the table but softly. His eyes were lowered with pain he did not want Sara to see. Looking up, Radhanath simply said, "Forgive me Sara, I didn't mean to sound patronizing."

After a brief silence, Radhanath, in an attempt to move their conversation along, gently prodded Sara toward the seemingly amusing thought he had interrupted. "Which other occasion were you going to tell me about when you've seen someone pass out?"

With a gentle sigh, Sara restarted, "Several years ago, I had traveled with Uncle Dick to visit his brother in Guyana, who worked as the manager at a sugarcane plantation there. I was about twelve or so at the time. Guyana is a country mostly dominated by swamps and trees, and there are a lot of free-ranging monkeys about." Radhanath noted that she was beginning to cheer up. "I had gone out to play with the other children. Cecil, one of my playmates that morning, started to tease a group of monkeys. We were making faces, and the monkeys were screeching and making faces in turn. Everyone was having a ball. Then suddenly, Cecil crumpled to the ground, and I noticed a pebble-sized fruit rolling away from where she fell."

As Radhanath screwed his brows in confusion, Sara said, "Well, can't you guess? One of the monkeys had thrown that fruit at her and managed to knock poor Cecil out."

Just as she was concluding her sentence, both realized that her anecdote had drawn an unintended parallel with the monkey, prompting Radhanath's face to light up with amusement and Sara's to blush. Unable to resist teasing her about it, Radhanath said, "Miss Langley, you must give the monkey more credit. I nearly broke my knuckles tonight!"

A mortified Sara muttered, "Please say no more, Mr. Sikdar!"

Using the brief pause that fell at their table, Radhanath looked toward where the brawl took place. The man he hit had regained consciousness and now sat at his old table, pressing ice to his chin. Unconsciously, Radhanath ran a hand over his own jaws, feeling a tingle where that man had hit him. Turning back to Sara, Radhanath found her head bent sideways, her face still a tad red.

As he watched her face, it crossed Radhanath's mind that there was a mesmerizing fluidity in her look – a quality that intrigued him mercilessly. Each time they met in the past, he had come away feeling besotted by how lovely she looked. However, when he tried to think of her in her absence, he realized that her beauty was fascinatingly subtle, that it was hard to capture the essence of her – the way her eyes spoke and her aura – in memory. It was impossible to recreate her magic when she was absent, as impossible as trying to shape water with bare hands. A jolt of resentment coursed through him at the unfairness of it all. *Oh, to see Sara's precious face more often like this, sitting across from him!* Conscious of Radhanath's ardent gaze, Sara sat with her eyes lowered, holding her face at a demure angle, and waited for Radhanath to look away. After a while when he still hadn't looked away, she raised her eyes to look at him directly again.

Sara spoke in that same husky voice. "Mr. Sikdar, I've been conscious of something between us, something intense, from that first day I met you."

Her questioning eyes waited for Radhanath to affirm her assertion, but he said nothing.

"I have never had another admirer – and there has been a fair number – however, never another, who has looked at me the way I have seen you look at me. You confuse me, Mr. Sikdar. With the Indians and the British at each other's throats everywhere now, you confuse me with your look. I hardly know you! I don't understand what it means or where…" Sara was forced to stop as a waiter approached their table with Radhanath's boiled beef and vegetables.

The waiter seemed keen to get away, perhaps spooked by his hitting a Brit. After laying out the food, he nervously turned to Sara to ask what she wanted. Presumably she made him uncomfortable as well, entertaining Radhanath at her table. Ignoring his nervousness, Sara asked for the *bhetki* casserole she loved on Evora's menu. Aware that Hindus don't eat cows, she had noted the plate of beef that sat before Radhanath with some surprise but didn't comment. Meanwhile, Radhanath had absentmindedly begun playing with the bread that had come with his dinner. When the waiter departed, Radhanath resumed, "Miss Langley, I wish I could help you understand what is happening between us. You said you hardly know me. The truth is you know me as well as anybody. I have spent most of my life wandering the outdoors. Roasted by the sun, soaked by the rains, and numbed by cold, I have kept myself busy tinkering with compasses and theodolites. Since I moved to Calcutta, my main occupation has been to burn the midnight oil doing mathematics."

Leaning back on his chair with a slightly faraway look, Radhanath continued, "I was born in Jorashanko, not ten miles from here. My father was a wealthy man, before he lost his fortune to his brothers. Mercifully, he managed to get me, and my brother educated at the Hindu school. That's where

I was exposed to Western culture. I got noticed for my skills in mathematics. It was mathematics that got me my job at GTSI."

After a brief pause, Radhanath muttered, "Over the years, my brother and I drifted apart. We don't talk anymore." At this point, he faltered to a stop, seeming at a loss for words.

Sara was listening with keen attention. Although she felt strongly curious about Radhanath's status from a romantic standpoint, she couldn't bring herself to ask the question. Abruptly, sitting up straight, Radhanath leaned forward to gaze into the eyes that had mesmerized him from day one. "So, Miss Langley, before I met you, even if my life was not entirely uninteresting, it was decidedly routine. My most cherished moment to that point had been to discover Peak XV, Mount Everest if you will, as the tallest point on Earth."

Sara became absolutely still, hearing the words Radhanath had not spoken. *Didn't he just admit, their meeting was more special to him than the grandest work of his life?*

Impulsively, dropping the bread he was toying with, Radhanath leaned forward to cover Sara's hand resting on the table with his. Sara froze. Her expression gave nothing away. Radhanath reached for her face with his other hand, apparently oblivious to where they were. He started to tenderly caress the blushing skin of her cheeks. After sitting paralyzed for a few seconds, Sara turned her face sideways in confusion, moving out of his reach. Her eyes fell on the glass windowpane, reflecting multiple images from the candle sitting on their table.

Sara whispered without turning to look at Radhanath yet, "So many reflections from one candle. Aren't they beautiful?"

By this time, Radhanath had withdrawn his hands. He was feeling a tad embarrassed for his impetuous action. Welcoming the distraction of Sara's question, he responded, "Believe it or not, Miss Langley, I was thinking about this very phenomenon as I was waiting at the foyer, earlier this evening. I got ample opportunity to figure out why it's happening. Shall I explain it to you?"

Turning back to look at Radhanath now, Sara tilted her head, encouraging him to elaborate. "You see, the glass of the window has a certain thickness. The two sides of the glass are like two walls around the material of the glass. The light from the candle gets trapped between the walls and bounces back and forth creating those multiple images."

Radhanath held the palms of his hands parallel to each other on the table, attempting to represent the two sides of the glass pane. "Imagine rays of light bouncing back and forth between my palms." Moving his chin to show the bouncing path of light must have felt awkward because he stopped with a pained look on his face.

To his surprise, Sara brought her own hands on the table imitating him. "All right!" said Radhanath. "So, your palms form the walls of the glass pane. Follow my fingers, I am going to trace the path of light from the candle."

Radhanath moved his index finger from the position of an imaginary flame and touched the backside of Sara's right palm. The dark skin of Radhanath's palms created a potent visual contrast against Sara's milky white. "The light enters the pane here. A part of the light is immediately reflected back to your eye, as it happens in the case of a mirror, forming the first image."

Moving his finger to touch the corresponding point on the inner side of the same palm, Radhanath continued, "The rest of the light enters the glass first through here…" Then touching a point on the inner side of her other palm he completed, "to reach the second wall here."

"From here, while some light escapes to the outside, the rest is reflected back to the first wall. There, it splits again, and part of it goes to your eye to form a second image."

While moving his fingers back and forth between Sara's palms, he said, "Each time the light bounces between these walls, some of it reaches your eye to form a new image. That is why you have those series of images behind the glass."

Looking up excitedly Sara said, "Do the images reduce in brightness because of light lost to the outside each time?" Radhanath nodded his head approvingly.

At this point, almost simultaneously with the previous shifty waiter arriving with Sara's *bhetki* casserole, a well-dressed Muslim gentleman also neared their table. With a slight bow, the man gave his name as Nusrat Hussein. Nusrat indicated he had come to Evora for Miss Langley. His *tanga* had been reserved to escort the madam to the ball at Chandannagar. A little regretfully, Sara responded, "I am sorry Mr. Hussein. I won't be needing the *tanga* after all. I have decided I won't go to Chandannagar tonight."

An uneasiness seemed to come over the man's face. As the waiter departed, Nusrat Hussein began again, "Kind madam, I was emphatically told to take you straight to the party. Please. You must come with me."

Sara's eyes flashed at the man's odd insistence. Firmly, she repeated, "Did I not say, I have changed my mind? Thank you for your trouble, but I will not be coming tonight. You may go."

Radhanath, who had been surprised by this man's arrival out of the blue, was about to speak up, but Mr. Hussein seemed to now accept Sara's decision. He left with a resigned but respectful bow to both. Pulling the *bhetki* casserole toward her, Sara said by way of explanation, "There is a midnight ball at Chandannagar where a couple of us were supposed to go from Calcutta."

Shrugging she added, "I did intend to go. That's why I am dressed like this."

Sara seemed curiously keen to get on, lifting her knife and fork to attack her *bhetki* casserole with sudden gusto. Also, Radhanath's dinner, having sat virtually untouched, had grown a tad limp. Sara urged Radhanath to start eating. Taking a bite of her fish, Sara said, "Rady, do you remember, on that walk at the hunting party, just before we brought the beehive down…"

Radhanath's eyes took on a soft light as he nodded; that night was among his most cherished even if it was ultimately harrowing. Sara continued, "You explained how it was tricky to measure the true height of Mt Everest because the light coming from it changes directions as it passes through the layers of our atmosphere?"

Starting to chew on the piece of the beef he had put into his mouth, Radhanath nodded again. "I was reminded of that when you explained about the multiple images from a single candle flame – how light goes back and forth between the walls of the window-pane," Sara elaborated. Then, almost reflectively she added, "I find it fascinating that light changes directions! Why does it do that?"

Encouraged by Sara's interest in the phenomenon, Radhanath decided to elaborate, "You'd be surprised, Miss Langley. The key principle is quite simple – light always chooses the quickest path to travel between two points. Say I want to go from point A to point B; ordinarily, I would follow the straight road between them. But if the straight road was busy, an alternate route could take me there quicker. It is as if light *knows* the quickest path to take. And it'll do that even if it has to change directions, bending away from the straight path to connect source and destination."

Radhanath found Sara's eyes gleaming with enjoyment in a manner he hadn't quite seen before. She teased him, "Are you saying light has a mind of its own?" An amused Radhanath shrugged in response – a tongue-in-cheek admission – that is indeed how nature worked, though he wouldn't have used those words himself.

Dropping her gaze to her plate momentarily, Sara admitted, "Nobody's ever told me these things about light, Mr. Sikdar." When she brought her eyes back to him, they shone with happiness. "I have often wondered about light when I stargaze, looking at those specs so far away. I imagine starlight also picks the quickest path as it travels through the atmosphere?"

Radhanath promptly answered, "That's exactly the reason they twinkle Miss Langley!"

He started to explain. "You see, the light from these stars, starting from billions and billions of miles away, are in a tremendous rush to get to you." Sara looked up at Radhanath, her chewing slowed, her eyes narrowed, trying to understand where he was going. "The path chosen by the very first ray produces the first image of the star. But then, because the atmosphere is continuously changing, that's not the quickest path in the very next instant. So, the next ray chooses a new quickest route, which means you are seeing the star at a slightly different position in the very next instant. The random change in the position of the image of the star is what causes it to twinkle."

As he finished his explanation, Radhanath tried to smile, "All because, when you look at a star, its light cannot wait to get to those beautiful eyes of yours!"

He had deliberately chosen to say something silly to finish on a lighthearted note, but it didn't come out like that. As he sat watching Sara, his breath quickened, and a wave of tenderness welled up inside him. Sara sat completely still, her eyes gazing into his. It was a moment when both suddenly grasped, they were at a crossroad in their lives; that no matter what, the path forward in their relationship would never be the same again. Neither registered how much time passed as they sat engrossed in each other. They regained awareness of their surroundings when a sudden commotion at Evora's entrance broke the spell.

Several British police officers had entered the restaurant. They rang a gong, trying to grab everyone's attention for an announcement they evidently needed to make. The violinist playing on the dais at the back of the restaurant came to a stop, as did all chatter, creating a sudden quietness. All eyes focused on the newcomers, waiting to hear what they had to say. Now, one of the officers started to speak, announcing that they were closing Evora down effective immediately. Apparently, British intelligence had credible evidence that there could be trouble from the natives tonight. The administration had carriages waiting outside to transport the Europeans in this room to various safe zones across the city.

These alarms, which began right after the uprising broke in the North, had grown more frequent as of late. Though the people were more accustomed to the drill by now, their attitudes toward these before and after the Bibighar massacre were markedly different. Previously, people tended to treat these as measures taken more out of an abundance of caution; nowadays, the mood was much more serious. The warnings, when they came, reminded everyone of all the horror stories they had heard, and the hours following were fraught with anxiety for them.

As the officer paused, a European man burst out pointing to Radhanath, "What's that native dog doing here? Why don't you shoot him? These bastards won't rest until they can repeat what they did at Bibighar."

Sara and Radhanath both recognized the speaker as the companion of the man Radhanath had punched earlier in the evening. Taking that man's cue, several other people hollered in a similar unruly vein. The officer that held the gong struck it again to bring order. "Please gentlemen. We have no time to waste. Proceed with the evacuation in a calm and organized fashion. Let the officers assist you. We are short-staffed. We need your cooperation to get through this. We have many more stops to make before our work is done tonight."

The people started to form a line to exit the restaurant. While Radhanath paid for their dinners, Sara collected her parasol from the doorman. When she spoke next, Radhanath caught a touch of annoyance in her voice, "Gosh, one more hoax. I am sure nothing is going to happen tonight. But we have to get out of here!"

Radhanath said, "I guess it's time for goodbye then. They will take you somewhere safe, I presume?"

Sara seemed unsure of what she was going to do next. Looking preoccupied, she asked, "And where will you go?"

Radhanath said, "Unfortunately, I won't be able to return to my rental at Beniapukur tonight."

As Sara turned to look at him questioningly, Radhanath explained, "They will definitely close Lower Circular Road down, which cuts access to my rental. And I can't get back to my office on Wood Street either – they won't let a native go through that side anymore. My best bet to exit the city is via Chowrungee, while it's still open. Things have changed these days. Calcutta is not safe for me right now."

Looking confused, Sara asked, "Not safe for you? Why not?"

The two had arrived at Evora's doorway by this time. As they passed, the officer supervising the evacuation spat, which landed close to Radhanath's boots. Flashing angry fire, Radhanath's eyes darted to the officer's face. The man had turned his eyes away, pretending to be busy guiding the British patrons leaving Evora toward the carriages. Turning his own face disgustedly away, Radhanath led Sara to the corner of the street in front of the restaurant and started to respond to her earlier question. It came out in a voice sharper than he had intended, "Miss, whether or not these alarms are hoaxes, it certainly creates opportunity for the British to abuse the occasion and seek revenge for what the mutineers have done. I can assure you that the curfew announcement will not reach everyone. People will be stranded in places where they aren't supposed to be. And if caught in the open, they can get shot. No one will ever question it."

Reading the shock on Sara's face, Radhanath elaborated, "Just a few days back, the battered body of a man from my locality was found on the street after one of these curfews. There's simply no telling what can happen. No one is held accountable."

Suddenly feeling tired and vexed, Radhanath said, "Why don't you go on, Miss Langley? Do take care. Hopefully, I will see you another day soon."

Sara bluntly insisted, "Well, if you need to get out of the city, where will you go?"

As the pressure to figure out exactly what to do next crowded his thoughts, Radhanath started to muse aloud, “I will head out via Chowrungee. It’s all I can do. If it was any earlier, I could’ve tried to go home to Chandannagar tonight. However, it’s too late. I’ll miss the last ferry. There’s a shady sort of inn I could try to get a room at, near Dumdum. But it’s not safe, and it’s really a dingy hellhole.” After trailing off, suddenly, Radhanath spoke with a soft chuckle, “Of course, if I am going as far out as that, I could very well go a little further and bunk at GTSI’s tower at Sukhchar. I have spent nights working there before.”

“Wouldn’t the tower be closed at this hour?” Worried about the developing situation, Radhanath had become distracted, thinking out loud for the past minute or so. He hadn’t realized he was being closely observed. With Sara’s voice piercing through his chain of thoughts, he turned to give her his undivided attention again.

“The tower is open and guarded round the clock. I have my GTSI badge on me, so I expect I will be allowed inside.” Curiously, Radhanath watched Sara’s resolute scrutiny of his plans.

“But I don’t have a badge. Will they let me in?” she asked mysteriously.

“I don’t understand,” retorted Radhanath, not entirely sure if he had heard her correctly.

Sara said, “I want to come with you. I love the idea of going to the GTSI tower right now.” Reminding Radhanath of the last occasion when their dinner at Evora was interrupted by the announcement of a curfew, she spoke with a touch of impatience, “They have had these silly hoaxes about a rebellion here at Calcutta so many times. I am not buying it. I have no desire to go spend the night in a crowded steamer right now.”

Gazing at Sara with an odd gleam in his eyes, Radhanath finally said, “Miss Langley, things are too uncertain for me at the moment. You will be much safer on one of those steamers under armed guard.”

Looking Radhanath in the eye, she firmly said, "Mr. Sikdar, thanks for your concern, but I can take care of myself. I was enjoying my time with you before this stupid alarm was sounded. Honestly, I have had enough of their fearmongering. I want to come with you. The idea of going to the GTSI tower at this time of the night, to watch the sleeping city from inside the tower, sounds absolutely fascinating! And look, the skies are clearing. The moon is rising. It could not be more perfect."

The ringing of a bell, as yet another carriage loaded with European passengers left for the safe zones, caused both of them to look in that direction. Radhanath turned back to the stubborn young lady, feeling torn. Suddenly, a rush of unfamiliar excitement coursed through his veins, and Radhanath found himself throwing caution to the winds, "You're on Miss Langley, let's get a *tanga* to take us up there then!"

Chapter Eighteen

21st August 1857, 6:30 PM

Meanwhile, at about the same time that Radhanath met Sara at Evora, a somewhat rattled Lawrence Cockerel stepped out of Reverend Stuart's house. He had been meaning to come see the Reverend lately. The inspector knew how much the mutiny weighed on the old man, especially the possibility of Calcutta falling to the rebels. Tonight, on his way home from the police station, Lawrence finally found time to stop by the vicarage. His meeting with Stuart didn't go well.

Earlier this morning, Gokul had also been to see the Reverend. He had grievously complained about Inspector Cockerel, relaying that Lawrence had almost choked him with his kerchief last week. Before he left, Gokul had filled the Reverend's head with how volatile Barrackpore was at this moment. Therefore, when Lawrence showed up, the agitated Stuart pretty much burst out at him. Stuart said, if not for the rain, he would have gone to see Lawrence by now. He insisted the inspector immediately hit Sepai Para with a search warrant. Based on what Gokul had said to him, the Reverend was convinced they were going to find weapons hidden there. Stuart lamented that if

Lawrence had not scared Gokul off with his drunken assault, Gokul would have gone to the inspector days ago with this critical information. As Stuart raged, Lawrence tried once or twice to get a word in, mainly to discredit Gokul's intel. Not only did the Reverend brush off the idea that these were false alarms, he grew indignant that Lawrence wasn't going to do a thing about Barrackpore. The poor inspector endured Stuart's tirade with tightlipped impatience. He was irritated that Gokul had filled the Reverend's ear with rubbish. No matter what he said, Lawrence found the father, who had lost his daughter and her family to the mutiny, impossible to placate.

It had started to drizzle by the time Lawrence stepped out from Stuart's. Fighting the feeling that his trip had been a waste of time, he hurried toward the *tanga* stand. Distractedly, he tried to remember something he thought he heard in the past hour from Stuart that had seemed important at the time. Just as he passed the grand Peepul near the *tanga* stand, it came to him. Gokul's reports mentioned a *zamindar* from the Dhanulia area – Chandrakanta Raychaudhuri. Apparently, that man had been spotted a number of times in the Sepai Para locality. Stuart's theory was the man must be inciting the rebels and funding their seditious enterprise; *what other business could a zamindar have there?* The inspector tried to imagine an affluent Bengali gentleman loitering in the shabby Sepai Para neighborhood. Perhaps this fact among all others warranted some kind of follow-up. Lawrence hadn't heard about this from any other source yet. Abruptly, the inspector decided he was going to swing by the Dhanulia *zamindar*'s estates. *It won't be much of a detour*, thought Lawrence, who was due at St Paul's Cathedral later tonight to meet the group he night-patrolled with. Since that wasn't until ten p.m., he had a couple of hours, at least, to check in with the *zamindar*.

Lawrence's *tanga* from the vicarage took over thirty minutes to arrive at Chandrakanta Raychaudhuri's family residence. In the meantime, after the brief drizzle, the rainclouds seemed in the mood for a pause. They were busy playing hide and seek; the winds blowing the occasional clump over the moon.

The *rajbàri* stood tall and fair with its front row of fluted Corinthian pillars glowing starkly in the moonlight. The rest of the house looked deserted and shrouded in relative darkness. Soon after the servant at the gate went inside to announce the visitor, a youngish *Dewan* appeared with a paraffin lamp to take Lawrence inside. As the man led the way along a veranda, Lawrence felt a little out of place with his wet shoes making an awkward noise on the sleek, Italian marble. He eyed the water-darkened, moon-washed courtyard to his right, astonished to find a peacock there, out on a nightly stroll. Then he walked into a luxurious living room, with oil painting covered walls and plush carpet, bathed in warm candlelight from the chandelier overhead. Irritated by the sight of his own scruffy reflection on the Belgian mirror hanging on the wall across from him, Lawrence lit a cheroot while he waited for the master of the house. He was a bit intimidated by the aura of money and privilege about the place. When the silk *dhuti panjabi* clad Chandrakanta finally walked in, the inspector sprang up without thinking. The dark-skinned, immaculately groomed curly-haired aristocrat, a far cry from the natives Lawrence was used to dealing with, greeted the inspector in impeccable English. Despite being surprised to see a police inspector in his house at this hour, Chandrakanta maintained a straight face. He answered each of Lawrence's innocuous questions patiently, waiting for the inspector to come out with whatever had actually brought him to the *zamindar*'s doorstep.

Lawrence, the man of law, had wanted to interrogate Chandrakanta, the suspect, but he struggled to assume the required high-handedness as he sat across from this well-educated, sophisticated man. At one point, a servant entered with a glass of *sherbet* for the guest. Lawrence picked up the drink without comment. After some chit chat, Lawrence finally asked his main question: "So Chandrakanta-*ji*, can I ask what has been taking you to the Sepai Para area of Barrackpore lately?"

Screwing his brows in apparent confusion, Chandrakanta commented, "Oh? Well, you see, some sepoys borrowed money through my estates. After

Mongol Pandey's execution, they seemed to have vanished. My men keep telling me they can't find anybody. I haven't seen a penny of what they owe me. When I heard that their families are still there, I showed up a couple times. I have no sympathy for that dishonest bunch. Thieves and liars, the lot of them!"

Pretending to reign himself in, a convincingly grumpy Chandrakanta then gently probed Lawrence, "However, why do you ask, Mr. Cockerel?"

Seeing Lawrence staring at him, Chandrakanta smoothly added, "I must admit I am impressed your men recognized me."

Choosing not to directly address Chandrakanta's comment, Lawrence looked down at the glass of *sherbet* in his hand, an enigmatic half-smile on his lips. His initial discomfort was morphing into a sort of mute recalcitrance. Chandrakanta's harsh words for the hapless folks that lived in Sepai Para had reminded Lawrence of Pannalal. And then, just as he felt irritated by the snooty aristocrat attacking one of those who he considered a friend, he remembered that he himself had a warrant out in Pannalal's name for aiding and abetting a *Sati* proceeding. Finishing the *sherbet* in his hand, Lawrence leaned forward to stub out the cheroot he had been smoking. And then, cutting his visit abruptly short, he stood up from the couch, ready to leave.

Lawrence had kept his *tanga* waiting while he met with the *zamindar*. Now he boarded it once more to take him to his quarters at Elysium Row for a quick bite before meeting with his night-patrol group. As the *tanga* hurried south, thoughts of the meeting with the *zamindar* swirled in the inspector's head. He wondered whether Chandrakanta had spoken the truth. Although he had caught himself reacting unpredictably to the natives of late, Lawrence still thought he understood them. But not Chandrakanta. That man was out of his league. The opulence in which Chandrakanta lived alienated Lawrence. The inspector felt instinctively suspicious of the bourgeois *zamindar,* even though he had discovered nothing concrete against the man. After some thought, Lawrence decided he wasn't going to disregard Stuart's warning entirely. He was going to take his patrol in the direction of the epicenter of these rumors – Barrackpore. As soon as he made that decision, Gokul's face came to his mind. Stuart had him installed in that area. If there was any truth to Stuart's theory about that *zamindar* conspiring to incite a rebellion, Gokul could be helpful. It occurred to Lawrence that with hard evidence in hand, not only could he stop the miscreants, but it could give him just the excuse he needed to throw that annoying bourgeois in jail. *That would be nice*, mused Lawrence nastily.

Meanwhile, as soon as Lawrence departed, Chandrakanta began to fret. *How much had the British figured about the mutineers' grand plan tonight?* Dubois, Chandrakanta, and a group of sepoys were due to set the GTSI tower ablaze in matter of hours now, kickstarting the Calcutta chapter of the rebellion. Ever since Chandrakanta started going to Sepai Para, he had his men spread rumors on what he was doing, to prevent too many questions. His cover story has been what he just told Lawrence. Now he wondered if it was good enough. What gave him confidence was Pannalal seemed not too worried. Pannalal insisted that none of those at Sepai Para were likely to blow the whistle. So, upon carefully going over his conversation with the inspector, Chandrakanta concluded the police didn't know anything concrete yet. Lawrence's demeanor for the entire time that he was with Chandrakanta was vaguely suspicious at best. In any case, it was rather late in the game for second thoughts. They had planned meticulously for tonight. Chandrakanta decided he had not seen or heard anything egregious enough for him to reconsider.

When the hour came upon him, Chandrakanta set out to meet Pannalal and his men. Having planned on avoiding the main road and using a route through the wilderness instead, Chandrakanta was on horseback tonight. He was worried with the rains starting earlier this evening. But thankfully, the rains had relented by the time he was ready to go, and the moonlight was adequate for him to see the trail. As his horse trotted along, Chandrakanta pondered over the events of this past week. Before he left, Nana sahib did have that secret meeting with the sepoys in Chandannagar. The men were thrilled to meet the legend in person. In his dialogue with the men, Chandrakanta witnessed Nana sahib playing upon the sepoys' religious sentiments, reminding them how their honor had been sullied by the East India Company's reckless deployment of the Enfield cartridges. Should they become successful, Nana sahib dangled the possibility of grand monetary returns. He also stoked their hurt pride, highlighting how poorly their loyalty had been rewarded by the Company, disarming and disbanding soldiers who fought side by side in the trenches with them. It was a learning moment for the more intellectually inclined Chandrakanta. The effect of Nana sahib's rhetoric on those who had come to meet the charismatic leader, including Pannalal, was unmistakable.

As Chandrakanta rode the tortuous paths going around the city, his thoughts turned to Dubois. Monsieur had asked his identity to be kept secret, especially from the sepoys. In fact, he had insisted everyone wear masks. It was clear that all he had signed up for was to light the tower. Then he wanted out. Dubois had already sent the material he was supposed to supply to Barrackpore. Tonight, per his plan, the sepoys were to wait near the tower, out of sight, ready with carts of paraffin-soaked mud, hay, and ingredients for the Greek Fire. Around midnight, Chandrakanta was to meet Dubois at the *tanga* stand near the tower, alone. The two would incapacitate the sentries guarding the tower before summoning the rest of the men. Then, while the men layered paraffin-soaked mud and hay on each floor of the tower, Dubois was going to prepare the Greek Fire. The men would then coat the walls of the building with the flammable liquid under Dubois' direction. Initially, Chandrakanta had resented Dubois rigidly calling all the shots, but he came around in the end. All that mattered was their rebellion's success. The brighter that tower burned, the better it was for them.

Chapter Nineteen

21st August 1857, 8:30 PM

Looking for a ride to take them to the GTSI tower at Sukhchar, Radhanath and Sara walked to the *tanga* stand at the intersection of Theatre Road and Chowrungee. With the curfew hanging over their heads, most *tanga* drivers were in a hurry to go home. The road closures meant that the tower at Sukhchar would have to be accessed via the native neighborhoods of Chitpur tonight, making it quite a long ride. After being refused several times, Radhanath finally found a *tanga* driver who agreed to go all the way. It was without a doubt the fare Radhanath named (almost thrice the regular amount) that thawed his reluctance. Soon as the price was settled, the driver could not resist revealing that he lived in the same direction, in fact beyond Sukhchar. But if not for them, he would have had to return with an empty carriage. The loquacious driver next inquired why the *memsahib* was going to the tower with Radhanath at this time of the night.

An amused Radhanath retorted that the *memsahib* did not like being imprisoned with the British; she had demanded to be taken to Sukhchar as soon as the curfew was announced. In reaction to his response, Radhanath observed a series of emotions play on the *tanga* driver's face. His initial wide-eyed disbelief morphed to empathy for Radhanath. *What could a man do, cornered by an unreasonable memsahib!* Then somehow sensing Radhanath wasn't being entirely serious, an injured look dawned on his face. And then, becoming stern all at once, the man turned away, his eyes on the road ahead, waiting for the two to board. Sara, who had been watching them, moved to climb inside the carriage. Radhanath followed, taking the seat next to Sara, leaving the seat facing them vacant. As soon as the two settled, the driver hit their horses. The beasts responded with a gallop, rushing down Chowrungee at top speed.

Sara's Bengali wasn't yet where she could entirely follow the conversation between Radhanath and their driver. However, she had caught enough to figure that the man had been a tad impertinent. Turning to Radhanath, she demanded to be told what was said and sat listening with a small smile playing at her lips. Afterward, she sat comfortably back into her seat, ready to enjoy the ride.

As they entered the dingy, native neighborhoods of Calcutta using the Kassitala-Chitpur Road, Sara eyed the rapidly changing scenery. With the rains stopped, people were out on the streets. It occurred to her that the curfew probably wasn't applicable here. As they passed the Kassitala shops (which got its name from the large number of butchers or *kasai* outlets in the area), Radhanath felt privately glad for the rain freshened air. It smelled much nicer than it usually did. Noticing a native inn that he hadn't known about go by, Radhanath thought, *it must do good business on nights such as this*. It was close enough to town to attract the natives caught in the curfew. Personally, he didn't expect this one to be any different from the one in Dumdum, which he had briefly considered for himself earlier tonight. These native inns were notorious for their small, hot, airless rooms, not particularly clean, and, most importantly, not safe. Their *tanga* continued on, passing shops selling saris, jewelry, and attar; most were in the process of closing down for the night. When they passed through the Kumartuli neighborhood, Radhanath noticed

Sara's eyes widen in awe, gawking at the unfinished, clay idols of gods and goddesses flanking both sides of the road.

Radhanath mused that he could not have anticipated the turn things took tonight, not in his wildest imagination. Sara's decision to come to the GTSI tower with him this late in the night, felt surreal. Radhanath could not help but admire her courage. It crossed his mind that ignoring the possibility of some kind of unrest despite the warnings from British police had perhaps not been a responsible thing to do. Sara's actions tonight echoed the same wildness of spirit that he had first encountered last year when she had suggested bringing the beehive down at that *shikar* party. His own faint objections had been swiftly overruled on both occasions. His heart began to race, something that had happened several times today, ever since he got together with her this evening. Radhanath stole a glance at the girl by his side – the one he now admitted to having fallen in love with. As their *tanga* passed by the Hooghly River, which hugs the contours of the city, Radhanath watched Sara gazing at the silhouette of the moonlit river. That same moonlight also fell on her cheeks creating a vision of incredible loveliness. He grew anxious, feeling displaced from the driver's seat of his own life, conscious of having little control over whatever happened next.

They raced down the increasingly deserted roads; by the time they crossed the circular canal via the Chitpur Bag Bajar Bridge to get on to BT Road, they'd left the last vestiges of the city behind. All they could see outside were bare fields, gleaming in the nightlight. The winds seemed to have dropped altogether. And just when it occurred to Radhanath that they hadn't spoken in a while, his eyes caught some lights moving on the road that curved ahead of them. Peeking out the window of the carriage, Radhanath saw what looked like a sizable procession carrying torches glowing in the dark, possibly headed toward them. Immediately, he felt a shiver go down his spine. *Who were these people? Could they be the ones about whom they were warned at Evora today?* Radhanath craned as much of his body as he could out through the window, his eyes peeled on trying to understand exactly what was happening. He shouted at the *tanga* driver, asking him to turn around and get out of the way of this procession, but the man seemed not to hear Radhanath over the noise that their carriage was making on the gravelly road.

Moving his body back inside the *tanga,* Radhanath helplessly turned toward Sara, who sat tensed, having noticed both the crowd and Radhanath's agitation. Clutching her shoulders urgently, Radhanath said, "Miss Langley, the warnings from the police may not have been a hoax after all. I am not entirely sure who we are seeing over there. For whatever reason, if I cannot get the *tanga* driver to stop, you should be ready. We will jump out from the carriage together."

Radhanath extended his left hand outside the carriage hitting as hard as he could, several times. He also started to kick the front wall of the carriage with his legs. Leaning out from the window on his side again, Radhanath saw he had attracted the driver's attention this time, and the man was looking at Radhanath curiously. Pointing anxiously to the crowd ahead, Radhanath wildly gesticulated that they should turn around. The expression that emerged on the *tanga* driver's face sank Radhanath's heart. Giving Radhanath a roguish smile, the driver turned his face away, continuing to move ahead.

He was going to let those men have a go at the memsahib!

Radhanath stared at the back of the man's head, paralyzed by the thought of Sara in the hands of the mob. Then, just as he braced himself for the next step he glanced at the mob one last time, hoping to gauge how close they were at this point.

A sudden jolt of doubt coursed through him. The crowd had indeed come closer, and in the light of the torches they held, Radhanath could now see the faces of those in the crowd. They were painted in loud colors; many were masked, sporting faces of animals or gods and goddesses. Eyeing their evidently playful bearing, a quick epiphany took a huge load off Radhanath's chest. There was no need to fear these men. They were the *Shong*! The last time he saw them was at the Charak fair with their anti-British act after the Mongol Pandey incident. This group tonight wasn't nearly as politically colored as that last one. Radhanath suspected they had been chartered by a rich *babu* for personal entertainment. The more he realized that they weren't in any real danger, the more relieved he felt, and an involuntary, awkward snicker emerged out of him. That's when he remembered Sara and pulled himself back inside the carriage.

Looking boldly at Radhanath, Sara said, "I am ready to jump whenever you say."

But then, as Radhanath explained things to her, she grew visibly relaxed.

As their *tanga* started to slow, Radhanath glanced out his window and noted that they were nearly at the frontier of the procession. The *Shong* that initially appeared to be blocking the entire breadth of the road, were parting to the sides to make way for their carriage. As the noise reduced with the slowing of the *tanga*, Radhanath heard their *tanga* driver calling to him. Popping his head out the window again, Radhanath saw the man pointing toward the procession with a bright, impudent smile. *The driver had known what the procession was about, perhaps because he was regular on this route*, realized Radhanath. He sat back, relieved, and his eyes strayed back to Sara, watching the painted, masked men in their fancy clothes with rapt attention.

Suddenly, the lady shrieked, with a little girl's enthusiasm, "What is that?"

Radhanath tried to follow her gaze and identify which specific character had caught her attention. When he couldn't, he asked, "Which one?"

With her eyes sparkling in excitement, Sara turned to Radhanath and beckoned him to move closer with her hand. "Come and have a look," she said.

As Radhanath leaned towards Sara's window, she pointed with her finger, "That one!"

For a moment Radhanath, much too conscious of Sara's face next to his, found it difficult to concentrate. A sweet smell seemed to pervade his nose messing with his focus. When he understood that she was pointing to a character wearing several fake human faces on both sides of his head, he slid back into his portion of the seat and said, "Oh! That?"

Still reeling from the effects of the scare they had just had, he answered distractedly, "Uh, that is an evil character in Hindu mythology, the Ravana, easily identified by those ten heads." Then hastily, he blurted, "That was something, wasn't it? For a moment there, I thought we were done for tonight." Sara turned to watch Radhanath with a puzzling expression. It took a few moments for the meaning of it to dawn upon Radhanath. *What horrible memories must this scare evoke for a Britisher with first-hand experience of fleeing mutineers!*

Once the *tanga* arrived at Sukhchar, Sara and Radhanath deboarded, careful to avoid the muddy puddles from the recent rains. The *tanga* driver, beaming unreservedly, was eager to explain the late hour *Shong*. His account was more or less in line with what Radhanath had already surmised – the merriment for the common people had been sponsored by a local *zamindar* to celebrate his son's marriage. The driver's face brightened as he got paid. However, in the very next moment, becoming conscious of the sentries from the tower coming up behind them, the driver appeared eager to leave. Bobbing his head side to side in farewell, the man hastily departed.

By this time, the sentries from the GTSI tower, who wanted to investigate the visitors at this odd hour, had come nearby. One of them recognized Radhanath and produced a military style curtsy. In the past couple months, when Radhanath was down here, he had often encountered this man Bhajan Singh on duty. Radhanath told Bhajan Singh that he had work at the tower tonight that could take a while. And then pointing to Sara, Radhanath said he would like Miss Langley to accompany him inside as his guest. Neither of the native guards on duty had any objections to letting a European woman in. As the two walked toward the tower, Radhanath briefly touched the GTSI badge sitting in his pocket; he had not been asked to show it. Neither had he been asked for anything, written or otherwise, for Sara.

Before they entered, the two stood looking at the square, white-washed building about seventy feet high, bathed in moonlight. Sara counted at least four floors with narrow rectangular openings cut into each wall to serve as windows. There seemed just one solitary lamp that glowed near the top of the tower, fixed to its street-facing wall. There was no wind at all at the moment.

Turning to Radhanath, Sara said, “You know, I’ve always enjoyed sitting on treehouses. It is amazing how far you can see as soon as you are positioned at a height above the ground, especially when there is nothing around for miles to obstruct the view.”

Nodding in agreement, Radhanath said, “We tell all our visitors that on a bright day, you can see up to St. Paul’s Church near Park Street from the top floor of this tower. I have. However, in this darkness, you won’t see very far, just a moonlit horizon.”

Entering the tower, Sara found herself in a chamber, approximately ten feet by ten feet. It was lit by a solitary paraffin lamp placed on wooden racks stuck to the wall. As she stood near the door, Radhanath went up to the racks to light one of the spare lamps to take up with them. Sara eyed the uneven bricks on the bit of the bare wall illuminated by the light from the one lamp burning. She soon discovered there was a ladder at one corner of the room. Moving to stand directly under the stairwell, she looked up to the top of the tower, but it was too dark to see all the way. In the feeble light that escaped up the stairwell, all she could see was the rough underside of the floor at the next level, and the dark hole through which the ladder passed beyond.

A paraffin lamp in hand, Radhanath came and stood next to Sara. After reminding her to be careful not to trip on the hem of her skirt, they started their climb up the ladder with Radhanath leading the way. Radhanath warned Sara about bats that lived inside the tower, so that she wouldn’t be caught off guard if one or two decided to fly by them. He also assured her that these creatures didn’t attack humans. Sara quickly discovered why Radhanath was speaking softly. A normally spoken word reverberated with a large echo inside the cavity created by the stairwell.

It was an arduous climb, to say the least. Sara watched their larger-than-life shadows dance ominously on the walls from the light in Radhanath's hand. Several times, unused to climbing so many stairs at once, Sara had to ask Radhanath to pause to catch her breath. At one point, a group of the rudely disturbed bats did go scurrying past them, close enough for Sara to feel a gentle breeze on her skin. Sara, who by this time had begun to feel as if her whole life was reduced to taking one mechanical step after another, was swiftly reminded by Radhanath not to get distracted. When they finally covered the four, straight flight of ladders to reach the topmost level, Sara could barely move her legs. Radhanath, perhaps because he was used to climbing these stairs, did not seem as affected.

Leaning tiredly against the back wall of the tiny room where she stood in semi-darkness, Sara noted the furnishings. A wooden desk with writing paraphernalia and a pitcher of water stood to one side. A massive, strange-looking instrument sat next to the window on the front wall with a stool by it. A white sheet covered cot stood against the back wall of the room, perhaps for the surveyors to take breaks between the long hours they slogged here. Placing the paraffin lamp he held on the desk, Radhanath lowered its flame. Then he opened the windows on all four walls of the square space. Soft moonlight flooded the interiors, along with the smell of moist night air.

Turning to Sara, Radhanath said, "Here we are, miss."

Sara was eyeing the massive instrument that certainly dominated the room. Mounted on a four-legged cast-iron structure, standing as tall as a man, the complicated-looking apparatus was made of solid metal with a round wheel-like base. Two narrowing columns rose from that base to support a pointed cannon-like arm, which Sara recognized as a telescope.

Seeing her walk over to the instrument with evident curiosity, Radhanath also went up to it. "This is a theodolite. It is the single most important instrument in a surveyor's arsenal. Mind you, this is very heavy. In fact, it needs to be heavy so that minor vibrations do not affect our measurements."

Pointing to the cannon-like extension, Radhanath continued, "And this is a telescope. It enables us to look at objects at large distances, so that we can measure the angle at which that object resides." Radhanath moved the telescope toward Sara inviting her to look through it.

Before doing so though, Sara went to the window where the telescope was pointing. Leaning on her arms, she looked out through the opening, trying to get a sense of what was visible to her naked eye from that vantage. She eyed the fields, the cluster of trees, and the Hooghly River in the distance. Then she came over to put her eyes on the mouth of the telescope, pulling the stool near the theodolite to sit herself. Radhanath added, "Although this is not an astronomical telescope, you can point it at the moon if you like. You can turn the eyepiece any way you wish, sideways or up and down. In this darkness though, there isn't probably as much to see on the ground, as there is in the sky."

The first thing Sara noticed as she stared through the telescope, were the black lines forming the crosshair. As she tried to turn the telescope toward the moon per Radhanath's suggestion, a sudden embarrassment flooded her mind. All her prior memories of handling telescopes were from stargazing with Dubois. Not appreciating those thoughts intruding upon her in this moment, Sara hastily turned the telescope lower, pointing it randomly at the horizon. *Of course, there wasn't much to see on the horizon this time of the night.*

Sara was about to turn away, when at the very bottom of the view, she discovered an orangish dot of light, right next to the vertical axis. For a moment, she stared hard at it, trying to identify what it might be. Radhanath, who didn't expect anything of relevance to be there at this time, light-heartedly inquired, "Exactly what are you looking at, Miss Langley?" Giving in to his amusement, he further added, "There are at best owls on those treetops where you're looking! Is that what you're hoping to spot?"

Sara did not hear Radhanath because by now, to her utter amazement, she found that the mysterious dot of light had started to move. With a racing heart, Sara double checked her initial impression. Yes, that thing was slowly and steadily moving upward, creeping along the vertical line that formed the crosshair. In a voice hoarse with excitement, Sara asked, "What is that orange light? It's rather low, close to the horizon. It is rising!" Still hunched over the telescope, she turned to glance at Radhanath.

"Orange light?" repeated Radhanath, perplexed.

Hastily, he came over to look through the telescope himself. Indeed, he saw the light. It seemed to be floating upward just as Sara had reported. Feeling Sara's hand gripping him in excitement, he moved to allow her to look through the telescope again. *What was that light?* His mind raced over the possibilities to explain what they were seeing. Meanwhile, the steadily moving luminous spec had Sara captivated. When it reached about three-fourth of the way to the top, Sara found it had stopped moving. And then, she saw it was twinkling, not unlike stars. Sara wondered whether it had been twinkling all along.

Looking at Radhanath huddled next to her, she relayed, "It stopped moving!"

As Radhanath moved in to look through the telescope one more time, he started to speak, "Miss Langley, I do believe, we have been incredibly fortunate tonight!" Turning to her to continue, Radhanath said, "That dot of light you saw… How do I say this? That light isn't real. It doesn't exist where you think you see it."

Furrowing her brows, Sara asked, a bit agitated, "What do you mean?"

Radhanath waited silently allowing the suspense to build, his eyes twinkling in the moonlight. Then he started to explain, "We witnessed a very interesting phenomenon! You do know of mirages, right?" Sara bobbed her head in agreement.

"What we saw is similar. That dot of light is what we call a false image. Just like the mirage, it is not present where you think it is. In fact, that light, believe it or not, wasn't moving at all!" stated Radhanath mysteriously.

Sara started to protest, "Say what? But how can that be? We both saw it moving!"

"Miss Langley," began Radhanath, "I have seen this phenomenon only a few other times in my life, not here, but in other parts of the country. When you first mentioned the light, I wasn't sure what you were seeing. But then I figured it out. There's a semaphore tower at Uludanga, on the other side of the Hooghly River, exactly in the direction in which the telescope is pointing. If I am not mistaken, that light you saw is from that tower."

Sara asked, "You mean like this light here?" referring to the lamp that she had found burning on the roadside wall, near the top of the tower at Sukhchar upon arrival today. As Radhanath nodded in affirmation, Sara broke into an animated chuckle, her face bright with amusement. "Rady, that is totally insane. Are you seriously suggesting that that thing we clearly saw moving, was actually a light like this one, solidly attached to a concrete tower? That's impossible!"

Savoring the look of indignation on her face, Radhanath responded, "Miss Langley, I know the geography around here like the back of my hand. There is a huge mango grove where you are looking that blocks the view. Certainly, the Uludanga tower that stands beyond the grove cannot be seen from here. However, that is also the only tall structure with a light on it for miles in that direction. The light you saw has to be from that tower."

Sara looked back, her eyes narrowed, trying to make sense of what Radhanath was telling her. He further explained, "Something rare happened tonight. My theory is that the atmosphere in this area tonight achieved a special condition that allowed the light from that tower to travel through its layers and bend like an arch over all the intervening trees. That's why it was possible for your telescope to intercept it. Of course, since we are used to seeing light travel in a straight line, our eyes are fooled into thinking that the light is coming from the peak point of that arch. The source of the light thus appears to be located at a point higher than the height of the mango grove. It is quite an incredible phenomenon, Miss Langley; it's called the Fata Morgana."

As the astonished Sara looked at Radhanath intently, his lips curved into a shy smile. He cited, "I've never been outside India, but in the East Indies, I have heard people report sightings of ships flying in the sky. That's also caused by a type of Fata Morgana. I can't believe we—"

Before Radhanath could finish his sentence, Sara suddenly exclaimed, "Flying Dutchman! You mean the myth of the Flying Dutchman, right?" Excitedly, she continued, "I do believe we are talking of the same thing. There is this legendary ghost ship, the Flying Dutchman; sightings of it in the sky are still considered a bad omen, a harbinger of ill luck, by sailors in the East Indies. I had vaguely known that there was supposed to be a scientific explanation for that myth."

Before Radhanath could respond, Sara continued musing to herself out aloud, "So the light bent, leaping over the obstacles. And we saw something that is blocked by the obstacles, at a falsely elevated position. I am still confused though, why did it appear to be moving?"

Abruptly standing up with excitement, Sara said, "Wait, don't tell me. Is it because, when we were looking through the telescope, the atmosphere was in the process of changing to this special condition, such that it continuously altered the path of the light from that tower to here?"

Nodding his head to confirm, Radhanath further added, "Yes, in real time. And because the path of the light was changing, the apparent location of the source of the light was changing continuously as well, giving the dot the appearance of movement."

With her eyes glowing excitedly, Sara started to gradually raise her hands, palms upturned, "I can totally imagine, a ship, rising up from the seas into the skies. Whoosh! Oh, how spectacular!"

Then, she went on to quickly summarize, "So this is similar to what we were discussing at Evora then, isn't it? Light changed directions, straying from its usual path. And this time, it allowed us to see something that we cannot see under normal circumstances."

Radhanath elaborated, "And per what we discussed before, the light is bending to select…"

"The quickest path!" they completed in unison.

Narrowing her eyes again, she asked, "Er, why? Why is the bent path the quickest? It's longer, isn't it? But even then, it's quicker, because…"

Radhanath explained, "In this case, the longer path is quicker because in this special atmospheric condition, what happens is the following: The temperature near the Earth becomes colder than the temperature up at higher elevations. As a result, the warmer upper layers are suddenly less dense than the lower, colder layers. Light takes advantage of this to minimize its travel time, going upward through the less dense portions faster, before turning back to get to the telescope, effectively bending like an arch around the obstacles in its path that would normally block the light."

Sara asked, "Did it happen because of the rains?"

Radhanath said, "That's a good question. It may or may not be related. We can't predict when this condition occurs."

Nodding in understanding, Sara bent to put her eyes to the telescope one last time. The dot was still there. As she straightened, she ran her hands through her hair sweeping them to one side, walking over to the narrow cot in the room. Plopping herself on it, she stretched her legs out in front, contentedly. One side of her was shrouded in darkness, while the other was lit by a shaft of soft moonlight. Radhanath thought she looked completely enchanting. He felt the tower he had spent so much time in, was changed with this exquisite vision of her being here – now seared forever in his brain. Radhanath leaned back on the wooden desk, half-sitting on its edge. Sara moved her head to glance at him, her eyes glistening in the moonlight. He noted the beginnings of that faintly defiant expression that has happened several times tonight. He knew it meant she was trying to concentrate.

"You had to apply corrections to the measurements of Mount Everest to account for the bending of light, right?" she verified.

Nodding in agreement, Radhanath confirmed, "Yes, as light passed through the ever-changing layers of the atmosphere, it shifted the image of the peak around, causing errors in the direct measurements. It was a major headache for me."

Leaning back on her hands on the cot, Sara murmured, "However, in this case, the bending of light allowed us to see something that we can't see under normal circumstances."

Suddenly, Radhanath became acutely aware of the outline of her youthful body wrapped in the purple-blue silk, accentuated by the provocative pose Sara struck in that moment. Simultaneously, he also caught a confusing change in the tone of her voice. The combination stopped him from offering a response. He eyed her searchingly instead, trying to understand the change.

"Isn't nature enigmatic, Mr. Sikdar? Sometimes she is generous and revealing, showing you things that you cannot otherwise see, like the exquisite Fata Morgana! At other times, not so much, like choosing to conceal the true height of Mount Everest from direct observation," whispered Sara softly.

Radhanath found himself unable to look away. The magic in her eyes had him pinned. He approached the cot, conscious that despite his coming closer, Sara did not sit up, as if daring him. Bending to bring his face close to hers, he growled softly, "Why does nature remind me of someone I know, Miss Langley? Beautiful and enigmatic?"

Without pausing for breath, he challenged, "Why are you here, Sara Langley?"

Holding his gaze, Sara responded, "To know the man who discovered the tallest point on Earth!"

Desire stirred in Radhanath's blood as he looked into Sara's eyes and felt himself drowning. He touched her pale cheek with his fingers and began tracing a line to her trembling lower lip, where he let them rest a moment. Then, moving further down her exposed neck, his fingers came to rest at the neckline of her dress. He could feel her erratic pulse, promising him the earth and the moon.

Restlessly bringing his eyes back to hers, Radhanath asked, "You want to know me? Is it a wise choice? Why risk your safety with this Indian man in these uncertain times?" Her lips stiffening with disdain, Sara raised a hand to fondly touch Radhanath's face.

"I am not afraid!" she said.

Raising both her hands to cup his face, she sat up and moved to touch her lips to his. The sweet smell of her that he'd caught whiffs of in the carriage earlier, enveloped his senses. Abruptly breaking away, Sara stood up, and then slowly started to undress. Radhanath watched her with bated breath. When her clothes lay in a heap at her feet, he peeled his own shirt off and threw it on the floor. Then with both hands, he pulled Sara's naked body close. Her softness seemed to melt against the hard lines of his manhood. His left hand snaked to tightly embrace her waist and his right hand moved to hold her head as he passionately kissed her mouth, twisting his fingers through her tresses. Coming up for air, Sara moved her head to rest against Radhanath's broad-shouldered, brown torso. As her nose grazed the matted hair of his chest, she caught the warm scent of him, that she found both erotic and oddly comforting.

The two made love on the narrow cot. Later, as Sara lay on Radhanath's bare chest, he gently caressed her soft, smooth body, unable to stop, his heart overflowing with happiness. The clouds outside had started to rumble, promising more rain.

Chapter Twenty

22nd August 1857, 12:00 AM

It was close to midnight when Radhanath and Sara sat up on the top floor of GTSI's observation tower at Sukhchar, interrupted by the door to the tower squeaking open four floors below them. The noise was loud enough for them to hear over the rainclouds growling in the background. As they dressed hastily wondering who it could be, they heard footsteps coming up the ladder. Radhanath raised the flame of the paraffin lamp. Sara glanced at him askance, wondering if he was feeling embarrassed to be discovered here with her at this hour. Both assumed, whoever it was, must work for the GTSI since the sentries had not stopped them. Neither were prepared for the pistol toting masked intruder who appeared at the head of the stairwell. As Radhanath and Sara's hearts thumped with shock, they heard a very familiar male voice exclaim, "You!" Paralyzed, they watched the unexpected visitor, struggling to remove the black cloth covering his face.

When the man's face was finally revealed, an astonished Sara whispered, "Dubois!"

A few minutes ago, with the chloroform Dubois supplied, he and Chandrakanta had incapacitated the sentries outside the tower. Now, as Chandrakanta stood on watch, Dubois had come to confirm that the tower was unoccupied, intending to vacate it at gunpoint if necessary. After, they were going to summon the sepoys waiting in the nearby woods to go about setting the tower ablaze. Meanwhile, Dubois had a private *tanga,* with his change of clothes for the ball afterward, stowed away at some distance from the tower; a boat also waited on the banks of the Hooghly River to ferry him to Chandannagar as soon as his job here was done.

Looking blankly from Sara to Radhanath to Sara again, Dubois burst out, "Didn't the *tanga* driver meet you at Evora?" The desperation in his voice ricocheted jarringly along the length of the stairwell.

Taken aback, Sara bluntly responded, "Well, I changed my mind. What are you doing here with a gun and a mask? Why aren't you in Chandannagar?"

"*Sacrebleu*! You changed your mind!" Frustratedly, Dubois repeated after Sara. Then, turning to Radhanath, he said, "Rady, I don't know what she is doing here with you. Just take her and leave. Don't you have a house in Chandannagar? Go to Chandannagar. Whatever you do, don't go anywhere near Calcutta tonight."

Confused by the seemingly ludicrous turn of events, and irked by Dubois' manner toward Sara, Radhanath sneered, "What the hell is going on, Dubois?"

Breaking eye contact, "Mutineers from Barrackpore are marching to Calcutta. They'll take Fort William tonight," revealed Dubois curtly.

The shock of the news sobered Radhanath. From the corner of his eyes, he noticed the blood drain from Sara's face. His voice ice-cold now, Radhanath persisted, "How do you know this? Are you with them?

By now, Sara had grasped that the ball at Chandannagar had merely been a ruse to get her out of town. With a dark foreboding filling her heart, Sara asked, "Dubois, what are you doing here at this hour?"

Dubois retorted with uncharacteristic derision, "I could ask the same!" Taking a moment to compose himself, he said, "Look, you must go now." Jerking his head toward the tower's exit, Dubois said, "Go! Please go."

"Answer my question," demanded Radhanath irritably. "Are you with the mutineers?"

With impatience of his own, Dubois shot back, "Oh *Mon Dieu*, you listen to me carefully now. I don't have all night to talk. I am here to set this tower ablaze. That's the signal to kickstart the Calcutta chapter of the mutiny. Your friend Chan-dru-can-ta is waiting outside to help me. And don't waste your breath about it. We are going to do this, with or without your blessing."

Dazedly, Sara mumbled, "Tonight's warning wasn't a hoax!" She was finding it unfathomable that Dubois had joined hands with the mutineers after what they had been through together.

"Chandrakanta with the rebels! I should have guessed." Radhanath muttered, low under his breath. And then, taking a step toward Dubois, he tautly questioned, "What's in it for you? You want to burn this tower down? For God's sake, you work for the GTSI!"

Dubois shot back, "I believe in the Indian rebellion to which your countrymen – not mine – yours, are sacrificing blood and sweat. And there you are, pontificating, not able to see beyond your nose! Has it ever occurred to you that this tower is a brazen symbol of British rule on a land to which they have no right?"

Unable to contain her agitation, Sara interrupted. "Dubois, you're not a man that engages in wanton acts of destruction. I know you. Haven't you heard what they're doing to these insurgents? For heaven's sake, you will be executed. Let's do the sensible thing here; let's all leave."

Glancing coldly at Sara, Dubois said, "Don't patronize me!" Sighing disappointedly, he added, "You should've stuck to the plan we made. I hope you don't end up paying with your life for the poor judgement you showed."

Ignoring Dubois, Sara turned to Radhanath and pleaded, "He doesn't know what he is doing."

The censure in Radhanath's eyes sobered the girl. Her soft corner for Dubois had become impossible to ignore. The awkwardness in her manner underlined the nature of her affections.

"I disagree, Miss Langley. Monsieur Dubois knows. He has made a conscious choice to break the law. This whole enterprise is criminal; it's irresponsible. This tower is an edifice to man's intellectual aspirations. It's dishonest to politicize it," snapped Radhanath.

Dubois bristled, "Don't talk to the woman. Talk to me. I am right here. You think you're this great man of science, don't you? Well, let me break it to you – you are a blind, blithering idiot. You refuse to recognize how your British colleagues see you. Open your eyes and look around, Rady Sikdar. They think of you as a talented freak from an ignorant culture that they consider beneath them. You are a man that uses his hand to wash his black arse. That's who they see in your black face," sniggered Dubois.

Desperately, Sara shouted, "Dubois, what has gotten into you tonight?"

"No, no. Let him speak," Radhanath cut in.

Exhaling noisily, Dubois tucked the mask he was clutching in his hands into his trouser pocket. Having let off the steam that had abruptly built up inside him, he resumed, "Look Rady, I don't hate you. I have more respect for you than a lot of your GTSI cronies. But like your friend waiting outside, I feel frustrated, frustrated to stand by and watch how blind you are. The GTSI doesn't give two hoots about you. Not a soul will speak of you, of your contribution, or of your mathematical genius, the day you leave your precious GTSI. Already, there are those who are itching to bury you alive."

With an evil snicker, Dubois elaborated, pointing his finger toward Radhanath, "I have heard them say they're going to strike your name from all future editions of your precious Survey Manual. They will, however, keep those chapters you poured your soul into writing. All your hard work will be forgotten just like that!" said Dubois, snapping his fingers.

Radhanath moved a step closer to Dubois, towering over the shorter man as he spoke through clenched teeth, "You, Monsieur Dubois, have no understanding of what it means to serve science. My black face pities you! It's not about you or me or sycophancy to the British. It's about unravelling nature's truth. Scientists and engineers dedicate their lives to that purpose. That's why I care about this tower. That's why I care about the theodolite you stand next to, with total disregard. You of all people should've understood the significance of this place. Instead, you propose to destroy it with those who haven't a clue of what this is all about. Shame on you!"

Moving toward Dubois, Sara turned him by his shoulders to face her. Taking one of his hands between hers, she implored, "Listen to me, Francois. You must give up this idea of helping the rebels and come away with us right now."

Forcefully, Dubois disengaged himself. Moving back unexpectedly, he raised his pistol, swinging the gun in an arc, pointing first at Sara, and then at Radhanath. Then he said, "Get out! Now!"

Unmistakable sounds of gunshots filled the air at that precise moment, startling the trio. Sara rushed to the window on the street-facing wall and attempted to peer outside. However, the rain clouds they had been hearing for some time now, had covered up the moon. Sara could only see vague silhouettes moving in the darkness.

Looking baffled by the intrusion, Dubois muttered, "I don't understand the gunshots. The sentries are down already. These can't be the sepoys. We haven't summoned them yet."

Turning to Sara, Radhanath commanded, "Let's get the hell out of here. If we aren't already too late!"

Taking the paraffin lamp, he walked to the head of the ladder and started to descend. Sara, then Dubois, followed behind him. They'd just gotten down one floor when they heard the door to the tower thrown open and obvious sounds of people entering. As the three froze on the ladder, uncertain of their next move, Radhanath saw British police holding torches and guns come into view at the bottom of the stairwell. At the same time, a bullet whizzed past Radhanath. One of the officers had just tried to shoot the Indian holding the light on the top of the tower. The three instinctively jumped away from the ladder, onto the adjacent wooden platform of the third floor.

"Freeze, it's the police!" they heard a terse British voice command them.

When the police climbed up to their level, light from the torches they held fell on the three. The two officers that had come up the ladder gawked with wild surprise. They were a peculiar motley indeed – an Indian man with two Europeans, including a woman! While the rest continued to climb up the ladder to check the floor above, two men stepped on to the wooden floor to remain on guard with them. At this juncture, Inspector Cockerel emerged from the floor below.

Spotting Sara and Dubois, the incredulous inspector exclaimed, "Goodness! What are you doing here?" And then as his inquiring eyes took Radhanath in, he said, "And who the devil is this? He hasn't hurt you, has he?"

Dubois threw a wild look at Sara. When Sara spoke next, Radhanath could scarcely believe his ears. "Inspector," began the lady. Pointing to Radhanath she said, "Mr. Sikdar is an employee at GTSI. You see, Dubois and I left Calcutta as soon as the curfew was declared. We have invitations to a midnight ball happening at Chandannagar tonight. Since we had time before we are due there, we came here for Dubois to catch up on his work. Mr. Sikdar was working here when we arrived a while ago."

Lawrence turned to look at Radhanath in silence. Then he asked if Radhanath had any proof of his official status. Returning Radhanath's badge after a careful scrutiny, Lawrence turned to Sara, with a half-serious protest, "So you simply decided to ignore the curfew?"

With a nervous shrug, Sara defended, "Well, nothing has come off these warnings in the past. Besides the curfew was only for Calcutta, isn't it? We were going in the other direction."

Radhanath stood stunned; not only did Sara smoothly create an alibi for Dubois regardless of his culpability, but she also irresponsibly implicated him in that lie. *Had she any idea what she was playing with? And what were her plans to explain Chandrakanta? She had either completely forgotten or willfully decided to deny any knowledge.*

"You're quite a romantic miss. Adventurous too, I daresay!" said Lawrence, his voice now laced with sarcasm. The officers who had gone to check the floor above were coming down. They informed Lawrence that they had seen nothing suspicious upstairs. After they passed, Lawrence turned to Dubois and challenged, "You don't look like you were going to a ball, monsieur. Care to explain?"

Dubois laughed a short nervous laugh before responding, "Officer, we have a *tanga* waiting outside with a change of clothes for me. And there's a boatman by the riverfront you can question. He will tell you he's been reserved to take us to Chandannagar at one a. m. today."

"Hmm," said Lawrence. After a pause in which he stood thinking, Lawrence looked up and said, "Sorry Mr. Dubois, Miss Langley. You have chosen a terrible day for your ball! The native sepoys are up in arms tonight, keen to repeat the massacres they perpetrated in the North."

With an imperceptible tremble in his voice, Dubois asked, "What do you mean? We heard the gunshots. What's happened?"

Turning to Dubois, Lawrence said, "Would you believe that the sepoys were plotting to burn this tower down?!"

"Burn this tower down?" Dubois echoed Lawrence's words while Radhanath's eyes burned a hole on his face.

Lawrence elaborated, "Well, the natives have always hated these towers the GTSI puts up. They believe the surveyors have an ulterior motive with their telescopes – wanting to peer into Indian homes, gawk at the Indian women. Obviously, the decision to take this tower out is a symbolic strike against the empire. Fortunately, I was on my way to the cantonment at Barrackpore when we found a suspicious group of twenty or so, standing outside the tower. As soon as we neared, they opened fire on us. However, we managed to subdue them. I have yet to get the complete picture. There's no sign of the sentries that are supposed to be on guard. If they're found alive, they should be able to provide more clarity. From what I understand, the ringleader had come down before the others to clear the coast. The sepoys seem to think the leader was supposed to meet a second-in-command here."

Abruptly, Lawrence turned to Radhanath, eyeing him doubtfully for a few seconds. "If this isn't the man, then I don't know who that is yet," Lawrence mumbled. Then shrugging his shoulders, the inspector added, "Of course, it's quite possible that this second man was a no show tonight."

Lawrence resumed, "Anyway. When he was ready, the ringleader was supposed to signal for the rest." With a smirk, he alleged, "Well, let's just say, discipline isn't their forte. The lot of them showed up before they were summoned. Apparently, with their main man delayed, they decided to come out and have a look. We found the leader huddled with the sepoys when we arrived on scene. He was about to raise his rifle, but luckily our bullets hit him before he could open fire."

It wasn't hard to deduce Lawrence had just declared Chandrakanta dead. Simultaneously with that thought, Dubois also felt relief realizing Lawrence was looking for a native as the second-in-command. His insistence on remaining anonymous was paying dividends.

At this point, somebody said something downstairs, and the policemen, standing at various positions along the stairwell, relayed the information up to Lawrence. It was starting to rain again, not too hard yet, but they couldn't stand indefinitely in the rain. What should they do with the prisoners? Indicating that he was coming, Lawrence turned to Dubois and Sara to share one last detail,

"The strangest thing is, I had just met the man, the late ringleader, earlier this evening. Chandrakanta Raychaudhuri of Dhanulia – one of those filthy rich, bourgeois *zamindars*! Good riddance, I say!"

Sara and Dubois stared transfixed at Lawrence. Neither dared to look at Radhanath. Oblivious to the abrupt stiffness that had come over the three of them, Lawrence turned to Dubois and said, "I am afraid your work here is done tonight. You must evacuate, immediately." Avoiding looking directly at Radhanath, he flung the phrase, "You too!" in his general direction. Then, becoming irritated by the intense manner in which Radhanath was looking at him, Lawrence turned to Dubois with the question, "Are you sure he isn't with the rebels? Wears that same arrogant look I've seen on the likes of that dead *zamindar* downstairs!"

Tersely Dubois responded, "I know this man, Inspector Cockerel. He is GTSI's chief mathematician."

Grunting, Lawrence turned on his heels, leading the way down the ladder. Mechanically, Radhanath followed them, going behind Sara and Dubois.

Chandrakanta no more? The horror of it slithered inside Radhanath like a snake. As they exited the tower, a drop of rain touched his cheeks. From the size and feel of the drop, Radhanath knew that heavier rain was coming. Radhanath's eyes fell on the row of native prisoners, made to kneel by the side of the road, their hands and feet bound with twine. British officers and civilians from Lawrence's group of vigilantes stood with guns and batons in hand, guarding the prisoners. Horses tied to various trees around this cluster neighed softly, shifting uneasily from feet to feet. Then, as his eyes moved up, Radhanath saw his childhood friend, Chandrakanta, prominently strung up, hanging from the branch of a tree. Shining in the light of the torches, his dark lifeless face, framed by an unruly lock of curls, drooped at an awkward angle. Lawrence's men had made a fine example of his bloodied dead body – a reminder to one and all of the fate that awaits those who challenge the might of the Raj. Radhanath noticed the soldiers hanging nooses from several other branches, leaving little to imagination on what they intended to do with the rest of the men.

Radhanath's feet started to walk of its own accord toward the tree from which Chandrakanta was hanging, leaving Sara and Dubois behind. No sooner had he taken a few steps, he felt a strong blow to his face from the butt of a gun. He fell on the wet ground, his nose bleeding. The policeman who hit him, landed a kick on his ribcage for good measure, snarling, "Why isn't this dog restrained yet?"

Meanwhile, Sara had rushed to Radhanath's side. She knelt beside him, laying her hands protectively on his body. With haughty annoyance, she spoke to the policeman, "He is not with the rebels. He works for the GTSI." When Sara tried to help Radhanath up, she found him recoiling from her touch. Lawrence, who had noticed Radhanath's interest in Chandrakanta's corpse, now came forward.

"Did you know this man?" Lawrence asked Radhanath roughly.

Wiping the blood off his nose, Radhanath turned toward Lawrence and rasped, "Yes!" The expression on his face did nothing to ease the dislike Lawrence had instinctively felt toward Radhanath from the moment they met.

Meanwhile, Dubois, who had walked up to them, attempted to diffuse the tension, "Inspector, as you said so yourself, this man was a *zamindar*. Many people knew him. Again, I've known Mr. Sikdar as a brilliant mathematician for over ten years. He is not with the rebels."

Lawrence Cockerel, aware of the un-British manner of justice he was proposing to dispense, by hanging the prisoners without a trial, with European witnesses to the deed, decided not to challenge Dubois' assurance. Snorting, he moved away. Radhanath watched the hapless captives awaiting their fate. They sat with a mix of fear and resignation, eyeing the nooses soon to go around their necks. It occurred to Radhanath that luck wasn't about to favor those faces, brown like him, as it had Dubois who was clearly to escape unscathed, despite having been on the verge of a most brazen act of subversion.

By the time Lawrence's men were ready to commence with the executions, it had started to drizzle. Inspector Cockerel walked over to stand by one of the sepoys. The light from a nearby torch illumed the face of the kneeling man. He turned his head sideways, looking up at Lawrence through a light veil of rain. It was Pannalal Chettri.

Pannalal had attempted to prevent the sepoys from barging in on the scene before Chandrakanta came for them. Unfortunately, the men in an excited state had gotten worried when Chandrakanta was gone longer than expected. They had overruled Pannalal and gone looking for Chandrakanta. When interrogated by Lawrence's officers, Pannalal along with several others had refused to snitch on fellow sepoys by divulging further about their foiled plans. As a consequence, they now awaited their own death.

At that instant, a bunch of fresh British personnel arrived on horseback. Immediately after subjugating the twenty odd mutineers in front of the tower, Lawrence had dispatched a few of his men to both cantonments at Barrackpore and Dumdum to warn the authorities. These were men returning from Barrackpore to tell him that a huge ploy had indeed been foiled. The disarmed native sepoys were undergoing rigorous interrogation. A significant number of ex-sepoys, who had been banished from the Barrackpore area, were discovered inside Sepai Para, armed to the teeth. They were now under siege, walled in by the British, who had every confidence of being able to resolve this peacefully. The sepoys were not likely to risk opening fire, with their families trapped inside Sepai Para with them.

The newcomers reported that the Barrackpore cantonment could use reinforcements; they were waiting for men from Dumdum to join them. Lawrence instructed most of his men to head back to Barrackpore, taking with them the sepoys who had agreed to cooperate in lieu of their lives. Lawrence said, "Pump these fellows. See if you can extract anything further that we can use."

The men started to kick and prod the sepoys along, loading them on to the three carriages that had come with the convoy. After they departed, Lawrence came back to Pannalal. With many of his compatriots executed in the interim, Pannalal was one of the last ones waiting to die. Harshly, Lawrence growled to him, "Follow me!"

Pannalal looked curiously at Lawrence. With his hands and legs bound by twine, Pannalal stood up clumsily, and started to hop along behind the inspector. When they had advanced some distance to a wooded area not directly visible from the tower, Lawrence stopped. They were standing underneath a jackfruit tree, lush with seasonal fruit. Rainwater trickled down their body. There was a faint light from the cloud laden skies that allowed them to barely make out each other's face. Extracting a knife, Lawrence bent and slashed the binding on Pannalal's feet and wrists.

With no further words, he said, "Go!"

Pannalal stood looking toward Lawrence. Finally, he asked, "Why?"

Lawrence did not respond.

Pannalal whispered, "The rebellion isn't over. What if I join those in the North?"

Woodenly, Lawrence chewed out, "You cannot win."

Pannalal sighed. Before stepping away, he offered a sad smile to Lawrence, which Lawrence did not return. After Pannalal vanished, Lawrence stood there for a while, gazing blankly into the darkness. When he came back to the front of the tower, he found the hangings all completed. The remaining officers were cleaning up, preparing to leave. Suddenly, they heard horses' hooves. Soon, a huge convoy of soldiers under British command appeared on BT Road. These were the reinforcements from Dumdum who were on their way to the cantonment at Barrackpore. The loyal native sepoys were marching in the direction opposite to the one the rebels had so meticulously planned for tonight.

After the convoy had passed, a relative quiet returned to the front of the tower. The sound of falling rain intensified, as did the strength of the blowing wind. The torches around burnt more feebly now, succumbing to the increasing intensity of the rain. The wind had brought a strong stench of paraffin with it. Radhanath crinkled his nose, as he watched the lifeless faces hanging from the trees, buffeted by wind and rain. The mutiny had arrived at his door tonight.

A shadow could be seen moving in the midst of this, cautious and almost imperceptible. The stalker was none other than Gokul. He had followed the initial group of rebels from Barrackpore to Sukhchar and then stayed out of sight, watching the whole drama unfold as the police confronted the native men. With the thinning of the officers, he had emerged from his hiding. As the dying torchlight or the occasional lightning illumed the strangulated faces hanging from the trees, Gokul felt a peculiar rush inside, reminded of his *thugee* days.

Radhanath's eyes looked past Sara and spotted Gokul loitering on the scene. *What was that man – whom Chandrakanta had confided about to Radhanath years ago – doing here?* Radhanath wondered. In the orange light from the torches, Radhanath watched Gokul's face, looking up at Chandrakanta's lifeless body hanging from the tree. Gokul wore a curiously animated expression. One of the police officers was about to accost the unrestrained native man, but Radhanath noticed Inspector Cockerel nodding the officer off. *So, Gokul had immunity*, realized Radhanath. *Then he must have been an informant.* Radhanath's instincts said that Gokul had been instrumental in getting Lawrence to come out here at the epicenter of the mutiny tonight – an action that had ultimately led to Chandrakanta's death.

Radhanath's eyes followed Gokul, who was attempting to ingratiate himself with Lawrence. The inspector brushed him off like a fly. Radhanath knew of Gokul's conversion to Christianity many years ago and of his work with Calcutta's well-known Reverend Stuart. Watching him dart surreptitiously around, Radhanath pondered at the irony of it. All one needed to do was look at his face now, to know that Reverend Stuart's teachings has had almost no impact on the man. Tonight, Radhanath reflected with bitterness, *whatever Gokul had hoped to gain by cooperating with the British, the crazy bastard had no idea about the price he has paid.*

Inevitably, Gokul's eyes turned to meet Radhanath's. Curling his index finger, Radhanath signaled the man to come closer. Surprised, Gokul ambled over. He had noted Radhanath was the only other native man apart from him, who wasn't in shackles this evening.

When he got close, Radhanath pointed to Chandrakanta's dead body and asked, "That man hanging dead over there. Do you know who that is?" There was something in Radhanath's voice, perhaps the insane gleam in his eyes that shut Gokul up. *Radhanath was not looking for an answer from him.*

"Forty-two years ago," ground out Radhanath, "You spared the life of the young *rani* of Dhanulia. Remember that night?"

Gokul's eyes flashed with remembrance. With a twisted smile, Radhanath completed, "Nine months later, she gave birth. That man there is your son. His mother told him about you on her deathbed."

By this time, the rain had begun to pour in earnest. Lawrence was standing nearby with the warm rain rolling off his skin like blood. Sara and Dubois had sheltered under another tree close by. Despite the sounds of the rain, all clearly heard the revelation Radhanath had just made. A dumbfounded Lawrence looked from father to son.

"They gave you a cross to hang around your neck, a tawdry pardon for the unspeakable crimes of your past, and for that, you sold them your soul! Didn't you, Gokul?! Running to them with any information you can find on other natives, like a dog fetching to please its master?" Gokul stared blankly at Radhanath.

Pointing a prophetic finger toward his dead friend, Radhanath continued to anguish, "Your flesh and blood over there? See him?" Radhanath taunted

Gokul. "He never sold his soul. Despite the luxury of his circumstances, he stood with his fellow natives." Radhanath's voice, scratchy with raw emotion, rang in the ears of all listening.

"You poor fool!" Radhanath lashed out again. "You are blessed in your ignorance. You've never had to be around a white man less capable than you, bossing you around, putting words in your mouth, simply because they speak their mother tongue better than you ever could. You haven't had a facetious know-it-all stamp himself over your hard work. And then bask in the spotlight that should have come to you."

By this time, Radhanath was past caring about who his audience was. He spoke to no one in particular, his emotions simply pouring out of him. His voice rose a notch pointing to Chandrakanta's corpse, he said, "That is my friend over there. He chose to join the insurgents behind my back. But I know the hunger that fueled his rebellion! *I know*! His was a life scarred by rejection. I never…" Radhanath paused to swallow the huge lump in his throat. "I never told him that I understood his pain. I understand how it feels to be pushed aside simply because you are different."

The last torch had died. Gokul who had been standing spellbound, shocked by both the revelation and the naked anguish he saw in Radhanath's face, seemed suddenly to come to his senses. In the eerie light of the night, he was seen running toward Chandrakanta's dead body, fighting the fast and furious rains. Perhaps the nineteen-year-old Sunayani's face swayed before him from distant memory. Gokul had not understood most of what Radhanath said, save that the hanged man yonder was his flesh and blood. After a while, a sudden streak of lightning revealed Gokul with his arms wrapped around Chandrakanta's dead, limp legs. The father was maniacally kissing his dead son's feet, touching his head to them.

"My son! My son!" he wailed like a man possessed.

Chapter Twenty-One

About fifty kilometers upriver from Calcutta, the city of Chandannagar prided itself as a slice of France embedded in the heart of Bengal. By the mid-nineteenth century, the city's French-inspired, fun-loving ethos was viewed with amused indulgence by the rest of puritanical Bengal. Radhanath Sikdar had built himself a riverfront villa in Gondolpara of Chandannagar. Perhaps it was Chandannagar's decidedly uninhibited character that had attracted Radhanath, looking for a life beyond prudery and prejudice.

25th August 1857

Three days after the showdown at Sukhchar, Radhanath sat abruptly up, woken from a nightmare. He had been drowning in the rain-swollen Hooghly River in his dream. Discovering him groaning, slumped on a garden bench at his Chandannagar house this morning, his servant had tried to wake him. "*Katta*! *Katta*!"

The servant's urgent calls finally pierced through the fog in Radhanath's brain. Slowly, he returned to the present, soothed by the birdcalls and the freshness of the morning blossoming around him. Radhanath recalled stepping outside the house last evening to watch the sun go down on the river from his garden. He couldn't remember when he fell asleep.

Aware that his servant was watching him nervously, Radhanath stood up. Giving the man a weak smile to somewhat reassure him, Radhanath turned toward the gate, heading for the riverfront, intending to take a walk to refresh himself.

In front of the tower at Sukhchar that night, as Gokul wailed unabashed, holding the dead Chandrakanta's feet, Radhanath had hurried away from the scene, feeling compelled to put as much distance as possible between himself and everybody else. He wasn't conscious of where his feet led or the wind-driven rain pummeling at him. Lightning tore up the darkness through which he passed. Thunder roared like a caged animal. Before long, Radhanath found himself on the banks of the Hooghly River. The tumultuous, rain-bloated river hissed like an angry snake. Radhanath eyed the storm tossing and turning the dinghies, barely held back by their anchors. On a sudden impulse, he jumped onto one of them. With the knife he usually carried, he cut the rope that moored the boat and started to row. Hearing a stranger making away with one of their dinghies, the boatman waiting to ferry Dubois to Chandannagar raised alarm. The fishermen who were huddling in boats nearby, emerged from their shelters and hurried after Radhanath. When they nearly caught up with him, Radhanath gave in to the fury raging inside him. Abruptly throwing the oars away, he jumped headlong into the river. The horrified fishermen had shaken their heads, marveling that a man could be so foolish. This was suicide. Radhanath had swum with the frenzy of a madman, attempting to cut through the current. The wind churned waves lashed at him. The water rose above his head. With great effort, Radhanath came up gasping for air. But it was raining so hard that it choked him as he desperately tried to breathe.

After what felt like an eternity, Radhanath saw lights on his horizon. He realized he was probably nearing the opposite bank close to Srirampur. That light was probably from the Danish tavern thereabout, that he had seen when passing this section of the river in the past. Numbly, he thought perhaps they were having a ball, like the one Sara and Dubois had planned to attend in Chandannagar. That was the last thought Radhanath had, before fatigue had overtaken his senses. He has no memory of finally reaching the bank on the other side or stumbling up the steps of the *ghat*. Next morning, he had found himself in a crumpled heap under a tree. Cold and feverish, he had somehow gotten himself on a *tanga* and returned home to Chandannagar, which was on the same side of the river as Srirampur. A grief-stricken, restless Radhanath had not been able to sleep a wink since then. Yesterday evening, he had come out to take a stroll in his garden, hoping to find some peace. As he sat on a bench watching the sun go down, his sleep-starved body had mercifully given away. It was on this bench that his servant found him groaning next morning.

Now, headed toward the Strand promenade, Radhanath walked unhurried along the banks of the softly susurrating Hooghly River, watching it glint serenely orange in complete contrast to that night. Crows and gulls flew over his head, their familiar cries filling the air comfortingly. He could see several fishing boats dotting the waterway. Occasionally, he saw thin cotton towel clad throngs, busy with their morning ablutions. Once or twice a tooting steamer would grab his attention. Radhanath walked tiredly, with nothing planned for the day. He had wired GTSI two days ago for indefinite leave. When he reached the main section of the promenade, he paused. Leaning against a pillar on the embankment, he watched the tiny ripples forming on the surface of the river. An inconsolable sadness seemed to pervade his heart. He felt stranded, at the helm of one more day of life, not knowing what to do.

The plot to burn down the tower that was almost like a shrine for him, rankled. The reality of Chandrakanta's unconscionable death, gnawed at his soul. But Sara's deft change of storyline to save Dubois' hide, shattered him.

It had little to do with Sara's having a soft corner for Dubois. It was all about the much broader issue that Radhanath had grappled with his whole life. Effortlessly disregarding the evidence against him, Sara had chosen to protect Dubois because she trusted the man. What Sara did for Dubois, Radhanath had seen one European do for another throughout his career. It was inseparable from his constant awareness that he was not one of them – a painful awareness that came into sharp focus that night – as Radhanath stood shaken by the sight of his childhood friend hanging stiff and dead. He stood a powerless witness to one native man after another being murdered in cold blood. In those moments, something had snapped irrevocably inside of him.

Over the last two days, Radhanath was finally forced to confront a bitter truth about his life. His time among the Europeans had done nothing to resolve and had perhaps deepened, his fundamental insecurity among them. *Ultimately, the question always was, is there trust? Could that instinctive, irrational feeling that is the bedrock of all human relationships form between him and a European? Could Radhanath ever trust a European with his vulnerability or vice versa?* After working in the trenches for over twenty-five years with them, Radhanath believed, they had failed. At a fundamental level, they had never learned to trust each other.

Radhanath had largely succeeded in shoving the matter of unresolved trust under the carpet. He had built his life around the only religion he acknowledged – science. There was just enough trust between him and his colleagues, to serve science together. He had been grateful for the opportunities he had gotten among the Europeans, and he had not allowed the deficit of trust between them to bother him. In these last few days though, Radhanath became conscious of how he had been aware of a void. It was why he felt effectively excluded from their social life despite consorting with them. It was at the heart of the slights, the neglect, and the misunderstandings that kept coming up in his interracial exchanges.

But then, despite himself, Radhanath had become enchanted by the beautiful Sara who had somehow gotten through to him. Without being fully conscious of it, he had broken the barriers of interracial mistrust and forayed into realms of trust-based feelings. The incident at the tower had made him conscious that his feelings for Sara could never be isolated from the realities of his brown-skinned existence. Of all the doubts in his mind, foremost was his essential alienation from this Englishwoman's Englishness. Radhanath was reminded that there'd always be occasions when his intuition would be useless as far as Sara was concerned. Possibly he could never understand her well enough to be truly intimate.

The sun had risen higher by this time. Radhanath continued to watch the Hooghly River from his vantage on the Strand promenade. Noticing smoke rise from a point on the other bank, Radhanath realized he was looking in the direction of the burning *ghat* thereabout. It must be from a recent cremation. For the first time in his life, Radhanath appreciated how one can die inside and continue to live in the shell of the body. His existence these last few days had been nothing but. Sighing, he started back for home, choosing to go around town instead of retracing his path. As he passed a dairy farm, the familiar and comforting smell of fresh manure wafted to his nostrils. Radhanath knew the man who owned the dairy. He used to call Radhanath a *compasswalla,* using the nickname men of GTSI often suffered. The nickname was born from the gargantuan theodolite the GTSI surveyors typically carried around, which was incorrectly called a compass by the common people. Incidentally, George Everest used to hate this nickname. When Radhanath had casually told the dairy farm owner that he measured the heights of mountains, the man had looked back fascinated. How is that even possible, the man had wondered out loud. Radhanath never forgot the astonished look he had seen on the man's face that day. Before continuing to walk home this morning, Radhanath stopped by the dairy to drink a fresh cup of warm milk.

When Radhanath entered his house, his servant mentioned a *memsahib* had come looking for him and was currently waiting in the garden. Astonished, Radhanath hurried there to discover none other than Sara Langley, bent, sniffing a column of exquisitely scented tuberose in bloom. Radhanath was struck by how lovely she looked, in a powder blue gown, navy capelet, and a sheer bonnet framing her face. As he approached closer, she straightened to look toward him, the ravages of the street apparent from the dirty hem of her dress. Radhanath noted the dark circles that had formed under those enchanting eyes he loved. Before he could say anything, Sara spoke in a voice gruff with pent up emotion. "You just up and left that night? When were you going to get in touch again?"

After the relentless angst of these past few days, Sara seemed to have restored Radhanath's ability to feel at least some form of pleasure. He experienced a familiar, sweet pain inside his chest. The memory of Sara on horseback from *Raja* Uday Singh's hunting party rose before him. Suddenly Radhanath felt she had, if anything, grown more beautiful in this last year, her experiences of life tempering her magic with depth. Radhanath did not answer Sara, continuing to watch her in silence. Then he invited her to come inside the house.

Sara followed Radhanath into his living room, sparsely but comfortably furnished. As he opened the shuttered French windows, light flooded in, and he asked, "How did you know where to find me?"

Radhanath heard Sara respond, "From General Waugh. When I inquired, he let me know that you are on indefinite leave and that he had no idea when you intended to get back. I arrived at Chandannagar yesterday and spent the night at *L'allumeur*."

A cheerful beam of sunlight fell upon the two, as Sara sat on a couch and Radhanath took a chair opposite to it. As she looked around her, her face brightened slightly with mischief. She said, "Nice! I like it. Much more spacious than the GTSI tower."

Her words were an obvious reference to the intimate time they had spent inside the tower. Watching her blushing cheeks, Radhanath felt his heart wrench a second time this morning. All he could offer in response, though, was a tired smile.

Noticing his reserve, Sara's face hardened with determination. "You must see that I had to save Dubois. I owe him my life. He helped me escape the mutineers from Jainagar. I couldn't let him hang," she pleaded.

After a pause in which no reaction came from Radhanath, Sara pressed onward, "I am sorry about your friend. But surely, you can't lay that on yourself, or me, or Dubois. He was killed by the police before anyone could possibly do anything. You see that, don't you?"

Radhanath said, "Yes, I know."

Impulsively, Sara stood up and came to kneel near Radhanath, placing her hands on his lap. Running fond eyes over Radhanath's face, she gently prodded, "Then why are you angry with me? Why have you made no attempt to get in touch?"

Sara felt Radhanath stiffen when she touched him. Her hands seemed to burn at the spot where it rested on Radhanath's knees. Slowly, they shrunk away, as Radhanath stared at her with deep sadness.

Abruptly, but unhurried, Radhanath broke into speech, "I am not mad at you. I have simply woken up to some things I had overlooked about you and me in the past. Dubois would have burned that tower down. But this did not matter to you. In that moment, you were a white woman saving a white man you understood entirely. You were only too happy to conclude that he wasn't thinking straight."

Radhanath's voice thickened with pain and rage, emotions stirred by trampled pride, trampled by those he had wanted to trust. "Can you not see what your actions meant? Could you have been as forgiving if Dubois was not white? Of course not! The contrast in your cultural identities would stand like a wall between you." Radhanath closed his eyes in an unconscious attempt at distancing himself.

When he opened his eyes again, Radhanath saw the warm vulnerability in Sara's expression faded. She was looking intently at him. With his heart beginning to race, Radhanath got up from his chair and walked to one of the windows. As Sara sat heavily on the chair he just vacated, Radhanath turned to face Sara, leaning his back to the window. He said, "I am not speaking in the air, Miss Langley. I have lived through this my entire life at GTSI. Incompetent Europeans are tolerated by their white bosses. Why? Because they understand each other. The little smiles, familiar body language, and common jokes smooth the bumps on the road that someone like me has no means to avoid. European candidates a thousand times less deserving, less qualified than me, get preference for positions at GTSI. My fate is to be stuck at four hundred rupees a month because I could never be one of you. I witnessed you succumb to that instinct that night at the tower. What if it was me with the gun? Planning to slaughter hundreds of British men and women? You found it in yourself to save Dubois because you trusted him. Are you sure you would have found it in yourself to extend me that same benefit of doubt? You might've discovered you don't understand me well enough. What then?"

With a rueful smile, Radhanath concluded, "I am not judging or blaming you. I realize it is not possible to escape that instinct. No one can. Finally, I understand why I will always be too Indian for the English."

With a self-deprecating sneer, he added, "I have also understood, a little too late and with infinite sadness, that I've become too English for the Indians."

Sara recognized the look on Radhanath's face. It was similar to the one he wore that night in front of the tower when he was speaking to Gokul. It was a look of unmitigable regret and despair, for all that was unfair, for all that he cannot change. His feelings seemed too deep to warrant any argument. With a heavy sigh, Sara closed her eyes and tried to imagine the scene from just a few hours prior that night, when they were dining at Evora, and Radhanath had looked at her with ardent affection.

Sara stood up, abruptly. When she spoke next, her bearing was icy and regal. Her voice held a contempt Radhanath had never heard in them before. "Have you thought where we would be if the rebels had not attacked the tower that night, Mr. Sikdar?" she asked. Radhanath narrowed his eyes.

"Do you know what I think? I think you are a coward. Eventually, you would have found this same fear inside of you no matter what. This same mistrust of treading on unfamiliar waters would have triumphed inside you. You criticize me for showing faith in Dubois because he is white like me. And yet, you refuse to show faith in me because I am not brown like you! How is that even logical? I made a practical decision to save the only life there that I could have saved. I will not apologize for it." Sara's eyes flashed with pained anger.

The silence between the two lengthened. Finally, Sara said, "I do not know if our relationship ever had a future. I do not deny that you have gone through a lot! But I will tell you this. You are not as extraordinary, as I once believed." Turning on her heels, she left Radhanath standing alone. Radhanath watched her walk away, making no attempts to intervene.

Epilogue

The Indian Rebellion of 1857 petered out before it began, at least in Calcutta. It raged for some time in other parts of India but was ultimately crushed everywhere, and the British consolidated their rule of the subcontinent. The horrors unleashed in the wake of the mutiny, remain a massacre of extraordinary cruelty in the history of the nineteenth century. More than half a million people died, the overwhelming majority of them, Indians. In 1858, the governance changed hands from East India Company to the Queen of England, and India prepared for another century of British rule.

In the days following the mutiny, Park Street *thana*'s Lawrence Cockerel was seen less and less at his longstanding, native haunts. The one exception was Shashibala, whose company he continued to solicit. Lawrence's friend, Reverend Stuart finally came to terms with the loss of his daughter and her family. And in its aftermath, his missionary zeal seemed to suffer a decline. By and by, Reverend Stuart allowed Reverend Banerjee to take over most of his duties, seeking solace in prayer and contemplation for himself. Sitting in Stuart's church these days, Lawrence sometimes thought of Stuart's man Gokul, conspicuously absent from the pews. When Lawrence asked Stuart about Gokul, the Reverend had regretfully admitted to not knowing anything about the man's whereabouts these days. For some years, Lawrence would be reminded of Gokul when he happened to pass that banyan tree near Botu *babu*'s pleasure palace where Pannalal had pointed the man out to Lawrence and where Gokul used to sit and tell stories about Jesus to the natives. Lawrence never saw Gokul again. Sometimes going past Bishwambhar's shop, Lawrence would think of Pannalal and the good times they had there. However, he did not enter Bishwambhar's shop. Neither did he ever attempt to look for Pannalal.

Shashibala remained as aloof as ever about who ruled over the land she was born into, too busy living her life of debauched drudgery, which, for her, was the closest to living a free life anyway.

Immediately following the showdown at the tower, Dubois had slipped away to French controlled Pondicherry in the south of India. While waiting for things to cool down in Calcutta, he used to fret that the British would eventually discover his involvement in the mutiny and hang him. Dubois agonized over whether he should return to France or go back to GTSI in Calcutta. Though he hated the thought of facing Radhanath, he was confident that Radhanath would not give him away, not deliberately.

After Sara Langley left that morning, Radhanath did not seek her out, not at *L'allumeur*, not ever again. Neither did Sara. With her Uncle Dick passing away toward the end of the year, Sara came into some property, whereupon she decided to return to England. For next several years, Sara would pursue private education in the natural sciences, honing an interest she always had. And eventually she would settle with a British professor of mathematics.

Despite many rumors floating around, D'Orgoni's forces never showed up on the shores of Bengal. No one knew if Nana sahib ever got to meet with D'Orgoni. Or, whether Nana sahib was dead or alive.

After the mutiny ended, the resistance to adopting Everest's name for Peak XV seemed to disappear all at once. Whether or not Peak XV had a local name didn't seem important anymore. Mount Everest had become a household name in the Western world, much as Surveyor General Waugh had hoped it would, in his letter that surfaced in the *India Chronicle* in May of 1856. For the next several years, Waugh was felicitated internationally for Mount Everest.

Radhanath Sikdar remained chief mathematician at four hundred rupees a month for the remainder of his tenure at the GTSI. He got no promotions, or pay raises, which Chandrakanta had once hoped for him. Radhanath gave up his rental at Beniapukur and commuted from Chandannagar to Calcutta these days. When he sometimes went past Evora, he noticed that the restaurant was not doing well. In the wake of the mutiny, people shunned places that accommodated both natives and Europeans under the same roof. Radhanath had heard rumors that Signor Alfonso was contemplating shuttering Evora after its three decades of existence.

Radhanath hardly went inside Evora himself, except if ambushed by one of Bengal's unpredictable *Kalboishakhi* storm. While waiting for his food to arrive, the lightning would draw his eyes outside the window where the trees stood writhing in the storm. When it grew abruptly dark outside, his eyes would linger on the windowpane, hypnotized by the infinite reflections generated from the solitary candle sitting at his table. Before he knew it, Radhanath would be transported to that evening in Ananta Bugyal among the Himalayan mountains, when he had experienced the strangest of feelings. For the first time in his life, looking into the eyes of an English girl he had just met, Radhanath had felt *seen.*

Acknowledgements

We are grateful to our editor Miss Emily Hoang for her thorough and detailed editorial inputs, her thoughtful suggestions that has materially improved the book.

We owe a huge debt of thanks to Mrs. Sanjukta Bhattacharya for developing the artwork used in the front and back cover of this book.

Thanks to Mimi Gupta, Harrison Leong, Suchandra Goswami, Shuman Majumdar, Sukhendu Majumdar, Bedatri Dutta Roy Chowdhury for reading the full manuscript and providing feedback.

Thanks to Bidisha Sen, Sarmistha Bhattacharya, Anusua Mukherjee, Arunima Dasgupta, Phillip Harris, Madeleine Flamiano, Trish Hegerich, Chitra Divakaruni for reading the first two chapters of the manuscript and providing feedback.

Thanks to the above-mentioned, and Heather Majumdar for feedback on cover design.

Swapnonil Banerjee
Nivedita Majumdar

List of Important References

1. Lahiri, A. (2016) *Radhanath Sikdar and Colonial Science.* Samsad Books.
2. Keay, J. (2000) *The Great Arc: The Dramatic Tale of How India was Mapped and Everest was Named.* HarperCollins.
3. Chakraborty, B., De, S. (2014) *Calcutta in the Nineteenth Century: An Archival Exploration.* Niyogi Books.
4. Singha, K. (1861) *Houtom Pechar Naksha* (Roy S., Translation (2008): *The Observant Owl Hootum's Vignettes of Nineteenth-century Calcutta*. Permanent Black.
5. Masters, J. (1951) *Nightrunners of Bengal*. The Viking Press.
6. Patri, P. (1984) *Choray Mora Kolkata.* Ananda Publishers.
7. Younger, C. (2020) *Wicked women of the Raj: European Women Who Broke Society Rules And Married Life.* Harper Collins.
8. Allen, C. (1975) *Plain Tales from The Raj*. Time Warner Books UK.

Glossary

A

Achha bolunto

You tell me

Ayah

Maid

Arrêtez

Stop it

Arreh

Wow

B

Babu

Neo-urban, rich Bengalis

Baksheesh

Tips

Banchot

Sister fucker

Bandhani

Tie-dye textile

Beedi

Tobacco in dried leaf

Benarasi

Popular bridal wear

Bhago

Get lost

Bhai

Brother

Bhang

Indian cannabis drink

Bhetki
Asian Sea Bass

Boishyo
Third of the four main castes in Indian society

Bon soir, mon ami
Good evening, my friend

Brahmin
First of the four main castes in Indian society.

Bujhini
I did not understand

Buransh
Rhododendron

C

Compasswalla
Person carrying a compass

D

Dewan
Minister

Delicieuse
Delicious

Dholak
Indian Drum

Dhuti
An Indian man's sarong

Doi
Yoghurt

F

Fado
Portuguese music tradition

Fakir
Ascetic who lives on alms

Fatua
Loose cotton men's shirt

G

Galabandh
High necked coat

Gari
Carriage

Ghat
Embankment

Ghomta
Sari covering the face of Indian women

Gora
White man

Gori
White woman

Gurung
A Himalayan tribe

H

Haveli
Islamic palace

I

Impossible
Impossible

J

Jatra
Indian theatre

Jeelipi
Deep-fried lentil cakes soaked in sugar syrup

Jhupri
Shanty

Ji
A respectful appellation placed after the name

K

Kacha
White no-stitch wrap son wears after parent dies

Kala jaiga
Dark corner

Kalboishakhi
Norwesters, tropical storms

Kaistho
Second of the four main castes in Indian society

Katta
Male head of household

Khansama
Muslim cook

Khemta
Indian dance tradition

Kobirej
Native medical man

Kobir-larai
Extemporal rhyming fight

Kulota
Girl who shamed her family

Kupi
Oil lamp

Kurta
Indian style relaxed-fit tunic

L

Lattu
Wooden top

Lucknowi
from Lucknow
Lungi
Men's long sarong

M

Ma
Mother
Marwari
from Marwar, India
Memsahib
Foreigner who is female
Merci
Thank you
Mujaras
Indian soiree

N

Nach
Dance
Namaskar
Hands joined in greeting
Nawab
Musalman lord
Non
No

O

Oh-ma
Goodness
Oui
Yes

P

Pagri
Indian man's headgear
Pajama
Indian style relaxed-fit pant
Panjabi
Loose tunic for upper body
Pantua
Deep-fried syrupy sweet
Paratha
Handmade Indian bread
Pardon
Pardon
Parfait
Perfect
Pulao
Indian-style fried rice
Punkah
Manual fans

Punkahwallah
Manual fan puller

R

Raja
King

Rajbari
Royal palace

Rani
Queen

Reshmi kebob
Skewers

S

Sacrebleu
My goodness

Sahib
Polite reference to males

Saishes
Horse groomsmen

Sati
Self-immolation by Hindu widows

Sherbet
Non-alcoholic drink

Sherwani
Knee-length long-sleeve coat

Shikar
Hunting

Shikari
Hunter

Shong
Peripatetic actor

Shradh
Hindu rites of passage

Shudro
Fourth of the four main castes in Indian society

Sitar
Indian music string instrument

T

Tabla
Indian drums

Tamasha
Performance by native artists

Tanga
Horse drawn carriage

Tappa
A local song tradition

Thana
Police station

Thugees
A deceitful robber clan

Thumri
An Indian song tradition

U

Ushnish
Cloth wrap worn on head

Z

Zamindar
Feudal landlord

Made in the USA
Middletown, DE
07 November 2022